WESTERN

Small towns. Rugged ranchers. Big hearts.

All In With The Maverick
Elizabeth Hrib

A Rancher Of His Own
Brenda Harlen

MILLS & BOON

Elizabeth Hrib is acknowledged as the author of this work
ALL IN WITH THE MAVERICK
© 2025 by Harlequin Enterprises ULC
Philippine Copyright 2025
Australian Copyright 2025
New Zealand Copyright 2025

First Published 2025
First Australian Paperback Edition 2025
ISBN 978 1 038 94550 1

A RANCHER OF HIS OWN
© 2025 by Brenda Harlen
Philippine Copyright 2025
Australian Copyright 2025
New Zealand Copyright 2025

First Published 2025
First Australian Paperback Edition 2025
ISBN 978 1 038 94550 1

MIX
Paper | Supporting
responsible forestry
FSC
www.fsc.org
FSC® C001695

Published by
Harlequin Mills & Boon
An imprint of Harlequin Enterprises (Australia) Pty Limited
(ABN 47 001 180 918), a subsidiary of HarperCollins
Publishers Australia Pty Limited
(ABN 36 009 913 517)
Level 19, 201 Elizabeth Street
SYDNEY NSW 2000 AUSTRALIA

Cover art used by arrangement with Harlequin Books S.A.. All rights reserved.

Printed and bound in Australia by McPherson's Printing Group

All In With The Maverick

Elizabeth Hrib

MILLS & BOON

Dear Reader,

In the small town of Tenacity, Montana, you'll find good hardworking people and Split Valley Ranch—the perfect place for sunset horseback rides across the pastures. It also happens to be a place where romance comes alive for Amy Hawkins and Josh Aventura.

Burned by love, Amy is only looking for a place to escape the limelight of her failed relationship, but what she finds instead is something even better. Josh has closed himself away, focusing on his ranch, until he meets Amy—who changes his life completely. But are they each willing to risk their heart again after going through so much pain in the past?

Amy and Josh remind us that opening up yourself after heartbreak is one of the hardest yet most rewarding things you can do, and that's something I think we can all relate to a little bit.

I am so excited to share Amy and Josh's story in my first Harlequin Montana Mavericks novel. I hope readers fall in love with the new characters who call Tenacity home, and enjoy reconnecting with old ones. So here's to second chances, dear reader, and to believing that the next best thing is just around the corner. If you enjoy this new addition to the Montana Mavericks series and want to talk handsome cowboys, you can find me on Instagram @elizabethhrib, swooning over my favorite books, or at elizabethhrib.com.

Elizabeth Hrib

Elizabeth Hrib was born and raised in London, Ontario, where she spends her nine-to-five as a nurse. She fell in love with the romance genre while bingeing '90s rom-coms. When she's not nursing or writing, she can be found at the piano, swooning over her favorite books on Instagram or buying too many houseplants.

Books by Elizabeth Hrib

Montana Mavericks: The Tenacity Social Club

All In with the Maverick

Hatchet Lake

Lightning Strikes Twice
Flirting with Disaster

Visit the Author Profile page
at millsandboon.com.au for more titles.

CHAPTER ONE

AMY HAWKINS KNEW a thing or two about working dangerous jobs.

As a rodeo star, she'd been bucked off the back of horses, slammed into gates by the roughstock, and stared down by bucking bulls. But stocking shelves at Strom and Son Feed and Farm Supply—the store owned by her sister's fiancé, Caleb, and his father, Nathan—was proving to be even more dangerous than getting between a cow and its newborn calf.

In the six weeks she'd been at the Tenacity, Montana store, she'd learned not to separate a grumpy ranch hand from his feed order. What she hadn't apparently learned yet was how not to mix up said orders.

"What happened now?" Faith said as Amy ducked behind the cash counter, using her sister as a human shield to hide from the surly man marching through the store with Caleb.

His face was beet red, his eyebrows pinched in a tight knot in the middle of his forehead. Amy couldn't tell if the color was from working out in the sun or if he was huffing and puffing over getting a truckful of feed back to his ranch before realizing it wasn't what he ordered.

"I might have sent the wrong order home with the MacPhersons."

"Not again." Faith checked the computer above the cash

drawer, the corner of her mouth twitching. "That's twice in two months."

"In my defense," Amy said, staring over her shoulder, "the MacPhersons' and the McPetersons' orders always show up at the same time."

Faith smirked, flicking her long, dark braid out of the way as she made an adjustment to the online order. "I'll handle it. Can you finish ticketing the clearance items in aisle two for me?" She passed Amy a roll of yellow stickers, each of them indicating a twenty-five percent markdown.

"Sure you wanna let me handle that alone?"

"Really? You can rope a calf in seven seconds but you can't put some stickers on some feed bags?"

"Of course I can. I just think it's funny when you get all those stress wrinkles across your forehead."

Faith smoothed her hand across her forehead, glowering at Amy. "You're lucky I like you," she said as Amy waltzed away. "Because you are definitely our worst employee!"

"I don't know... Pretty sure Caleb's angling to make me employee of the month."

"Doubtful."

Amy turned around and framed up a square with her fingers against the wall. "I think my face would look great right behind the register."

"As if. We might put your face up there as the first person ever fired from Strom and Son."

"Firstly, you're not paying me. This is free labor. So remember that when you try to fire me. Secondly, you'd miss me too much."

"Miss you hogging our guest room," Faith muttered as Amy walked away grinning.

To be fair, Faith had done Amy a huge favor, inviting her down to Tenacity. She hadn't quite known what to expect of the little hardscrabble town in Montana, but when Faith offered her the guest room, Amy had eagerly accepted. After a bad breakup, she'd been desperate to escape Bronco, leaving the crowded city and social media scene behind in exchange for some small-town refuge. From what Amy had seen so far, there wasn't much going on in Tenacity, and that suited her just fine. Spending time with

Faith and putting some work in at the store was about all the social activity she could handle right now. Besides, she'd learned recently that there were worse things than stocking shelves and ringing up orders for surly cowboys.

Heartbreak was certainly worse.

And rejection.

And finding out that the person you thought you loved had up and gotten married while you were apart.

That was definitely worse.

So, as far as Amy was concerned, stocking shelves was a dream come true.

There was something almost calming about stocking shelves. Maybe it was the repetitiveness of the motion. She appreciated the neatness and the order. She liked that everything had a place. Surprisingly, she also enjoyed the quiet, even if it meant taking the occasional order from Faith. If someone would have told her all that six weeks ago, she'd have laughed them right out of a rodeo arena. Now she was starting to crave the slower pace in Tenacity. The monotony. And especially the distance from her whirlwind life.

Amy stopped in front of a stack of feed bags, double-checking the brand before she started tabbing them with yellow stickers.

"Amy?" Faith called from somewhere in the store.

Strom and Son Feed and Farm Supply was a large, boxy building with shelves upon shelves of anything a rancher could ever need. There were bags of livestock feed for a variety of animals—cattle, sheep, goats, pigs. But also grain and fresh hay and corn. The building always smelled faintly sweet, a little like home if Amy was honest, which probably had something to do with how much time she'd spent mucking out horse stalls growing up. There were also feed buckets and salt licks and horse tack and an aisle with toys for enrichment.

"Yeah?" she said.

Faith appeared at the end of the aisle.

"Nathan said the new April shipment of feed came in. He's gonna get the guys to unload the pallets. Help me with inventory when they're done?"

"Sure thing," Amy said. Despite the earlier feed order mix-up, she'd been a quick study with Faith as her guide, and she was starting to know the business like the back of her hand. They made a good team, which wasn't surprising, considering they'd spent a lot of their life traveling the world's rodeo circuit together along with their other sisters, Tori, Carly and Elizabeth, before settling in Bronco not long ago. Because of that, they often fell into a natural rhythm, one that reminded Amy of being on horseback and barrel races and rope tricks.

To look at them, it would be hard to tell they were sisters. Faith had high cheekbones, beautiful dark brown eyes, clear brown skin, and was only about five foot two. Though what she lacked in height, she made up for with her spunky attitude. Meanwhile, Amy was almost five foot seven, white, with bright blue eyes and straight, shoulder-length brown hair she left loose unless she was riding. Frankly, Amy didn't share looks with any of her sisters. She didn't even share DNA, considering they were all adopted. But the way they could read each other and the way they all loved fiercely—those were the things that made them family. The Hawkins Sisters had always been known as a group of strong rodeo-riding women, and Amy liked to think they lived up to that.

Or, at least, she had. Amy had only been away from the rodeo for a short time, but some days she felt like a completely different person. Was that what Faith saw when she looked at her now? Someone looking to step out of the limelight? While living in Bronco had been nice, it wasn't exactly a quiet existence. With more of her family settling in the city, The Hawkins Sisters had become the talk of the town. It had become almost impossible for Amy to go out in public without being recognized.

But Tenacity was different. Here she didn't have to traipse around in sunglasses and baseball caps all the time, and most days she could forget that Truett McCoy—the cowboy turned actor whose posters graced the walls of young fans around the world—dumped her to run off and marry his costar back in February.

There were moments when that realization still hit her hard, though she did her best not to mope. Faith would only worry more than she already was.

Amy finished up her task and headed back to the cash desk to return the roll of unused stickers. As she did, she turned up the radio, the song ringing out over the store speakers. She hummed along, grabbing a small bag of feed to return to a shelf in aisle four. When the song finished, the radio hosts started chatting, and it took Amy a moment to understand why the hairs on her arms had stood up.

"Can we talk about everyone's favorite cowboy for a second?" one of the hosts said.

Amy knew immediately that they were talking about Tru.

"Oh my gosh, yes!" the female host said. "Let's."

"Okay, last we heard, Tru McCoy was linked to several women prior to his whirlwind marriage. Isn't that right, Cady?"

Amy glowered at the shelf. There was only one thing worse than falling for a cowboy, and that was falling for a cowboy turned movie star. Of that, she was certain. In recent years, Tru's name above a marquee virtually guaranteed a box office smash, and his popularity had skyrocketed. Everyone was talking about him. After the breakup, she'd avoided the magazines and the trashy entertainment news channels, but apparently she'd forgotten about the radio.

"Wasn't he also supposedly seeing some unknown rodeo star?" the male host said. "We all know Montana is bustling with them."

Amy bristled. That's all she was in the end? Just an unknown, unnamed rodeo star? Her chest constricted, and she felt like a fool. Damn Tru McCoy, and damn him again for making her feel this way. She blinked back the tears she could already feel gathering in the corners of her eyes. She couldn't keep letting him affect her this way.

The host continued. "But apparently none of that matters because according to sources, his heart has always belonged to his new bride. Isn't that sweet, Cady?"

"Almost as sweet as you, Doug. And we definitely like a man who knows what he wants. We'll be right back after the break."

What he wants? Amy thought. Ha! Anger pooled inside her. It was no wonder her emotions had been all over the place since arriving in Tenacity back in February. Just bringing up Tru's name made her a weepy, blubbering mess, never mind being reminded that she'd been second fiddle all along. It was embarrassing and insulting. But what was even more mortifying was her reaction to the news after this many weeks. She'd been through breakups before. And she likely would again. She just needed to stop thinking about Tru. All it did was upset her and exhaust her, and she couldn't spend all her time trying to sleep away these feelings.

"And we're back," the radio host announced. "Talking about everyone's favorite heartthrob, Tru McCoy."

Hearing that she was only one of his many women shouldn't have surprised her—this was what happened when you fell for cowboy-hat-wearing movie stars. But the tears still threatened to spill, and Amy tugged a little too hard on the bag of feed she was putting away. It slipped from the shelf suddenly, sliding right through her outstretched hands.

It hit the floor, splitting at the corner, and the feed poured out all over her shoes in a dusty pile, sending pellets and grain dancing across the aisle. Amy swore under her breath. At least, she thought it was under her breath. It must have been louder than she thought, because Faith appeared a moment later and that made her tear up harder.

"Everything okay?"

"It's all good," Amy said. "Just a little accident. No big deal, I've got it." She did her best to avoid Faith's eye. Though they'd never discussed her fling with Tru, and Faith had never directly asked about him, Amy suspected that she knew. Sisters always knew these kinds of things. It was one of those special powers they were gifted with. That and the ability to annoy you in three seconds flat. Still, mortified at her reaction, Amy shook off the tears and hurried to the supply cupboard to grab a broom.

What did they say? Never cry over spilled milk? And here she was almost crying over spilled cattle feed. If anything, Amy should be ecstatic that she'd dodged that Tru-shaped bullet. He'd clearly never liked her despite his many declarations, and the last thing she needed to be was tied to a snake of a man. She was more grateful than ever that they'd used protection when they'd finally slept together back around Christmas. She'd even taken a pregnancy test to be sure because she'd felt sick right after the breakup, and with her birth control, she hardly ever got her period. With that worry assuaged, now Amy was mostly just angry for getting caught up in Tru's charms in the first place. She wasn't naïve. She'd lived and breathed the celebrity world for most of her life. She should have known better than to trust a cowboy with a handsome smile.

Amy swept the spilled feed into a pile, then dragged over the garbage bin, crouching to scoop grain onto the dustpan.

A set of footsteps drew near. Amy looked up, expecting Faith, but instead she saw a man—talk about a cowboy with a handsome smile. His hair was cut just above the shoulders. Dark brown, like his eyes. It was the kind of hair that looked especially good swept back under a cowboy hat. Much like the one he carried in his hand. Not that she was thinking of cowboys. Nope. Amy had strictly sworn off cowboys. But with his dusty blue jeans and snug T-shirt and olive complexion, she couldn't help but stare. He tilted his head, his gaze lingering, and for a moment, Amy wondered if he'd recognized her as one of The Hawkins Sisters. He wandered a little closer, and she prepared for the question, wincing internally.

"You know," he said. "If you get a couple of chickens in here, they'd take care of that for you no problem."

Amy blinked up at him, then she laughed, caught off guard by his comment. It was a real, deep belly laugh. She couldn't even say why she found it so funny, but as the sound faded between them, she almost couldn't remember why she'd been such an emotional mess. "You're probably right." She got to her feet. "Unfortunately, we're fresh out of chickens."

"You sure? You checked the back?"

"Almost positive. The only chicken you're going to find back there is Faith's chicken salad sandwich."

"Probably not as helpful in that form."

Amy bit her lip. A *funny* cowboy. Now that was a dangerous combination. "No. I wouldn't say so." She glanced at the flatbed cart he'd left at the end of the aisle. "Do you... Can I help you find something?"

"I'm looking for a fortified cattle feed. It used to be over there by the door."

"Oh, right," Amy said, leading him out of the aisle and toward the far end of the store. "We're doing some rearranging of the stock. Well, Faith and Caleb are. I'm just a lowly grunt worker."

"As if," Faith snorted from behind the cash desk as they passed. "I'm not forcing you to be here. Hi, Josh," she called, waving to the man that followed Amy.

Josh, huh?

"I do good work for you," Amy replied. "You should appreciate me more."

Faith smiled a little smile. "I guess I shouldn't bring up the earlier order mishap or the fact that you just wasted an entire bag of feed?"

"Take it out of my nonexistent salary," Amy teased.

Faith crossed her arms, smirking. "I just might."

Amy reached the far aisle and turned down it, lifting her hands in a kind of ta-da motion. "Here you go. Not sure which kind of feed you're looking for, but all the fortified ones are here."

"Thanks," Josh said, scanning the shelf. "I haven't seen you around before," he added before she could walk away. He grabbed a couple bags and tossed them on his cart. Thick veins ran up his muscled forearms. "Uh…"

"Amy," she supplied. "I came down to visit Faith back in February. Haven't really gotten around to leaving yet, so I figured I better earn my keep."

He smiled at her. It was a soft smile. The kind that might get her heart fluttering under different circumstances. He had one dimple in his cheek and lines by his eyes that told her he smiled often.

"And you?" she said. "You must not come by the store a lot."

"Only about once a month," Josh said. "To stock up on supplies. Sometimes I have Caleb arrange to deliver the larger orders if I can't get away."

That was likely why they hadn't crossed paths yet. "Get away?" Amy prompted.

"From my cattle."

"You have a ranch?"

"Yeah, Split Valley." He raised his hand and gestured in a vague direction. "Up on Juniper Road?"

Amy bit her lip and shrugged. "I'm not super familiar with town yet. I haven't been out much if you don't count the store."

"Right," Josh said. "Well, Split Valley Ranch used to belong to my parents. When they retired, I took over."

"Carrying on the tradition?" Amy said. She could appreciate that. She and her sisters had rodeoing in their blood.

"The Aventuras have been on that property for as long as anyone can remember."

"Josh Aventura," Amy said, mostly to herself. "Do you have any horses up at this ranch or just cattle?"

"A few horses. Makes getting around the property easier at times if I don't need to take a truck out for repairs or something. And it's easier to round up wayward cattle. Plus I just like to ride. Have ever since I was a boy." He pulled another bag of feed off the shelf and added it to his cart. "What about you? Ride much?"

Amy almost laughed in his face. Did rodeo star Amy Hawkins ride? Her brows rose. He really had no idea who she was. *What a treat*, she thought, her gaze traveling up his forearm as he reached for another bag of feed. Her eyes landed on his biceps before she managed to tear her gaze away.

"You never answered my question," he pointed out.

"I do ride," she said. "It's actually one of my favorite things."

He flashed her a smile. "Yeah?"

"Yeah." This was usually about the time she'd say something about the rodeo, and his eyes would get wide as realization struck. *A Hawkins Sister! Of course!* But Amy bit back the rest of her explanation. It was refreshing having someone be interested in her without the name attached. Without knowing who she really was.

"So you came down to visit from… Where? Bronco?"

"How'd you know?" she asked.

He flicked his head in her direction. "Just a guess. But you look like a city girl."

Amy glanced down at her attire. Sure, maybe her jeans were a little more expensive than what they wore around here, and her button-down was high-end, but she blended. Right? "What about you? Ever been to Bronco?"

He nodded. "A few times, especially when I was younger. But with the ranch I don't have a lot of time for traveling."

That was understandable. Amy suspected he also didn't have time for a lot of things, like TV and radio and following what Tru McCoy was getting up to. He seemed like the type of guy who could really care less about Hollywood gossip. Where Tru had to be the center of attention in every room, Josh struck her as a little gruff, a little quiet. And with his dusty boots, there was certainly nothing flashy about him. He really didn't seem to have any interest in charming anyone, certainly not her, and maybe that's exactly why Amy *was* so charmed by him.

Faith had been telling her for weeks to get out of the house and meet people. Amy had brushed her off more times than she could count, but right at this very moment a part of her strongly considered asking Josh out for coffee. It had been a long six weeks since everything had ended with Tru, and Josh seemed like he might be interested in her enough to say yes. If she could manage to pry him away from his cattle.

But as she watched him load the last few bags of feed onto his cart, she reconsidered. She no longer felt like she could trust her own judgment after the Tru situation. Maybe Josh was just being friendly. Tenacity was small; people took a genuine interest because they cared, not because they were trying to flirt. Maybe she'd read far too much into a handsome smile.

"Ready?" she said as Josh finished up. "I can ring you up at the cash desk."

Josh nodded. "I think that's everything."

They walked to the front of the store together. Amy stood behind the register and totaled Josh's order.

Josh paid, his eyes lifting to meet hers briefly. Amy tore the receipt free and handed it to him. She might be mistaken, but for a second he seemed to linger, like he wanted to ask her something. Then he just smiled and said, "Good to meet you, Amy. I appreciate all your help today."

"Of course. I was happy to. If you don't mind telling Faith

that the next time you see her," she teased. "I'm gunning for employee of the month."

"Well, I don't know how you could possibly have competition."

"That's what I keep saying."

They chuckled and Josh ducked his head, that dimple in his cheek deepening as he pushed his cart across the store. Amy watched him until he disappeared out the door.

"You know," Faith said, coming up behind her. She leaned her chin on Amy's shoulder. "I think that's the most words I've ever heard him say in all the time he's been coming in here."

Amy glanced at her. Faith wore that shrewd look she got when she was sussing something out.

"I'm serious. The best Caleb and I usually get is a polite grunt of acknowledgment. If Iris is around, sometimes she'll inquire after his parents and he'll give her a nod and a shrug." Iris was Caleb's mother. "Personally, I didn't even know the man was capable of that much conversation."

"Oh, come on," Amy said.

"I think he liked you. Who knows why?"

Amy scoffed. "Rude."

"You should have asked him for coffee."

"I was just being nice. *He* was just being nice."

"You asked if he had horses. You were getting down to the things that matter."

Amy laughed. She did have a soft spot for a man who loved to ride as much as she did. "I was trying to get you a sale. Now Caleb's gonna have no choice but to put my picture on the wall."

"We're probably not gonna see Josh back here for a month. You have four weeks to work up the courage to ask him out."

"Why are you so obsessed with me getting out to meet people?"

"Because it's good for you. And because you can't sit home every night watching *90 Day Fiancé*."

Amy made a vague hum of agreement. She was developing quite the evening routine. "I really was just trying to be friendly."

"You could have continued being friendly over coffee."

"Your suggestion is noted and I have chosen to ignore it."

"I swear I'm setting you up with the next single cowboy that walks in here."

"Good luck with that," Amy said.

"You know, sometimes I have good advice," Faith said, walking around the counter as a customer flagged her down for help. "You should listen to me every now and then."

"What was that?" Amy said, reaching to turn up the radio again. "I couldn't hear a word you said."

Faith rolled her eyes. "You're thirty-five. I thought you'd outgrow being annoying by now."

"And that assumption was your first mistake." Amy planned on annoying Faith well into old age. But even as she stood there, knowing it was best to leave handsome cowboys alone, she couldn't stop her thoughts from straying back to Josh.

CHAPTER TWO

THERE WAS SOMETHING special about a Montana spring.

Josh knew that the mountains would still be covered in snow, but every day the valleys grew more lush and green, filled with the buds of new wildflowers. The snowfall had been heavy this year, forcing Josh to start the herd on hay to supplement the leftover forage the cattle nosed at from the previous growing season. But even the acres of land around his property had started to flourish, allowing him to finally move the cattle on from winter feeding activities.

Now the ranch was in the thick of calving season which usually began at the end of February and wrapped up in early May. As a boy Josh had learned not to get attached to the new little additions to the herd, and though he still heard his father's words echo in his head—*these aren't pets, son, they're our livelihood*—Josh maintained that all these calves running around the property as the world blossomed made his heart light.

Or maybe he was particularly thoughtful today.

Perhaps that was it.

Spring made him think of new life and new life made him think of family, and he imagined what it would be like to have what his father had: a woman he could adore and a kid (or a couple) that he could dote on. When Josh's dad had finally retired and handed the ranch over to him, it came with a piece of advice.

He'd said that at the end of the day, all that really mattered was not what Josh did with the land, but that he had good people to call home. *Not a place*, he'd said. *People.* At twenty-four, when Josh had been given the ranch, he hadn't thought much of that. He'd been determined to carry on his father's legacy, to make Split Valley Ranch something he could be proud of, and he'd jumped into the sweaty, backbreaking work with all the vigor of a young man. But now he was thirty-six, and Josh was thinking about his father's words a lot lately.

Mostly he was thinking about the way his last relationship had crashed and burned. Josh didn't think he was asking for too much, but so far life hadn't been kind to him as far as romance was concerned. In fact, he'd had his heart kicked around a cow pasture a couple of times. Frankly, he'd prefer to be the night-calver for a whole season, stuck waiting up all night for heifers that might have trouble birthing, more than he would like a repeat of that dating experience. Josh had sort of come to terms with the fact that this was his lot in life: his land and his cattle.

So why couldn't he get Amy out of his head?

"What's your deal?" his friend Noah said from the other side of Josh's truck as they loaded the bed with supplies. Josh had noticed some downed portions of the fence when he was driving into town the other day and Noah was here to help with the repair. The cattle weren't currently using that pasture, but it was best to repair these things when he found them. If not, he'd forget about it in the chaos of the ranch until he drove out to find the cattle on the road one day.

"What are you talking about?"

Noah shrugged. "You're quieter than usual. That's all."

"And that's saying something!" Noah's brother Ryder laughed. He crossed the porch, a toolbox in his hand, clunking down the steps in his work boots. "What he actually means is you're brooding worse than a hen."

Noah inclined his head toward Josh as if to say *he's not wrong*.

Josh sighed, leaning against the bed of the truck. Noah and Ryder Trent were some of his best friends. Their family owned and operated Stargazer Ranch, and though Josh had been a couple years ahead of them at school, once he took over Split Valley, he'd become better acquainted with the brothers, frequently bumping into them at the feed store and at the Tenacity Social Club on his nights off.

"Is something wrong?" Noah asked. He crossed his arms, his flannel shirt bunching at his elbows. He looked tired, dark circles lingering beneath his eyes, though as a single dad to triplet toddlers, he always had that look about him. Between working the ranch and looking after his boys, Noah didn't have a lot of time for socializing, so Josh appreciated these visits even more. He also appreciated that they were willing to help out with a quick repair. It would save him from having to pull the ranch hands away from their work—he always employed a couple during calving season.

"Nothing's wrong," Josh assured him. "I'm just...thinking. That's all."

Ryder scoffed. "Thinking? In my experience," he said as he placed the toolbox in the bed of the truck, "only two things make a man sigh like that. Women and money. And I doubt the ranch is about to go under, so that only leaves one thing."

"Maybe those are the only two things you're thinking about," Noah said. Ryder was known for his roving eye. Josh was pretty sure he'd already dated every eligible woman in town.

"No," Ryder said, clapping Noah on the shoulder. "I also think about how I can rile up my nephews right before bedtime."

"You're horrible."

"I keep things interesting." He climbed into the back seat of the truck.

Noah caught Josh's eye, shaking his head briefly. Josh closed the tailgate, then they both loaded up. Josh drove them down the long gravel drive toward the road, heading for the western border of his property.

"Okay," Ryder said. "Start talking. Who is she?"

Josh glanced in the rearview mirror. Ryder wore that cocky smile of his. The same one he used to woo the ladies in town. Luckily, they'd started getting wise to his tactics.

"It's no one."

"Sure," Ryder said.

Josh felt a flush creep up his neck. He might be the strong

silent type, but he was usually pretty open with his friends. He just didn't know where to start. He'd spent all of fifteen minutes with Amy at the feed store yesterday, yet he couldn't seem to shake the thought of her.

Josh wasn't usually one to brood over women. He'd learned a long time ago that no good came from it. But there'd been a moment yesterday, while Amy was cashing him out, when he'd considered asking her out for coffee. He'd panicked, obviously, and turned tail, rushing out of the store as fast as he could. The problem was, he liked Amy, quite a bit. She'd been interesting and sweet, laughing at his pathetic jokes, and the words *cattle rancher* hadn't sent her running from him, unlike his past relationships. He just wasn't sure what to do about these feelings now. Despite wanting someone to share his life with, he'd come to the conclusion that looking for love only ended up with his heart stomped on. And he wasn't interested in living through that again.

"You know I've got a nose for these things," Ryder said. "I knew Renee and Miles had a thing before they even realized it. Trust me, I'll figure out who you've been talking to."

Noah and Ryder's sister, Renee, had recently found love with Miles Parker. But that's not what was going on here. "I haven't been talking to anyone," Josh said. "I talked. Singular. One time. To someone."

Ryder whooped from the back of the cab. "About time. You're getting as bad as Noah."

"I don't have time for dating drama," Noah said.

Josh glanced out the window, the fields rushing past. He thought he'd made his peace with his land and his cattle. But as much as he loved his work and the land, it was still a lonely existence, even for a man who had learned to enjoy the solitude.

"Okay, but who is she?" Ryder said.

"She's new in town." Josh's eyes lifted to the rearview again. "You don't know her."

Ryder's brow arched. "You sure?"

"Don't go getting any ideas." Josh slowed and drove onto the shoulder of the road, nearing the portion of downed fence. "Her name's Amy. She's working down at the Strom feed store."

"Aww, *Amy*," Noah and Ryder chorused together.

"I hate you both." The truck bounced through some deep potholes, the supplies rattling around the bed of the truck, and the brothers broke into fits of laughter.

"Sorry," Noah said, trying to keep a straight face. "It was just the way you said it, all doe-eyed."

"Shut up."

"Tell us about Amy," Ryder interrupted.

"Nothing much to tell."

"Must be something to tell if she's got you this infatuated already," Noah pointed out.

Josh pulled up next to the fence. "I'm gonna make you both walk back to the ranch."

He got out of the truck. Noah and Ryder followed him to the back of the truck, unloading new fence posts and wire. "Can you blame us?" Noah asked, grabbing the tools. "How long's it been since you were last interested in someone?"

"A while," he muttered.

Honestly, it had been longer than Josh would care to admit. He wasn't a very exciting or adventurous man, and he liked his life the way it was. And that was maybe his downfall. When the woman he'd last seriously dated finally admitted she hated the idea of being trapped in this small town, in this world of ranchers and cattle, Josh had let her go without a fight. How could he possibly hold on to someone who wanted more out of life than what he could offer?

Now she was probably chasing rich cowboys across Montana. Which was for the best.

He turned his gaze to the property line. Split Valley stretched out before him in rolling pastures and meadows caught in a sea of sunlight. The cattle barn loomed like a dappled gray mountain, and the roof of his homestead rose up in two small peaks. Beyond that he could just make out the bulk of the herd, a mass of dark shadow, grazing in the farthest pasture. Maybe this was too simple of an existence for some people, but Josh never failed to be struck by its beauty.

"Give me a hand here," Ryder barked, breaking Josh from his thoughts.

He gathered up one side of the wooden post and helped Ryder carry it over to the fence, replacing the beam that had likely come down during a late winter storm. Noah brought over the toolbox and had a wheel of wire under his arm.

"Watch that there," Josh said, pointing out the rusty nails sticking out of the old beam. Ryder slipped on a pair of work gloves and dragged the old beam off to the bed of the truck.

As Josh set the new beam in place, his thoughts drifted back to his past. He worried now that a romantic partner was always going to expect more than he could provide. More adventure. More money. More thrilling things than what Tenacity had to offer. And as far as Josh went… He knew he was usually too quiet and too much of a homebody. He preferred the outdoors, getting mud on his boots in the pastures, to being cooped up in some stuffy building or surrounded by crowds of people. His social circle was small, and he liked it like that. Sure, maybe that all made him a bit boring, but was the idea of settling down with him that unfathomable?

"I think this'll hold," Noah said, packing earth around the base of the post. "Not going anywhere barring another wild storm."

"Hopefully we won't have to worry about one of those until the summer," Ryder said.

"Looks good," Josh agreed, giving the beam a shake. It held steady, so he released it, collecting supplies as Ryder and Noah strung new wire to keep the cattle contained. When they were finished and everything was packed back into the truck, they all climbed into the cab. Josh took the long way back to the ranch, doing a quick perimeter check, making sure no other posts had come down while he had Ryder and Noah with him.

"So… Amy," Noah said after a beat.

Josh laughed and shook his head. "There really is nothing to tell."

"Well," Ryder said, "maybe you should make a move and change that."

Josh hummed thoughtfully. Should he? Should he have asked her for coffee? Or maybe to lunch? Would she have said yes?

"Look," Ryder said. "I know you love living in Lonely Valley, but it's okay to venture out of it every now and then. It's good for you even."

Josh snorted. Split Valley Ranch had earned its name from the small creek that crossed through the property, but in recent years Ryder had taken to calling it Lonely Valley or even Bachelor Island on occasion.

"I'm not the only one living in Lonely Valley right now," Josh said pointedly.

Ryder smirked. "I'm not lonely. Trust me. And Noah already has too many obligations to attend to. But you... You need this."

Josh reached the long gravel drive and drove them toward the house. Once they'd unloaded the truck, they relaxed in the chairs on the porch. Josh went inside to retrieve a couple of beers as a thank-you. When he returned to the porch, Noah looked up at him and said, "We think you should go for it."

"For what?"

"Amy."

"I barely know her," he said. He actually needed to get her off his mind.

Ryder reached for his beer. "That's the fun of it. Getting to know someone."

"Besides, what's the harm in asking her out?"

Josh could think of a lot of things. Maybe she'd flat out refuse. Maybe she'd agree and then realize he wasn't all that interesting. Would she though? She'd been surprisingly easy to talk to. He opened his beer and took a long sip.

"Remember what you said at the Fur-Ball?" Noah said.

He recalled the fundraiser for Loyal Companions, a local animal rescue organization, but nothing else. "Not particularly. No."

"You said you weren't looking for Mrs. Right, just *Ms. Right Now.* Ring any bells?"

Josh shrugged. "Maybe."

"Exactly," Ryder cut in. "This doesn't have to be anything serious. Everyone deserves to have a little fun now and then. Even the president of Lonely Valley."

Josh snorted.

Noah shifted in his chair to face Josh. "Look, all I'm saying is if you feel like you hit it off with this woman, why not ask her out?"

"Because it'll probably end badly. So avoiding the whole thing seems wiser."

"Sure, if you never put yourself out there, you'll maybe save yourself the heartache, but you also might miss out on something really great."

Ryder laughed, almost choking on his beer. "Listen to the two of you, carrying on like the Quilting Club. Josh, you know what your problem is? You need to get laid and stop thinking so much."

"We can't all be a Lothario," Josh muttered.

Ryder grinned and nudged Josh's shoulder. "I'm serious. Every lady likes a grand gesture. Do something spontaneous, get her attention, and I'm telling you, she's yours."

"I don't know." The idea of doing anything particularly bold made him uncomfortable, especially without knowing if Amy was in any way interested.

"Better than you sitting around here moping with the cattle about it."

"I'm not moping."

"What would you call it then?"

"Look at it this way," Noah cut in. "If you don't ask her out, Ryder will probably try. So just think of it like that. You're saving the girl from a far worse fate than you."

Josh burst into laughter as Ryder scowled at his brother. Noah spilled his beer down his shirt from snickering so hard.

IN JOSH'S EXPERIENCE, telling himself not to think about something only made him want to dwell on it more. And he was beginning to think that he wasn't ever going to be able to shake Amy from his thoughts. He'd tried in a lot of ways since his conversation with Noah and Ryder a couple days ago. Really, he had. He'd thrown himself into his work. He'd gotten up earlier and went to bed later. He'd started projects he'd been putting off, and even made an effort to pop into the Tenacity Social Club to catch up with his neighbors.

The problem with ranching was it left him with a lot of time to think. Cattle weren't the best conversationalists, so his mind wandered. And no matter how often he redirected them, his thoughts inevitably returned to Amy.

His phone buzzed in his pocket, and Josh yanked it out, eager for the distraction. An image of his mother filled the screen. Josh answered it. "Hey, Mom. Thought you and Dad would already be on your way."

"Hi, honey. We just boarded the ship, but we don't depart for another couple of hours. They need time to get all the passengers and luggage on board. Can you believe your father almost misplaced his passport this morning?"

Josh checked his watch. Seattle was only an hour behind Tenacity. His parents would be destined for Alaska before lunch.

"Your father's disappeared in this breakfast buffet somewhere. I've never seen so much food. Harry!" she shouted suddenly. "Harry, get over here. Josh is on the phone!"

Josh laughed. He could just imagine his father heading straight for an all-you-can-eat platter of bacon. His mother would be spending the entire trip hounding him about his cholesterol.

"Anyway," his mother continued. "We just wanted to check in before we left. I don't know when our next chance will be. I'm sure reception will be spotty once we're out at sea."

"Right."

"How are things going?"

"Good. The ranch is good. Calving season is on track."

"Mmm hmm," his mother said. "And is that all?"

"What are you talking about?"

"Don't pester the boy, Margaret," he heard his father say in the background.

"Quiet, Harry," his mother said. "I'm talking about this young lady that you've met."

Josh's jaw dropped. How the heck did she know about Amy all the way in Seattle? "I don't... I don't know—"

"Don't play that game with me, son."

"What game?"

"I spoke to Iris Strom. She mentioned that Faith said you'd been in the store, talking to some girl named Amy."

"Yes, because she works there." Josh sighed. Sometimes

small towns were just too dang small. "She was helping me find the feed."

"Well, is she—" His mother cut off. "Oh, Josh, I have to go. Your father's found the bacon. Harry! Harold, that's enough."

He laughed. "Okay, Mom. You two have a good trip."

"I'll send you pictures. And don't think I've forgotten about this Amy person. I want to hear—"

"Think that reception's getting a little spotty, Mom."

"Nice try."

"I've gotta go. Love you." Josh hung up before his mother could finish her sentence about Amy. There was nothing to tell, because they'd only had *one* conversation. And after the way things went with his last girlfriend, he didn't need to get his mother's hopes up.

Despite all that, Amy was still there, hanging out at the edge of his thoughts. Josh figured there was only one thing to do. He rushed through the rest of his chores and got into his truck, then drove down to Strom and Son Feed and Farm Supply.

He pulled into the parking lot, glancing at the front of the building.

What the hell was he doing?

Josh cut the ignition.

He hadn't driven all the way out here just because his mother had asked about Amy. Okay, not *just* because his mother had asked. It was because he didn't know how else to get her off his mind. That was the only reason. He needed to be able to focus on the ranch, and he couldn't do that if she kept popping into his thoughts.

Maybe Noah and Ryder were right. He should ask her out. What did he have to lose? His heart thumped in his chest. Putting himself out there again felt like a big step, one he didn't know if he was ready to take. But he'd already come this far. It would be ridiculous to turn back now without even trying.

CHAPTER THREE

AMY STOOD ON the top of a stepladder in the middle of aisle three, the back of her hand pressed to her lips as a wave of nausea as strong as an angry bull threatened to bowl her over. *Where the hell did this come from?* She didn't know if it was the lingering scent of hay that Caleb had just restocked in the warehouse or something on one of the shelves, but the cloying scent was turning her stomach like a blender. Amy clutched the shelf in front of her and took a deep, steadying breath.

She wasn't actually going to be sick, was she? Right here? In the middle of the store? She was too far away from the bathroom. She'd never make it. Her best bet would be to head for the trash can behind the cash desk but even that would be a risky dash.

Amy squeezed her eyes shut, willing everything in her stomach to settle. The nausea swept through her again, lingering on the back of her tongue, and she was almost afraid to swallow. Amy didn't often feel like this. The only time she did was during early morning rodeo training when she was doing a lot of activity and hadn't eaten enough.

And sure, maybe she'd skipped out on breakfast this morning. But who could blame her? Faith had been trying to stuff some turkey bacon-shaped something on a whole grain bagel in her hand, and that had sounded entirely unappealing. Though Amy usually turned her nose up at most of Faith's healthy choices—

flax seed, quinoa, steel cut oats. It all just tasted like cardboard as far as Amy was concerned. Faith would have to pry real bacon out of her cold, dead hands. Amy had intended to grab breakfast when she got to the store. There was a cute little diner up the road that she'd been meaning to try for weeks, only she'd started stocking shelves and now it was almost lunchtime.

Still, this wasn't exactly the most arduous of tasks, and she'd skipped breakfast before, surviving on nothing but coffee and creamer. She shouldn't be feeling nauseated and slightly dizzy and tired.

Why was she so tired all of a sudden?

Amy fought off a yawn, worried that if she opened her mouth, it could be disastrous as far as the nausea was concerned. She clutched the shelf and took a short, even breath in through her nose. Then another. And another.

Slowly, the uncomfortable wave passed and Amy breathed easier.

There. All better.

She clearly needed to get some fresh air and some food into her. She'd no sooner thought about food than the nausea was back, so strong Amy clasped her hand over her mouth, certain she would be sick this time. *Okay, time to take a break*, she thought. From stocking. From the store. From the overwhelming scent of sickly-sweet hay. She just needed to get away from it all. But moving felt like a really bad idea.

What she needed was a distraction. Something to take her mind off the way her stomach was churning and bubbling, and the goose bumps that flushed down her arms, and the prickly heat that was suddenly creeping up her neck.

The bell over the front door jingled and Amy really hoped it wasn't a customer that was going to need her help. She didn't really feel like she was in any condition to be gathering up orders or showing people around.

"Well, look who it is!" Faith's voice soared over the sound of the bell, tinged with surprise. "Or should I say, look who the horse dragged in?"

"Sorry, I just came from the barn." That voice was familiar. Amy craned her head, looking down the aisle from the top of the stepladder. She couldn't quite see more than the corner of the cash desk. "I didn't even think about changing."

A figure stepped into view. Tall. Broad-shouldered. Long brown hair swept back, showing off a strong jawline. It was *him*.

Josh Aventura.

In the flesh.

Again.

The man her sister thought she should have asked out for coffee the other day. The man who she'd been thinking about nonstop since. It had been months since a man had occupied her waking thoughts. Certainly not since the early days of seeing Tru, and now in hindsight, he'd obviously been haunting her.

She tried to bite down on the smile that stretched across her face. She couldn't quite tell if she was thrilled to see him again, or if that was just the nausea, fluttering away in her chest. She reached onto the shelf and pulled a pallet of cans closer, facing the labels out to the front. What was Josh doing back here so soon anyway? Faith had said it would be close to a month before he'd be back for supplies. Perhaps he'd forgotten something.

Amy looked his way again.

She certainly hadn't forgotten how effortlessly handsome he was. It really was unfair for him to look that good after likely spending all morning with his cattle on his ranch.

He brushed at his shirt, knocking away dust.

"I'm kidding," Faith said. "I was just surprised to see you in here twice in one week. I'd say to what do we owe the pleasure? But usually when a customer returns that quickly it's with a complaint. Something wrong with the product we sold you?"

"No," Josh said, shaking his head. "No problem."

"So what? This just a social call?" Faith walked around the end of the cash desk, crossing her arms as she looked up at him. Her lips puckered, and Amy knew she was trying not to grin. "You checking up on your neighbors?"

"A man needs supplies," Josh said, so low Amy could barely hear him. His shoulders hunched up by his ears.

Faith threw her head back and laughed. "You know damn well we only see you in here once a month."

Josh dropped his hands to his hips. "Maybe I forgot a couple of things last time."

"Oh yeah? Like what?"

Amy shook her head. Poor Josh. She'd been on the wrong end of one of Faith's interrogations more times than she could count. If she wanted to know something desperately enough, Josh didn't stand a chance.

"Do you always harass your customers?" he asked gruffly.

"I'm not harassing, I'm showing a vested interest."

Josh reached out for one of the stands by the desk, pulling something from the display rack. He laid it on the desk.

"Wool sheep shears?" Faith said. "For a cattle ranch."

"Maybe I'm branching out," he said. "Or maybe I'm doing a favor for a neighbor. You want my money or not? Cause there's another perfectly good feed store up the road."

Amy smirked. Growing up on the rodeo circuit with a lot of sisters and cousins, Amy had quickly learned to compete with strong personalities. Josh might have been the gruff, quiet type who usually kept to himself, but Amy liked that he didn't take any of Faith's flak.

"Oh, I'll take your money," Faith said, clicking her tongue. "No need to act like you've got a burr in your saddle. I'm just saying... Sheep?"

"She giving you a hard time?" Caleb called, strutting across the store with Nathan and a pair of cowboy boot-clad ranchers in tow.

"Nothing I can't handle," Josh said.

Caleb slowed by the desk, leaning over to peck Faith on the cheek. He was incredibly tall, with deep brown skin, carved cheekbones, and an abundance of muscles from dragging around heavy bags of feed all day. Amy's heart swelled at the sight of them together. She really couldn't be happier that Faith had ended up with someone as kind and as doting as Caleb. Faith might give her a hard time, as sisters do, but she deserved all the happiness she'd found with Caleb.

"Be nice to the customers," Nathan called before carrying on. "I don't need them running off to the Feed and Seed."

Amy knew Nathan was joking. For as small as Tenacity was,

with the sheer number of ranchers that lived and worked in the surrounding area, there was definitely a need for more than one feed store in town. Though each store still seemed to have their own loyal, longtime customers.

"I'm just reminding Mr. Aventura here that he runs a cattle ranch, not a sheep ranch."

Caleb hummed. "Maybe he's branching out."

Faith rolled her eyes so dramatically Amy could see it perfectly from where she stood. She muttered something that sounded like *"Men,"* as Caleb wished Josh a good day and headed off after his father and the customers.

Faith turned her gaze back to Josh. "You want me to ring these shears up for you now?"

Josh turned, glancing around the store. "Not quite yet. I've got a couple other things to look for."

"Yeah, for that sheep ranch you're starting." Josh turned away from the counter, and Faith picked up the shears, placing them on the display shelf once more. She turned around and shot Amy a look, her lips curling into a smug smile.

Amy knew exactly what Faith was thinking, and resisted the urge to roll her own eyes at Faith's insinuation. She couldn't deny the fact that she was pleased to see Josh back in the store so soon, but it's not like he'd returned just to see her. He was a busy, hardworking man, and even if he didn't need sheep shears, they'd spent all of fifteen minutes together. Surely she hadn't made any type of worthwhile impression on the man.

He certainly made one on you though.

Amy pushed that thought aside. It disappeared quickly, lost in another wave of nausea, though this one was not nearly as bad as the first. She sucked in a sharp breath just as Josh's voice reached her.

"They pay you to stand around on top of stepladders all day?"

Amy turned her head. Josh had appeared from the other end of the aisle. He glanced up at her, the corner of his mouth lifting, a sack of feed tucked under one of his arms.

"Well, hello to you too, cowboy. I don't get paid at all, remember?"

"Ah, that's right." He took a step closer, and she could make out the way his brown eyes shone under the sunlight spilling in through the skylights. "You're just standing around out of the goodness of your heart."

"I am not *just* standing around," Amy scoffed. "I happen to be facing the product." She gestured down the aisle to all the cans she'd neatly arranged. "I'm even arranging it by expiration date."

"Oh, well, I'm sorry now for interrupting such vital work."

"You should be. I'm giving up my precious time to talk to you."

"Still haggling Caleb for employee of the month?"

Amy laughed. "As if there's any real competition. So, I hear you're branching out into sheep?"

"You do a lot of eavesdropping up there, huh?"

"Only on the interesting conversations. So, sheep?"

"What is it with you and Faith getting on my case about the sheep? Do I not look like I could handle some sheep?"

Amy's heart fluttered beneath her ribs. She suspected he hadn't really come to the store to secure supplies to start a sheep ranch. But before she could really wonder about what had brought Josh back so soon, a wave of dizziness consumed her. It started at the top of her head, like someone had cracked an egg right against her skull. The sensation slithered down her spine, rolling out across her body. She clutched the top of the stepladder as her head spun. This wasn't Josh having this effect on her, was it?

No, that would be ridiculous.

She didn't swoon over men.

Not even cowboys like Josh, who looked at her with big brown eyes and a smile that could knock the air right out of her lungs.

She'd learned her lesson.

Amy took a step down the ladder while she still had her balance. And another. She just had to get her feet back on solid ground. Then her stomach would settle and her head would stop spinning.

Right?

She reached up, palm to her forehead. Her mouth was dust dry. Her feet hit solid ground.

"Amy?" Josh said, his tone soft, concerned. She'd closed her eyes again so she couldn't see his face, but she felt his hand on her shoulder and that stirred more sensation in her gut. "You doing okay?"

"Fine," she squeaked in a voice that was too tiny to be her own. Then everything shifted sideways. Her head, her body... Her hip hit the stepladder, jostling it aside, and she was certain she was going to hit the floor next, but instead she crashed up against a wall of sturdy muscle.

Josh's arms wrapped around her upper arms, holding her upright with the kind of strength that would bruise, but Amy's other alternative was slumping straight to the floor. Her legs felt like sandbags, heavy and useless, and exhaustion surged through her, clinging to her bones.

"I don't think you're fine," he said. "You're the same color as my mother's china."

Oh, he was comparing her to porcelain. If she squinted maybe she could take that as a compliment. Porcelain was shiny and lustrous. Surely he didn't mean she was as pale and gaunt as she currently felt? One look at his face and she knew better.

"I really am fine," she insisted, trying to shake off the dizzy spell. Before she could, the nausea returned full force and Amy tried not to heave on Josh's boots.

"Okay," he said, sounding even more concerned. "Let's find you somewhere to sit down, huh?"

Amy let Josh guide her out of the aisle. She didn't have the strength to do anything else. She was like a rag doll in his arms.

"Faith!" he called. "Can I get some help?"

Amy heard panicked footsteps and Faith's sharp cry as she rushed over to meet them. "What happened?"

She took Amy by one arm, Josh kept to the other, and together they helped her into the chair behind the cash desk.

"What's going on?" Faith asked, pressing her hand to Amy's forehead the way their parents had when they were young. "You're not coming down with something, are you?"

"It's nothing," Amy said, shrugging her off. She didn't need Faith fussing over her like this. She especially didn't need her doing it in front of Josh. She'd practically already collapsed into the man's arms. That was enough mortification for one morning. "I got a bit dizzy coming down the ladder. That's all."

"It was a little more than nothing," Josh cut in.

"Dizzy?" Faith said. "Since when do you have a problem with heights?"

"I don't," Amy said. "It's probably because I didn't eat this morning." This was like trying to barrel race on an empty stomach with low blood sugar.

"You should have eaten that bagel I made you."

Amy wrinkled her nose as fatigue clung to her. She sighed. "I'm good now. I swear. I'll just get some food into me." She tried to stand, only to be hit with a shaky bout of weakness. Maybe she hadn't gotten enough sleep last night? That plus skipping breakfast might have been enough to make her feel like crap.

"I think I should take you home." Faith glanced up at the customers in the store. "Caleb should be finished with those ranchers soon. Do you think you can wait a little bit?"

Amy didn't want to admit it, but going home and crawling back into bed sounded like a dream. "I really am fine. I can drive myself back to your place. It's not that far."

"No!" Josh said at the same time Faith declared, "Absolutely not!"

Amy shrugged away from the force of their combined outburst. Faith's brows arched as she regarded Josh.

"I can drive you back to Faith's if you want," he said.

Faith's brows rose even higher, probably matching Amy's. "That's okay," she hurried to say. She'd already troubled him enough for one morning.

"You're sure it's no bother?" Faith said, completely ignoring Amy's huff of protest.

Josh shrugged. "Your place is on the way out to my ranch anyway. I'm driving by regardless."

Amy frowned. What was happening here? First of all, she was fine. Second of all, she was a big girl. She didn't need other people making decisions for her.

"You know what, that would actually be super helpful," Faith said. "Amy, I think you should take him up on his offer. You look like you're about to keel over."

"Gee, thanks," she muttered. But as much as she wanted to argue, to tell Josh and Faith exactly where they could stuff their good idea, she just didn't have the energy. Something had zapped it from her. "All right, fine. I'll take the lift."

"Great," Josh said. "I'll go pull my truck around front and be right back."

"Thanks again, Josh," Faith called after him.

The moment he was out the door, Amy's eyes cut across to Faith. "Don't do that," she all but hissed.

"Do what?" Faith asked, playing with the end of her long braid.

"Meddle."

"I don't know what you're talking about. I'm just trying to get you home safe and sound."

"By sending me off with a practical stranger?"

"Don't be ridiculous." Faith laughed. "Everyone knows everyone in Tenacity. And Josh wouldn't hurt a fly. You don't have to worry about him."

"The other day you said you'd barely ever heard the man speak more than a few words."

"Yes, in that gruff, stoic, lonely cowboy sort of way. Not in like a serial killer way."

Amy rolled her eyes. "Wonderful."

"You'll be fine. Seriously. But call me if you start to feel worse after he drops you off and I'll come home and take care of you."

Amy grumbled. She didn't need Faith to take care of her, and she especially didn't need her sister trying to set her up with a man while she was trying her best not to hurl all over the interior of his truck.

CHAPTER FOUR

"STAY PUT FOR a second. I'll give you a hand," Josh said as he pulled into the empty driveway at Faith and Caleb's place. A sun-bleached porch wrapped around the front of the property. It was a cozy, modern farmhouse filled with rustic country style. A wooden porch swing hung at one end of the house and two wooden rockers at the other. Vertical white siding covered the exterior of the house, stretching up to twin peaks with square windows. Amy thought it was the perfect little house in many ways. Right now it was perfect because her bed was just inside.

When Josh cut the ignition and the truck stopped rumbling, Amy felt like her insides were still shaking. Josh hopped out, hurrying around the front of the truck to collect her. He reached her door before Amy had even had a chance to open it.

"You don't have to escort me," she said as he swung the door open for her. "I'm perfectly capable of walking myself inside." She took a beat to make sure she was steady, then stepped out of the vehicle. It was a long way down and Josh caught her as she hit the ground. Amy resisted every urge to huff. She was not an invalid. And she'd only been a *little* dizzy. Now she had Josh tripping over himself to help her, and she felt silly. She also felt a little of something else as the heat of his hands pressed against her upper arms. Something that made her heart skitter in her chest. But she wasn't going to think about that or the flush that was creeping up her neck as Josh looked down at her, smiling a crooked smile.

Then he put a respectful bit of distance between them. "I don't mean to impose my help, but you do know that Faith will have my hide if I don't get you safely in the house, right?"

"What was that?" Amy said as an uncomfortable prickle of sensation washed through her. It wasn't quite dizziness, but it swept away her thoughts and made her stomach queasy. What the hell was going on? The feeling crept up on her, then receded, and she took an exaggerated breath, trying to get control of herself.

"Amy? You good? Not gonna hit the pavement on me, are you?"

The way he said her name sent a shiver through her—delight, maybe?—and Amy wanted to shake herself. *Get a grip, girl! He's just being friendly.* "I'm fine," she managed.

"You say that so often I'm starting to not believe you." He held out his arm to her. "I know you're insisting you don't need my help, but just humor me. Until we get you inside?"

Amy reached for him, latching onto his arm like one of those big suckerfish she and her sisters used to fish out of the river when they were young. She supposed this was the better alternative to fainting cold on the driveway. She had no doubt that Josh would catch her if she did in fact pass out, but how mortifying would that be? Then he'd have to drag her limp body inside while he called Faith and that was something she'd rather avoid.

"How're you doing?" Josh asked as they wandered up the driveway.

"Good."

"You don't sound very convincing."

Because with every step she felt like she was balancing on two spindles instead of legs.

"If it would make things easier I could just carry you inside."

Amy snapped her head up. "Don't you dare, Josh Aventura."

"Yikes! What'd I do to deserve the full name?"

"It's to let you know that I mean business."

"Noted." He pursed his lips and nodded. "Not a girl to be swept off her feet."

Amy snorted at that. After Tru, the last thing she wanted was someone swooping in and trying to dazzle her. Though she knew very well Josh had meant those words literally not figuratively. Amy doubted he had any plans to try and dazzle her. They still hardly knew each other.

"How about we agree to this then?" Josh said. "I will not offer to carry you unless there is an obvious threat to life or limb."

Amy leaned into the hold she still had on his arm. "I suppose that's reasonable. I don't think I'd be in any shape to refuse you in those particular circumstances."

"Glad you see it my way," Josh said. He looked over and she studied the way his hair parted, falling in soft waves on either side of his forehead. It was more than long enough to run her fingers through, and her mind wandered. She thought about the way it would feel to tangle her hands in it before she reeled herself in. She was already fighting dizziness, no need to make it any worse. His brown eyes studied her in return. Amy watched the way they crinkled, the lines by his eyes holding something like mischief.

Back at the store, Faith had given her the impression that Josh was a quiet man. The kind who kept to himself. But looking at him now, she was starting to think that Josh was anything but quiet. He expressed himself in a multitude of little ways—the curl of his smile, his narrowing gaze, the way he cocked his head at her, the way his thumb stroked her forearm. Amy thought Josh was saying an awful lot. Most people were probably just too busy to notice.

They reached the porch steps, and Amy thought Josh might leave her there, but he inclined his head toward the door. "We're going all the way," he said. "I don't intend to cross Faith."

"Probably for the best. You already had her in a fit over those sheep shears."

"Exactly. You wouldn't want me to face her wrath again so soon?"

"I see now why you offered to drive me. Trying to stay on her good side."

Josh looked over at her, his lips twisted. "I wasn't really after sheep shears," he admitted as they walked up the steps to the door.

"I figured," Amy said. She fumbled with her house key, finally getting it in the lock. "Seemed like a jump to go from cattle rancher to sheep rancher."

"Well, it's for the best probably. And I suppose I got what I wanted in the end anyway."

"But you left empty-handed."

"Not quite."

Amy's head snapped up, gazing into those brown eyes, and her breath caught. He couldn't mean… She stumbled against the doorframe. Great. Now she was dizzy all over again. There was no mistaking the fluttering in her chest this time. Nerves and adrenaline and excitement and… *Who are you to make me feel like this, Josh Aventura?*

He leaned toward her, huffing a laugh. "Thought you were perfectly fine."

Amy reached between them, turning the doorknob and shoving it open. "Might have spoken too soon."

"Where do you—" Josh started to say.

Amy pointed to the plush couch in the living room. It was soft fabric and swallowed her as Josh deposited her onto the cushions. She sank back with a heavy sigh.

"I think you're a little worse than you're letting on," Josh said.

"I'm really not," Amy tried to assure him. "It's just coming in waves. I'll be fine in a minute, after some rest." She touched the back of her hand to her forehead. Despite the weird cluster of symptoms, she really didn't feel sick. But she was clearly going to have to make sure she ate a proper breakfast in the mornings. She *was* getting older. Maybe her body was changing and telling her to take better care of herself. Maybe she was going to have to start eating Faith's turkey bacon. She wrinkled her nose.

Josh turned and headed for the door.

"Thank you!" Amy called after him, scrambling to sit up. "For the ride and for…well, everything." She wished she had the energy to work up more of a thank-you. She should at least offer him something to drink for his troubles, but she didn't have it in her. And that was a shame because she really liked talking to Josh. Amy ran a hand through her hair. Damn Faith and her need to interfere. She hadn't even gotten around to asking Josh out for coffee yet, and after today she wasn't sure she ever would.

He'd obviously had more than enough of her. Probably couldn't wait to get back in his truck and flee to his ranch.

She heard the door close, but to her surprise, Josh was still standing there. *Oh*. He toed out of his boots, then turned to face her. "Where's the kitchen?" he asked, lifting his hand to gesture down the hall. "Through here?"

Oh! Amy propped herself up a little more. She could do this. If Josh wanted to stay a minute, she could rally. "Would you like something to drink? Can I get you—"

Josh was by her side in an instant, settling her back into the cushions. He wedged one of Faith's fancy, frilly pillows behind her back. "Don't get up," he said. "Just make yourself comfortable."

Amy smirked up at him. He was so close she could count the dark stubble on his cheeks and chin. "I think you stole my line."

The corner of his mouth twitched. "You might be surprised to hear it, but I actually know my way around a kitchen pretty well. And before I go, you at least need some water. Maybe you're just dehydrated."

"Josh, I can get it. Really. Please don't trouble yourself."

"Sit," he said in that gruff way of his. It sounded like an order. "I won't take any arguing."

Amy frowned after him as he made his way to the kitchen. She felt odd, having Josh wait on her in Faith's house, but she didn't want to offend him after he'd gone out of his way to help her. Plus, a silly little part of her liked that she got to indulge in his company for a little while longer. She sank back, listening to cupboard doors open and close. She could hear him puttering around, shifting glasses, and then the squeak of the sink tap. When he returned to the living room, he had a tall glass of water in his hand.

"Drink," he said as he handed it to her.

"Is that another order?"

"A strong suggestion."

Amy took a sip. It was refreshing, but she wasn't parched, so she doubted her dizzy spell had anything to do with being dehydrated. "Thank you," she said anyway. "For this. For driving me home."

He studied her again with those deep brown eyes, and Amy felt her cheeks flush. She didn't know why, but under the strength of his gaze, she felt oddly cared for.

"You need something to eat," he finally said. "How about some toast and sweet tea?"

"The water is plenty," she said, but he was already making his way back to the kitchen.

"I assume you *like* toast?"

"Who doesn't like toast?" she called.

"According to my grandmother," Josh said, his voice carrying across the house, "a good piece of toast could settle your stomach and all your woes."

"She sounds like a wise lady."

"She was. She also used to keep sweets in her purse for whenever she visited the ranch. Some for me. Some for the horses."

Amy came from a long line of strong, stubborn women—especially her mother and grandmother—so she could appreciate how fondly Josh spoke of his grandmother. She closed her eyes briefly, listening to the sounds of Josh moving about the kitchen. She imagined him at the counter, strong shoulders, perfectly parted hair, those forearms... The toaster popped and her eyes flew open. Heat pooled in her chest. Maybe it was better not to be imagining those sorts of things.

Josh returned a few minutes later with some buttered toast and sweet tea. He handed it to her, and Amy sat up. "Looks like the color is starting to come back to your cheeks," he noted.

That only made Amy flush harder. The color was back for all the wrong reasons. "I think I'm feeling much better. You don't have to stay."

"Right," Josh said, giving her a curt nod. "I'm glad to hear it."

Amy felt the energy in the room shift as Josh turned toward the door.

"Wait," Amy said suddenly. "I'm sorry, that felt abrupt. I didn't mean to rush you out, especially after you were kind enough to make me something to eat. I hope you didn't think that." She was messing up this entire thing.

"I didn't think that," Josh said. "But I'm also not trying to overstay my welcome."

"You're not," Amy said. "It's not that I want you to leave. I just figured you probably had more important things to be getting on with. I'm sure the ranch needs your attention."

He shrugged. "Well, even if I do, I'm still happy to sit a spell with you. If that's something you'd like, of course."

Yes! she wanted to shout. *Stay for a spell. Stay with me.* She didn't want this to end just yet. "I would like that very much." His face lit up at her words. "How about we sit on the porch though? I think I could use a bit of fresh air again."

"Sounds good." Josh helped her up and carried her sweet tea and toast out to the porch.

Amy settled into one of the wooden rockers. The day was sunny, the air cool but not chilly. She let the energy settle into her, let it wash away her earlier dizziness. She felt better out here with the endless blue sky stretching across town. It was the perfect kind of day, actually, made all the better by the fact Josh was here.

The fact that he wanted to be here was something Amy was still trying to wrap her head around.

"Can I get you anything else?" Josh asked.

"No, but will you at least get yourself a drink? I'm feeling like a terrible host."

"Please don't," Josh said. "We're here because you weren't feeling well, not so you could wait on me."

Amy smiled up at him. "Just get some sweet tea, please?"

"If it'll stop you from stressing."

"It will."

He disappeared into the house again. While he was gone, Amy picked away at her toast, even the crusts, which she usually left behind, finding herself ravenous. When had buttered toast ever tasted so wonderful? Josh returned with a glass in hand.

"Happy now?" he asked, plopping down in the rocker next to hers. He kicked his legs out, the toes of his boots worn and dusty.

"Yes," Amy said, grinning. Caleb and Faith often sat out here like this in the evenings, after the store was closed and dinner was cleaned up. More than once, Amy had thought about how lovely it must feel to sit in the quiet company of someone you cared about. "So, do you get any time to do this out on that ranch of yours? Or is it just work, work, work all the time?"

"You know, I usually put the cattle in charge and they take care of things for me."

"Oh, of course. I'm sure they're running the ranch right now."

"Keeping it in top shape," Josh agreed.

"No, but really?" Amy said.

"I mean, do I kick back on the porch and relax? On occasion. Usually only if I have people stop by for whatever reason. When it's just me, I usually have a running list of things that need to get done around the property and I just fill my time. It's the kind of job where you're never really caught up, if that makes sense. There's always some wayward cow getting stuck in the creek or some storm tearing down fences or supplies that need to be gathered."

Amy nodded. "I guess you could say *I'm* the one doing *you* the favor. Forcing you to relax in the middle of the day."

Josh sipped his sweet tea, hiding his smirk. "This was all for my benefit then?"

"It's looking that way."

"I see. Guess I should be thanking you."

"It's the least you could do," Amy said. "After the big show I had to put on to get you here."

Josh chuckled. "I am glad you seem to be feeling better."

"The toast worked wonders."

"Now that's a best kept secret, so don't go spreading it around."

"Oh, I would never." Amy pretended to lock her lips and toss the key away. She glanced back at him. "Tell me about Split Valley."

"What do you want to know?"

"Tell me about the horses. You said you have a few?"

"Well," Josh said, "There's Bella and Bitsy. I've had Bella since I was a teen. She's older and grumpy now, but still my best girl. Bitsy likes who she likes and bites everyone else. But we're working on it."

Amy laughed. "Sounds like quite the character."

"Oh, she is. And then there's Mac. Short for Macbeth, because he's just full of drama. But he's also very sweet and gentle, and as long as I sneak him a treat every now and then, I can usually get him to keep the melodrama to a minimum."

Amy loved the way he talked about his horses. There was warmth and affection, and she very much wanted to meet this little herd. His voice was soothing as he carried on about their personalities, about Bitsy not being allowed near visitors, about the oddball things that horses do. Amy could have listened to him talk all day about everything and nothing. As it was, everything sounded so much more interesting. He could have been telling her about the clouds in the sky and she suspected she'd still be hanging on every word.

"So how long have you been riding?" Josh said. "You mentioned it the other day at the store that it's one of your favorite things."

"I started learning... Gosh, I must have been three or four," Amy said. "But I'd been around horses my whole life." She glossed over The Hawkins Sisters stuff again because she wanted Josh to know her without all the glitz and glam.

"Did you get yourself a tiny little pony?"

"That's exactly what I had!" Amy laughed. "Me and all my sisters. We used to fight over who got in the saddle first."

"I'm trying to imagine a tiny you, kicking up dust and wrinkling your nose when you didn't get your way."

"I try not to scrap with my sisters anymore," Amy said. "I don't think I ever outgrew the nose wrinkle though."

"It's okay." The corner of his mouth quirked in that half smile. "It's cute."

Amy chased away her blush with a huge gulp of sweet tea. Josh either didn't seem to notice, or politely chose to ignore her, carrying on the conversation. They kept talking and before Amy knew it, over an hour had passed and Josh showed no sign of leaving.

Amy basked in the perfection of the weather and his company. In the back of her mind, though, a small, annoying thought couldn't help drawing her attention to Tru. He had seemed sweet too, once upon a time, and she'd foolishly trusted that sweetness.

When she'd met Tru last October at the Golden Buckle Rodeo held at the Bronco Convention Center, Amy had thought he was something special. He was the kind of person who gave you his full attention when you talked, making you feel like you were the only person in the room. And when he'd singled her out for conversation, Amy was not only flattered but shocked, falling for those false charms so fast she was surprised she didn't land flat on her face.

Josh seemed different in so many ways. In all the ways that mattered, perhaps. But her heart skipped for him the way it had once raced for Tru, and that made her nervous. Still, she tried to imagine Tru dropping everything, putting his entire day on hold, just to take care of her the way Josh had today, and she couldn't—so that had to mean something. Didn't it?

Amy pushed the thoughts from her mind, determined to enjoy what was left of their afternoon together. Only when Josh left, did Amy realize how refreshed she felt. It was almost as if Josh had lifted some sort of darkness off her, and that was certainly more than she could ever say about Tru McCoy.

CHAPTER FIVE

"IT'S NOT WEIRD," Josh said to Bella as he removed her tack, tossing the heavy saddle over the gate. He picked up a brush and swept it across her broad back, her roan coat gleaming in the early morning sun that spilled in through the barn door. "I'm just gonna swing by and see how she's feeling after yesterday."

Bella snorted, the sound muffled with her face in her feed bucket.

Josh had a habit of talking to his horses. He hadn't noticed until one of his hired hands pointed it out one day, and they'd all had a good laugh about it. Josh supposed he talked to most of his animals. He spent a lot of solitary time out here, with nothing but the cattle and the horses as company, so some one-sided conversation was expected. Besides, the horses never complained. As long as he bribed them with a bucket of oats and a thorough brushing, they were content to listen as long as he needed.

"It's the neighborly thing to do," he continued. "I know we're not *technically* neighbors, but it'd be rude of me not to inquire. Wouldn't it? I mean, I use the feed store every month. Don't you think it would be weird *not* to say something?"

Bella's ear twitched.

"That's not particularly helpful," Josh said, giving Bella a firm pat.

He'd been thinking about Amy since the moment he'd gotten up this morning, wondering how she was faring, if she was feeling any better, if she'd be back at work today. He tried to tell himself it was just genuine concern, but a small part of him knew it was more than that.

He'd spent the better part of yesterday afternoon with her, sitting out on the porch, and Josh honestly couldn't remember when he'd enjoyed himself more. It had been a perfect spring day, but the truth was that it was the company that had been so pleasant. It could have been blowin' up a storm and he'd still have enjoyed himself just the same. Frankly, Amy was the only thing occupying his thoughts, and he'd come to the conclusion that the only way to stop said thoughts was to see her again. When he'd left her yesterday, the color had come back to her cheeks and she laughed freely at the stories he told her about wayward cattle on the ranch.

But he couldn't shake the desire to see her again. To make sure she really was feeling better.

"It's not weird," he said again as he locked Bella's stall and hung up the tack.

It was perfectly normal to be concerned about a neighbor. A charming, sweet, interesting neighbor. Not to mention beautiful. Because he'd be lying to himself if he didn't acknowledge the way Amy's pretty smile, directed right at him, made his pulse skip like a frog into a creek bed.

He thought again about what Ryder and Noah had said the day they'd visited. *Go for it.*

And why the hell not? Josh asked himself. They'd had a good time yesterday—him and Amy—after she was feeling a little better. Perhaps they'd have an even better time if he worked up the nerve to ask her to lunch.

Because it's going to hurt, a voice whispered inside his head. *It's going to get messy and she'll stomp all over your heart.*

Hush, he wanted to tell the voice. He glanced at his watch. If he was going to check up on Amy and maybe catch her before lunch, he had to go now. Josh darted inside to change out of his dusty riding clothes. He wetted his hands and ran them through his hair, making sure everything lay flat before he hurried back out to his truck. The quicker he went, the less time there was for him to talk himself out of this idea.

Josh followed the long gravel drive out to the main road, passing the sign for Split Valley that sat carved in thick, polished wood next to the entrance of the property. Growing up on Juniper Road, Josh had watched ranches come and go, most falling on hard times. There were few that had endured the economic hardship Tenacity had been plagued with. But there were acres of land to the west of the Split Valley that belonged to the Coreys. Josh had always been close to them, having practically grown up with their grandson, Shane. And to the east was the property that had once belonged to the Woodsons. Fences lined the road, wood and wire and steel, keeping the animals contained and marking out property lines. At this time of year, the first wildflower blooms were stretching out of the ditches in thick clumps.

Josh had always appreciated growing up out here, just beyond town. Out where the world quietly shifted from one season to the next. And though he'd come to appreciate that reliable change from winter to spring, he sometimes thought it might be nice to have someone in the passenger seat to enjoy it with him.

He reached town after another minute, his truck trundling along Central Avenue. He passed The Grizzly Bar with its weather-beaten benches and large orange door. Next door was the Silver Spur Café where Josh had spent a good many mornings enjoying coffee and eggs. Town Hall rose up right in the middle of everything, that old busted clock tower looking out over the town. Then there was Tenacity Drugs & Sundries, and the Tenacity Social Club, built in the basement of the same building that housed their post office and barbershop. The businesses that survived in this hardscrabble town did so out of pure grit and determination. He drove past the Feed and Seed and a while later pulled into the parking lot of Strom and Son.

Josh hopped out of his truck and quickly checked his hair in the reflection of the window, then walked into the store.

He nodded to Nathan as he passed by with a box of nutritional supplements and spotted Faith at the front counter. She glanced up, and her eyes narrowed slightly, the corners of her mouth quirking.

"You again?" She placed a hand on her hip. "Here for more sheep shears?"

Josh clicked his tongue. Faith was far too astute for her own good. No point in lying. He leaned against the counter. "I actually just wanted to see how Amy was getting on after yesterday."

"Huh," Faith said. "Did you?"

Her gaze almost made him squirm. Maybe he should have stuck with the lie.

"Well, I suppose you could ask her yourself," Faith said. She inclined her head in the direction of the warehouse. "Amy's out back."

"Right," Josh said. "Thanks."

He could feel Faith's eyes on him until he passed through a door and out of sight, disappearing into a back lot where a supply delivery was being unloaded from a large box truck. He spotted Amy right away, her dark hair hanging just past her shoulders, tapping a pen against her chin. She had a clipboard in hand and her lips moved like she was counting under her breath.

He cleared his throat as he approached so he didn't startle her.

Amy's eyes widened. He hoped it was a good surprise. Then her face broke into a smile. "Well, hey there, cowboy."

He liked the way she called him *cowboy*. He liked it too much, probably.

"I didn't think I'd see you again so soon."

"Hope I'm not interrupting anything," Josh said. "I sort of just wanted to check in and see how you were doing."

Amy flushed. "I'm actually feeling much better," she said, tucking the clipboard under her arm. "And Faith wouldn't let me leave the house this morning until I'd eaten a turkey bacon sandwich. So no spontaneous fits of dizziness either."

"Turkey bacon?"

"I've been trying to sneak real bacon into the house since I got here back in February. Faith won't budge."

"Wow, you really are suffering."

"Thank you," Amy said. "No one else seems to understand my plight."

"Really though, I don't know how you can bear it."

Amy laughed, and he caught a flash of teeth. She did look

better. Brighter. Glowing even. It was such a sharp contrast to yesterday that Josh actually sighed, relief washing through him. He knew he'd been worried, he just hadn't realized *how* worried. "I'm glad you're feeling better."

"Well, I've also been keeping up with my sweet tea and toast," she said. "And it's been working wonders."

He chuckled under his breath, charmed that she remembered what he'd said about his grandmother.

"You didn't come all the way here just to check up on me, did you?"

"I might have."

Amy ducked her head, her hair obscuring the deepening flush in her cheeks. She held the clipboard to her front, like it might stop his words from reaching her. "You really didn't have to do that. Your help yesterday was more than enough."

"I know." Josh shrugged. "But I wanted to." And he wanted to keep talking to her. Even now. "Is it busy today?" He gestured to the skids of supplies. "I mean, do you still have a lot of work to be getting on with here?"

Amy glanced. "Not too much more actually. I was almost done when you turned up."

"You think you could leave for a bit?"

She arched her brow.

"For lunch," he clarified.

"Are you asking me out for lunch, Josh Aventura?"

"If that's something you'd be open to," he said. "If you're not, then I will just be on my way. And we can both pretend I was never here asking awkward questions." He started to back away but she caught him by the wrist. Warmth flooded through him at the touch.

"I'd love to go to lunch with you," she said sweetly, and Josh's heart lobbed against his ribs. It was so forceful he worried she might be able to see it beating right through his shirt.

"Great. That's really… Okay then." He waited for Amy to finish up her counting, then they headed back through the store together. Amy stopped briefly to speak with Faith who was eyeballing him over Amy's shoulder, her eyebrows rising higher and higher. Josh wasn't sure what that look meant, but he averted his eyes just in case.

When their conversation was finished, Amy followed him out to his truck and he drove them back down Central Avenue to the Silver Spur Café. They'd just missed the lunch rush, which meant it would be quiet inside, but they should still have enough time to eat before the café closed for the day.

"How's this?" Josh asked as he stopped in the parking lot. There weren't a plethora of options in Tenacity, but he could vouch that the food was good. Definitely not a five-star experience. It actually might not even compare to what she was probably used to having up in Bronco. But the owners were kind, and he'd never once heard a bad word about the service. "I know it's not much," he continued. Damn. Maybe he should have planned this out more. It was his first time asking her out. Should he have sprung for something better? Should he have cooked?

"This is perfect," Amy said. "I'd been meaning to check it out, just hadn't gotten around to it yet."

Josh nodded and took his keys from the ignition, emboldened by Amy's words.

They walked inside, greeted by cozy booths and wooden tables and an eclectic mix of cowboy paraphernalia tacked to the wooden ceiling beams. There were photos of people from town in frames adorning the walls behind the hostess stand. Ranches and ranchers. Young couples and old. Newly married folks and babies. It summed up Tenacity pretty well.

"Cute," Amy said, studying one of the photos.

They were seated quickly, and he briefly glanced at the menu, but put it aside knowing he was going to order his favorite. The brisket burger.

"There are too many options," Amy laughed, lowering her menu. Her blue eyes twinkled in the low light overhead.

"What have you narrowed it down to?"

"Maybe the chicken club with the pickle spears on the side."

"Good choice."

Their waitress came over and talked Amy into also getting their homemade soup. When their food arrived, he was pleased to see Amy eating with gusto, again reassured that she really was feeling better.

"So, is this place like a Tenacity staple?" Amy asked, studying the photos on the walls again. "Been around since the beginning of time sort of thing?"

"I've actually been coming here since I was a kid," Josh said. "I've lived in Tenacity my whole life. Never left town. So it's been around at least that long."

"Not for college or anything?"

"No, I took over the ranch from my parents in my early twenties."

"And you never wanted to leave?"

He shook his head. "This place might not work for some people. But I've always been content with what the world had to offer me right here." Though, of course, a nice woman, a partner in this life, could only make it better, but Josh had come to the conclusion that that ship had probably sailed. Still, with Amy sitting across from him it was easier to dream of a future that looked like that. "What about you? Get out of Bronco much?"

"Actually," she said, wiping her hands on a napkin and giving him a sheepish little smile. "I've done a lot of traveling with my family. Like an exorbitant amount. For work mostly."

"So, you're not really a feed store shelf stocker?" he teased.

"No, I'm...actually in the rodeo business like Faith."

"Wait! I knew Faith was one of The Hawkins Sisters, but I didn't realize you were also one of *those* Hawkinses." He tipped his head, staring like he was seeing her for the first time. He'd seen dozens of posters promoting local rodeo events, highlighting The Hawkins Sisters with their rhinestone cowboy hats and lassos. But even knowing Faith's connection to the rodeo, he'd never once considered that Amy might also be involved. It seemed so obvious now. "I don't know how I didn't put two and two together." It was literally in the name. The Hawkins *Sisters.*

"Yeah. I'm sorry I didn't mention it before. I just... When I bump into people that's usually the first thing they bring up. And if they're rodeo fans, they want pictures and autographs. But you didn't say anything, and at first I just thought you were being nice. But then I actually wondered if you really didn't know who I was. You just seemed to see *me,* without the name and the family and the fancy rope tricks. And I kind of wanted to keep existing in that bubble for a minute."

"I really had no idea," he said. "I feel kind of like an idiot now."

"Don't," Amy said. "Please. It was my choice not to tell you."

Josh watched her wring her hands together. He hadn't meant to make her uncomfortable. "If you don't want to talk about it, we don't have to. I can steer clear of the conversation."

"Oh, it's nothing like that. I love my family. Don't get me wrong. But sometimes it's nice just to get to be Amy, if you know what I mean?"

"Sure."

"But I don't mind talking about it."

"So… A Hawkins Sister. That's…wow." He was impressed not only by her rodeo prowess, but also by her worldliness. With his ranching responsibilities, he'd never been able to travel far. In fact, he might even be a little intimidated by how vastly different their worlds now felt. But he really did like her, and Amy genuinely seemed interested in him, so he tried not to dwell on how his simple life could possibly measure up to hers. "You said you did a lot of traveling?"

Amy nodded. "Faith and I and one of our sisters Tori spent a lot of time in South America during our last rodeo tour. Our other sisters Elizabeth and Carly were in Australia with some of the Hawkins cousins. So, you know," she laughed, "we get around."

"Which of all your trips was your favorite?"

"Definitely a show we did down in São Paulo, Brazil, near a community called Barretos where they have this local cowboy festival. They were just so excited to have us there and the crowds had so much energy. There's just something about when the crowd is excited and your heart is beating and you can feel the power of the horse beneath you. Really makes me remember why I love it so much."

To Josh it all sounded exciting and glamorous, and though he knew he could never compete with all that adventure, he was intrigued by her stories. "São Paulo is a long way from Tenacity. A different world entirely." He chuckled and said, "Probably much more charming, too."

"Oh, I don't know about that," Amy insisted. "Tenacity has its charms, I think."

He guffawed. No one had ever called Tenacity charming before, at least as far as he'd heard, and he was tickled that she would say that.

"I think it's mostly just that I've had my fill of big cities," Amy said. "For a long time the circuit and the travel and the performing was what I thought I wanted."

"Not so much anymore?"

She shrugged, her nose wrinkling in that adorable way. "I think some peace and quiet would be nice now. Tenacity seems like the perfect place for that."

Josh nodded. "A person can find peace here," he agreed. "But it can also be lonely sometimes."

Her smile thinned. "I've come to understand a thing or two about loneliness recently."

Her words were soft and sad, and Josh reached over to take her hand, to comfort her, but before he could, Amy flinched away, and he felt like an idiot. Lord, what was he doing? "I'm sorry." He cleared his throat. "I didn't mean to be so forward." Maybe he was reading things wrong and Amy was only humoring him with lunch. With conversations on the porch. With sweet smiles and pink cheeks and… Before he could fret anymore about overstepping, Amy shook her head.

"No. I'm the one who should apologize." She frowned. "It's just, I've recently gotten out of a bad relationship and I guess I'm just a little cautious."

Josh nodded. "Of course. No need to apologize."

They went back to eating.

"I really am glad you asked me to lunch," she said.

"Yeah?"

Amy nodded. "Yeah."

"Good," he said softly, and for the life of him, Josh couldn't figure out who had been foolish enough to let Amy get away.

CHAPTER SIX

JOSH TURNED INTO the Strom and Son parking lot without really thinking about it.

He'd been to the post office to check up on a package, and seeing the feed store, his thoughts had immediately turned to Amy, and before he knew it, he was parked and walking through the door.

There was a bounce to his step and a giddy flutter in his chest as he stepped inside. When had this become his favorite spot in Tenacity?

"Welcome to Strom and Son," he heard. "How can I—" Faith popped out of an aisle, took one look at him, and grumbled. "We're gonna have to put a bell on you so I stop wasting my breath. Amy's in the office."

"Would she mind some company?"

"Well, why don't you ask her and find out." Faith shot him a funny little smile before wandering off.

Well then, Josh thought. Faith might like to pretend that seeing him here was a nuisance but she also seemed to be going out of her way to encourage…whatever this was.

What was this?

He headed for the back office. The door was ajar, the sign posted said EMPLOYEES ONLY. He obviously liked Amy's company. His mother would call him smitten.

Noah and Ryder would say he had a crush.

But the word *crush* didn't feel quite right, he decided, as he knocked, peeked inside and spotted Amy. The sight of her smile stole his breath away. It was somehow more than just a simple crush, and that thought made him feel ridiculous. Like he'd jumped into a rodeo ring without ever having learned how to ride a horse first. He felt like he'd skipped some crucial steps somewhere. And yet explaining away his feelings as a simple crush wasn't possible.

He liked Amy Hawkins.

That much was true.

But he liked her in a way that didn't make sense to him.

It was too much, too fast.

Only he didn't know how to undo it. *Take it slow*, he told himself. *Don't jump into this*. Problem was he'd already taken a running leap off the diving board.

She sat in a chair behind a long, wooden desk, holding a granola bar. There was an uneaten apple on the desk. "Hey there, cowboy."

He leaned against the doorframe. "Not interrupting anything, am I?"

"No." Amy gestured with her granola bar. "It's my new mandatory snack break." Her lips quirked at the corners. "Faith's been on me since the other day."

"That doesn't surprise me. She seems like a stickler for that sort of thing."

"She worries too much."

"Because she cares?"

"Remains to be seen," Amy joked. "So back for more—"

"If that sentence ends in sheep shears you might want to re-think it."

Amy's eyebrow arched dramatically. "Careful, cowboy. If you keep swinging by like this for no reason I might start to think you *want* to see me."

He huffed. This woman knew damn well he wanted to see her. "Maybe I do."

Amy hummed thoughtfully. "Can't imagine why."

"Isn't it obvious?"

She shrugged.

"If I get in good with Faith's sister I might qualify for the friends and family discount."

Amy guffawed. "Oh, of course. I'm on to your schemes now."

"Good."

"You know, you're less charming when I know you're just using me for your own personal gain."

Josh crossed his arms and cocked his head. "Huh."

"What?"

"You think I'm charming."

Amy flushed like she was only now just realizing what she'd said. "Past tense," she muttered. "You *were*."

"I don't think that matters." He stared at her, and he swore the flush spread down her cheeks to her throat. A place he'd very much like to press his lips. He wanted to see if her pulse fluttered under his kiss. He wanted to—

"Well, I also think puppies are charming and seniors that sing in barbershop quartets. So don't let it go to your head. Might not be able to get your cowboy hat on anymore."

"Worried about my ego?"

"Yes. With that head of hair you don't have much room to work with."

So she thought he was charming and had good hair? If he was ever in need of a compliment he knew where to come. She met his eye and held his gaze for a long moment. "I didn't just come here to get my ego stroked."

"No?"

"I actually swung by because I was wondering… I mean, I had a really nice time the other day. At lunch."

Something about her softened, and Josh wanted to sweep her into his arms. "I did too," she said.

He nodded. Reassured. "Good. Great." He cleared his throat. "I thought maybe you'd like to go for a ride then? Up at my ranch. We could take the horses out, I could show you the property. It's a nice, easy trail. Though I suppose you're not one to shy away from some rough terrain."

Amy lit up. "I'd love that actually."

"Perfect," Josh said. If he'd known that, he wouldn't have taken so long to spit it out. "I guess I'll pick you up later? At Faith's?"

"Sure."

He smiled, backing away from the doorway. "See you then."

"See you, cowboy."

Josh turned, heading for the exit, practically buzzing with energy. He clapped a surprised Caleb on the shoulder as he passed him. "Hey, man. How's it going?"

"Hey?" Caleb said.

Josh was out the door before he could say any more. The faster he got back to the ranch and finished up with the chores, the faster he could get back to Amy.

JOSH PULLED INTO Caleb and Faith's driveway several hours later. He'd run later than planned, thanks to a complicated calf birth that required a call to the local large animal vet. But as Josh's father used to say, mother nature changed her plans for no one, so he'd texted Amy, telling her he was absolutely still coming to pick her up, just a little later than anticipated.

There was still enough time left in the day for a ride, plus if the weather cooperated, it should make for a pretty decent sunset. And who didn't like a nice sunset?

When Amy appeared on the porch, Josh got out to meet her.

She wore jeans, a jewel-toned plaid shirt, and a black puffer vest. It wasn't exactly cold, but at this time of year the temperature did drop the closer it got to sundown. Her hair was pulled back too, tied off in a high ponytail, and he admired the long, graceful line of her neck as she came down the steps.

"How are mother and baby?" she asked.

"Everyone's doing well. Doc said there should be no issues going forward."

She grinned at that and he walked her around to the passenger side of the truck, opening the door for her. "You didn't have to get out," she said, giving him a look that was both amused and a little exasperated. "I am fully capable of opening my own door."

He leaned against the open door. "I know that, but I wanted to."

"Well, just don't expect any more ego stroking."

"I would never." He grinned at her, already basking in the pleasure of her company.

"So, are we gonna go ride some horses?" she said. "Or are you gonna stand there and keep staring at me?"

Josh laughed. He liked how cheeky she could be. How bold. "What would you say if I decided I just wanted to keep staring?"

"Hmm. You're not supposed to ask that question." She reached out, nudged him out of the way and closed the door.

Josh rounded the front of the cab and climbed into the truck, starting the ignition. "But I did ask," he said, backing out of the driveway.

"Then I would say you're wasting precious horseback riding time."

"I don't think any time with you is ever wasted."

Amy opened her mouth. Closed it. Her cheeks pinked. "Just drive, cowboy."

"Did your words get tangled?"

She snorted.

"I mean it, you know. If you didn't want to come to the ranch, I would have done anything else. I just...wanted to spend some more time with you."

"And I wanted to spend time with your horses."

He barked a laugh. "Glad we cleared that up."

They grinned at each other again as Josh went racing down Juniper Road to the ranch, the fields on either side of them painted a soft green in the late afternoon sun. He'd driven this road thousands of times, but now he wondered what Amy saw when she looked at it. Did she think the fields looked like rolling green waves? Could she smell the honeysuckle that wafted from the meadows? Could she hear the buzz of insects on the wind?

"How was the rest of your day?" he asked.

"Well, Faith put me to work discounting old stock."

"Fascinating."

"I know. I'm allowed to put big yellow stickers on everything I can reach from the ground." Amy huffed. "I think since the other day she's afraid to let me near a ladder or lift anything heavy."

"Have you been feeling poorly again?" Josh asked, suddenly worried.

"No, I've felt fine. She's just...overprotective sometimes. Sisters, you know."

He tilted his head thoughtfully. "Wouldn't know. I'm an only child."

"Oh," Amy said. "I guess it's like... When you're young, you affectionately want to kill your siblings all the time. For everything. Stealing your clothes. Breathing too loud. Eating your food. Talking to the boy you like. And then you sort of, I don't know, grow up a bit. And you hit this place where they're suddenly your best friends and you'd do anything for them. Fight off the world if you had to." She laughed to herself. "It probably sounds strange."

"No," Josh said. "It sounds...nice." He didn't know what it was to have siblings, but he imagined he'd feel the same if he did. "Is that what Faith was doing when she invited you down to Tenacity? Fighting off the world?"

Amy hummed in agreement. "Letting me hide from it more like. One of their employees actually just went off on maternity leave, so it sort of worked out timing wise. Caleb and his dad needed an extra set of hands a few days a week, and here I was. But I appreciate them letting me bunk in for a while all the same."

"Guess you can't complain too much about them putting you to work then."

Amy laughed. "I really can't."

They turned onto the ranch, driving down the long stretch of gravel, the rocks nicking off the bottom of the truck. Josh parked and hopped out. Amy climbed out before he could even dare to open her door again. The look she gave him told him she knew exactly what he'd been thinking.

"So, this is it," he said, gesturing from the house he'd grown up in to the massive barn that housed his cattle.

"Why is it called Split Valley?"

"There's a creek that runs through the property," Josh said. "We'll pass it on our ride."

"Oh, that's lovely."

"It's the bane of my existence actually."

"What? Why?"

"The calves like to get themselves stuck down there."

Amy laughed. "You're telling me you have to mount calf rescue missions?"

"At least a couple times a year. Ranching is all fun and games until you're trekking through knee-deep water after some baby that's still too new to know not to run away from you."

"I'm gonna need to see that in person because it sounds hilarious."

Josh inclined his head toward the barn, the brown-gray structure towering over them. "You want to meet today's newest addition?"

"Do I want to meet a tiny, mooing ball of fluff? The answer to that is always yes."

Josh's pulse fluttered at her enthusiasm. He hurried after her as she set off for the barn door. Inside it smelled of... Well, cows and churned earth and damp straw. He led her through the building, pointing out the feed storage and various calving boxes for the expectant mothers, each of them filled with soft bedding. They walked further along a concrete aisle, coming upon a gate. He swung it open, admitting them into an area with another calving box. He'd left the mother and baby inside after the vet had come by to help with the birth and was pleased to see that both mother and baby seemed to be getting on fine. The calf was nestled down in the bedding, his ears twitching.

"Oh my God," Amy said softly. "He's so little."

"He came a bit early by the looks of things but he'll do just fine. Mama here will make sure of it." Josh kept an eye on the mother as Amy gave the calf a little pat, her face lighting up. They weren't pets. Josh knew that. But they sure were cute.

"Do you ever get used to this?" Amy said.

"Never."

"I've roped a lot of calves in the rodeo ring but they're older. This one's so precious."

"Come on," Josh said. "Let's go check out those horses before you fall in love with the little guy. My father always said you can like 'em but you can't love 'em."

"Guess not when it's your livelihood," Amy said. She reached her hand up and let Josh pull her to her feet.

She followed him out of the calving box and down into a different part of the barn. When they reached the horse stalls, they were greeted by Mac, who stuck his head over his gate for a head scratch.

Josh obliged. "This is Mac. Our resident drama queen. And that's Bella in there," he said, pointing her out in the next stall. "And Bitsy at the end."

Amy walked up to Bitsy's stall, biting her lip as she gave the horse a long look.

"Maybe you wanna take Bella out," Josh cautioned, worried as Amy opened the gate to Bitsy's stall. "Like I said... She's not the friendliest." Amy reached her hand out and Josh braced as Bitsy nosed forward. *Please don't nip at her, Bit. I'm trying to make a good impression.*

But Bitsy simply sniffed and then nuzzled Amy's hand.

Josh came up behind her, still on edge, but Amy reached her other hand up, rubbing down Bitsy's neck. "I don't know how you did that."

"You need to have some more faith in me, cowboy. I do know how to charm a horse." She ran her hand along Bitsy's back, giving her a solid pat.

"You sure you want to ride her?"

"Just get me some tack," Amy said, accepting the challenge.

Josh shook his head. This might go terribly. He left the stall and returned with all the necessary tack. As Amy got Bitsy saddled up, Josh turned to Mac, doing the same. When they were done, he watched Amy climb into Bitsy's saddle, clicking her tongue. Bitsy headed for the door and Josh followed.

"We'll head up along the edge of the property line," he said, gesturing to a fence. Amy shifted around in her saddle. "You okay?"

"Yeah, sorry. It's just been a couple months since I've been on a horse. It always brings me a certain kind of joy when it's been this long. I get a little antsy. It's taking everything in me not to dig in my heels and gallop full-out."

"Can you try not to give me a heart attack? Bitsy's behaving for you now, but I think it's best if you ease into that sort of thing."

Amy laughed. "Worried about me?" She clicked her tongue and Bitsy trotted ahead.

Josh's stomach flipped. He liked this. He *really* liked this. He liked that he'd made her happy. He liked having her here. He liked having company on this usually lonely trail.

When Josh caught up with her, Amy was patting Bitsy on the side of the neck. "I am a little worried she's gonna try and throw you."

"She would never." Amy cooed down at her and Bitsy's ears twitched. "Though it would not be my first time falling off a horse."

"I suppose it's a hazard of the trade?"

"It doesn't happen often, but it *does* happen. I think I'm more careful now. When I was younger, I could be thrown and bounce back up like nothing had happened. Now, I'll be a walking bruise."

"Ever broken anything?"

"My collarbone," Amy said. "Once. And my wrist." She gestured with her left hand. "Got my hand tangled in a rope and got dragged by a steer. I was back on a horse before the cast had even finished setting."

Josh's eyes widened. Amy was tougher than he thought.

"I can't imagine doing that now. So Bitsy and I are going to be good friends. Aren't we, girl?" Bitsy chuffed like she understood.

They crested the far ridge of the property and started up along the fence that kept the cattle off Juniper Road. Josh kept one eye on the fence line, forever looking for wear and tear that might need fixing. But mostly he watched the way the evening crept up on them, painting Amy in the early colors of sunset. It brought out hints of red in her dark hair and the flush in her cheeks and the blue of her eyes. For a beat he wished he could somehow preserve this moment. Him and Amy and the world around them beautifully still.

His heart raced at the thought.

"So, riddle me this," she said. "How does a man like you, with a place like this, end up out here all alone? Is it a choice or…" She let the rest of her question fade.

Josh tilted his head, wondering how to answer.

"If I've overstepped, just say so," Amy said.

"You haven't," he assured her. Past relationships weren't usually something he wanted to dwell on, but for some reason he wanted to tell Amy. Maybe just so he could explain that he was a good guy who'd simply stumbled on some bad luck as far as love was concerned. "I guess recently I'd just kind of given up on looking."

She nodded. Bitsy weaved so close he could have reached out and touched the piece of hair that had escaped Amy's ponytail.

"I... My last relationship sorta made me want to *not* try again. I thought things were going well, but Erica felt trapped here with me. So she took off for bigger and better things and... I'm still here," he said. He didn't know if he was explaining it right. "Don't get me wrong, I want to be here. This place is what makes me happiest. I just don't really need my heart stomped on again."

"I'm sorry that happened," Amy said. She glanced out across the fields. "I don't know how anyone could feel trapped here."

"I suppose the same way I'd feel totally out of my element if I was dropped in the middle of some big city."

"Still, I'm sorry you couldn't find a way forward together."

"I think in hindsight it's easier to see that maybe we weren't as great together as I always thought we were. Maybe we didn't match up in the right ways. I was content with this," he said, gesturing out at the ranch, at the gold dappled fields, at the sunset-gilded earth. "And she wanted... I don't know if *more* is the right word," he said, "because I think this is an awful lot for someone to be happy with. I guess she just wanted different things, better opportunities than what Tenacity could offer, and we didn't realize that about each other until it was too late. It was gonna hurt regardless by that point."

"I think it's easy to get caught up in who we *think* someone is. Especially when we're not really looking."

"What do you mean?"

She shrugged. "I guess it's just easy to see what we want to see. That's all."

He knew she wasn't referring to Erica rather an experience of her own. Again, he wondered about this guy who had hurt her.

Wondered where he was now. What he did for a living. How he had walked away from this. From *her*.

"I like it here," Amy said.

"Yeah?"

"You were right. It's peaceful."

They fell in line beside each other again, their horses weaving together then apart.

"How does one get into rodeoing in the first place?" he asked. "I mean, I realize you're part of the Hawkins clan, but do they just line you up as kids and teach you rope tricks?"

Amy laughed. "Sort of. As a kid it just seems like fun and games and you can't wait to get on a horse. I remember spending hours watching my grandmother Hattie in the arena. She's the one who started it all, proving that anything men could do on the rodeo circuit, she could do better."

"She sounds incredible."

"Oh, she's a hoot," Amy said.

"So, how do you get from Hattie to you?" Josh asked, trying to place The Hawkins Sisters he'd always heard about with the real-life Hawkins sister sitting next to him.

"Well, Hattie's husband, Roscoe, died in a rodeo accident shortly after they were married."

"That's terrible."

"I'm sure it was," Amy said, "losing him so soon, and Hattie spent most of her childbearing years on the road, so she ended up adopting four adolescent girls. My mom, Suzie, and my aunts Josie, Hannah and Lisa. Hattie obviously taught them everything she knew, and they traveled with her on the circuit, performing and making a name for themselves as The Hawkins Sisters."

"What a legacy for Hattie to start," Josh said, impressed by the strength Hattie had clearly inspired in all her children and grandchildren.

Amy nodded in agreement. "And not just The Hawkins Sisters legacy, but even the tradition of adoption. My grandmother started that, and it's been carried on by the whole Hawkins clan. My parents adopted me and Faith, who you obviously know, but also my three other sisters, Tori, Elizabeth and Carly."

He hadn't realized she had so many sisters. "Was your dad in the rodeo, too?"

"Yeah," Amy said. "But he was forced into early retirement by a leg injury."

"Rodeoing really is in your blood."

Amy smiled. "Exactly. I spent so long surrounded by it, so long wanting to be a part of it, that by the time I realized it was something I was making a career out of, I already loved it too much to stop."

"So there was never anything else you wanted to do?"

"I don't think so. It gave me the best of everything. Time with my family." She chuckled. "Sometimes too much time. And travel. A job I loved. But in the typical sense of working some regular nine to five, I guess that was never in the cards. Working at the store is the closest I've gotten. I like being outside too much. Like being with the horses."

Josh took that in. "But there must be a bit of the glitz and glamour that you miss."

Amy shrugged. "There were definitely perks to everyone knowing your name sometimes. But the older I've gotten, the more I've realized I want other things out of life. In a way I feel like I've maybe waited too long."

"For what?"

"Oh, you know, the typical things. Marriage, kids, white picket fence. And I know I'm not that old yet, and adoption is definitely something I'd consider, it's just a feeling inside me. Like I want to settle, but I keep ending up with people that don't want me or don't want that."

I want you, he thought, almost shocking himself right out of the saddle.

"And, well, you know. It's hard some days to know you want this thing so badly, but not know where you're supposed to look to find it. Or how long you'll have to wait for the right person to come along. Or if they ever will." She laughed. "I never used to worry about these things. I think this last relationship crashing and burning just really put things in perspective for me. Or, really, the lack of those things in my life."

Josh shook his head.

"What is it?"

"I'm still trying to figure out what kind of man let you go."

Amy scoffed. "You wouldn't believe me if I told you."

"Well, he made a mistake. A big one. One day he's gonna wake up and realize that."

She flushed the same pink as the horizon line. "I don't think so."

"I mean it."

"Thanks," she said quietly. She kept her gaze on Bitsy. "But frankly I hope I never have to see him again."

"Is he on the rodeo circuit?"

Amy hummed. "Not quite. He's sort of in that world, though. Of glitz and glamour as you said."

A world Josh would never know anything about. He wondered if Amy could ever really be okay with that. If he even stood a chance.

He hoped so.

CHAPTER SEVEN

"MORNING, COWBOY," AMY said as she met Josh on the street in front of the Silver Spur Café. He leaned casually against the wall of the café, hands tucked into his jean pockets, a jacket over his flannel shirt and his hair swept back beneath a Stetson. She sucked in a sharp breath. He really was the most handsome man she'd ever seen, and not for the first time she wondered what it would be like to walk down the street and hold his hand or to run her fingers along his stubbled jaw. A wave of heat washed over her, and she shoved those thoughts aside before they could gallop into dangerous territory.

"Not quite morning anymore," he said.

"You're right. Afternoon, then." Amy smiled up at him. "Should I assume we're not going to lunch since you told me to wear good shoes?"

"You assume correctly. I wanted to take you somewhere, if you're up for it?"

"Are you going to tell me where?"

He winked as he looked down at her, his eyes shadowed by the brim of his hat. "If I say no is that going to sway your decision?"

Amy hummed, narrowing her eyes. "What are you up to, cowboy?"

"Nothing, I swear." He crossed his finger over his heart. "I promise to ensure you enjoy every second of your afternoon."

"Well, in that case," she said, "lead the way."

He grinned and set off down the sidewalk, pausing long enough for Amy to fall in step beside him. Josh led them past Town Hall and the few businesses on Central Avenue before turning down an alleyway next to the Little Cowpokes Daycare Center. He cut across the parking lot behind the building, heading for a grove of trees that was fenced off. Amy slowed as they reached a gap in the fence.

"I'm starting to wonder if I agreed to this too quickly," she said as Josh slipped through the fence to stand in front of an overgrown trailhead that was blocked by a wooden gate. A no-entry sign was nailed to one of the beams.

"It'll be fine." He hopped the gate with all the grace of a mountain lion, then turned around, waiting for her.

Amy slid through the gap in the fence and stopped on the other side of the gate. "There's definitely a sign that says we shouldn't be in here."

"Do you always do what signs tell you?"

"Typically." She laughed. "I've always assumed they're there for a reason."

Josh held his hand out for her. "Then you're just gonna have to trust me. This is one sign you can ignore."

Amy bit down on her lip as butterflies exploded in her chest. She didn't want to ignore *that* sign. She wanted to trust Josh. Not just with this, but with all the feelings bubbling up inside her. She laid her hand in his, and he squeezed once before releasing her so she could scale the gate. At the top, he took her by the waist and helped her down. His fingers pressed against her sides, and her skin heated where he touched her.

"You're sure you can be away from the ranch this long?" she asked as he stepped away. She stared into the trees, the branches parting slightly, revealing a worn trail cutting through the brush. "Aren't there afternoon chores and such?"

"There are always chores, but I've got my ranch hands covering for me." He glanced over at her as they started down the path. "I wanted to see you."

I wanted to see you.

Amy felt like she'd swallowed soap bubbles. Like the elation didn't fit in her chest. She bit down on her cheek to keep from grinning too hard. "Maybe I wanted to see you too."

"Did you?"

"Yes. But only to ask how Bitsy's doing."

Josh huffed playfully. "Of course. Now that you mention it, though, she's been all out of sorts with me since the other day. I think she misses you."

Amy nudged his arm. "I told you she was my girl now."

"Well, she used to be *my* girl. Which is why I need you to come by the ranch again sometime. Set her straight for me."

"I'll do my best, but I can't make any promises. We clearly have a bond that can't be broken."

Josh held aside a branch for her to pass. "I can't believe you've usurped my relationship with my horse."

Amy smirked. "Get used to it, cowboy. Bella and Mac are next. So, how's your day been? Other than Bitsy giving you the cold shoulder."

"No calving emergencies so far. Everyone is doing exactly what they're supposed to be doing. How's the store been? Busy?"

"Not too bad. Though we do have this one customer that keeps coming back again and again."

Josh opened his mouth to say something, but Amy plowed on.

"The weird thing is he never actually buys anything."

Josh snorted. "All right. All right. I get it."

Amy bumped his arm with hers. "To be clear, I don't mind."

"Good. I didn't plan on stopping anytime soon."

They emerged onto a wider trail, this one running along a trickling stream. Josh inclined his head, and she followed him downstream.

"You gonna tell me where we are now?" Amy asked. "Or where we're going?"

Josh gestured to an old, weather-beaten sign. "This is one of the trailheads that would have connected to the Tenacity Trail. When I was a kid, there was this big plan to revitalize it and really put the town on the map."

"And that never happened?"

He shook his head. "No. There was an incident. The money meant to fund the revitalization disappeared. And when the money disappeared, so did the folks interested in restoring the trail. Soon one small business after another folded. It was a really hard time for folks. A lot of people had to leave town, try their luck elsewhere. Most young people took off for cities with actual industry in order to find jobs."

"That's horrible," Amy said.

"Watch your step." He held his hand out, helping her over a downed tree. "Those who stayed struggled to make ends meet. I guess in a lot of ways that hasn't really changed."

"I didn't realize." They climbed down a short embankment, using the tree roots like stairs. "Tenacity has so much small-town charm."

"That's the people," Josh said. "They make all the difference and look out for each other. It isn't until you really start to look around that you see how run-down the town actually is."

Amy considered that as they came upon a pond. Streams of sunlight broke through the canopy of leaves overhead, spotlighting growths of new wildflowers.

"Oh, Josh," she said, taken aback at how pretty and peaceful the place was. "This is...wow."

"I used to walk the overgrown trails as a boy and stumbled upon it one day. In the summer I'd hunt for crawfish along the banks." He bent down to pick up a stone from the edge of the water then skipped it across the surface. "I don't get out as much now, with all the work responsibilities, but next to the ranch, I think it's my favorite place in the world."

She could understand that. He was the kind of person who valued quiet, or at least a good place to think, and she couldn't imagine anywhere better.

"It's beautiful," she said.

"I've never brought anyone else here." He looked back at her, and Amy's heart skipped a beat. "Sometimes I'm selfishly glad that the revitalization never happened. I might have had to share this place with other people."

"Thank you for sharing it with me," she said softly. "You didn't have to."

"I wanted to."

Amy didn't know what to say to that, so she just nodded and

let her hair fall in front of her face, hiding her blush. Once they'd had their fill of the burbling stream and the chilled, honeysuckle-tinted breeze, they made their way back to the trail.

She let Josh help her up the embankment. She didn't need it, but it was an excuse to hold his hand, and she took it any chance she could. At the start of the trailhead, Josh lifted her down from the gate once more, and Amy committed the thrill of it to memory. Her heart hadn't beat this hard for someone in a long time.

Maybe ever.

They passed behind the squat brick buildings along Central Avenue and cut through that alley next to the Little Cowpokes Daycare Center. People came and went from a few of the businesses, and Amy considered how difficult life must have been since the plan to revitalize the trail fell through. Still, they smiled and waved, and Josh lifted his hat. The people here were bonded by much more than by being neighbors. They were bonded by hardship.

"Do you ever wish you'd left Tenacity like a lot of the other young people?" she asked.

"It's not something I wished for necessarily. But when I was younger, I did wonder if there was another life out there I was meant to live. You know…just travel and wander and see what happens."

"As someone who did a lot of traveling and wandering, the thought of belonging somewhere, of having roots and familiarity… It's kind of nice. I really have no idea what it's like to walk down a street and look up and know the person you're passing. Or what it's like to be able to ask them about their family and their kids."

"That is nice," Josh agreed. "Being somewhere people know your history. Where friends feel more like family."

Amy nodded. Bronco was great, especially now that a lot of her family had settled there, but there was something to be said of a place where everyone would know her name and not just because she was a Hawkins sister.

Josh fit here so perfectly, and she couldn't help wishing that she'd fit here, too. Someday. When she left Bronco, she didn't think Tenacity would be somewhere she'd want to stay for long.

It was supposed to be a pit stop on her road to heartbreak recovery. But now, well… Josh's hand lingered near hers, and Amy thought about how easy it would be to take it. To lace her fingers through his.

She wondered if he'd pull away. If she was being too forward. Reading too much into this.

"Back to the ranch for you?" she asked as they wandered down the sidewalk, neither of them seeming to be in a hurry.

He nodded. "Back to the store for you?"

She shrugged. "I might pop by. See how things are going. Might also just go back to Faith and Caleb's and call my mom since it's been a while. She likes her regular updates."

Josh laughed. "Mine, too. My only excuse right now is she's on a cruise with my dad. So reception isn't great."

"Oh, where are they traveling?"

"Alaska," he said. "They'd been saving for the trip for a while, and I want them to enjoy these years as much as they can. While they can. My dad's got pretty bad arthritis, which acts up a lot."

"Is that why you ended up taking over the ranch?" Amy asked.

"Partly," Josh said. "Also because, well… I was a little bit of a surprise. My mom was pretty convinced she couldn't have kids, and then I showed up when she was almost forty. My parents like to joke that I ran them ragged for those first twenty years."

"I doubt that," Amy said. "A quiet thing like you?"

Josh smirked. "You didn't know the terror I was when I was young. Anyway, by the time they were pushing sixty, they were already feeling ready for retirement. I was old enough to take on the responsibility by then, so I took over and my parents rented a small place just outside of Bronco to be closer to my dad's rheumatologist."

"Well, I hope they're having a great time."

"Me, too." He stopped walking. Amy hung back, looking at him. "There's something I've been wondering."

"What?"

"Do you think… Is there a time limit on you staying with Faith and Caleb?"

Amy raised her brow, a bit surprised by his question, wondering if he was asking for the reason she thought he was asking. "Despite what my sister might say, she loves having me here. So I don't think so."

"You got any designs on leaving?"

Her pulse raced. "Why? Would that inconvenience you?"

"Someone's gotta keep Bitsy on the straight and narrow, and she's clearly not listening to me."

"Right. The horse." Amy couldn't help the smile that stretched across her face. "Any other reason I should stick around?"

Josh took a step forward. They were close, maybe too close, and she looked up into his eyes. They were deep brown, with flecks of hazel. She could have counted each striation.

"Because I want you to?"

"Is that a question or…"

"No."

"No what?"

She could smell his soap and see the stubble along his jaw, and she lost her breath suddenly, looking at his lips.

Josh was gazing at her like he might just lean down and close the distance. But then a horn wailed, and the spell broke. Amy sucked in a sharp breath. Had he really been about to kiss her?

Josh was now glaring at a pickup truck that had stopped on the side of the road. Two men hopped out of the truck and came over to greet them.

"Amy," Josh said as they drew near, "this is Noah and Ryder Trent."

"In case it's not clear, I'm the good-looking younger brother," Ryder said, reaching for her hand.

Amy shook it.

"So, this is Amy," Noah said, also shaking her hand. He had a kind smile but looked exhausted. "We've heard a lot about you."

"Have you?" she said, glancing at Josh, who was now conveniently looking everywhere but at her.

"What're you two up to?" Noah asked, smirking like he knew exactly what they'd *almost* been up to.

Josh cleared his throat. "Took a bit of a break from work this afternoon. We just got back from walking the old trailhead."

Ryder made a face. "That's definitely a...choice."

Amy and Josh laughed in tandem. "It was nice," she said.

"You don't have to pretend for us, Amy," Ryder said. "Blink twice if you need to be rescued from this guy and his horrible attempts to show you around town."

"Really," she insisted. "It was great."

"Nah," Ryder said, looping his arm through hers. "For example, if you'd allow me to escort you this way—" he steered her down the sidewalk, gesturing with his hand "—I'd like to draw your attention to this here alleyway where our little Joshy had his first kiss."

"I didn't know this kind of tour was an option," Amy joked with Ryder. "Tell me more."

"How about we don't," Josh said.

Noah needled him in the side, making Josh flinch. "What were you, Joshy? About fourteen, I'd say. A whole group of us saw it."

Josh dropped his head into his hand and massaged his brow. "Which is why we don't need to relive it."

"I think Amy would like to hear the story," Ryder said.

"Actually, I would *love* to hear the story," Amy teased.

"I hate you both," Josh muttered to the brothers.

"He was shaking so bad I don't know how he even stood up straight," Noah said.

"I imagine you were an adorable, sweet-talking young man," Amy told Josh.

He laughed. "Oh, I was shy as anything. Couldn't get a word out. Luckily there's not a whole lot of talking needed when you're kissing."

"It went well, then?"

"Lord no." Ryder cackled. "They never spoke again after that."

"Anyway, this was my first job outside the ranch," Josh said, pointing out the barbershop.

"Stop trying to change the subject," Noah said.

"I'm not. I'm just saying, I swept up after school sometimes for extra cash."

Ryder winked. "'Cause he clearly wasn't sweeping up with the ladies, if you know what I mean."

"Okay!" Josh said, steering Ryder away. "I think she's heard enough."

Amy could just make out what they were saying from where she stood.

"Not gonna be able to call you president of Lonely Valley much longer, am I?" Ryder said.

"I think you need to go back to work."

"I'm serious, man. This is good for you. I've been saying forever that you needed to get back out there after... What was her name? Erin? Eliza?"

"Doesn't matter," Josh muttered.

Ryder looped his arm around Josh's shoulders. "That's the spirit."

Josh shrugged him off, practically escorting Ryder back to the truck. Amy would have laughed at the sight if not for the giddy butterflies dancing in her chest. Josh's friends clearly thought she was a good thing. It reassured her to know they approved of...whatever this was.

"It was good meeting you," Noah said, pulling Amy's attention. "We'll have to catch up later. We've got plenty of stories about Josh you probably want to hear."

"I'd like that," she said, then waved as the brothers drove off. She didn't miss Ryder shooting kissy faces in Josh's direction through the window.

Josh cleared his throat. "I'm really sorry about them."

"Don't be. They seem like great friends."

"For the record, you can't trust ninety percent of what Ryder says."

"Sure." Amy winked at him. "I think you just don't want me to have access to all this insider information."

"I'll tell you whatever insider information you want." Josh smiled at her so warmly she could have melted against him. "I should be getting back though."

She didn't want him to go.

"I'll call you later," he said.

Amy nodded. "I sure hope so."

Josh backed away down the sidewalk, like he wasn't quite ready to stop looking at her. Or maybe that's just what she was telling herself. When he turned around, Amy slumped down on the nearest bench, feeling like she needed to catch her breath.

FAITH DUMPED THE basket of washing on the bed between them, and Amy reached for a towel, folding it neatly and setting it aside. Next she picked up a few pillowcases, folding them into perfect little rectangles. She usually hated doing laundry, but at least with Faith as company it felt like less of a chore.

"Why do you always avoid the fitted sheets?" Faith asked as Amy tossed one sheet-looking clump back into the pile.

"Because they require an advanced degree in mathematics to fold."

Faith cocked her head and shook out the sheet. "Grab that end and help me."

Amy did, dutifully following Faith's directions as they folded the sheet.

"So, I can't help but notice that you were out with Josh. Again."

"Is there something you want to ask?" Amy said, hearing the unsaid questions in Faith's voice.

"Did you have a nice time on your walk?"

"I did," Amy said. "He took me down part of the Tenacity Trail."

Faith wrinkled her nose. "That old, overgrown thing?"

Amy laughed. "Part of the trail leads to a clearing that Josh is fond of. I guess he used to go there as a boy. It was quite beautiful."

"If you say so."

Amy hummed. It was a shame that the revitalization of the trail fell through. More people deserved to enjoy the beauty that Josh had shown her. Even so, she felt like she'd been given another small glimpse into Josh's world, and she was eager for more.

"You've been spending an awful lot of time with him," Faith said. "I wondered if maybe it's turning into more than friendship?"

Amy matched up a pair of socks before meeting Faith's eye. "I'm not sure if us talking or hanging out or whatever's happening now was ever just friendship."

"Okay!" Faith climbed onto the bed. "This is the good stuff. Keep talking."

Amy sat down, disturbing the laundry piles. "I don't know. Everything feels so easy with him. Even the silences. And he's sweet and thoughtful and my heart races when I hear that bell over the door in the store. I'm always hoping it's him. And the other day on the ranch when we went riding..." She trailed off. "Is it ridiculous to feel this way already?"

"No," Faith said. "*I* don't think so. These things sort of just happen the way they happen. Time isn't necessarily a factor. When it's with the right person, when everything clicks and makes sense, you feel like you've known them your whole life. Like there was already a hole carved out for them, just waiting to be filled."

Amy knew part of her was talking about Caleb now, and she grinned at her sister's soft expression.

"Do you think Josh feels the same?" Faith asked.

"I mean, I think there was definitely a moment today."

"A moment? What kind of moment?"

"You know."

Faith shrugged.

Amy huffed. "The kind where you lock eyes and it feels like you're just a breath away from stumbling into a kiss for the first time."

"He almost kissed you? Where?"

"On the street. When we came back from our walk. A couple of his friends showed up before we got around to it, but I was pretty sure it was going to happen."

Faith wrinkled her nose and groaned. "*Amy...* Don't let the first time be on the street where you'll obviously be interrupted."

Amy laughed. "I can't exactly curate it. The moment happens when it happens. Anyway, it caught me a little off guard, but not because I didn't want it to happen. I just didn't realize how much I wanted it to happen." In many ways, it seemed like they'd only just met, and yet Josh showed up in her life and parked himself at her side and hadn't strayed far since. Part of her felt like being with him was the most natural thing in the world. When they were apart, she missed his company: his soft, gruff words. His thoughtful questions. That dark stare. The way only one of his cheeks dimpled when he smiled. As the list went on in her head, Amy flushed. She'd wanted to kiss Josh very much. She sort of wished she could just go back to that moment. She would have closed the distance and pressed her lips to his, just to know if he felt all the same things she felt. Were there actually sparks there? Or was she just imagining everything?

"Well, you deserve to have some fun," Faith said.

"I am having fun."

"You know, I was so worried about you moping around here, I got Tori, Elizabeth and Carly on the phone."

Amy rolled her eyes. "You did not drag them into it."

"Tori told me to get you on the dating apps. She even offered to make your profile."

Amy huffed. "I can't believe you four are having secret meetings without me."

"And that's not even the group chat Elizabeth started."

"There's a group chat I'm not in?" Amy demanded.

Faith burst out laughing. "I'm just kidding. Of course not." She narrowed her eyes playfully. "Or am I?"

Amy whipped out her phone. "I'm messaging Elizabeth right now to ask."

Faith nudged her. "I really am kidding. But I've given the girls the low-down on Josh. They all agree it's a good thing. He's brought your spark back. I've missed it."

Amy wanted to deny it, but she knew Faith was right. She felt more like herself now than she had for months. She picked up a pair of her jeans, shaking them out and tugging on the waistband a bit. "I need to stop putting my clothes in your dryer," she said. "I think they're shrinking."

"There's nothing wrong with my dryer."

"It's on like turbo heat mode or something."

"If your clothes are fitting a little more snugly, maybe it's all these visits with Josh and a distinct lack of rodeo training."

That was fair, Amy supposed. She was used to a more rigorous training schedule when she was on the rodeo circuit. She'd grown complacent with her simple life since coming to Tenacity: helping out at the store and being with Josh. But it had also been such a nice change of pace, part of Amy wondered if some snug jeans were a worthwhile exchange. Maybe it could always be like this.

Maybe Josh was supposed to be something more permanent in her life.

That thought was quickly overwhelmed by another thought. Was she rushing into these feelings too quickly?

"What are you thinking?" Faith asked. "You've gone all quiet and that's never a good sign."

"I don't know. I think there's still a small part of me that feels like this is too good to be true." As wonderful as all this felt, she knew she should slow down. Hold off. Pull back.

Tru rose to the forefront of her mind. When she was away from Josh, it was easier to remember how wretched Tru had made her feel. The problem was, it wasn't like that at first. In the beginning, Tru was a total gentleman. He'd said he liked to keep his private life out of the spotlight, and Amy had been dazzled by the lengths he was willing to go to protect her from the media. He'd seemed every bit as kind and honest as his movie persona as he'd wined and dined her!

She cringed now, reliving the memory of him saying she was like no one he'd ever met. She'd fallen hard, sucked right into his trap. In all those weeks, he never once pressured her for sex, but it had gotten to the point that she was *dying* to sleep with him. He kept saying she was "worth waiting for," and Lord, had that just made her swoon harder. Around Christmas, he'd jetted her off to St. Barts, a little island paradise where they could finally be together away from the prying eyes of the media. Amy truly thought she'd found something wonderful with Tru. Only after New Year's, Tru had to fly off to Europe to film, and though he still kept in touch, as the weeks went on, communication eventually dropped off entirely. It was like a knife to the chest, and only now was Amy starting to realize the full extent of the wound Tru left behind. She'd trusted him, and not only had he basically dumped her after sleeping with her, he'd done it by marrying another woman. She was a damn fool, and that's what worried her about her own judgment when it came to Josh.

He couldn't possibly be this wonderful. Something had to be amiss.

It was true, he helped ease the sting Tru McCoy left behind. But what if he left his own wound? Amy didn't think she could handle that again. Not this soon. What if it turned out he didn't feel the same? Could she trust these feelings? Could she trust Josh?

"What if it all goes wrong?" she said.

"What if it doesn't?"

Amy flopped on her back, toppling laundry piles. "Does life really work like that?"

"I mean, it did for Elizabeth and Jake, and Tori and Bobby. Not to mention Brynn and Garret, Audrey and Jack, Corinne and Mike," she said, listing off their sisters and cousins.

"Okay, okay."

"It also seems to be working out for me and Caleb," Faith said thoughtfully. "So I'd say so. Besides, I really do think you should give Josh a chance. Don't talk yourself out of something that could be so good."

"Sometimes I worry that we're different—maybe too different?" she said, trying in vain to keep the concern from her voice. Josh lived in his small corner of the world, and Amy had ventured out to explore all of it. More than that, what she really worried about now was that she didn't exactly know who she was away from a rodeo arena. What if Josh didn't like the person she'd become? What if he wasn't interested in her if she wasn't this glamorous Hawkins Sister anymore? Though that seemed like a silly concern. He'd liked her before she told him who she was. Right?

"Your differences are probably what's drawn you together," Faith said, derailing Amy's worries. "Josh needs a little adventure in his life and maybe you want someone grounded."

"Maybe you're right."

"Gosh! Feels like I've been waiting my whole life for you to say that."

Amy snorted, but despite her concerns, one thing was clear. She was going to keep seeing Josh. Maybe he'd only end up hurting her in the end, but Amy was speeding along this barrel run, too far gone to stop it now.

CHAPTER EIGHT

"SHE REALLY LIKES you," Josh said, failing to hide his smile as Amy rubbed Bitsy down with the stiff-bristled brush. They'd gone for a ride earlier this morning as the sun was coming up. Josh had been surprised at how eager Amy was to get out of bed early enough to watch the sunrise. When he'd picked her up this morning, greeted by a beaming smile, his heart had landed right in his stomach, kicking up butterflies. There seemed to be more and more of them swooping around his gut every time he saw her. "You didn't even have to ply her with sugar cubes to brush her."

"Of course she likes me. We've been over this." Amy ran her hand along Bitsy's silky coat. "What's not to like? I'm an excellent rider. And a fantastic conversationalist."

"Rider, yes. Conversationalist..." Josh started to tease.

"Watch yourself, Josh Aventura."

Amy looked at him over her shoulder, a few strands of her dark hair coming loose from her ponytail. Josh wanted to reach over and brush them aside. Her eyes were bright, the corner of her mouth turning up playfully. Gosh, she was pretty when she smiled. She was pretty all the time, but something about her lit up around the horses. It was like she didn't have a care in the world.

It was no wonder Bitsy liked her. Bit was a stubborn, picky horse, and usually the last one Josh would let someone ride, but

Amy had taken to her almost instantly, and Bitsy hadn't so much as huffed in displeasure.

Josh wanted to believe that Bitsy was a good judge of character, and as he looked at the chocolate-brown mare, her dark eyes clear and glassy, he wanted to believe that she was telling him that Amy was one of the *good ones*. One he should hang on to. One he could trust not to stomp on his heart.

How was it possible that the world could make so much more sense with one person around?

He'd grown more than fond of these rides with Amy. He liked wandering the outskirts of the ranch, their horses weaving back and forth as they talked about nothing and everything. He liked looking over and seeing her there, comfortable on horseback, comfortable with him. Grinning as the sun stretched across the property, shading her eyes to see the cattle way off in the distance. He liked talking to her, more than anyone else in his life, and he never worried about the stretches of silence. Already he felt assured in the quiet spent with her.

He wanted more of that. Conversation and quiet and early morning rides that left his boots dew-stained and his cheeks warm.

"Thank you for having me out again," Amy said, patting Bitsy on the forelock. She'd hung around after the ride and followed him around the ranch while he and his ranch hands completed the morning chores. She'd visited with the tiny calf again who she'd nicknamed Romeo, and had even offered to help muck out the horse stalls. Hours had passed and she still showed no sign of leaving, and frankly Josh wasn't complaining.

"Of course," he said. By now she had to know how much he enjoyed her company. They'd been together almost every day for the past couple of weeks. There was a part of him that wished she'd never leave. "You're welcome here anytime."

She glanced over at him where he leaned against the stall door. "You mean that?"

"I wouldn't have said it if I didn't mean it."

A touch of pink washed across her face. Gosh, he liked that

too. He liked making her blush. Liked knowing that he wasn't the only one affected.

"I don't miss the rodeo and the training as much as I thought I would," Amy said thoughtfully, putting the brush down. She gave Bitsy one more pat then turned to him. "But the horses..." She shrugged. "That's different."

"I think Bitsy would appreciate having you out more often," he said. "To visit. To ride."

"Is she the only one?"

Josh's heart thumped in response. "I'm sure the cattle would appreciate seeing more than my ugly mug on occasion, too."

Amy laughed. "It's far from an ugly mug and I think we both know that."

"Trying to give me a compliment?"

"Probably trying and failing, cowboy," she said. She looked up as Mac stuck his head over his gate, looking for pats. "You might regret inviting me to pop by anytime."

"Oh, yeah? Why?"

Amy flashed her teeth at him. "I'm gonna teach this lot about barrel racing."

Josh snickered, the buzz transforming in his chest, and he realized his phone was ringing. "Bella might be too old for that," he said, pulling out his phone. "She's delicate now."

"Well, maybe she'll just supervise."

"Hold that thought," he said, answering the call. He stepped away. "Hey, how's it going?"

"Didn't wake you, did I?"

On the other end of the line was Shane, longtime friend and grandson of Josh's neighbors, the Coreys—Black ranchers that had lived in Tenacity for generations. Josh and Shane had grown up running around their respective family ranches together, getting in and out of trouble, jumping off hay bales, driving heavy-duty ranch equipment, and generally causing mischief. Shane's grandparents had been good friends with his own parents, and Josh was more than glad that Shane had come back to town after a stint away.

"You know I'm up with the sun."

"Didn't know if things had changed in your old age."

Josh snorted.

"You got a minute to help out an old friend?"

"What's going on?"

"Part of the fence came down last night and some of the herd got out. Could use your help wrangling up cattle and getting the fence repaired. And before you hang up on me, Gram says she'll make it worth your while."

"I would have done it out of the goodness of my heart," Josh said. "But I will allow Angela to bribe me."

"Good. You got time now?"

"Yeah, just wrapping something up," he said, glancing Amy's way where she was giving Mac's muzzle a rub.

"Would *something* happen to be that girl you were telling me about?" Shane asked.

Josh could hear the grin in his voice. He didn't say anything, but Shane knew him too well.

"She's there right now, isn't she?"

"And here I was just thinking I might let you meet her."

"Bring her," Shane said. "Gram'll be ecstatic."

"You're right," Josh said, then paused thinking it through. "On second thought, Angela might be a lot."

"Can't back out on us now."

"I don't want to give you the chance to scare her away."

"Gram!" Shane bellowed on the other end of the phone, and Josh could hear him plodding across the porch. "Josh is bringing his new woman!" There was a murmured reply and Shane yelled again. "The woman he's been seeing. Yeah, the one I told you about!"

"Great," Josh muttered.

Shane snorted. "If you don't bring her now, you're gonna get an earful."

"Yeah, thanks for that." He sighed.

"Didn't you miss me, Joshy?"

"To be honest, right now I'm not really sure why I was so excited for you to come home. I'll be over soon."

"With Amy."

"To be determined." He hung up on Shane and tucked his phone into his pocket.

"Everything okay?" Amy asked, glancing up at him as he approached.

"Just the neighbors. They need a hand—some of their cattle got out."

"Oh," Amy said. "Does that happen a lot?"

"More often than you'd think. They sort of like to play follow the leader with bad ideas."

Amy chuckled.

"Do you mind if we make a little detour on the way back?" Josh asked. "If not, I'm happy to drop you off first."

"No, of course not," Amy said. "I'd like to meet your neighbors."

"Great," Josh said, glad she was up to going, and not just because it would prevent him from getting the third degree from Angela. He was mostly just glad to get to spend some more time with her. "It shouldn't take too long. *Hopefully.*"

They packed up the truck—Josh brought his tools and some extra lumber just in case, though he suspected Otis would have everything they needed—and drove over to the Coreys'. Otis Corey, Shane's grandfather, was the salt of the earth. He'd had gray hair and wrinkles for as long as Josh could remember, and he wore it as well as he did his plaid shirts and denim overalls and cowboy boots. He was the type to put you to work while giving you advice. Josh had always had immense respect for how hard he worked and the morals he'd passed on to his own children and grandchildren. His wife, Angela, Shane's grandmother, was the tenderhearted, tough, no-nonsense counterpart. She had a warmth that instantly endeared her to you, but she wasn't afraid to set you straight, as she'd done on numerous occasions for Josh and Shane, especially when they were getting up to no good.

"So," Amy said as Josh drove down a gravel road, dust spiraling in their wake. "Give me the crash course. What should I know?"

"Okay, well," Josh started. "Shane Corey. We practically grew up together. He's been living near Helena and just returned to

Tenacity after a bad breakup. His grandparents own the ranch. Otis, steady, wise, will look at you like he's staring straight through to your soul."

Amy chuckled. "Got it."

"And his wife, Angela, she's the co-owner of Little Cowpokes Daycare Center in town. She also makes the best mac and cheese in Montana—ask anyone. And if you think you've had better…" He eyed her seriously. "No you didn't."

Amy grinned back at him. "Eyes on the road, cowboy."

"I could drive these roads blindfolded."

"Please don't," she said. "There's an awful lot of cattle roaming around."

Josh turned back to the road and realized she was right. The Coreys' cattle had gathered at the edge of the road, some of them roaming back and forth. Josh slowed so there wouldn't be any accidents, and hung his head out the window, whistling and calling out to get the cattle to move out of the way. He looked at the break in the fence.

"I wonder what happened," Amy said.

"Might have come down in the last storm we had." It was the wetter part of the year still, with temperatures varying from cold enough to need gloves to warm enough to shed your coat. They'd lucked out with nice weather this past week though, and he'd spent a good portion of it outside with Amy. "Or the board was loose and an adventurous cow decided to make a break for it."

Amy turned in her seat to watch the cattle disappear as they turned onto the Coreys' property. "They sorta look like they're waiting to be picked up for a night out."

"It'd be great if they'd just realize that they could walk back the way they came."

"Now why would they make it easy for you?"

"Because I'm a nice guy." The tires crunched over more gravel. He pulled up beside an old weather-beaten truck that both he and Shane had driven up and down this road as teens. He wasn't all that sure it actually functioned anymore or if it had merely rusted in place.

"Hey," Shane called as they got out of the truck. He came clomping down the porch steps and clapped Josh on the shoulder, pulling him into a hug. His thick black hair was shorter than it had been last time Josh had seen him, which was probably Angela's doing, and he'd apparently decided to try out a neatly trimmed beard. It suited him, Josh thought, as Shane broke away, making him look older. At least until Josh spotted that too-bright smile that usually meant mischief. Then it was like they were kids all over again. But this time Josh suspected Shane was looking at him that way because Amy came walking toward them and not because he had his mind on a prank.

"Shane, this is Amy," Josh said, introducing them.

"Good to meet you," Shane said, shaking Amy's hand. "I've heard a lot about you."

"This is becoming a regular thing now," Amy said, probably referring to the fact Noah had told her the same thing.

"Don't worry. I've only been told the best," Shane assured her.

He flashed Amy a smile that usually made women swoon and Josh nudged him. He didn't need any other competition.

"So, getting tired of our poky little town yet?" Shane asked.

"Not quite," Amy said. "It's got a few interesting things going for it."

Shane threw his head back and laughed. "I hope you don't mean this guy."

"Josh said you moved back from near Helena?"

"Yeah. A breakup chased me out."

"I can sympathize there."

"A girl after my own heart. Or whatever pieces remain," Shane joked.

They walked up the porch steps and Josh introduced Amy to Angela as she popped out the door, greeting him with a hug. She was short enough for Josh to rest his chin on the top of her head for a beat. He pulled away, noting new strands of grey by her temples and new wrinkles by her eyes, but her hug had felt as sturdy as ever. That was Angela Corey in a nutshell: sturdy, fierce, with the patience of a wrangler breaking in a wild bronco. Except when it came to his love life, of course.

"You hungry?" she asked, pushing a few curling strands of hair from her face. "Look hungry to me. Come inside."

"Gram, we have to go get the cattle," Shane interrupted.

Angela waved him off. "Where're they gonna go? Not like they're gonna hitch a ride into town."

Shane rolled his eyes.

"I saw that," Angela said even with her back turned.

"I'm gonna go grab the supplies for the fence," Shane said, eyeing Josh. "Finish up here and come find me."

Angela went into the kitchen to get plates as Josh guided Amy through to the dining room.

Amy motioned over her shoulder. "Should we offer to help or..."

"No," Josh said. "Just let her do her thing."

Before Josh had a chance to say anything else, Angela returned, putting a plate of mac and cheese down in front of each of them. It was the same dishware he used to eat off of as a boy with the little daisy patterns around the edges. It was nice to see that some things never changed. He glanced at Amy as she tucked in. It was also nice to see that some things did change.

"I've heard it's the best in Montana," Amy said as Angela sat down across from them.

"You heard right," Angela said.

Josh took his first bite and waited with bated breath for Amy's reaction. Her eyes widened and suddenly she was gushing about how good it was. Josh let out a breath of relief. Not that he expected Amy *not* to like it, but Angela was serious about her cooking and Josh loved Angela like his own grandmother, and he wanted her to like Amy.

Angela gestured to the china hutch in the corner which displayed an eclectic mix of trophies and ribbons. "I've been perfecting the recipe longer than you've been alive. To award-winning results, as you can see."

"You should have opened up a restaurant instead of a day-care."

"There's still time," Angela said. She winked. "Maybe when I retire."

Josh laughed. Otis and Angela were both in their seventies and the thought of them retiring anytime soon was almost as ridiculous as someone not liking Angela's mac and cheese.

"So, you haven't been in town long?" Angela said, and Josh

winced. She had her serious face on, and Angela wasn't one to beat around the bush with pretty conversation. If she wanted to know something about Amy, she'd ask her directly. Josh felt like he needed to run some sort of interference. How could he get Amy out of the house?

"No," Amy said. "I came down in February to visit my sister, Faith."

"And she's marrying the Strom boy. They're a nice couple."

Amy nodded. "I think so."

"And what do you do for work?"

"I'm on the rodeo circuit, actually."

Angela raised a brow, impressed. "What did you say your last name was?"

"Hawkins."

Angela's eyes widened.

"Angela—" Josh cut in.

"It's fine," Amy said at the same time Angela said, "Don't you have some cattle to wrangle?"

Josh knew when not to push his luck with this woman. He stood up, looking down at Amy. She gave him a little smile that he took to mean, *I'll be just fine.* And he had no doubt she would. Amy wasn't a damsel. From everything he'd seen, she was strong and independent and feisty and even that day at the store, when she'd felt sick, she'd been stubborn about letting him help her.

"Guess I'm gonna go wrangle."

"I'll help Angela with the dishes," Amy said, "then I'll come out and join you."

Josh nodded. "See you in a few."

He left the dining room, taking a detour to the bathroom to wash his hands. From there he could hear the rattle of dishes as Amy and Angela moved into the kitchen.

"So, a Hawkins Sister," Angela said. "Not much rodeoing going on in tiny little Tenacity for you."

Josh knew Angela was fishing for information.

"You're right," Amy said. "I miss the arena and my other sisters. But it's been a nice break from Bronco."

"Is it only a break?" Angela wondered.

Amy sighed. "Honestly, I'm not sure. I *think* so. Faith kind of invited me down because I was having a tough time after a breakup."

Angela hummed in understanding. "We know all about break-ups around here. I mean, don't get me wrong, I'm glad my grand-baby's back. But Shane's been going through it."

"I figure I'll sit out a few rodeos and make my way back to Bronco eventually. My ex isn't exactly on the circuit, but I don't even want to chance running into him right now."

"I think getting some space is the right thing to do for most folks if you can. It helps clear your head."

"I guess that's what I was after," Amy said. "A clear head and all that."

Josh turned off the water and leaned against the bathroom sink.

"You think you found it?"

"I'm starting to." Amy said softly.

"Well, for the record, I think you two make a lovely couple," Angela said.

Josh shouldn't have been eavesdropping. His mother had taught him better. Heck, Angela would probably scold him if she knew. But he was frozen, his breath coming shallow and uneasy, like he'd just run across the pasture.

"Oh," Amy said, laughing softly. "No, it's not like that. We're just… We're friends, I suppose."

Josh's pulse skipped in his chest. Just friends? Weren't they more than that? Didn't she feel it? He certainly did. And from where he was standing, he wanted to be much more than just friends. These feelings he had for Amy… It might sound ridicu-lous, but they were so much stronger than they should have been after only a couple of weeks together, but sometimes when a thing was right, it settled into your bones and couldn't be altered.

That's what being with Amy felt like. She was a breath of fresh air that had spread through his lungs and revived him.

It was right, this thing between them. He knew it was; he just hadn't wanted to push her for anything, afraid that she'd bolt like a spooked horse, trampling his heart along the way. But hearing her say that they were just friends… The words boiled in his gut like an acid soup, burning and bubbling. He looked at his face in the mirror, knowing that even after this short while, losing Amy would crush him.

"You don't sound so sure of that yourself," Angela said.

"Maybe there are some feelings there," Amy admitted. "At least on my end."

The emotion inside Josh shifted so fast he almost fell back. Had she just admitted to having feelings for him? A herd of cattle could bust through the door and he wouldn't care. His entire being delighted in Amy's little confession.

"Only *some* feelings?" Angela clarified.

"No. A lot of feelings actually. More than I probably should have. Though I don't think he knows that."

"I've known Josh for a long time, and judging by the way he looks at you, there's nothing friendly about it," Angela said pointedly.

Josh should be mortified, but all he could do was smile.

CHAPTER NINE

A PERFECT MONTANA sunset painted the sky, the creamsicle clouds framing the pastures in pillows of crisp orange and rosy pink and sunflower yellow. It reminded Amy of cotton candy, and she almost felt like she could reach out and pluck a handful from her place on the porch.

She'd been at Split Valley for the better part of the afternoon. When Josh had invited her out riding, it had been an easy yes, but when he'd asked her to stay for dinner... Well, how could she possibly turn down a glorious spring evening like this? Josh had been quick to suggest burgers, prepared with all the fixings, and Amy wondered if he'd been working up the nerve to ask her to stay one of the other evenings they'd spent together. He'd seemed delighted when she agreed, giving her one of those dimpled smiles, and Amy knew in her gut that her feelings for him had spiraled way past friendship. She'd said as much to Faith and to Angela Corey, but this was something else. She didn't just like Josh.

What she felt... It was something more.

And the thought of him not feeling the same way almost made her want to be sick.

But then Josh looked up from the grill where he was flipping burger patties and grinned at her in a way that made her doubt such a thing was possible. Happiness welled inside her. That, and a fierce hunger. Her belly rumbled.

"Was that your stomach?" Josh laughed.

"Maybe." Amy touched her belly. "I didn't eat much for lunch, so this is a treat. I actually didn't realize how hungry I was."

"Well, glad you brought your appetite. Burgers are almost done. You want cheese and bacon on yours?"

"Is that even a question?"

"Right. We've talked about how Faith is making you suffer the turkey bacon."

"*And* whole grains," Amy added. "She should have to answer for her crimes."

"I'll put a couple extra pieces of bacon on for you then. So you can indulge."

Amy dipped her head in thanks. He was so effortlessly thoughtful. Bacon. It was such a silly thing to get emotional over, and yet she blinked back a sudden wave of tears. God, what was wrong with her? She tried not to stare at him as her cheeks flamed hotter than the grill. "I'm glad I don't have to corrupt you to my bacon-loving ways."

"No worries there. I am a red meat carnivore through and through. Poultry has its place. Just not on my burger."

"Can I do something to help?" Amy asked.

"Grab the plates? And the condiments," he said. "They're on the counter in the kitchen. Unless you'd rather eat inside. I just thought that it's shaping up to be a nice evening and we might as well keep enjoying it."

"Definitely," Amy agreed, heading for the house.

"Oh, there's potato salad too," he called.

Amy tossed a look over her shoulder, impressed.

"Don't get too excited. Angela made it."

"I'm learning so much tonight."

"I may not know my way around the kitchen that well, but I do know my way around the grill."

Amy winked. "And that's what really matters."

She slipped through the door. Walking through Josh's space didn't feel foreign the way she thought it might. It was comfortable, filled with old wooden furniture and little touches of home she figured had been left over from his mother—the checkered throw blanket tossed over the back of the couch, the cute framed cross-stitches hung along the wall, the family portraits. In the kitchen, she gathered up the essentials for dinner and took them outside, along with a glass of sweet tea for each of them.

"You were blond," she said, coming back to the porch.

"Huh?"

"As a boy. You had blond hair."

"Oh." He ran a hand through his hair, and she appreciated the way the locks parted on either side of his face. "Guess I was. It darkened up by the time I started middle school. You snooping at the family pictures?"

"Can't be snooping when they're hanging out right in the open."

Josh plated up the burgers, and they dressed them up to their liking, then sat side by side in the Adirondack chairs, watching the last of the sunset wash across the sky. It felt like such a simple thing, being there together, eating dinner, but it also felt like everything. Amy didn't know how else to describe it. How else to express the overwhelming bubble of contentment that rose up inside her. The swell of peace made her feel like she was floating. And if that was the case, she never wanted to come down.

"Good?" Josh asked, catching her eye.

"Really good," she said. "You were right. You know your way around the grill."

"I had to figure out some way to survive bachelorhood."

"Has it… Have you…" Amy wasn't quite sure how to ask what she wanted to ask. "Feel free to tell me to mind my own business," she started again.

Josh sat up in his chair. "It's okay. You can ask."

"Has it been that long since… there was someone important in your life?"

Josh opened his mouth, closed it. He sucked in a deep breath, letting it out again. "Yeah. A good long while. My previous relationship, the one with Erica, she was the last woman I was serious with. And I'm not very good at being *non-serious*, so I haven't really been dating around or seeing anyone. I'm just not so good at the going out thing and being around heaps of people all the time. I'm my best self here. On the ranch. Where I can be outside. And I appreciate that's not everyone's cup of tea."

"Well, I like *this* Josh," Amy assured him. The corner of his mouth quirked, and a coil of desire swept through her. It was getting harder to shoo these feelings away when she was with him. She wanted to run her fingers along his stubbled jawline and taste the heat of the day on his lips.

"What are you thinking?" Josh said, peering deeply into her eyes.

Amy huffed. "About how strange fate can be."

"You mean how you can stumble into the right person when you least expect it?"

"Something like that," she said.

"You feel like the right person."

Amy opened her mouth, closed it, swallowing down her gasp.

"Are you okay?" he asked.

She nodded. "Sometimes you say awfully sweet things, cowboy. And it catches me off guard."

"I didn't mean to make you uncomfortable."

"No, you didn't," Amy said. "I just—"

"What?"

"I don't know," she said honestly. There were a lot of things she wanted to say right now. But what if they ruined everything? What if Josh didn't really mean those words? Tru had used pretty words too. *You feel like the right person.* If she was wrong, this would devastate her. She caught Josh's eye, trying to untangle her thoughts. *Do you like me the way I like you, Josh Aventura?* "I guess I'm worried I'm going to say something that'll ruin this. And I've come to the realization that I don't want to lose you."

"Why would you lose me?" he asked.

"You've been really sweet to me these past weeks, Josh." His brow pinched as she said it. "But I'm not sure I like you as a friend. As only a friend, I should say. I'm not sure I ever did." The words left her in a rush, and suddenly her insides felt hollow and achy. She wanted to fill the space, fill the silence, with something. Anything. But there was nothing to do but watch the emotions shift across Josh's face. His brow furrowed, and his mouth opened, but no words came out as he struggled through confusion and then another emotion Amy couldn't confidently identify. Surprise, maybe? Was there a hint of a smile on his lips?

"So what you're saying is…"

"That I like you an awful lot," she whispered. "More than should be possible this soon." God, she wanted to bury her face in her hands, but she resisted the urge. Resisted the urge to get up and run right off the porch. Had she ever felt this way about Tru? Filled with this heart-pounding, edge-of-her-seat desire and fear and hope? She couldn't remember. Tru felt like lifetimes ago. Lifetimes that didn't matter in a world where Josh existed.

"Amy." Josh reached between them and caught her hand. "I want you to know that being here, with you, feels right in a way that I'm not sure I've ever felt."

Her breath caught. "I feel the same way."

Josh rose from his chair, crossed the short distance and leaned down, giving her plenty of time to stop him. To push him away. To tell him he'd gotten his wires crossed, but she didn't, and Josh cupped her jaw with his hand and kissed her softly.

It was only a brush of lips.

Barely even a kiss.

But it was everything.

"Was that okay?" he asked.

"Yes," she breathed.

"Good. I didn't want you to leave here tonight not knowing how I felt."

He kissed her again.

Sensation shot through her. It was electric, just that touch, and she gasped. If it all went downhill from here, then so be it. But at least she'd told him—shown him—how she felt too.

As Josh pulled away, Amy rose out of her chair. He gathered her into his arms, pulling her in for another kiss. She was reasonably tall, but he was taller, and she had to press up on her toes to deepen the kiss, tilting her head and sinking into the feel of him.

Josh's hands smoothed up and down her back. Then he turned his head slightly, breaking the kiss. Amy heaved in a breath of air as Josh pulled away enough to lean against the railing. He kept his hands on her hips, but the distance between them left room for conversation again.

"I've been dying to do that for weeks," he said, a little smile flickering across his face.

She giggled. She couldn't help it. "Why didn't you?"

"I was afraid I'd spook you."

She snorted. "Like a skittish little horse?"

"Yes. Or that I'd chase you away." He leaned down and pecked her on the corner of the mouth. "I'm still not convinced I won't."

"You won't," she assured him. She couldn't believe she was saying those words after Tru, but Josh made her want to be bold. Or reckless. Maybe both. "And, unlike Bitsy, I don't bite. You could have told me sooner."

"I didn't want to pressure you into anything." He pulled back again. "We can take this as slow as you want. I realize that you only got out of that relationship a few months ago."

Amy curled her fingers in the fabric of his shirt, tugging him closer. "That doesn't matter anymore. And I think we've been taking things slow," she said. "Considering how we both feel." Now that she knew, now that she had him like this, she didn't want there to be any more distance. She wanted to be with Josh. Here. Now. She reached up and nipped at his jaw playfully. "We don't have to stop."

Josh groaned, pressing his face against her neck. She could feel his warm breath against her skin and it was wonderful. "Are you sure?"

"*You* don't have to stop."

"Amy, I mean it. This doesn't have to happen now. It won't change how I feel."

"I think you should stop talking and kiss me already."

He did, both hands on her cheeks, and Amy felt like she was floating.

Josh deepened the kiss again, his tongue looking for entrance, and Amy let her lips fall open, let herself sink into the bliss that crept through her veins. Her heart was beating so hard, and she was breathless, and for a few moments, they let themselves be breathless. Neither of them speaking.

"God, I want you." Josh looked at her, tucking a strand of hair behind her ear. "Do you want to go inside?"

"Well, otherwise I'm gonna start stripping out here," she

teased. "And I'm not sure that's a show you want your cattle to see."

Josh laughed. "They'd be scandalized for sure." He took her by the hand and led her into the house and straight upstairs to his bedroom. Amy tried to look around, tried to catalog the rustic wooden furniture and the cowboy hat hanging off the bedpost and the smell of cedar, but she was distracted as Josh's fingers trailed up beneath her shirt.

"You made your bed," she said, impressed.

"I always make my bed. Don't you?"

"Only because Faith would be grumpy if I didn't." She kissed him. "I don't see a point if I'm just gonna mess up the sheets again."

"Because that's half the fun. Give us a second to get horizontal and I'll show you just how much fun." His hands snaked up her shirt, skimming the underside of her breast. "I think this is in the way."

Amy's shirt was on the ground before she could work up words for a reply. Josh pressed against her, his hands suddenly everywhere, and she could feel the length of him. Amy tugged on his belt buckle and Josh got the message, shrugging out of his clothes while she shimmied out of hers.

They touched and caressed as they did, sending electric shivers through her body. Lord, she wanted him.

Josh reached for her again, his hands running over bare skin. "Are you on—"

"Yes," she said. "But I think we should still use a condom."

"Got it," Josh said, reaching for a drawer by the bedside. There was the crinkle of a wrapper as Amy sat down on the bed, reclining back on her elbows just so she could look at him. Every tanned, muscled inch.

He grinned at her, taking a step closer to the bed before leaning down to press a kiss to her knee. Amy fell back, eyes closed, enjoying the sensation of his lips moving from one leg to the other, slowly inching toward the place she wanted him most.

"This okay?" he said, and Amy practically arched off the bed.

"Josh, I swear if you don't touch me—"

And then he did, with his lips and his tongue, and Amy

moaned. It was good, he was so good, that she practically forgot her own name as she trembled against him. He continued his way up her body, the weight of him enveloping her, and Amy kissed his lips as he settled between her hips.

"You're sure?"

"Yes," she said, and then Josh slid against her, making love to her as only a cowboy could. She arched and panted against his ear, and when she came undone, it was to the sound of her name on his lips.

Amy floated there for a long while, in the soft aftermath, content to be held.

"Did I tucker you out?" Josh asked eventually, his words a grumble as he pressed a soft kiss to her shoulder.

"I was almost asleep," she hummed. "Unless you want me to leave?"

"Don't you dare. You should message your sister though. Let her know you're staying the night so she doesn't think I kidnapped you."

"Good idea." Amy rallied enough to dig her phone out of her jeans, half hanging off the bed.

Josh's hand wrapped around her hip, holding her in place. She smiled at that.

Won't be home tonight. Don't wait up, she texted.

Faith responded immediately. Amy! Oh my God, tell me everything!

Good night, Faith, she wrote, putting her phone away before her sister could start grilling her with questions. Questions she would be happy to answer tomorrow, when she wasn't lying in Josh's bed. She rolled back over into Josh's waiting arms.

He tucked her against him, and for the first time in months, Amy felt safe and wanted. As far as a partner went, maybe for the first time in her life.

CHAPTER TEN

JOSH WOKE BEFORE his alarm, the way he did most mornings, and lay in that blissful suspension between sleep and wakefulness, where he was both completely aware and fully capable of drifting off again. If not for the years of early wake-up calls to tend to the cattle and the horses, he might have been tempted by the thought of another hour. But he was used to rising with the sun, and today would be no different.

Except, it *was* different.

He stretched, suddenly aware of an unfamiliar ache in his bones. Josh was used to hard work. His muscles had long grown accustomed to the effort of labor on the ranch—trekking long distances around the property, lifting hay bales, maintaining the facilities. But this morning was different. He ached in a way that told him he'd perhaps had too much of a good thing, and then the previous night came crashing back. Dinner on the porch. Telling Amy how he felt. Kissing her. Taking her to his bed. Well then, that explained the odd exhaustion that clung to him, and Josh couldn't be happier. He grinned to himself as he sleepily reached beneath the covers for her.

Only, his hand brushed nothing but empty space, and his eyes flew open.

Josh turned his head, finding Amy's side of the bed vacant. He reached out again, feeling along the space she'd occupied.

The sheets were rumpled but cold, and worry flared to life inside him. He already missed her presence, and his entire body ached with her absence. He waited for the sleep fog to clear, but confusion settled over him like a strangling weight and he frowned, sitting up on his elbows. With two fingers he rubbed the sleep from his eyes.

What was going on?

When they'd fallen asleep last night, Amy had been tucked up against him, warm and content in his arms. She'd told her sister she was staying the night.

So what had happened between then and now?

Maybe she'd reconsidered staying with him, or regretted their night together, and snuck away. No, she wouldn't have set off on her own. Someone must have come to pick her up. But wouldn't he have heard someone come down the lane? Tires weren't exactly quiet on the gravel. None of it made sense, and his heart sank.

Last night had been wonderful as far as he was concerned. Holding Amy in his arms, watching as she drifted off to sleep... He couldn't have asked for a better end to the night. And after everything she'd said, why would she run off?

I like you an awful lot.

Her words played on repeat in his mind. He'd said that being with her felt right and she'd agreed. So when had it all gone wrong? Had he somehow failed to live up to her expectations? Did she finally realize that he was just some average cattle rancher? That to be with him would mean being stuck here too?

Josh flopped down on his back, staring at the ceiling, wishing the ground would open up and swallow him whole. He couldn't believe this was to be his lot in life again. He couldn't believe he'd lost Amy when he'd only just found her.

Then he heard the squeak of the pipes in the wall. Someone was running the water in the bathroom.

The bathroom! Of course. Josh almost burst out laughing. What a fool he was, panicking. There was no reason to panic. Amy had simply gotten up to use the bathroom. He pressed his hand to his face, massaging the worry lines from his forehead. He really had to let go of these fears. Amy wasn't his ex. He wanted to be able to trust her with his heart.

Then Josh heard a different sound and he sat up.

Was that retching?

He strained his ears, listening for that unpleasant sound again. Everything was quiet, and then… Yes, Amy was getting sick.

Why was she sick?

A moment later the toilet flushed and then the pipes squeaked and clattered again as the water in the sink ran. When he heard the bathroom door pop open, he looked to the hall. Amy appeared in the doorway to the bedroom, a hand pressed to her stomach, ashen-faced. She clutched the doorframe with her other hand, her fingers blanched.

Even from here he could see a slight tremble.

Immediately Josh rolled out of bed and gathered her to him. She felt clammy. Her body sagged like it was too weak to hold her up.

"I thought you'd left."

"Only made it as far as the bathroom," she said, and he could tell she was trying to make a joke.

He pushed her hair back from her face. "Are you okay?"

"I'm sorry," she muttered. "I think I have to go. I'm not… I'm not feeling well."

"Of course. I'll uh…" Where were his keys? No, first he needed pants. "I'll drive you back to Faith's."

He dressed as quickly as he could, then helped get Amy downstairs and into the truck. There was a moment when he thought she was going to be sick again, right there on the driveway, but once she was sitting in the passenger seat, she rolled the window down and half leaned out, breathing in the fresh air.

Josh was filled with competing emotions. He was worried and anxious that something might really be wrong, and also disappointed. Last night he'd envisioned waking her up with breakfast. He wasn't a miracle worker, but he could manage eggs and bacon and coffee. Now he just wanted to get her back to Caleb and Faith's so they could figure out if she needed to see a doctor.

Was it a bug?

Or something she ate?

Oh… *Oh!*

"God, I hope it wasn't the burgers." Josh pressed on the gas, speeding down Juniper Road, spitting dust in his wake.

"No... No, I don't think so," Amy said. "If something was wrong with the meat, you'd be sick too. But you feel fine?"

He nodded. He did feel fine. Right? He took a deep breath, trying to assess if he somehow felt unsettled. Nope. He felt fit as a fiddle. "So far so good."

"See," Amy said, sucking in shallow little breaths that made him nervous.

He still wasn't convinced this wasn't somehow his fault.

"And besides," she said, "you're a great cook."

"Wasn't much cooking involved," he noted. It wasn't the potato salad, was it? Lord smite him for even suggesting such a thing. Of course it wasn't Angela's potato salad. He'd eaten it the day before. Again, if there was something wrong, he'd be just as sick.

"It wasn't your dinner. The burgers were delicious." Amy pressed her face into her hands. "God, I'm so embarrassed."

"Don't be," Josh said, still wondering if he'd inadvertently poisoned her. "Please don't be. I had a wonderful time with you. This is just—"

"Mortifying," Amy cut in.

"It doesn't change one second of the time we spent together. Don't think that." Amy leaned her head out the window again. Josh looked between her and the road, to the way her entire face pinched, a tiny crease appearing between her eyes.

"I'm sure I just caught a stomach bug somewhere." She groaned. "Oh God, I hope I didn't give it to you!" Her eyes flew open, startled as she looked at him. "Josh, I'm so sorry."

"Don't worry about me."

"How can I not worry? The first night we spend together and I infect you with some horrible stomach germ."

"You didn't infect me with anything. We don't even know what *this* is yet."

"I hope not. Cause I really do feel awful." Amy paled and reached one hand out for the dashboard to brace herself.

Josh pressed on the gas a little, trying to shake the thought that fate was laughing at him. Here he'd found this wonderful woman, and she was ridiculous enough to like him back, and now he'd given her food poisoning or something. Ryder and Noah were never going to let him hear the end of this once they found out how his latest romantic entanglement crashed and burned. He could almost hear them now... *Remember that one time the girl literally left your place throwing up? You made her sick to her stomach?*

Josh grimaced just as Amy groaned, pressing the back of her hand to her lips.

"Do you need me to..." Josh started, trying to figure out how to best help her. "Should I pull over?"

She shook her head, eyes squinted, and sat back in her seat. "No, keep going. I'm okay. I think it'll pass."

"Will it?"

"I don't know. Let's talk about something else."

"Okay, sure. What?"

"I don't know. Distract me."

"Distract you. Right." He could manage a story. "Did I ever tell you about the weekend when Shane and I almost crashed a truck into the side of Otis and Angela's barn?"

Amy snorted. "Having met Shane, I'm not even a little surprised."

"Hey, I was the voice of reason in this situation. Even at nine years old I knew it wasn't going to end well."

"You were nine?" she said, her voice rising.

"Yes. You know country kids. You learn to drive almost anything by the time you're tall enough to reach the pedals."

"So what happened?"

"Shane was a short little thing and couldn't quite reach the brakes." He shot Amy a grin as she laughed.

"You're kidding."

"I wish I was. But, you know, once we got going it was too late. I still remember us ripping through the pasture, screaming as Shane blindly tried to slam his foot down on the brake pedal. And I'm like looking over the dash, being our eyes, grabbing the wheel to dodge the cattle, and we go ripping through a hay bale and as that clears, right at the last second I spot the barn, and just yank the wheel and we careen past it, still screaming. It was the closest I'd ever come to living out an action movie."

Amy shook with laughter. Josh did too, remembering the

feeling of the truck slamming to a stop as Shane finally got his foot on the brake.

"Then what?"

"I could hear Angela hollering all the way from the house. Next thing I do is look out the window, and there she is, marching straight across the pasture toward us. To this day I swear there was steam coming out her nostrils."

"What did you do?"

"The only thing I could do. I bailed out the side of the truck, ditched Shane to deal with his grandmother, and went running home. You would have thought I was a track star."

Amy laughed again. "You didn't."

"That woman put the fear of God in me. I wasn't about to let her catch me."

"And so that was it?"

"Oh no. Otis drove over to our place later, talked to my parents about what happened. Or what *almost* happened. No one was impressed. Shane and I spent many weekends after that mucking out stalls on both properties. Angela made sure we were too busy to have any more time to get up to that kind of fun."

"She put you on the straight and narrow path."

"Oh, absolutely. Who knows how many derelict trucks I would have taken for joyrides in my youth without her intervention."

Amy shook her head and Josh was pleased to see that she didn't look quite so ashen. He pulled onto Faith's street and into the driveway, throwing the truck in Park.

"You don't have to get out," Amy started to say.

"Like hell I don't." He hopped out of the truck and met her at her door. She was already half out of the truck. "You think I'm just going to dump you on the doorstep?"

She wobbled a bit and he wrapped his arm around her, helping her to the door.

It flew open before they reached it, and Faith's smile slowly fell from her face. "Uh-oh," she said to Amy. "You look awful."

"Gee, thanks," Amy muttered.

"Don't worry," Faith said. "I'm sure it'll pass."

But before Josh could say as much as a goodbye, Amy darted into the bathroom again.

CHAPTER ELEVEN

DESPITE FAITH'S DECLARATION, it did not, in fact, pass.

Not for a while.

Faith stood behind her, asking a thousand questions, none of which Amy was capable of answering while she was hunched over the toilet. Finally Faith got the message and excused herself, leaving Amy in relative peace for the next half hour.

Thankfully, the nausea receded, and on shaky legs, Amy went to the sink to splash some cold water on her face. What a long morning it had already been and the sun was barely up. As she looked at herself in the mirror, she could make out the dark circles that hugged her eyes. It looked like she'd pulled an all-nighter on the road between rodeo destinations instead of a night wrapped up in Josh's arms.

She took a deep breath, comforted by the thought of him, if not still a little mortified.

At least her stomach had settled.

For now.

Amy washed her hands and left the bathroom, careful with every step, somehow afraid to trigger another bout of nausea. But as she reached her room and sank down on her bed, she was feeling a little better.

"Here," Faith said, appearing in the doorway. The tie at the end of her braid was coming loose. She passed Amy a glass of water.

"I'm almost afraid to drink anything."

"Little sips," Faith said, the way their parents had when they were younger. "The last thing you want to do is get dehydrated. Then it'll be off to the hospital in Bronco."

Amy grumbled. Faith was right. That's the last thing she wanted. She brought the glass of water to her lips, realizing how dry her mouth was, and took a small sip. The water went down her throat like sandpaper. She winced.

"How are you feeling now?" Faith asked.

"Exhausted. Though my stomach feels settled for the first time since this morning. Then again, maybe this is just a short reprieve. Who knows?"

"Was it something you ate?" Faith said.

"No." Amy shook her head. She repeated what she'd said to Josh. "I'm thinking it's a stomach bug, maybe." Though she was already feeling much better than she had been ten minutes ago. But just in case... "You should keep away from me. I'm already worried I gave whatever this is to Josh. I don't need you and Caleb to catch it too." Amy flopped back on her bed. "God, how can I feel so horrible and so wonderful at the same time?"

"Good night until this happened?" Faith asked. "You didn't respond to any of my texts."

"How could I? Josh was right there. Did you think I was going to start gushing about him while he was lying beside me?"

"You seemed really happy to ignore me."

"I was." She sighed heavily. "It was honestly the best night, Faith. Possibly the best night of my life. And I know that sounds ridiculous, but things were just different with Josh. I mean, it's new and exciting, but there's also something that feels..."

"Right?" Faith said softly.

"Yeah," Amy said. "Like I was finally where I was supposed to be, and everything just made sense."

"Good thing Josh didn't hear you say that. It'd go right to his head."

"It's not just the sex though." Amy laughed.

"I know," Faith said, sitting down next to her and patting her knee. "I get it."

Amy smiled a bit. She probably did get it. Maybe she'd felt the same way with Caleb. It was like a giddy bubble had swelled in her chest, making her light and buoyant. Like nothing could bring her down. Until this morning. "If only I didn't get sick!" Amy covered her head with the pillow. She wanted to scream. "Like, how embarrassing is that? You sleep with a guy and then throw up in his bathroom."

Faith drummed her fingers against her lips. "Amy, what if it isn't a stomach bug?"

Amy tossed the pillow aside, sitting up on her elbows so she could look at her sister. Faith was studying her, lips pursed, eyes narrowed, like she was puzzling something out. She opened her mouth, then closed it again. Amy tilted her head. "What are you talking about?"

Faith cleared her throat. "I hate to even ask this. And please don't take it the wrong way. But is it in any way possible... I mean... Do you think you could be pregnant?"

Pregnant? She huffed a laugh. Really? Pregnant? She shook her head. "No." She sat up all the way. "No, I'm not. I mean, the last time I was with anyone was back around Christmas. We were careful, thank God," she muttered. "And I took a pregnancy test weeks ago, just to be sure because things didn't work out between us, and it was negative." But by "weeks," Amy realized she meant almost three months ago. She'd taken that pregnancy test back in January. Still, it wasn't possible that she was pregnant with... *Tru's baby.* Oh, son of a—

Amy stared at Faith, wide-eyed, shaking her head in disbelief. "It can't... *I* can't."

"Oh, honey," Faith said, taking her hand. "You know those tests aren't always accurate. Or maybe you simply took it too soon or maybe it was a false negative."

"No." Amy couldn't do anything but keep shaking her head.

"Think about it. It would explain all of your odd symptoms. Maybe it would even explain this bout of sickness that doesn't seem to be a stomach bug or food poisoning."

"Morning sickness?" Amy said. "But I haven't been sick every morning."

"No, but that's not always the case for every woman. Maybe you've been really lucky so far. But there's been other signs, Amy. Think about it. Maybe one-offs, but when you add them all up together—" Faith counted things off on her fingers. "That dizzy spell you had a few weeks ago in the store, and you're always complaining about being tired. You've also been weepy, which is really out of character for you."

Amy shifted to the edge of the bed, clutching the mattress as the pieces fell into place. She'd really thought that dizzy spell was because she hadn't eaten. And of course she was tired; she spent every spare minute she wasn't at the store with Josh. And she'd always chalked the weepiness up to being dumped by Tru. But then she thought about the fact her clothes had been feeling tighter too. Her heart galloped in her chest, the beat rushing by her ears like the crash of ocean waves.

What if Faith was right and the test had been wrong?

"Have you been getting your period?" Faith asked.

Amy shrugged. "With my birth control it's virtually non-existent, so I wouldn't even know. That's why I took the test. To be sure." As reality settled over her, terror set in, and Amy's voice trembled. "God. Not now!" She covered her face with her hands. "Not when things with me and Josh are getting so good."

"Okay," Faith said diplomatically. She got to her feet, pacing in front of Amy. "Let's not panic about anything. We don't even know for sure yet. So, here's what we're gonna do. You're gonna shower so you feel more like a human, and I'm gonna run out to the drugstore to pick up a pregnancy test. Then we'll regroup, okay?"

Amy didn't say anything.

"I'm gonna go now. Try not to freak out while I'm gone."

Amy nodded. "Right. Okay." A plan. She could handle a plan. The not freaking out part… Well, she wasn't making any promises about that.

Faith left for the Tenacity Drugs & Sundries, and Amy got in the shower, scrubbing until she felt like herself again. Was that what this was? Morning sickness? *Don't think about it,* she thought as a wave of panic launched up her throat. Nothing was confirmed, and until it was, she'd be freaking out for no reason.

When she was done in the shower, she dressed and brushed her hair. By then, Faith had returned. She handed Amy a bag full of tests.

"Isn't this a little overkill?"

"Do you want to be sure or what?"

Amy took one of the tests, popped into the bathroom, and peed on the stick following all the directions. When she was done, she opened the bathroom door, and she and Faith paced, waiting for the results with bated breath.

It came back positive.

"No," Amy said. She grabbed another test and took that one. It also came back positive and the panic inside her skyrocketed. Amy went to grab a third test but Faith stopped her. Stared at her.

"Amy," she said softly.

Amy slumped against the bathroom wall. She was pregnant. This whole time she'd been pregnant. She was going to have a *baby*. A million thoughts raced through her mind. A baby? She couldn't have a baby. She hadn't been taking care of herself properly these past months. She tried to think back to every potentially foolish decision. Had she had a drink these past four months? She'd definitely been horseback riding. And she obviously hadn't been to see a doctor. Weren't there vitamins she was supposed to be taking? Or like…things she was supposed to be planning for? Birth? Lamaze classes? She didn't know how she was supposed to be breathing!

She was sort of hyperventilating now and that clearly wasn't right. She was also thirty-five. Did that make her a high-risk pregnancy?

"What are you thinking?" Faith asked.

"A really bad word," Amy said.

Faith chuckled softly and leaned against the wall beside her. "That's fair. I probably would be too."

"I can't believe I was so stupid."

"You weren't though. You did the things you were supposed to do. Used protection. Checked. It's just one of those flukes. You know, the zero point one percent chance or whatever it is."

"Of course it would happen to me."

"I know you haven't had long to process this news, but do you know what you're going to do now?" Faith nudged her shoulder. "Whatever it is, just know I support you and Caleb and I will be here. And all of your sisters will."

Amy had no idea what she was going to do. Of course her family would be supportive. She wouldn't expect anything else. But there was so much more to this. Tru-shaped complications that she hadn't ever considered. Having his baby would mean that she would be forever tied to that man.

The corner of Faith's mouth twitched uncertainly, and she took Amy's hand, squeezing it. "Amy, you don't have to tell me if you don't want to. I did my best to stay out of the relationship when it was happening, and I don't mean to pry now, but is the baby Tru McCoy's?"

Amy nodded miserably. "The movie star and newlywed," she said with a dramatic flourish. "And I'm now apparently his baby mama."

"Wow," Faith said under her breath. "We suspected maybe you two had a thing."

"Who?"

"Oh, me, Tori, Elizabeth, Carly. We used to talk about it all the time. But I never expected this to be the result."

"Yeah. You and me both." She could only imagine how he'd respond to the news when he found out. How was she going to tell him? Did she even want to tell him? She hadn't spoken to Tru in months. He'd likely already forgotten who she was, and maybe that was for the best. Maybe there was no need to drag him back into her life.

Besides, there was something haunting her more than the thought of confessing she was pregnant to Tru and that was telling *Josh*. Where did she even begin? As she sat there, she pictured his face and tried to imagine how he would take the news. Would he feel lied to? Betrayed? Worst of all, would he look at her differently now?

Amy couldn't shake the feeling that she was about to lose him and everything they'd been building together.

It was all over, wasn't it? Horseback rides around Split Valley

Ranch and lunch at the Silver Spur Café and sunsets wrapped in each other's arms.

It was all about to change.

What a mess she'd made.

CHAPTER TWELVE

"OKAY, LET'S TALK this out logically," Faith said, clapping her hands together. She paced in front of Amy, fingers drumming against fingers as she buzzed her lips together, clearly at a loss.

"Not sure there's much logic to it," Amy muttered, staring down into her mug of now lukewarm tea.

They'd relocated to the kitchen table around midday as Faith had tried to get Amy to eat something. The only thing she could stomach at the time was toast, especially with the news swirling through her thoughts, and that made her think of Josh and the tea and toast he'd made for her the last time she was sick. At that memory, she'd immediately broken down in a bout of uncontrollable tears which had sent Faith into a panicked scramble, and she'd whipped up a loaf of chocolate walnut banana bread.

Amy had a little chuckle about it now—her tears, Faith's anxious baking. What a pair they were. She wasn't sure there was anything particularly funny about realizing you were having a baby months into the pregnancy, but she was two slices of banana bread deep now, and the chocolate seemed to have improved her mood slightly. Either that or she was finally going into shock.

"Why are you laughing?" Faith asked. She stopped pacing.

"I don't know. Sugar rush, maybe."

Faith frowned, sitting down next to Amy. "Do you want anything else? I can make... I don't know, whatever you're craving. Or I can go pick something up."

"How about you just go back to December and tell me not to sleep with Tru. Actually, go back to the Golden Buckle Rodeo and don't even let me talk to the guy."

"I wish I could. Honestly, I'd like to give the guy a good talking to after the way he treated you. Never mind the fact that you're now pregnant with his child."

The front door opened and closed and Faith fell silent.

Caleb walked into the kitchen, home from the store for lunch. He slowed, and took a good long look at them: Faith clutching Amy's hand, looking half-murderous, Amy wearing a mix of disgust and regret. Caleb picked up the sandwich Faith had left on the counter for him and took a bite, all without taking his eyes off them. "So... do I want to know?"

Faith released her hand, stood and kissed Caleb on the cheek. "I love you," she replied, "but now is not the time to ask questions."

"Okay, well, now I'm concerned."

"Just trust me. Eat your sandwich and leave in ignorant bliss."

Concern pinched his features. "Is everyone okay?" he asked. "Your sisters? Your parents?"

Faith opened her mouth to respond as Amy slumped against the table. "I'm pregnant," she cut in before Faith could answer.

"That," Faith said, looking from Caleb to Amy.

"Huh," Caleb said. He took another bite of his sandwich. The concern shifted to confusion. "*Huh?*"

"Yeah," Amy said. "That's about how I feel."

"I'm not sure what I'm supposed to say next." He clearly meant that Amy didn't look very enthusiastic, so perhaps the default *congratulations* was the wrong choice, and he would be right.

Amy couldn't even imagine hearing that word right now. And what about when other people found out? It would be all *Oh my God, congrats, this is so exciting!* said in high-pitched voices. She'd be hugged and squealed over and she didn't even know if she wanted any of that. What she really wanted was to find the nearest horizontal surface and bury herself in blankets. She didn't want to emerge until someone figured out what to do about this mess.

"You don't have to say anything," Faith told Caleb. She ran her hand up and down his arm. "Actually, no questions or comments is probably preferable at this time." She pecked him on the cheek again.

"Understood."

He put his plate on the counter and stuffed the rest of his sandwich in his mouth. "I guess if you need anything, call me." He shot Amy a sympathetic smile before heading back to work.

"Okay, what was I saying?" Faith asked as the front door closed again. She returned to her place at the table.

Amy propped her head on her hands. "That we should be logical about this."

"Yes. Logical options."

"Which are?"

"Well, one, do you want this baby?" Faith asked simply. "I guess that's where we need to start."

Amy pressed one hand to her stomach. To the space she imagined this little life had been secretly growing inside her. If you'd asked her last week if she had any plans to become a mother in the next year, she would have said no. Not when she was still trying to sort through heartache. But now that the opportunity had presented itself... No, now that reality had busted down her door screaming, *I'm here*, things were different.

The question was no longer *if* it happened in the future.

It had already happened.

"Okay, I'm having this baby," Amy said. "Where does that leave me?"

"Well, as far as I can see it, option one, you call Tru and tell him the truth. You tell him he's going to be a father and see how he takes it. And then the two of you make decisions from there about who does what and how much involvement he has in raising your child."

Amy wanted to throw up again. "I'm sure that'll go over so well with his new bride."

"Hey, that's not on you," Faith said. "That's a problem for him to sort out."

"Right. Let's hear option two."

"Option two." Faith bit her lip, perhaps considering her words. "You say nothing. You raise this baby without Tru's influence or interference."

"And what if the baby grows up and wants to know who their father is? Then I'll have to do all this in ten years anyway. And by then my child could resent me."

Faith shrugged. "Maybe you'll feel more prepared to handle Tru in ten years."

"But then I'll still have to explain to this kid why I lied. Why I kept their father a secret." Lying to her child right out of the womb didn't feel like something she wanted to do. She sighed heavily. No, she was going to have to call Tru. She was going to have to be brave and do the adult thing and tell her ex-fling that she was carrying his child. Amy's stomach flip-flopped uncomfortably.

There was a knock on the door and Faith stood to answer it.

She breezed out of the kitchen and back in so quickly Amy blinked in surprise. Faith's teeth were clenched.

"What?"

"It's Josh," Faith said. "I peeked out the curtains."

"Oh, crap! He's probably coming to check up on me." Her pulse raced more than it had at the thought of calling Tru. She wasn't ready to face Josh yet. "What do I even say to him?"

"Nothing," Faith said. "You don't have to tell him anything yet."

Amy ran her hands through her hair. He'd stopped by on his lunch break to check on her. And though the sweetness of the gesture made warmth flood through her momentarily, it was quickly replaced by cold dread. Would he hate her? Would he stop talking to her once he found out she was carrying another man's child? Tears welled in the corners of her eyes. "I don't want to lose him."

"I can tell him you're not up to seeing anyone," Faith offered. "I'll tell him you're in bed and that should buy you some more time to figure out how you want to do this."

Faith's suggestion was enticing. She wanted nothing more

than to put off this conversation, but telling him she was in bed wouldn't keep Josh away.

"No," Amy said after a beat. "He'll just worry more and stop by again later." It would be better to get this over with now. Let him see that she was fine. Then he would leave and she could figure out what the hell she was going to do.

"You're sure?"

Amy nodded, though truthfully, she wasn't sure of anything. Hiding under a pile of blankets was sounding better and better by the second.

Faith left her side and a moment later returned with Josh trailing behind her. His face relaxed the moment he saw her, and the only thing Amy wanted to do was sink into his arms and forget about everything else. At least for a little while. Faith gave her a little nod and slipped out of the kitchen, giving them some privacy.

"Hey," he said as he crossed the kitchen. She stood to meet him. "You look better than you did this morning." He reached for her, his hands gentle as he stroked a piece of hair behind her ear. "Faith said you still aren't feeling great?"

Amy tried to mask her anguish as he enveloped her. His words were too soft and his body too warm, and she couldn't hold it together. A sob broke free and her shoulders shook. God, she was losing it.

"What's happened?" he asked, holding her tighter. "Is it something bad? Amy, tell me what's going on." He pushed her away enough to see her face. Amy couldn't stop the traitorous tears from leaking down her cheeks. "Whatever it is, it'll be okay, I promise."

And then she couldn't stop herself. She hadn't intended to tell him, not before she knew what she wanted to do, but she couldn't help herself at his tenderness. The words just tumbled out. "I'm pregnant," she said, almost choking as she did. "I'm... going to have a baby."

Josh blinked down at her and she could tell he was processing. Probably thinking the words *a baby* over and over again in his mind the same way she was.

"I had no idea," she continued, feeling like she needed to explain, like she needed him to understand that she hadn't meant to string him along or trap him in any way. "The last time I... God. I used protection. I'm not walking around sleeping with every guy I meet if that's what you're thinking."

She went to turn away but he caught her by the arms. "That's not what I was thinking."

"I swear I didn't know. I would have been up-front with you if I did. I never meant to keep this sort of thing from you."

She could see the questions in the pinch of his brow. He probably had so many. So did she. But he only asked her one: "Do you love him?"

Amy hadn't been expecting that. Of all the things she expected Josh to want to know, she never expected that to be the first question he asked her. Did she love Tru McCoy? She laughed, startling them both. "No! Gosh, no. I don't. I've come to realize that our grand relationship was nothing but an illusion," she muttered. "A part he played like in one of his movies." At this, Amy clamped her hand across her mouth. She hadn't intended to out her baby's father like that. She was screwing up everything.

Josh frowned. "I don't... His movies? I'm not sure I quite get that reference."

"Maybe for the best," she said.

"Amy." Josh's tone was pleading. "Talk to me. Please."

She sighed. She'd been truthful with him so far. What was the point in lying now? She looked up at him through watery eyes. "Have you ever heard of Tru McCoy?"

Josh's jaw went slack. "Are you being serious right now? You mean Hollywood heartthrob Tru McCoy?"

"One and the same," Amy mumbled. "Though heartthrob sort of wears off when you get to know him."

"Tru McCoy is the father?" Josh said, clearly still stunned. "Wait, didn't I just read somewhere that he got married?"

Amy nodded, unable to meet his eyes. "Yes, to one of his costars. Within weeks of breaking it off with me. So that tells you how faithful he was. And how much of an idiot I am."

"Oh, Amy." Josh cursed. "That son of a—"

"I understand if this might change things between us," she

said, cutting him off. "I get that this is a lot. It's so much to process. Maybe too much."

"I'm honestly not sure what to think right now." Josh shook his head slowly, his eyes unfocused. "But I think I should probably get back to the ranch," he said. "Chores and stuff."

"Of course." Amy bit her tongue to keep the tears from falling again. She knew it was too much for him to handle. "Yeah, you should get back."

"I'll, uh… I guess I'll talk to you later."

"Sure." She nodded as he left the kitchen. Would they talk later? Or was this goodbye? Watching him walk away now, knowing she might never see him again, was too hard, and she turned away to save herself some of the heartache.

This was just like when everything fell apart with Tru all over again.

No, Amy thought suddenly. No. Somehow, this was so much worse.

CHAPTER THIRTEEN

JOSH HAD NEVER been skydiving before but he felt like he'd been pitched out the side of a plane without a parachute.

He was just falling, falling, *falling*.

And he wasn't sure when he'd hit the ground.

Or how much it would hurt.

He hurried out of Faith's house without so much as a goodbye or a wave in Amy's direction. He had one singular focus, and that was to exit that kitchen before he looked Amy in the face and said completely the wrong thing.

A baby?

Amy was having a baby with a movie star. And not just any movie star. Tru McCoy. The blond, blue-eyed, ruggedly handsome cowboy of everyone's dreams. Regardless of how it had ended, at one point, he'd been the cowboy of Amy's dreams. Somehow putting a face and a name to Amy's ex-fling made everything worse. That was the man who had dumped her to run off and marry someone else. That was the man who had hurt her.

He was also the man that had apparently knocked her up.

Josh massaged the ache between his eyes. It thudded in the middle of his forehead. Was this the weight of his anxious thoughts? Or was his head just coincidentally going to explode? It felt like a thousand thoughts were ricocheting around his brain, and Josh had no idea what he was supposed to do now. What was the right thing to say in this situation? He tried to imagine being in Amy's position. The last thing he'd want was other people's advice, and platitudes would feel hollow. Besides, how could he sit there and promise everything would be okay when he didn't even know if that was something she wanted to hear?

Was she angry?

Scared?

Shocked?

Judging by the look on her face and the fact she'd broken down in tears, she wasn't exactly happy about this, so he was certain *congratulations* probably wouldn't go over well. But what else did you say when someone announced they were pregnant? He didn't even know where to start. Besides wanting to knock some sense into Tru McCoy, he wasn't sure he was the right man for the job.

What did he say now that the woman he lov—

Josh wrenched the door of his truck open. Leaving was for the best. He needed to screw his head on straight before it twisted off completely.

Josh climbed into his truck, backed down the driveway, and headed to the ranch, throwing himself into afternoon chores. By the time evening rolled around, he wasn't any closer to knowing what to say to Amy. He let out a heavy sigh that rattled his lips, got back into his truck, and started driving.

What he wanted most of all was to be a loving, supportive boyfriend—because that's what he was now, wasn't he? They'd been tiptoeing around this thing, around these feelings, for weeks, and Josh sort of thought that after what Amy had said last night, things between them had gotten a lot more serious. And if that was the case, and he'd read the signs clearly, then he was as good as her boyfriend. And as her boyfriend, he wanted to know how Tru could have left her like this?

Clearly he was never serious about her, likely stringing her along the way only some big-time, sleazy Hollywood actor could. And though Josh didn't know what it was like to have the father of your baby run off and marry someone else, he did know what it was to have his heart stomped on, so as torn as he was about the news, he was also sympathetic to what Amy was going through. And he was also a little ashamed of himself for just walking out on her.

Wasn't that what Tru had done?

God, he was better than this. Josh pounded his fist against the steering wheel.

He *was* better. He was just... Scared? Worried? Completely out of his depth?

He knew things were different now. They'd changed the moment the words had left Amy's mouth. He just wished he knew *how* they'd changed. Was everything that had happened between them meaningless now? Had all the moments and feelings and smiles and laughter been for nothing?

No, he reasoned. *It didn't need to be*. Tru had left Amy. He didn't want to be in her life. He'd chosen someone else. So this didn't change anything.

But as soon as he had that thought, another question rose to the forefront of his mind. What if Tru didn't want to abandon Amy once he found out she was having his child? Yes, he did just get married. And yes, he'd chosen someone else. But maybe becoming a father would force a change of heart. Maybe he'd come to his senses and see the error of his ways. He'd finally realize how wonderful Amy was and want to start this family with her.

And where did that leave Josh? Would he want to stand in Tru's way if he decided he wanted to be a real father?

Yes! Josh's heart shouted. *A thousand times yes.*

But that wasn't the right answer. He'd never want to deprive Amy and her baby of the baby's father. That was jealousy talking, and Josh knew he wasn't handling this well. He'd walked out on Amy, he was jealous of Tru McCoy, and he really wanted a drink. That might not help him in the end, but it was the only real plan he'd come up with.

His eyes drifted down the road, past the shops on Central Avenue to the sign for the Tenacity Social Club. It was a former speakeasy turned gathering place in the basement of the building that housed the town's post office and barbershop. Local musicians often performed, but Josh was most interested in the fact that he might be able to drown his sorrows there on a weeknight.

He turned into the parking lot, got out of his truck, and walked inside. It was a dimly lit space, filled with dark-stained tables. There were no televisions mounted to the ceiling here or craft brews on the menu, and Josh liked it that way.

He nodded to people he knew, which was practically every-body. Tenacity was small, but the crowd here was even smaller. The kind of place where everybody knew your name and your daddy's name and your granddaddy's. Josh didn't know if he was quite in the mood to sit down and join any of them, so he opted to take a seat at the bar instead. The bar itself was an old wooden plank with lovers' initials carved into it. It read like a who's who of Tenacity, and Josh's stomach turned thinking about Amy as his fingers brushed over the carvings.

"You look like you just got kicked by a horse," Mike Coo-per said as he offered Josh a beer from behind the bar. He was a fellow rancher who often moonlighted as a bartender. He was younger than Josh, with brown curls, and a kind smile. Mike had the kind of soft, sympathetic stare that often had Tenacity locals spilling their guts, especially after a few drinks.

Josh huffed a humorless laugh. "Sorta feels that way."

"You know, this job's made me pretty good at listening." He took a couple glasses and filled them, passing them down the bar. "If you need an ear or just someone to bounce things off of, I'm not a bad option."

Josh dipped his head. He appreciated the sympathetic ear, but he wasn't about to spill Amy's business all over town. In a place like this the news would spread like wildfire and the ru-mors would twist and turn until it was impossible to set people straight. The last thing Josh wanted was to chase Amy out of town.

He just sipped his drink and brooded. "Not sure talking it out is gonna help much."

"That's fair," Mike said. "You can only talk around a problem so much. Sometimes you just need to take action."

If only Josh knew what that action was.

He drank his beer, and his thoughts swirled worse than be-fore. The drink likely wasn't helping. He could go back to see Amy. Or at least call her. But after watching him walk away, would she want anything to do with him? And if he did call, what would he even say?

It was a stupid decision, but Josh told himself that another drink might help clear things up. He knew it was a lie but he could pretend for a few minutes. "I'll take another when you've got a second," he said to Mike, downing the last gulp and pushing his empty bottle back across the bar.

Mike handed him another beer on his way by with a tray of drinks destined for a table in the back. When Mike returned he started cleaning glasses.

"Do you ever think love can be hell?" Josh said.

"Figured that's what you were in here about."

"Isn't that most of your patrons?"

Mike nodded. "It's either love or land out here."

Josh almost wished it were something to do with the ranch. He could handle that. Matters of the heart were so much more complicated. Just when he thought everything was going so perfectly, just when he thought that Amy might turn out to be *the one*, the universe charged in and wrecked it all. Maybe he really wasn't suited for love. Maybe it was time he stopped looking for Mrs. Right or Ms. Right Now or Ms. Whatever.

Josh snorted. "It's definitely not the land."

"I didn't think so." Mike sighed. "I'm not a stranger to it myself, so I know that feeling."

"Been there, done that?" Josh asked.

Mike winced, his mouth pulling into a tight line. "It's really hard to find the right person, isn't it?"

"It sucks." Josh drained his beer. "Can I get another when you get a chance?"

"You can. But you're gonna trade it for your keys," Mike said, holding out his hand.

"Ah, right," Josh said. If he was going to keep drinking, then he wasn't going to be driving. He took the ring out of his pocket, slipped his key fob free and passed it across the bar. Mike dropped it in an empty glass fishbowl that sat on the counter behind him.

"You have someone you want me to call to come pick you up when you're done with this one?" he asked, uncapping another bottle and sliding it to Josh. "Or with however many drinks you need to drown out your thoughts?"

Josh's first thought was to call Amy, and he almost said as much. But that was selfish of him. He'd practically run out on her when he didn't know what to say, and now what? He was going to ask her to come and get him? To drive him home because he'd drunk a few too many instead of talking to her? How pathetic.

"You know what, I'll just call a taxi," Josh said, rethinking his plan. The service, affectionately called the Tenacity Shuttler by locals, was operated by a few ranchers who moonlighted on the side for extra cash. And though Josh knew he still shouldn't be behind the wheel, he could at least stay sober enough to call his own ride. "Do me a favor, and brew me a coffee too?"

Mike nodded. "Sure thing."

Josh took out his phone. He was confused enough about how he felt about Amy, he didn't need to leave here drunk. He opened his contacts and called the local taxi company. They picked up on the third ring. "Yeah, hi, this is Josh Aventura. I'm at the Tenacity Social Club and need a lift to 100 Juniper Road."

Mike looked up when he ended the call. "Hey, how long have you lived out on Juniper Road?"

Josh laughed and shrugged. "My whole life."

"Are there any rocks on Juniper Road?"

Josh looked at him funny. He'd just asked about rocks, right? He hadn't had that much to drink. "Plenty of them. Why?"

Mike shrugged. "It's probably nothing, but… When you were a kid, did you know Barrett Deroy?"

"Yeah, I knew *of* him." Barrett had left town about fifteen years ago with his family under a cloud of suspicion following the 'incident'. He was accused of stealing the thousands of dollars from Tenacity Town Hall meant to restore the Tenacity Trail. Town was never the same, and most people still blamed him for how rundown Tenacity had become in recent years. "Barrett was friends with Brent Woodson, who lived on one of the neighboring ranches."

Mike frowned. "Brent Woodson, as in Mayor Woodson's son?"

Josh nodded. He was very confused. Why were they talking

about rocks and Barrett Deroy? As far as he remembered, when Barrett's family fled, they were persona non grata, and no one had heard hide nor hair from them since.

Mike leaned closer to him. "Does 'Look Juniper Rock' mean anything to you?"

Josh frowned. "Is that a real question or just something you do to mess with the customers?"

"Yeah, it's a real question. 'Look Juniper Rock,'" he repeated. "Is it ringing any bells?"

Josh thought about it for a minute and then said, "The Woodsons had a bunch of boulders at the edge of their property. The Stoolers live there now. Hasn't changed much in that time, but I don't remember the rocks being anything special. I couldn't imagine why anyone would want to look at them."

Mike took in his words, nodding along like everything Josh was saying was important. "Do you mind if I take a moment and call Diego Sanchez? Diego's great-uncle has been doing some private investigating for Diego's sister. She's trying to track down the Deroy family. I think this might be a clue!"

"Huh... Well, be my guest," Josh said. If Mike wanted to call Diego about some rocks, who the hell was Josh to stand in his way? Who the hell was he to anyone? He certainly wasn't Amy's husband or this baby's father. He reached into his pocket for some money and paid his tab. "I'm gonna go catch my ride."

Josh got to his feet as Mike turned away to make the call. No, he wasn't a husband or a father, but in that moment, it shocked him just how much he wished he were.

CHAPTER FOURTEEN

AMY PACED THE length of the kitchen, half a sandwich in one hand, and her phone in the other. She'd been staring down at Tru's contact info for the better part of an hour. It was funny. When Tru had broken things off with her to spontaneously marry his costar, she'd been devastated and heartbroken, but in the midst of all that she'd never gotten around to deleting his contact info. Now she wondered if that was fate's little way of saying they weren't quite done with each other yet. Okay, so it actually wasn't very funny at all. Amy would have much preferred never to speak to the man again.

"Do you want another sandwich?" Faith asked, standing at the counter next to Caleb. They'd been puttering around with dinner, but Faith had stopped to make Amy a sandwich when she realized she hadn't eaten anything but toast and banana bread. Amy didn't know how to tell her she wasn't all that hungry. She was full of dread and doubt, and she didn't know what to think about Josh, and with all that swirling around inside her there couldn't possibly be any room left for food.

She shook her head. "I've still got this half."

"But are you still hungry? You must be hungry. You've hardly eaten today."

"And now you're eating for two," Caleb added.

"I've been eating for two for months apparently."

Faith hummed. "I wonder if you'll have any cravings."

Amy shrugged. She wasn't much concerned with food cravings at the moment.

"You definitely have aversions. And that's a thing too, I think. Like turkey bacon. You can't stand the stuff. Must be why you always wrinkle your nose at me whenever I cook it."

Amy looked at her, deadpan. "Are you serious right now?"

Faith licked peanut butter off the end of her knife. "What?"

"Disliking your turkey bacon has nothing to do with being pregnant. Trust me." She shook her head, trying not to laugh. It felt like such a silly thing to laugh at, especially right now, when she was trying to work up the nerve to call Tru, but she couldn't help herself. "That had everything to do with you choosing a subpar bacon variety." Amy stopped laughing suddenly. "You know, Josh and I had a good laugh about that last night." She put her phone down on the kitchen table and slumped into a chair. Last night already felt like a million years ago. So much had happened since then... So much had happened to rip apart this thing she and Josh were building.

"Oh, Amy," Faith said. "He'll be back."

"I'm not sure he will," Amy said, more to herself than Faith. If this was her reality, she needed to come to terms with it. "You didn't see the way he ran out of here."

"He cares about you," Faith said. "I can see it in the way he looks at you. Trust me. You haven't seen the last of Josh."

Amy shook her head. "Even if I have, I can't really blame him, you know? I'm sure he feels blindsided and maybe even like I lied to him."

"But you didn't," Caleb said. "You had no idea about the pregnancy when you met him."

"*I* know that. And I hope he knows that. But it doesn't change the fact that we fell for each other. Maybe even imagined a future with each other. Heck, I know I was starting to. All the while this big secret was growing between us. And now suddenly everything we thought we knew is different."

"Not everything," Faith said softly. "Not the way you feel about each other."

"I don't know," Amy said. How would Josh really feel about

hanging around her while she was carrying another man's child? "It might not be something he can get past." Saying the words out loud, she hoped would make them hurt less. It was a logical argument. Something she should expect may become a reality. But it didn't make them hurt any less. They spilled over her lips like sand, rough and grainy, getting caught between her teeth and making her throat burn.

"Just give it some more time," Caleb suggested. "A man like Josh is a quiet thinker. Let him process everything that happened today. Then he'll come back around, you'll see."

Amy blinked back tears. It was useless though. They fell and she swiped her hands over her cheeks.

"Oh, Amy," Faith said. "Don't cry. Please."

"I'm not sad," she said, sniffling. "I'm angry. I'm angry that after all this time Tru McCoy is still somehow screwing me over."

"You don't need to call him right now. You can take some time to process everything, too. Josh isn't the only one who's had a world-altering bit of news dumped in his lap today."

"No. I need to call Tru because I need a plan going forward. It's been almost four months already and I can't just wing it. I'm having a baby and that baby deserves a plan. I need to know if Tru wants to be part of that plan so I can just move on with my life, I guess."

"What can I do?" Faith asked.

Amy rubbed the last of the tears from her eyes. "Get me some olives."

"Olives?"

"Yes."

Faith laughed, and Amy did too.

"Okay, we'll just run to the store before it closes." She took Caleb by the arm. "You text me and let me know if you suddenly develop a hankering for any other random foods. But we'll just cover the gamut. You know, peanut butter, pickles, salty, sweet, savory."

"Thank you," Amy said. Faith walked over and pulled Amy up into a hug.

"It's gonna be okay. You know that, right? Whatever happens.

Because you've got me and Caleb and the rest of our family. And this baby is going to be so, *so* loved."

Amy nodded. "I know."

Faith kissed her cheek. "We'll be back in an hour. Try not to let Tru McCoy rattle you. He's not worth your spit," she called over her shoulder as she headed for the door.

Caleb lingered, giving her a long look. "You know, his movies aren't even that good." And with that, he followed after Faith.

Amy waited until she heard the door close and the car start in the driveway before she picked up her phone again. It was time to stop dreading this and just do it. She had to tell Tru he was going to be a father, and she had to do it today, to save her own sanity.

Oh God.

She was going to be sick again.

She pressed the back of her hand to her lips and breathed hard. *Calm down.* Faith and Caleb were right. Tru McCoy wasn't anything. He was just like any other man. Hollywood heartthrob. Those words meant nothing. It had all been one grand farce in the end, probably to get her into bed. Her and however many other women he was schmoozing on the sidelines.

When the anxious wave passed, she hit Tru's contact number and lifted the phone to her ear. With each unanswered ring, her heart raced faster and faster. Maybe he was on set somewhere and away from his phone. Or he could have changed his number since they'd been together.

Then the call rang through to voicemail and she heard Tru's voice for the first time in months. It startled her, sending an unpleasant shiver up her spine. Part of her was secretly glad he didn't pick up. How awkward would that conversation have been? She would have stumbled over her words. He would have been confused hearing from her after all this time. It was better like this. She would leave him a message with all the details. That way he could get over the shock of hearing about the pregnancy first. And then they could speak about the baby when and if he called her back.

"Hi, Tru," she said as the phone beeped. "It's, uh, Amy. Hawkins," she said as an afterthought. Who knew how much of an impression she'd really left? "Sorry to bother you like this. I know it's unexpected, but…" She hesitated. She couldn't tell him about the baby like this. Not on a voicemail. "Can you give me a call when you have a chance?" she said, the words rushing out of her. "It's really important. Uh, okay thanks. Bye."

Amy pulled the phone away from her ear and winced. Well, that was somehow both better and worse than she'd expected. Nothing to do now but wait for the horrible moment he replied. Amy hadn't even had a chance to put her phone down before it started ringing. Tru's name popped up and her eyes almost bugged out of her head. He was already calling her back!

"Dammit," she muttered under her breath. She thought she'd have a little more time—maybe even a day—before he returned her call. She answered the phone, somewhat stunned. "Hello?"

"Amy, hi!" Tru said, his voice booming through the phone. Even after listening to the voicemail, it was still a shock to hear it. "It's been a minute."

"Yeah, you could say that," she said.

"How are you?"

"I mean…" Where did she even start with that question?

Tru plowed on without letting her answer. "Look, I'm really sorry about the way things ended with us."

"Tru, that's not why I'm calling," Amy hurried to say. "I—"

"I know I didn't do right by you. Trust me. I know. And I'm so glad you reached out. I wanted to, honestly. I just didn't know how to make things right. But when I saw you call, I knew this was my chance."

"Your chance for what?"

"To fix things with us," he said, like it was the most obvious answer in the world. "My romance with my costar was ill-advised."

"Your romance?" Amy practically choked on the words. "Tru, it wasn't just a romance. You *married* the woman!"

"And it was a stupid decision. One of the stupidest I've ever made."

"Tru. Look, there's something—"

"We've already filed for divorce."

Amy touched her hand to her forehead. Her thoughts were

all over the place. *This* was her child's father? "I don't know what to say."

"Then don't say anything. Not over the phone. Not like this. Can I come see you?" he asked.

What the hell was she supposed to say to that? "Tru, wait," she said. Better to just spit it out and tell him the news before this went too far.

"No, I've decided. I'm coming to see you. To apologize in person. Let me make it up to you, Amy. I'll fly to Bronco," he said. "I'll come there and you'll see. You'll see how sorry I am. How much I've changed."

Amy frowned. He was talking a mile a minute. And changed? In four months? "I... I'm not in Bronco, I'm in Tenacity right now—"

"Perfect." He cut her off. "I'll come to Tenacity then. Tomorrow. I'll see you tomorrow." He hung up before Amy could say anything else.

She blinked down at the screen and contemplated calling him back, but wouldn't it be easier to have this conversation in person anyway? Before she could make up her mind, her phone rang again. It was Josh this time, and she gasped. She hadn't expected to hear from him again today after the way he rushed off.

She answered, her heart pounding. "Hi."

"Hey," he said. She could hear the murmur of voices. A lot of voices. He must be in town somewhere. A door opened and closed with a thud, and the voices died away. "I'm sorry about how abruptly I left," he said as the silence lingered.

"It's okay," Amy said. "I don't blame you for your reaction. I'm still in shock about it myself."

"Right." Some more silence. "Well, I've done some thinking, and I'm going to follow your lead here. Whatever you want to do, I will support you."

"Oh?" Amy said, a little taken aback.

"I mean it."

"Okay, that's, um... Well, it's good to hear. I actually just called Tru to try and tell him about the baby." She wrinkled her nose. She shouldn't even be telling Josh this. It would make everything worse. "He didn't really let me get a word in, but he's coming to town tomorrow. I suppose in many ways it might be easier to break the news like that instead of over the phone."

Josh got very quiet again.

"You still with me?" she asked. Maybe she shouldn't have told him Tru was coming. But she didn't want to lie to him.

"Yeah," he said, but she wasn't sure he was. Then he said, "Okay. That's…uh, good, I suppose. That'll be good. For you to tell him."

"Yeah."

"Well, um, you get some rest and call me if you need anything."

"Okay," she said. "I will. Thanks."

She hung up and stared down at the phone. Somehow this felt just as bad as him walking out.

CHAPTER FIFTEEN

JOSH CLIMBED OUT of the taxi at the entrance to Split Valley Ranch and gave a little wave as the car peeled off. With just three cars in their roster, the company was kept busy, even in a town the size of Tenacity. There was always someone that needed a ride or a delivery made, which left little time for chatting or meandering, which Josh preferred.

Especially right now. The last thing he needed was the driver asking him any leading questions.

One wrong slip and his business would be all over town.

Did you hear Josh Aventura got beaten out by a movie star? That guy never stood a chance. What was he thinking?

Josh grimaced at the unfamiliar voices that filled his head. He doubted anyone would really say that, at least not to his face, but he couldn't shake the dread as he lumbered down the gravel drive to the house. He'd opted to get dropped off at the road. He needed a good walk and some fresh air to clear his head, but it wasn't clearing much of anything.

Josh stuffed his hands in his pockets, feeling every bit as pathetic as he probably looked. He'd barely worked up the nerve to call Amy before he left the Social Club. Moments before the taxi showed up, he'd realized he needed to apologize for rushing out on her the way he had and for making excuses instead of processing the way he was feeling in the moment. He knew that leaving things to linger would only end up making them both feel worse.

But hearing that Tru McCoy was coming to Tenacity tomorrow was like a kick to the gut. He hadn't realized Amy would move so quickly with the news, but he supposed she couldn't really afford to wait. The baby had been a surprise, so there was probably plenty to sort out, first of which involved telling the father.

The father. He thought the words over and over, grumbling every time. Tru didn't deserve to be the father of this baby. Josh wanted to be supportive. He wanted to follow Amy's lead with this. At least, that's what he'd told himself upon walking out of the bar. He'd been so sure of himself when he dialed her number. But now the thought of Tru coming into town to sweep Amy off her feet was both devastating and nauseating in turns. It filled Josh with a wicked heat that swelled in his head and made his cheeks burn. He'd never hated someone he'd never met before. Frankly, he'd never hated anyone.

But Tru McCoy left a bad taste in his mouth.

His dad would tell him to take a step back and assess the circumstances with a clear head, reminding Josh that he was far too close to the situation if he was having thoughts like that. But that *was* the problem. He was already too close to Amy. Too close to simply step aside and pretend like none of this mattered.

He didn't want to stand aside.

He wanted to be here for Amy and the baby, but did she even want that from him? Or had everything that happened last night just gone out the window? Tru was about to ride into town like a knight on a white horse, making her promises Josh couldn't hope to match in his wildest dreams. Of course Amy was going to choose him. Why wouldn't she? Tru could offer her so much more than he could.

Tires crunched on gravel, drawing up behind him and breaking Josh from his melancholy thoughts. He perked up, turning as headlights blinded him momentarily and a vehicle pulled up close. He hadn't been expecting company, and he jumped aside.

Shane hung out the window of his truck, one hand on the wheel, creeping up slowly. "Hey, man. Everything okay?"

Josh squinted at him in the near darkness. "Hey," he said, unable to muster an ounce of enthusiasm. "Yeah."

"Saw your truck down at the Social Club. I popped inside, thought we could have a beer together, but Mike said you'd already gone home in a taxi."

"Yeah."

"You could have called me, you know?"

"Not a big deal," Josh said. Truthfully, he could have called a lot of people. He didn't though, because there was only one person he'd wanted to talk to, one person he'd wanted to be with, and anyone else would likely have asked about why he needed a ride home on a weekday. Well, maybe not Shane. He probably wouldn't even have judged Josh for it. But Josh was still getting used to having him back in town.

"So everything's just fine despite you looking as stormy as those clouds up there," Shane said. "Am I understanding things?" He cut the ignition and the truck stilled.

"About the gist of it," Josh muttered.

Shane snorted and got out of the truck. They fell in line next to each other, walking back toward the house slowly. "I can tell when you're lying, you know. I *have* known you long enough. You get all broody and avoid looking at me."

"I'm not lying," Josh said. "Relatively speaking, everything is fine. No one's hurt. No one's dying. The ranch is trucking along. You know, on a scale of one to all the cattle escaping, it's not that bad."

"Girl trouble then," Shane said with a nod.

Josh did look at him then, but only to roll his eyes.

"Don't try denying it. I could see those slumped shoulders a mile away. And I should know. I became very familiar with that look every time I clocked myself in a mirror lately." He bumped Josh's arm. "Feels just like old times, huh? When we were both in high school and couldn't get a date to save our lives."

Josh shook his head, smiling despite how wretched he felt. It did sorta feel like old times. But they were kids back then, regardless of how grown up they'd felt. Plus with their shifting infatuations from week to week, there was always someone new to get hung up on. Josh didn't want to think about anyone else.

He wanted Amy, and only her. He sighed. "This feels different. Like there's more at stake."

"Because it's real now," Shane said. "Because it matters. *She* matters."

He was right. If this thing between them didn't matter, Josh would have stepped aside the moment Amy told him she was expecting. He would have wished her luck with everything and chalked these past weeks up to a good time. And maybe that's what he should still do. But something inside him refused to acknowledge that option. He couldn't walk away from her; he just didn't know where he fit anymore.

He thought it might be by her side. But was there room there with Tru?

"I'm guessing you and Amy didn't fully break it off," Shane said.

"No," Josh said immediately. "We're not... At least, I don't think so. I mean... It's complicated." He huffed a humorless laugh. How cliché. "How can you tell?"

"I figure you'd be more of a wreck if you had. I saw the way you looked at that girl when you came by the ranch. It's all Gram could talk about after you'd left. How you'd finally found a good woman who would do right by you."

Josh didn't know how to respond. Even Angela thought they were good for each other, and that meant a lot.

"So what is it?" Shane asked. "Did you find out she has a long-lost boyfriend somewhere she's still pining over? Oh, God, she isn't married, is she?"

Josh shook his head. "No, um... She's pregnant." He had no intentions of telling Mike at the bar or anyone else, but Shane was different. He used to be able to tell Shane everything. Anything. And even though Shane had been away for a while, that hadn't changed. He trusted him not to go blabbing all over town. He even trusted him to keep this from Angela. "Sorta took her by surprise. Unplanned. Unexpected. All that." At the look on Shane's face, he added, "It's not mine. She's about three or four months along I would figure."

"Wow," Shane said, the word leaving his mouth on the end of a whistle. "I was not expecting that."

"Me neither."

They walked in silence for a beat, reaching the house. Josh slumped down on the porch steps. He felt like he was carrying sandbags on his shoulders.

"And she really had no idea?"

"No. And I believe that. I don't think she would have let things get this far without telling me." She'd been adamant that she hadn't lied to him, and Josh saw no reason not to believe her.

"Must be a shock to the system. For both of you."

"Yeah."

"And the father… Is he," Shane winced, "around?"

"He's alive and well, if that's what you're wondering. I'm not quite sure about the state of their relationship." Amy said that it wasn't good, and he'd left her, hadn't he? He'd chosen some-one else. Married that girl, even. But how did you say no to Tru McCoy? If he wanted back in this baby's life…

"That's rough," Shane said.

"I'll say."

"Well, from where I'm sitting, you've got two options. One, you walk away. You let her go. She moves on. Has her baby. Plays happy house with her kid and the baby's father."

Josh didn't like that option. "And two?"

"You fight for her."

"Did you fight?" he asked, wondering about this girl that Shane had chased across Montana.

"For a while, yeah. We had our problems. Not surprise preg-nancies, mind you. But we tried to make it work. *I* tried."

Josh wanted to try. He did. But the real question was, did Amy want him to fight for her? Did she want *him* when she could have Tru? The more he thought about it, the more ridiculous it sounded. Why would she ever choose him over Mr. Hollywood Heartthrob? Josh didn't think he could handle that rejection. He didn't think he could bear to fight and lose. To let Amy *and* Tru stomp all over his heart.

"You gonna be okay?" Shane asked.

Josh glanced around the darkened property. There were still a couple chores to do. So even if he wasn't okay, there were things to be getting on with. "I suppose so. I gotta check in on the cattle once more before bed."

"You want help?"

"Nah. It'll be good for me to keep busy. Get my mind off Amy and the baby."

"If you need anything," Shane said, getting to his feet, "let me know. Even if it's just a lift to the bar tomorrow to pick up your truck."

"Thanks," Josh said. "That'd be great actually. I'll call you tomorrow."

"Sounds good."

Josh watched Shane walk back down the drive to his truck. When he was gone, Josh forced himself to his feet. All he wanted to do was go inside and go to bed and hope some of this turned out to be a bad dream. But the animals needed things and they didn't care much for matters of the heart interrupting their dinner. Josh switched into his dusty, muck-covered work boots and headed out to the barn.

He called in the cattle, making sure they were fed and watered. Then he popped down to the horse stalls, mucking them out quickly before he called them in for the night.

When he was finished, he stood in the doorway of the barn and whistled. Bella and Mac trotted toward him. Bitsy stood out in the field, just a shadow against the blue-black sky, as stubborn as ever. Josh got the other two horses settled in their stalls before he returned for Bitsy, marching out across the field to get her. He brought a halter with him and strung it over her head so he could guide her back.

"Can we not do this tonight?" he said. It wasn't lost on him that Bitsy had bonded so well with Amy these past weeks. Was she missing her favorite person too?

She huffed in his face, and Josh took that as a yes.

Josh led her back to the barn as raindrops started to fall. They pattered against the roof as he got Bitsy into her stall for the evening. She immediately dunked her head in the bucket of water, taking large gulps. Josh leaned against the gate, watching her for a moment. Bitsy had really taken to Amy, but without her here, she got on with business as usual. Maybe that's what he needed to do too.

Maybe Tru coming tomorrow was for the best. It was certainly best for Amy. For her child. It didn't matter that his heart ached at the thought. He could never compete with the glamour and jet-setting. He couldn't give Amy or this baby everything they deserved.

Shane had said he could fight for Amy, but if he stood in Tru's way, all he'd be asking Amy to do would be to give up a life of certain luxury.

Josh thumped the stall door. "Night, ladies. And Mac," he said, listening to the soft braying of the horses as he left the barn, slumping through the rain to the house. He was soaked to the bone before he reached the porch, but that didn't matter. It was just another box to check off on the long list of things that had sucked today.

What really sucked was the fact that he couldn't stop envisioning everything he could have had: Amy moving into his place. Her clothes in his closet. Maybe a horse of her own in the stables.

That was probably the hardest part of today. Giving up that dream. It was foolish of him to let his mind plan for a future.

To long for it.

To want it.

Because this was what happened when he let himself want something. Charmingly handsome movie stars came bursting in to tear it all down.

Josh ran a hand through his damp hair. But why should he have to step aside? Why should he have to give up on this dream? On Amy?

He wanted her.

So, until she told him to go, shouldn't he keep trying for this future?

Then again, how could he possibly be her first choice? He'd never been anyone's first choice, and he needed to prepare himself for that reality.

CHAPTER SIXTEEN

AMY DIDN'T KNOW what to do with herself and had taken to dusting everything in Faith's house. Multiple times. Bookshelves and furniture and windowsills and little figurines that sat out on the coffee table.

Everything was spotless. It had already been spotless.

But that didn't stop her from swapping out her rag for a clean one and starting all over again.

She heard Faith huff from the kitchen. Amy had already been explicitly told to sit down and relax. *It's not good to stress the baby like this.*

Honestly, Amy figured her baby would understand. This was an impossible situation and the only way to keep her nerves in check was to keep her hands busy.

Tru had texted her earlier in the day to let her know that he was jumping on a flight to Billings. He texted her again when he landed and sent her a picture of the rental car he'd ordered. It was some fancy thing that had no business being in Tenacity.

Worst of all, that car would bring him right to Amy. And wasn't that a horrible thought.

Her anxiety had been multiplying all afternoon, and she could feel the uneven, uneasy trembling of her heart against her ribs. It didn't even beat, it just shook.

But why was *she* nervous? She already knew about the baby.

She'd already been sitting with this news for a day, playing out what her future might look like over and over. Sometimes the murky figure by her side looked like Tru. Sometimes it looked like Josh, and her heart gave a little leap of joy. Then again, sometimes it looked like neither of them, and she'd quickly found herself accepting that as a possible reality.

So it was Tru who should be nervous. He should have paused to question why an ex was reaching out to him after all this time.

Though she doubted it even crossed his mind. If things had already soured with his wife, then Tru was probably just looking to slide back into his life pre-marriage. And that meant rekindling his former romances. Amy had come to terms with a lot these past few months, and she was under no delusions about Tru. He wasn't ever the man she thought he was. The kindness and sweetness had all been an illusion. In reality, he was an oily, slippery snake, and she had to remember that. Because while he was out there, whispering all the right words in her ear, jetting her off to private islands, there were how many other women in his contacts?

Her gaze drifted to the clock on the wall as the hour ticked down. Billings wasn't that far from Tenacity. Tru would be here anytime now. She dusted with more vigor until she heard the unfamiliar rev of an engine. Then everything inside her seized up like ice.

"Is that him making all that racket?" Faith asked, hurrying down the hall to peek out the curtains. Wisps of hair pulled free from her braid as she stealthily took in the view. "What the hell kind of car is that?"

Amy joined her at the window, watching the car recklessly race down the street. How had she ever found him impressive?

"Looks like a Porsche," Caleb said, peeking over Faith's shoulder.

"He's gonna hit one cow pie and end up spinning off into a ditch."

"And we will not be here to see it," Caleb said. "Because this is the first day off we've had together in forever and we have a date."

"We do." Faith glanced over at Amy. "Are you gonna be okay without us?"

Amy smiled a bit. "Of course. You two go have fun. This is something I have to do on my own."

"You got this," Caleb told her. "Remember. His last movie only has a thirty-three percent audience rating on Rotten Tomatoes."

She did have this. Right? Amy watched Tru get out of his car, slipping a finely made cowboy hat on his head. He dripped in finery. His leather boots gleamed and the belt buckle at his waist sparkled in the sun. It probably cost as much as that souped-up car he'd rented.

"I can't believe that's my baby's father," Amy muttered to herself. She should have known better. She'd met her fair share of men like him on the circuit, and now she felt like an idiot for not seeing him plainly. Maybe she'd just been so desperate for it to be real.

That thought touched something in her. She'd never said that out loud, but the truth was she was getting older and the little flings on the road hadn't felt right anymore. She'd wanted something stable and real. She'd wanted someone to want her the way she thought Tru had wanted her. When that fell apart, Amy didn't think she'd ever put herself out there again, and that's when Josh had stumbled into her life. She hadn't been expecting him. But he was everything that Tru wasn't—stable, real, and he wanted her. Or, at least, he had. It didn't really matter either way, because here Tru came to ruin it all over again.

Amy buzzed her lips together. "Better go get this over with." She slipped on her shoes, stepping out onto the porch.

Her hand danced over her lower belly quickly. *Here goes nothing, baby. Actually, here goes everything.*

Tru lifted his hand in greeting and flashed her a brilliant smile.

She couldn't believe she'd ever swooned over that smile. Though she'd grown quite partial to another smile lately. A closed-mouth smile with just a hint of mischief, lips curling at the edges. Eyes creased and twinkling. Every part of her wished it were Josh walking up the driveway toward her because this felt like a certain kind of nightmare. Amy never imagined seeing Tru again outside of a billboard or TV spot, and she'd certainly never envisioned him waltzing through tiny Tenacity. Her stomach flipped uncomfortably.

"Hey there, Hawkins," Tru called. He'd always called her Hawkins with affection. Or maybe she'd only thought it was affection and he was using it to keep some semblance of polite distance between them.

"Hey," Amy called, shifting from one foot to the other. She folded her arms across her chest to keep the nerves from unraveling. "You made good time."

"I didn't want to hang out in Billings too long. Once word gets out that I'm around it's gonna be nonstop pictures and autographs." He waved off the thought. "You know how it is."

"Right," she said. She did know how that was. Not to the same degree as Tru, of course. But that part of her life also felt so far away. Like it belonged to a different Amy. An Amy that hadn't started to build a life in Tenacity.

"Besides, the only person I really wanted to see was here. So I might have been a little heavy on the gas pedal."

Amy tried to smile but it didn't come out right. Tru might wish that he'd taken his time when he found out what she had to say. Her hand fell to her stomach again. Just a momentary brush. She'd been doing that a lot since yesterday, suddenly conscious of this tiny life she had growing inside her.

Tru surged up the steps toward her, and before Amy had even opened her mouth to ask him to sit down, he'd swept her up into his arms. Amy's skin crawled. It felt wrong. These arms. They didn't belong to the right person. But suddenly Tru was kissing her, and Amy's thoughts were ringing like alarms in her head.

Her eyes widened as she forced her head back. She hadn't been expecting this kind of reception.

Tru must not have noticed the look of utter shock on her face because he was too busy hugging her, whispering words into her neck. "It's so good to see you." His breath tickled her ear and she shivered. Not the good kind of shiver. The warning bells kept ringing. This wasn't going the way she'd planned. "I've missed you, Amy. So, *so* much."

She wriggled out of his arms. Delicately. Trying not to hurt him despite the way he'd treated her. She knew the kind of shock this was about to be. "Tru—"

"I know. *I know,*" he said, shaking his head and dropping his hands to his hips. "What right do I have to swoop in here like this? To kiss you like this? I know what you must be thinking and what you're going to say to me now, but I beg you to hear me out." He snatched up her hands, squeezing them. Running his thumbs over her knuckles. "The marriage. It was wrong. I knew it was wrong the moment it happened. That the only person I wanted to be with was you. I knew we were making a huge mistake. *I* was making a huge mistake. I just didn't know how to stop what I'd started. I didn't want anyone to get hurt, but I was a coward, calling that love when I knew it wasn't." He blinked at her, those big blue eyes like shimmery pools of deceit. Oh, he was good. Too bad she'd watched him do this act on the big screen. "Will you ever forgive me? Could you ever?"

"Tru, I—"

He wrapped his hands around her shoulders, pulling her close again, running his hands up and down her back. "I want us to be together, Amy. More than anything."

Amy hesitated, overwhelmed by everything. All she could think about was Josh and the way he touched her, held her. His smile. The way he laughed. The way he made her *feel*. But this was a scenario she'd never considered when she'd called Tru. A few months ago, she might have been overjoyed at Tru's declaration, but that was before Josh, before she'd really thought about who Tru was and what she deserved. Now, Josh was the only one consuming her thoughts. Still, if her baby's father wanted to make this work, shouldn't she want to try *something*? Shouldn't they want to be at least cordial for this little life they'd created? She took a step back, breaking out of his hold again. She needed space to think.

Actually, she needed a stiff drink.

But that was a no-go for the foreseeable future.

"What do you say?" Tru said. "Forgive me?" He smiled that smile that made women across the country pull their hair out screaming. The same smile that had once had her desperate for his attention. Now it didn't even set her heart racing.

"Tru," she started again. "Before you make any big decisions or big declarations, there's something you should know." He beamed at her, nodding. "I'm pregnant and it's yours. I'm sorry I didn't tell you sooner. I just found out myself."

That beaming smile dropped from his face. "You're... What?" he said, the corner of his mouth twitching like he expected her to shout "gotcha."

"I'm pregnant," Amy repeated, letting the words sink in.

Tru's face fell further and further. The shock ended in a frown, his brow pinched. He looked like she'd just hit him over the head with a skillet. Guess he wasn't as good of an actor as he thought. He turned pale and started stammering about dates and condoms and how could this have happened? Then he quieted, rubbing at the scruff on his jaw. "You say you're pregnant, but how do I really even know it's mine? I mean, it's been months since we were together."

Amy sucked in a sharp breath. This was not the response she was hoping for. Frankly, she didn't know what she'd been hoping for. But it did clarify things in her mind. "I will try not to take offense at the accusation that I might have been sleeping around while I was with you."

"That's not what I—"

"It is what you meant," Amy said pointedly. He didn't argue. "Anyway, I will gladly submit to a paternity test, if this is something you want, Tru. But from the look on your face, it's obvious that you don't want this child. And if you don't want this child, then you don't really want me either." She didn't think he ever did. She was just some pretty thing to warm his bed.

"Look, Amy, I could..." Tru swallowed hard. He glanced around, like someone might overhear them at any moment. "... give you the money."

"Money for what?"

"To take care of it."

Wow. She'd considered the reality that Tru wanted nothing to do with this baby, but she never thought he'd ask her to 'take care of it'.

"That won't be necessary," Amy said calmly, knowing he wasn't referring to child support.

"Listen, I—"

Amy put her hand up, interrupting him. "I will not hold you responsible for a child you want no part of," she said. "If that's what's really worrying you. I won't blow up your life and your career. But I also won't 'take care of the problem' the way you're suggesting." The moment she'd realized she was pregnant, she knew deep down that wouldn't be an option she was taking. She'd always wanted to start her own family, whether biologically or through adoption. She also had enough financial resources to care for a child. She didn't need Tru or his fame or his money. She would have this baby on her own and she would love it enough for both of them.

"Come on, Amy. Think about how much fun we could have together. I'm not ready to be a father right now."

Amy arched her brow. That much was obvious.

"Are you really ready to be a mother?"

His question didn't make her panic the way she thought it might. She knew next to nothing about having a baby or raising a child, but it didn't fill her with fear. There were definitely nerves and excitement and a little anxiousness. Was she ready? Was she prepared? No. But she *would be* ready when the time came.

"Think about it," Tru said, taking her hand and painting a picture of the life they might have. "You could travel with me." He tucked her hair behind her ear. "And I could treat you to the finest things."

Only until he found someone new. He was probably just waiting for the ink to dry on the divorce papers. Amy wanted more for herself. More for her child. And she definitely wanted better than Tru McCoy. She looked up at him and sighed. "I think it's probably time for you to go, Tru."

He nodded once, turned from her, looked back, then set off down the porch steps. He didn't even bother to argue with her and perhaps that was the most telling of all. She was never anything to him, just a good time.

He walked down the drive to his rented car and swung the

door open. He looked up at her one more time. "Call me if you change your mind."

"I won't," she said. "I promise."

Tru climbed into his rental.

Amy watched him pull down the street. In a way, she supposed she owed Tru a debt of gratitude. He had given her the gift of clarity.

She pulled out her phone and called Josh. He didn't pick up.

She ended the call, wondering if she'd lost two men in one day.

One thing was certain: she was going to have this baby. Regardless of whether she had anyone by her side to help raise it.

CHAPTER SEVENTEEN

SOMETIMES JOSH HATED the damn creek Split Valley Ranch was built on. Not for the first time over the years did he consider filling the entire thing in with gravel.

He closed the passenger door of his truck with a hard thud, a coil of rope slung over his shoulder. He marched across the pasture to the edge of the creek, stopping just short of where the ground dipped sharply toward the water.

He looked down at the small calf that waded through the water, tail flicking. It looked up at him, making soft snuffling sounds.

"How'd you get yourself down here, huh?"

The calf responded with a half-hearted moo before carrying on down the creek.

"Now don't go wandering," Josh called as he carefully made his way down the short embankment. It was still slick with mud from the winter thaw and his boots slipped. He caught himself, his hand sinking into muck. He huffed and carried on.

He'd spotted the calf earlier on a ride around the property. Usually a baby this small wouldn't stray far from its mother, so it must have been thirsty, and instead of using one of the water troughs, it had tumbled down the incline for a drink only to find it was a lot harder to get out again.

When Josh reached the creek bed, he winced. Water soaked

through his boots and the bottoms of his pants. The creek was shallow for this time of year, barely up to his knees, but the calf darted away from him, forcing Josh to chase it.

"You're lucky you're cute," Josh muttered, surging forward and catching the calf by the scruff. It fought against him, making displeased sounds. He was a fluffy little thing, his coat a deep russet brown. When he looked up at Josh it was with two shiny black eyes. "Behave," Josh told the calf. "Or I have half a mind to leave you down here."

The calf did not behave. It butted against his thighs as he attempted to get the rope secured so he could pull the little thing out of the creek. Every time he managed to get the rope over its head, the calf would shake it off. He needed one hand to hold the animal still, but he needed both hands to get the rope in place.

"You know who'd probably be really good at this?" Josh muttered. "Amy. She'd have you roped in seven seconds flat. But I can't call her because Tru McCoy is in town, learning that he's about to be a father. So it'd be really great if you could just cooperate, okay?"

The calf mooed softly and rammed its head against Josh's thigh, clearly unimpressed with being detained. Josh wasn't that impressed either when the calf shook him off and went running down the creek.

"Don't be like that," he called. "This is for your own good." He trudged after the calf. The bottoms of his jeans were heavy and dragging.

The calf turned and mooed at him again. A little warrior's cry.

"I know, I *know*," Josh said, taking slow, careful steps so as not to startle the calf into running farther down the creek. "But sometimes we have to do things we don't like. Which is why I'm here with you while Amy talks to her ex. Did I mention he's a movie star?"

The calf lowered his head and lapped at the water. Talking to it seemed to help. If he got used to Josh's presence, maybe he'd calm down enough to let Josh do his job.

"I obviously want what's best for her, you know? Even if what's best for her and the baby is Tru." Josh took the opportunity and lunged. He got his arm around the calf again, and this time he hung on. The calf bucked and reared back, trying to pull his head free as Josh strung the rope around him again.

"Not that I *actually* think Tru's what's best for her," he said through gritted teeth. "He sounds like a scumbag, all things considered. Like the guy knocks Amy up and immediately goes off to marry someone else. Sure, maybe he didn't know. But how are you just casually sleeping with someone while planning your nuptials with someone else? Who does that? He definitely doesn't deserve her."

The cow mooed. Maybe in agreement. Maybe because Josh pulled the rope tight. *Finally!* He stood, stretching the muscles that ached in his lower back. The calf made a few half-hearted attempts to bolt, but Josh held tight to the rope and he eventually settled.

Josh gave the little thing a pat on the head. "I'm not sure I deserve her either. Or, really, that I can provide the kind of life she deserves. Tru could give that to her though. He's got the money and the connections. And he already belongs to the world Amy is used to."

Josh staggered forward through the water, tugging on the rope. The calf resisted, tugging in the opposite direction. He was a strong little bugger.

"I can't give her those things," Josh continued. "Film premieres. And fancy dinners. And nights out in cities I've never even heard of."

Josh pulled harder on the rope.

"I… Am I supposed to just let her go?" That's not what he wanted. But he also didn't want this ache in his chest to worsen. He didn't want an Amy-sized heartbreak to get over. He didn't want his feelings to get dragged through the mud. And he certainly didn't want to be Amy's second choice—the consolation prize she settled for. If there was any part of her that wanted Tru… Well, maybe it was best, for his own sake, that Josh just stepped aside and let them figure this parenting thing out.

His arm flew forward suddenly as the calf launched into a run. Josh braced himself but it was too late. The calf took off like a shot, yanking Josh off his feet and face-first into the muddy water. He groaned, his clothes soaked through, his cowboy hat floating a few feet away.

The calf turned around and looked at him, prancing back and forth like they were playing a fun little game.

Josh grimaced, climbing to his feet. "I'm not gonna forget this."

Dripping muddy water, he snagged the rope, and climbed out of the creek, pulling the calf along. Once they crested the top of the muddy embankment, he set the calf loose. It went skipping across the pasture to join the other cattle and hopefully find its mother. Josh glared after it, wiping water from his face. He could taste mud on his tongue. What a day this was turning out to be.

Maybe it was time to consider putting up a fence to stop the cattle from getting stuck down there. He marched back to his truck. All he wanted to do was head to the house and take a long, hot shower. Maybe call Shane and see if he felt like a beer so he could take his mind off Tru McCoy.

His phone was blinking with notifications when he settled in the driver's seat. He picked it up, realized it was a missed call from Amy, and his heart skipped a beat.

There was no voicemail, so he called her back immediately.

"Hey," he said when she answered.

"Hi, cowboy." She sounded tired.

"Sorry I missed your call. I was..." *Getting bested by a calf a third of my size?* "Dealing with a little cattle situation on the ranch."

"That's okay, I know you're busy."

Not too busy to talk to you, he wanted to say, but he didn't know if that was the kind of thing she wanted to hear right now. "How'd everything go with Tru?"

"About as good as I expected, honestly."

Josh held his breath. What did that mean?

"Tru's gone," she clarified. "And I'm pretty sure he won't be back."

"So he didn't—"

"Want anything to do with the baby? No."

The rest of his breath left him in a rush. "I'm sorry, Amy."

"It's probably for the best. I'm not sure he'd make a great father right now. Or ever."

He was apologizing and part of him meant it. Amy deserved someone who was going to take responsibility for the child. Tru should have been that person. He had all the means to be that person. And the fact that he'd already failed Amy more than once made Josh angry. But there was a larger part of Josh that was quite relieved to hear this. Elated, even. If Tru was out of the picture, did that mean he and Amy could go back to the way things were? That they could just pick up where they'd left off?

But could he really compete with the memory of a movie star? Could he get over being the person she settled for? Mostly he wondered if she could really be happy living a quiet life in Tenacity when she was used to a life of adventure. Josh worried that he knew the answer to that question and it filled him with defeat. "I really am sorry things didn't work out with Tru," he said.

"I'm not," Amy said quietly.

Silence lapsed between them, and Josh didn't know how to fill it. What the hell was he doing? He wanted Amy. But she couldn't possibly want him in the same way, especially not now that she was expecting a baby. She needed support and structure and so many other things he didn't even know about.

"Well," she said. "I'll let you get back to cattle stuff."

"Right. Yeah... I better do that."

"I guess..." Her words lingered for a long moment. "I'll talk to you later?"

"Yeah," Josh said awkwardly. He had no idea when later might be, and he felt horrible about that as the call ended. This didn't feel like a goodbye, but he also wasn't quite sure what they were anymore. Here he was ragging on Tru for not stepping up, but Josh didn't know the first thing about having a family of his own, so how could he possibly be any better than Tru McCoy?

CHAPTER EIGHTEEN

"YOU WANT TO stop for food?" Faith asked as they turned onto the narrow stretch of highway leaving town.

"There's not really anything worthwhile between here and Bronco," Amy said. "Just that little shack of a diner with the stale coffee."

"And the oatmeal cookies that taste like cardboard. Yeah, I know. I meant when we get into Bronco. Might be nice to have some options for a change. Don't get me wrong. I love Tenacity, I really do. But—"

"They don't have your favorite chickpea falafel wrap?"

Faith glanced at her, a smile on her face. She reached over and squeezed Amy's hand. "It's gonna be a good day. Everything's going to turn out fine at the doctor's. So I think we can make time for a little fun, too. Maybe we can even swing by the arena if you're feeling up for it. Visit with the horses. Catch up on all the rodeo gossip."

It felt like eons since Amy had been in the Bronco Convention Center or set foot in the arena. She brushed her hand across her belly. It might be a good long while before she had another chance. "Well how can I say no to that?"

Amy had never fully appreciated Faith's ability to soothe nerves. She'd been up all night thinking about this OB appointment, tossing and turning as anxiety-inducing questions ricocheted around her brain. They were on their way to see Dr. Rangely, an obstetrician who worked out of Bronco. Amy had also grown quite fond of Tenacity, but her options for medical care were more limited there than they were in the city. Plus she'd wanted to be seen as soon as possible and Dr. Rangely had an opening in her schedule.

Now that Amy knew about the baby, she was certain she'd done something wrong. Many things, probably. Her thoughts turned protective. She just wanted everything to be okay. This poor baby had already been rejected by its father. Somehow Amy had to do and be enough for this child.

"Hey," Faith said, breaking her from her anxious spiral. "Really. Everything's going to be fine."

"I just feel like the baby's not even here yet and I'm already screwing this up somehow," Amy said.

"You haven't screwed up anything. I bet you that if you talk to any new parent they feel the exact same way."

"I didn't even bother to notice I was pregnant for four months, Faith. All the signs were there."

Faith shrugged. "You had other things on your mind." Her eyebrows wiggled. "Josh-shaped things."

Amy frowned.

"How's that going by the way?"

"It's not," she said, a little defeated. "We honestly haven't spoken much since the day Tru left. I thought it might reassure him, knowing that Tru wasn't going to be around to get in the middle of what we had going on. He seemed happy about that part at least. But he has sort of retreated since then." Almost a week had passed since their phone call, and though Josh texted her on occasion, things felt different. There was a distance there she didn't know how to fix. "I think it kind of dawned on him that I was still gonna have this baby. And that being around me, being *with* me, automatically included that now."

"Amy, I don't think Josh is—"

"Of course he is. He's probably wondering if he could raise another man's baby. Wouldn't that be what you were thinking?"

Faith grew quiet. Contemplative.

"I don't think there's anything I can do but give him space,"

Amy said. She wasn't going to beg him to want her. The same way she hadn't begged Tru to want this baby. It would hurt if Josh ultimately stepped away, but she would survive it. She *had* to survive it. There was someone more important than herself to think about now.

"I think you need to have more faith in Josh."

Amy smirked a bit. "That's your advice? Have faith."

"Hey, if anyone's qualified to give that advice, it's me."

"I think I'd rather just be practical, and not live with some fairy-tale hope right now."

They passed a sign for Bronco. Amy glanced at her phone. They'd made good time, but they wouldn't be able to squeeze in lunch before the appointment. That was fine though. Amy was too nervous to eat. Just as she was thinking it, her stomach made a noise to the contrary.

"Well," Faith said. "You be practical and I'll hold out enough hope for both of us. Josh is a good man."

"I'm not disputing he's a good man. But I also once foolishly thought Tru was a good man."

Faith snorted. "You were clearly off your rocker with that one. Even I could have told you to tread lightly there. And I was a big Tru McCoy fan until recent events."

"I fell for the oldest trick in the book. Listening to anything that sweet-talking snake had to say." Amy's pulse skipped as Faith pulled into a parking lot outside a squat red-bricked building with Bronco Medical on the side in fancy silver letters. "I just don't want to do that again."

Faith parked and turned to face her. "Okay, listen here. Josh Aventura is nothing like Tru. Yes, he's a gruff, stubborn man. And maybe it's gonna take him a minute to realize the good thing he's got here, but he *will* realize it, Amy. Just don't give up on him yet."

Amy flashed her a tight, close-lipped smile. She wanted to believe Faith more than anything, but the best thing to do was have reasonable expectations. It would soften the blow when it landed. "I haven't given up. Not completely." She glanced out the window and back. "I just have other things on my mind."

"Speaking of other things. Let's go see how this little avocado is doing."

Amy chuckled. "Avocado?"

"Oh, yeah, I was reading on this app that the baby is the size of an avocado now or something."

"Explains why all my pants are tight."

They got out of the car and walked into the building. Amy was greeted by a receptionist who took her name and checked her in. Then they sat down in the faux-leather chairs that filled the waiting room. Amy glanced around at the other patients, wondering how many of them had been unexpectedly knocked up by famous movie stars. Maybe there was a club for that sort of thing.

"We should get a pony."

"Hmm?" Amy glanced over at Faith.

"For the baby. It's gonna have to learn to ride sometime."

Amy tilted her head, briefly resting it on Faith's shoulder. "Let's just focus on getting to the due date before we start teaching it rope tricks."

"I am so excited."

Amy was lucky. What did she need Tru for when she had Faith?

"Amy?" a nurse called, waving her back. She was short, with a full head of gray hair and wore her glasses on a chain around her neck.

Amy liked her immediately. She hopped up.

Faith caught her hand and squeezed. "I'll be here when you get out."

The nurse led her to an exam room and had Amy change into a gown. She took some vitals and some blood and chatted with her, completing a basic history. Then she asked Amy to pee in a cup. When the doctor came in, she shook Amy's hand.

She was a tall, middle-aged woman with dark, curly hair.

"Doctor Rangely," she said. "But you can call me Gloria."

"Amy. Nice to meet you."

"So, babies," the doctor said, grabbing a seat in a swivel chair.

"Babies," Amy repeated.

"Your first?"

"Yes."

"And are we happy about that?" There was no judgment in her voice, and Amy suspected the doctor asked most of her patients this question. Their answer likely determined the direction of the conversation.

"It was definitely unexpected, and I'm not going to say I wasn't shocked, but yes... I'm happy."

"Okay, then. I'd like to do an ultrasound. Just to see where we're starting off since this is your first visit with me."

"We're gonna see the baby?"

Dr. Rangely nodded. "You bet." Amy reclined back on a table, her heart pounding, as the doctor rubbed cold jelly on her stomach. She tried to imagine what this would have been like if Tru had decided to play parent. Would he be standing here next to her, holding her hand? She couldn't picture it, but she could picture Josh and her chest ached. Dr. Rangely adjusted some equipment, pulling a monitor into focus as she moved the ultrasound wand over Amy's skin. Amy watched the screen, trying to make sense of the unrecognizable blurs.

Suddenly a swooshing sound filled the room.

"Is that—"

"The heartbeat," Dr. Rangely said.

"The heartbeat," Amy replied softly. The swoosh raced faster than Amy expected. "Is that...good?"

"That's normal. It's a very strong heartbeat."

Amy wanted to burst into tears. And she did. "I'm sorry," she muttered as she was handed a box of tissues. Everything was just so uncertain. She didn't know where she stood with Josh or how to fix this situation or if there was any chance she might get him back, but the baby's heart was strong. How could everything be so wrong and so right at the same time? "I guess I just wanted to make sure everything was okay. After not knowing for so long, and not doing the things I was supposed to do—"

"Everything looks really good, Amy," Dr. Rangely said. "I promise. Nothing out of the ordinary for this far along."

"I was reading some things on the internet and it said you weren't supposed to be horseback riding. But then some other websites said you could. And I did. Go horseback riding, that is. But that's before I knew about the baby."

Dr. Rangely rubbed the back of Amy's hand where it rested on her stomach. "It can be a risky activity, especially for people who aren't used to it. But your file said you worked the rodeo circuit, right?" Amy nodded. "Well, seeing as you do it regularly, I'd say you were probably okay."

Amy let out a sigh of relief.

The doctor removed her gloves. "You and the baby look healthy. But I'd like you to hold off on the horseback riding going forward. You're into the second trimester now, and you're technically high-risk because of your age. You're fit but we want to be as careful as we can."

"I can do that," Amy said.

Dr. Rangely sat down at a desk, making notes on a laptop. "We'll get you scheduled for the anatomy scan next. We'll be able to tell you the sex at that appointment if you want to know."

"When's that?"

"Between eighteen and twenty-two weeks."

Amy felt her breath leave her. At the next scan she'd learn if she was having a little boy or a little girl. This was all becoming more real by the second, and she couldn't help wishing for Josh. Wishing that he'd been here with her, listening to this baby's heartbeat, the baby they might raise together if any part of him still wanted her. But could he ever want her enough now to make that work? Emotion filled her chest and it was hard to breathe.

Dr. Rangely turned to her. "Now, do you have any questions for me?"

"Oh, so many," Amy said. "Is it true the baby is the size of an avocado?"

"A BABY!" ELIZABETH said as they crowded into a booth. "I can't believe it. Congratulations again. I'm going to keep saying that. I'm so happy for you. I know you've wanted this for a while."

"A secret baby!" Tori added, nudging Carly. "This is like one of those episodes of *I Didn't Know I Was Pregnant*. I keep trying to get Bobby to watch it with me, but he just thinks it's ridiculous."

"Oh my God, you're so right!"

"I always wondered about those stories," Faith said, sipping her sweet tea. She'd gathered up all their sisters at Lulu's BBQ for lunch, surprising Amy after the doctor's appointment, and Amy's heart was full to bursting. And not just because she was starving, and Lulu's ribs were her favorite of anywhere in Bronco. "Like how do you reach nine months and not know you've grown a whole child?"

"Well, I *do* know I'm pregnant now," Amy said. "And according to Dr. Rangely, the baby is officially the size of an avocado."

There were squeals of delight around the table, and Amy had to hush her sisters so as not to disturb the other customers with their excitement. It had been an emotional morning, hearing the heartbeat and missing Josh, but despite everything, Amy was looking forward to welcoming this baby into her life, and knowing that her sisters supported her was the biggest gift of all.

"Your little avocado," Elizabeth said on a sigh. "I remember those days. Enjoy these moments. Pregnancy will go faster than you think. I'm not saying it's all sunshine and rainbows—"

"Yes, the morning sickness made sure of that," Amy said.

The corner of Elizabeth's mouth turned up. "I don't miss that, but there are definitely other moments you'll miss. Feeling the baby kick for the first time, watching your bump grow."

Amy smiled softly, considering her words. Elizabeth had lost her first husband, but she'd remarried Jake McCreery, and between them they now had five kids. If any one of her sisters should be offering parenting advice, it was definitely Elizabeth. "Well, I can't say I'm looking forward to giving up horseback riding for the foreseeable future—" she laid her hand on her stomach "—but I suppose some sacrifices are worth it."

"I guess that's you off the rodeo circuit for a while longer," Tori said. "At least for the duration of the pregnancy and some maternity leave."

"Yeah." Amy sighed. "I wasn't in any big rush to get back to it, honestly. At least, not until this nonsense with—"

"Yes!" Carly interrupted. "Let's talk about Tru. How is the baby daddy doing?"

Tori hushed her, looking around like their conversation might attract the paparazzi.

Amy's eyes cut across to Faith, who threw her hands up. "Like I was going to be able to keep that a secret."

"It's not like we didn't know," Elizabeth said diplomatically. "Or we at least suspected you two had something going on. When we learned you were pregnant and how far along you were, it wasn't hard to put two and two together."

Amy grumbled. "I was a fool. I know, I *know*."

"You were in love," Tori said, patting her hand. "There's a difference."

"What I can't understand is why a man with Tru's money and resources can't be bothered caring for his child," Carly said. "It's not like you're expecting him to tote the baby down a red carpet in a stroller. But he could at least kick over a bit for formula. Or set the kid up with a small trust fund for school or whatever."

"Caleb says he's too full of himself to genuinely care about anyone else in his life," Faith said.

Amy nodded. "I can't help thinking that maybe his rejection was a blessing in disguise. I mean, Tru's not cut out to be any kind of parent. That became more than obvious when I last saw him. And throwing this baby into the limelight, for the tabloids to exploit before the baby can even understand the situation, feels cruel. If there's one thing I want to be able to do as a mother, it's protect this child. Even if that means protecting them from their own—"

"Father?" Carly cut in.

Amy hesitated. "He's not, though, is he?" She'd been thinking more and more about this since the ultrasound this morning. Lying there on the exam table, alone, she'd come to the conclusion that Tru was *not* this baby's father, not in the sense that he should be. "He might have donated his DNA, but he's never going to do all the things a father is supposed to do."

Her sisters nodded, and Amy knew they understood. Maybe better than most. Being adopted really gave them a different perspective on what family was. It had nothing to do with DNA or blood. All that mattered were the people who stuck around in the end.

The people who chose you.

"Tru didn't choose me or this baby. So, I don't plan to tell him when the baby is born. He won't be at the hospital with me. I don't even plan to write his name down on the birth certificate." She would tell her child, one day, when they were ready to hear the truth, but until then, she didn't see a reason to weigh them down with the disaster that was Truett McCoy.

"Is there someone else's name you want to write down?" Elizabeth asked quietly, eyeing her over a plate of corn bread.

Amy opened her mouth, closed it, emotion clogging her throat. It was so hot and tight she couldn't get the words out. Tears gathered at the corners of her eyes. When she thought about that moment, about bringing this little life into the world, the only person she saw by her side was Josh.

"Oh, honey, I didn't mean to make you upset." Elizabeth reached across the table and squeezed her hand.

"It's not you," Amy said. "Honest. I'm just... I'm missing Josh. I feel like we were moving in a really good direction and now it sort of feels like I've been bucked off the back of a horse. I don't really know where we stand or where to go from here."

"Well, that's easy enough to figure out," Tori said.

Amy looked up at her.

"You know exactly what to do when you get bucked off."

"Get up, dust yourself off and get back on the horse," her sisters chorused, making Amy chuckle.

"Advice from the great Hattie herself," Tori said, raising her glass of sweet tea.

"I'm not sure that applies here," Amy said.

"Of course it does," Tori said. "Has Josh explicitly said he doesn't want to be with you?"

"Well, no," Amy said. "Not in so many words."

"Not in any words," Faith cut in.

"Has he stopped answering your texts?" Carly asked.

"No. He hasn't really called much in the last week, but he's messaged to check in. I've been trying to give him as much space as I can."

"And did you ever think that maybe he's trying to do the same thing?" Elizabeth suggested.

Carly nudged her under the table. "It sounds like he's still interested, Amy."

"I agree," Tori said. "And as far as I'm concerned, you have to get back on the horse."

Try again, Amy heard in Hattie's voice. *Don't let fear stop you from reaching for something you love.* Frankly, she knew Hattie had been talking about reaching for the reins, but maybe her sisters were right. She shouldn't give up on her and Josh yet.

She just didn't know how to reach for him. It felt unfair to dump this kind of news on Josh and expect a decision so quickly. If she was going to ask him to choose her and this baby, she felt like she needed to give him the appropriate amount of time to process. But how long was that? Weeks? A month?

Maybe she'd just put it off forever. That would be easier than getting rejected.

"I think you're scared," Elizabeth said, squeezing her hand again. "And that's understandable."

"What if he doesn't choose me?" Amy blinked heavily. "I don't know if I can do this."

"That's what loving someone is," Elizabeth said. "It's giving them the ability to hurt you but trusting them not to. I know it's terrifying, but I really think you need to put your faith in Josh now. You need to give him a chance."

"Regardless of what happens," Tori said. "You'll always have your family. We'll be here for you and this baby."

"Trust me, Amy," Elizabeth said. "If he's the right man for you, it'll work out. But it can't work if you don't fight for it."

CHAPTER NINETEEN

THE MORNING HAD started off reasonably cool, but after a couple hours of standing under that Montana sun, lugging lumber back and forth, Josh was sweating. He took a swig from his water bottle, kneading his back. In an effort to take his mind off Amy, he'd decided to tackle the bridge repair on the eastern end of the property. It was the bridge the cattle used to cross the creek to reach the furthest pasture, and after the winter they'd had, Josh had noticed a couple of the boards rotting.

But once he'd pried up the first few, he figured he might as well just change them all, only that had turned into a bigger job than he'd anticipated. Now he was not only drenched in sweat, but his mind had started wandering, inevitably landing on Amy. All he wanted to do was call her, but something scared him off. He couldn't shake the thought that he wasn't good enough for her. And if she was only settling for him, then he'd always play second fiddle to Tru McCoy. Maybe these were ridiculous thoughts, but it's what rattled through his brain with every strike of his hammer against wood.

Josh collected another board from his truck and carried it across the bridge. He carefully dropped it in place, then secured it with half a dozen nails. He was just hammering in the last one when he spotted a cloud of dust coming up the drive.

"About time!" he said as Shane drove up and parked next to

the creek. He'd called in a favor when he realized the repair job had gotten away from him, and Shane had agreed to pop over to help. "I expected you an hour ago."

"Sorry," Shane said. "Thought we could use some more reinforcements."

The truck doors opened, and Noah and Ryder climbed out.

"What're you doing here?" Josh asked as they retrieved their tools from the bed of the truck.

"Heard you'd decided to remodel the property instead of dealing with your feelings," Noah said, walking over and clapping him on the shoulder.

Josh glared at Shane. "Really?"

"Look, I didn't tell them everything. The details are for you to disclose," Shane reasoned. "I just needed some backup."

"Because clearly you and Amy are having troubles," Ryder said, "and it's bumming you out, man."

"It's not bumming me out," Josh muttered.

"You're bummed." Ryder took him by the cheeks and looked back at the others. "Isn't this the face of a man who's bummed?"

"Never seen anyone more bummed," Noah agreed.

Josh shrugged him off. He wasn't bummed. He was devastated, but he didn't really want to get into that. The whole point of this job was to get his mind off Amy, not talk about her even more. "I can't believe you brought these two fools with you," he muttered to Shane.

"I can't play relationship expert all by myself," Shane told him as he grabbed a board from Josh's truck and carried it over. "I needed someone with more experience getting rejected." He dropped the board in place and nudged Ryder. "Right?"

Ryder scoffed. "Not funny, man."

Shane steered Ryder in Josh's direction. "Here is your walking, talking example of what not to do in these kinds of situations."

"I'll have you know, I'm happily single," Ryder said. He gestured to Josh. "Does this man look happy to you? He's way past my tried-and-true method of 'get in and get out before the feelings get their hooks in you.'"

"Agreed," Noah said, hammering nails into the board Shane had just placed. "He's been hooked."

Ryder set off for another board, and Shane leveled Josh with a stare. "I know this isn't what you were expecting today," he said, readjusting his Stetson. "But this way we get the bridge repaired faster, and maybe you'll listen to someone else since clearly you didn't take my brilliant advice."

"What brilliant advice?" Josh said. "You gave me two options the other night. You said I could walk away or I could fight for her."

Shane gave him a *duh!* look. "And what exactly are you doing?"

"Well, I'm… I'm…" Josh put his hands on his hips, staring off at the cattle in the distance. What the hell *was* he doing?

"That's what I mean," Shane said. "You clearly haven't walked away from Amy. And you're not over her. So why aren't you out there trying to make this work?"

"Because I don't know how to make this work," Josh said with a grunt. He wasn't a star-studded, high-rolling movie star, and he didn't know how to prove to Amy that he could offer her more than Tru ever could. Tru would always be wealthier. He'd always be famous. He'd always be this baby's biological father. And just because Amy had said that Tru walked away didn't mean things were over between them. Tru could have a change of heart, decide he wanted to know his child, and maybe Amy would fall for that charming smile all over again.

"Look, it's a little difficult to give you advice when I don't know what's going on," Noah said.

Josh sighed. These were his best friends. And the news was bound to come out sometime. He trusted them enough to hold their tongues until it did. "She's pregnant."

Ryder barked a laugh, giving Josh's shoulders a squeeze. "You two made quick work of that."

"It's not mine."

"Damn," Ryder said, his tone shifting from congratulatory to conflicted. "Sorry. I didn't even think."

"You don't often before you open your mouth," Noah said to him.

"No, it's okay," Josh cut in before Ryder could respond. "It was a shock to all parties involved."

"So, that's what this is all about, then?" Noah continued. "Why things are so complicated?"

"Exactly. I was serious about Amy. I *am* serious about her. But now there's this baby and her ex, and I just don't know where I fit into that picture."

"So, the other guy's still around?" Ryder said.

Josh hummed. "I mean... He was. But I'm not so sure anymore."

"Has he asked you to back off?" Noah asked.

"No."

"Has Amy asked you to back off?" Shane clarified.

"No," Josh said again.

Ryder ran his hand through his hair, scratching at the back of his head. "Okay, I know I'm not exactly the person to be asking about committed relationships here, but seems to me like you want Amy, she wants you, and instead of making that happen, you're sitting here with your cattle. Have I got that right?"

"That's not what's happening," Josh said.

"That's exactly what's happening," Shane muttered.

"Sounds to me like you're feeling sorry for yourself," Noah said. "You need to knock that off, follow your heart and go get your girl back."

Josh huffed. Last time he'd followed his heart, Erica had stomped on it on her way out of town.

"You got company coming?" Shane asked as a car turned onto the property.

Josh whipped his phone out of his pocket and checked the time. Had the day really gotten away from him that quickly? He'd been expecting visitors, he'd just planned to be a little less sweaty when they arrived. "Yeah, actually. I've got a meeting."

"Then I guess we'll let you off the hook for now," Ryder said, poking Josh playfully in the chest. "But next time we talk, you better have good news for us."

"You just focus on yourself," Josh said. "I heard you're cycling through women so fast your mother's stopped asking their names."

Noah snickered, leading Ryder back to Shane's truck.

"Call me later," Shane said. "I'll come out and help you finish up."

"Thanks," Josh said. "And thanks for this, I guess." He wasn't really in the mood for advice, but Shane's heart was in the right place.

"Just sit with what we said for a while," Shane said. "You'll figure it out."

"If you say so." Josh waved as they left, then quickly packed up his tools and the excess lumber. He tossed it all into the bed of his pickup and drove over to the house. Mike Cooper had messaged him earlier in the day, asking if it was okay for Stanley Sanchez to swing by. He wanted to follow up about the conversation Mike and Josh had at the Tenacity Social Club regarding the rocks on the old Woodson property. Josh didn't know how he'd found himself in the middle of Stanley's investigation, and he wasn't sure what kind of help he could be in the search for the Deroy family, but he'd agreed to talk to the man. He figured it was another way to keep his mind off Amy, though clearly his friends were determined to keep his thoughts there anyway.

He sighed, getting out of his truck.

"Hey there!" a man called, stepping out of his vehicle. He was older than Josh had expected, tufts of white hair visible under his black cowboy hat. He wore denim on denim and a leather vest.

"Hi," Josh said. He headed over to greet him.

The man stuck out his hand. "Stanley Sanchez."

Josh shook his hand. "Josh Aventura. Good to meet you. Mike said you'd be coming by."

A door thudded and Josh looked up to see a woman come around the vehicle.

"This is my grandniece, Nina," Stanley said.

Josh recognized her as the daughter of Tenacity locals Will and Nicole Sanchez. She was tall, with dark hair that reminded him of Amy. And a smile that reminded him of Amy. And...this not thinking about Amy thing was not going so well.

"Hi," she said, smiling at him. "Hope we're not interrupting your work."

"No." Josh glanced over his shoulder. "I mean, there's always work but that doesn't mean I couldn't do with a break. So, Mike said you wanted to talk about what I told him?"

"Firstly we wanted to thank you for giving Mike that tip and for your part in helping us find 'Juniper Rock,'" Stanley said.

"You found what you were looking for then?" Josh said.

Stanley tipped his head back and forth. "The people who live there now are not keen to let us on the property. I think they got spooked by the word *investigation*."

"Right," Josh said. The Stoolers weren't the chattiest of neighbors as far as Josh was concerned, but they'd always seemed reasonable. Then again, if someone told Josh they were investigating and wanted to poke around his property, he might have gotten weirded out too. "That's too bad."

"We were hoping that you might be able to pave the way for us," Nina said. "You being neighbors and all."

"What we find there could end up having ramifications for the whole town," Stanley added.

Ramifications for the whole town? That seemed like a good enough reason to try. Besides, what did Josh have to lose? He had no stake in the game. And if he helped a neighbor in the end… "I don't know them well," Josh cautioned. "They're quiet neighbors. Mostly keep to themselves. So I'm not promising any miracles, but I'll give it my best shot."

Nina grinned so wide it made him think of Amy again and his chest ached. "Great!" She clapped her hands together. "You have no idea how much this means."

Josh glanced down at his sweaty, dusty clothes. "I'm gonna change real quick. Probably better to make a good impression if they've already turned you down once. I'll be right back. Then we have to make a pit stop."

"WE DID ALL that for some mac and cheese? I don't see how this is going to help," Nina said as they arrived on the Stooler property. It hadn't changed much since it belonged to the Woodsons from what Josh could remember. There was a large barn at the back of the property and a pair of tall silos and a long, winding drive that disappeared to a massive garage. Josh held a tray of Angela's mac and cheese in his hands.

"This isn't just any mac and cheese. This is the best in all of Montana," Josh said. "Trust me. If that doesn't convince the Stoolers to let you have a little look around the property, then nothing will. Plus I practically had to sell Angela my soul to get this." And dodge a lot of awkward questions about where Amy was. Shane had been tight-lipped about Josh's woes and that had just made Angela more suspicious. She'd given him the *look*— the same look his mother would have given him if she was in town—and Josh had felt the combined weight of Angela's disappointment mingle with his own.

"Well," Nina said, "let's hope this magic dish does the trick."

They walked up to the door, with Josh flanked by the Sanchezes, and he felt like a kid again, dragged into one of Shane's silly schemes. Nina rang the doorbell, and they waited. Josh didn't know why *he* was so nervous. A moment later, the door opened.

Mr. Stooler looked back at him, lifting the reading glasses off the end of his nose. He looked past Josh to glare at Stanley and Nina. "I thought I already told you two I wasn't interested in having people poke around my property."

"We don't mean to give you any trouble," Nina said. "Honest. I'm just trying to figure out what happened to someone I really cared a lot about."

Mr. Stooler didn't look convinced by her plea.

"Fifteen minutes," Josh said. "That's all we're asking. Then we'll be out of your hair. And as a thank-you, I've got some of Angela Corey's mac and cheese here." Josh lifted the tray, making his offering.

Mr. Stooler's eyes darted to the tray. "Angela's, huh?"

Josh bit down on his grin. This dish really was magical.

"Darrel, just let them look around already!" a woman called from inside the house. "What do you care about the rocks at the edge of the property anyway?"

Mrs. Stooler came to the door, two heads shorter than her husband, but with the attitude to make up for it. She took the tray of mac and cheese from Josh. "Thank you. This was a lovely gesture. You didn't have to do this." She nodded toward the driveway. "Well, go on and have a look. Take as long as you need."

Mr. Stooler gave them all a gruff nod. "I'll come out and join y'all in a minute."

Stanley tipped his hat. "We're mighty grateful. Won't be long."

They turned and the door closed behind them. "Let's make it quick," Josh whispered to Stanley. "In case Mr. Stooler changes his mind."

They marched off down the driveway, to the very edge of the property line, where large rocks were piled up, some as tall as him. Josh remembered driving past as a kid, watching the Woodson boy climb on them.

Stanley and Nina separated, inspecting the different groupings. Josh stared after them as they started to feel around in the grooves.

"What exactly are we looking for?" he asked.

"We'll know it when we see it," Stanley said.

Josh laughed and shook his head. "Sure." He wandered between the rocks, his mind drifting to Amy. He wondered what she was up to today. How she was feeling. If things with Tru were still status quo. He missed her. He wanted to hear her voice more than anything.

He reached for his phone almost without thinking.

Stanley picked up a long stick and started tapping on some of the smaller rocks, bending close to listen to the sounds.

What would he even say if he called? *How are you* seemed rather empty when what he really wanted to say was *I miss you and I want you.*

Stanley tapped along another batch of rocks and froze when one echoed back strangely.

Josh slipped his phone back into his pocket and joined him. Nina hurried over. The rock was about as high as Josh's knee. "False bottom?" he said.

"Sounds like it." Stanley gripped one side of the rock. "Give me a hand here."

Together, Josh and Nina helped Stanley shove the rock over, exposing what was very clearly a false addition to the stone based on the color difference. Stanley whipped out a small pocket-knife that dangled from his key ring and pried the bottom open.

The metal creaked and groaned, rusty after all that time of sitting in the wet earth.

When the bottom flew off, Nina gasped. Inside was a wadded-up roll of money and a folded-up note. She reached in and carefully unfolded the paper. She cleared her throat, reading it out loud. "'You got the wrong man.'"

"Well, I'll be damned," Stanley said.

"Do you think this means Barrett didn't do it?" Nina said. She sounded on the verge of tears.

"I think the only thing we can be sure of is that someone believed they'd accused the wrong man," Stanley said. "And that's enough to question everything."

"What d'you got there?" Mr. Stooler called, walking over. He spied the roll of money in Stan's hand. "My God." His eyes widened. "That should be ours, now. You hear? It was found on our property."

"We'll have to turn the funds over to the authorities," Stanley said. "It's evidence. Once that's cleared, they can decide who to allocate it to."

Mr. Stooler huffed a bit, but he couldn't argue that logic.

Stanley rose to his feet. "You want me to call them out to take a look or will you?"

"Suppose I'll do it," Mr. Stooler said. "It's my land anyhow." He inclined his head and he and Stanley set off for the house.

Josh smiled as Nina smothered a grin behind her hand. She was still defending Barrett after all these years. "You do know that it's still possible that Barrett could have put the money—and that note—there himself."

Nina solemnly shook her head. "I've always thought that the Deroys' sudden departure from Tenacity made no sense. And I'm choosing to believe that this note proves Barrett never would have done something so horrible to the town. I know there's still so much more to the investigation but—"

"All these years later, you still have that much faith in him?" Josh asked.

She tilted her head, a funny little smile coming over her face. "Yes. Do you still have faith in you and Amy?"

Josh flinched. He knew Tenacity was a small town, he just

didn't realize how fast word about him and Amy had spread. He supposed they'd been seen out together...a lot. And he'd been hanging around the feed store more than necessary. Still, he was a little surprised that Nina knew about their relationship.

"I obviously don't know exactly what's going on with you two, but you really do look miserable."

Josh sighed. "Can't deny that."

"Why don't you go do something about it?"

Josh laughed despite himself. "It's that easy, huh?"

"It *is* that easy. Well," she smirked, "it's a hell of a lot easier than unearthing false-bottomed boulders on the Stoolers' property."

She was right about that. And about Amy. Heck, it was the same thing Shane, Ryder and Noah had tried to tell him earlier, he'd just been too stubborn and miserable to listen. But maybe he'd just needed these little nudges in the right direction to get his act together. Because if the guys were telling him to go for it and Nina was still fighting for Barrett after all this time, then he could sure as hell fight for Amy.

He excused himself from Nina, took out his phone and dialed. But it wasn't Amy he called. Not at first. It was his mother.

"About time, Joshua!" she said when she answered the phone. "Your father's just about eaten his weight in pickled herring and every time we stop in a port, I get an update from Iris Strom. First you and Amy are seeing each other. Then you're not."

"I'm hopefully about to change that," Josh said.

"What's going on?"

"I've been a fool and it's taken me this long to screw my head on straight, but I felt like I needed to talk to you and Dad first, so you don't think I'm jumping into something without thinking it through first."

"That's not like you," his mother said. "Why would we think that?"

"Because... I want to be with Amy. I want to make a life with her." The truth was, he wanted Amy, even if she'd chosen someone else first, even if he'd only ever be her second choice. He might not be able to hold a candle to Tru McCoy, but he wanted to take care of her and her child. He thought that she could be happy with him, and that they could have a good life together. And maybe those were all foolish things to think, and she'd reject him anyway, but he knew what his heart wanted, and he at least needed to try.

"Oh, Josh! That's music to my ears."

"But there's something you should know." Josh swallowed. There wasn't really a delicate way to break this news. "Amy's pregnant."

His mother gasped.

"It's not mine," he rushed to say before she could get carried away. "But I… I want it to be. I know we've only just met, and I haven't even introduced her to you and Dad yet, but she's the one. I *know* she is. And I want to raise this baby as my own. If Amy will have me, that is."

He stopped talking, taking in the silence on the other end of the line.

"Do you think I'm still being a fool?" he asked.

"Do you love this girl?" his mother replied.

"Yes," Josh said. "More than anything."

"Then that's all that matters."

"But do you think I'm ready to be a dad?"

His mother chuckled softly. "Josh, none of us is ever ready. Look at me and your father. You showed up later in life and we still weren't ready. But we loved you, and we figured it out. And you and Amy will, too. Remember what your father told you? All that really matters at the end of the day is that you have good people to call home. That's all we've ever wanted for you. So, if you've found your person, you hold on to her tight. Right?"

"Right," he said, fighting the emotion that swirled in his chest.

"Now, you go fix things with Amy," his mother said. "Because I want to meet my grandbaby when the time comes."

Josh laughed, pressing his hand to his forehead. Maybe he'd only been looking for Ms. Right Now before meeting Amy, but she was Mrs. Right…his Mrs. Forever. He knew it down to his boots. She was the only one for him. And the old Josh might have let her go without a word and retreated back into his world of cattle, but it was time to risk his heart again and go after what would make him truly happy.

"Oh, I can't wait to tell your father! He's going to be thrilled. We both are, Josh. We love you."

"Love you, too, Mom."

"Call me later with good news?"

"You bet." Josh hung up, finally ready to call Amy, adrenaline surging through him. He sure hoped he'd be calling his mother back with good news. His hands shook as he found Amy's number in his call log. He hit Dial.

Part of him worried she might not take his call, but she answered after the second ring.

"Hi," he said.

"Hey there, cowboy," she answered, a mix of surprise and relief in her voice.

"Do you think we can meet up in person?" he asked. "To talk?"

There was a pause. "Where?"

"The ranch?" Josh suggested. At least there they'd have privacy.

"Okay," Amy agreed. "I'll see you soon."

CHAPTER TWENTY

AMY FELT LIKE a shaken soda bottle as she turned off Juniper Road and down the gravel drive leading to Split Valley Ranch. Nerves coiled in her gut, and her hands trembled against the steering wheel of her car. The shakes were so bad by the time she pulled up beside the house that she had to sit in the driver's seat and take a few deep, calming breaths. In through her nose. Out through her mouth. And again. In and out.

Elizabeth had told her to fight for him, and she'd wanted to call him for days. But that fear of rejection had planted itself inside her chest and refused to move. Every time she'd tried to pick up the phone, she'd been overwhelmed with the image of Josh pulling away, of him turning his back on her. So she'd resigned herself to giving him more time. She tried not to take up space in his world even though that's all she wanted to do. That didn't stop her from missing him though.

She'd done her best to keep busy with Faith and the feed store and planning for this baby. There was so much to do. So many unknowns. She was grateful for all her sisters and the constant stream of parenting and relationship advice trickling down the group chat since their lunch at Lulu's. She'd missed them and had loved seeing them, but truthfully, she'd found herself missing Tenacity even more. She'd missed the small-town happenings and the quiet and seeing the same people day in and day out. She used to love the city. When had her heart shifted?

The moment I met Josh, she told herself.

She missed him everywhere. Sitting on the porch in the evenings with tea and toast. Bumping into customers in aisles in the store. Mostly she missed being here with him, riding through the pastures, nothing for miles but them and the Montana skyline.

She touched her belly.

There would be no more riding for a while.

And there might not be any more Josh after today.

That last thought churned in her stomach worse than any morning sickness. If Josh had come to the conclusion that he simply couldn't raise another man's baby, this would be the end of them.

Amy blinked, fighting off tears. *Dammit.* If she started crying now, she'd never be able to stop. She'd be a blubbering mess before Josh even uttered a hello. *If* he said hello. She'd been playing out this moment in her mind, trying to anticipate what Josh might have to say. Amy fought the urge to believe that he'd leave her like Tru, but unlike with Tru, she'd understand. Josh hadn't signed up to be a father to someone else's kid. And regardless of what they wanted, Amy was about to be a mother. Tears grew heavy in the corners of her eyes. She swiped at them with her fingers. *Get it together, Amy.*

This news had blown in like a twister, disrupting both their lives, and it wasn't fair of her to expect Josh to pick up those pieces or to try to salvage this relationship. She imagined the situation in reverse. What if Josh had sprung a kid on her? To fall for someone only to watch their past creep back in and change everything you thought you knew about them. Her first instinct might have been to step away too.

She supposed there was no more putting it off though. It was time to find out if there was anything left to fight for. Amy climbed out of the car and walked around the side of the house, up the porch steps.

Josh leaned against the railing, looking out at the barn. He had a beer in his hand. He left the bottle on the railing the moment he spotted her. "You came!"

"Of course I came." She noticed a few more beers scattered about. *Uh-oh.* Had Josh needed some liquid courage before dropping the news that this was over? Her heart gave a dull, hollow thump, and she resisted the urge to rub at the spot where her chest ached. Fear made it difficult to swallow, and heaviness welled behind her eyes. She didn't know if she wanted to scream or cry or curse Tru McCoy until the cows came home.

"How are you?" he asked.

"Good." Her gaze drifted past him briefly. "Having a bit of a party?"

He looked over his shoulder at the empty beer bottles. "Oh, no. More like a celebration, I guess. I, uh, got roped into some detective work with Stanley Sanchez and his grandniece, Nina. We were just celebrating a clue that panned out. Sort of a big deal for the town. At least, Stan says so."

Amy's eyes widened. Of all the things she imagined Josh doing in their time apart, detective work was not one of them.

Josh shook his head. "Anyway, I'll tell you about it later."

Amy's heart startled to life, rattling with anticipation. More than anything she wanted them to *have* a later.

"That's not what I called you over to talk about," Josh continued.

Right. Was this it? Should she prepare herself for the blow? Amy wasn't sure anything could prepare her. She'd been hurt by Tru, but losing Josh would be different. It would devastate her. She hadn't wanted to admit that to herself, hadn't wanted to face the heartbreak before she had to, but now there was nowhere to hide.

"How is the..." Josh looked down between them, his voice softening. "How is the baby?"

"Baby's doing well." She flattened her hand against her stomach. "I had an appointment with a doctor the other day." Did he even want to know these things if this was over? His eyes found hers and held them. "Up in Bronco. She did a bunch of tests. Everything's right on track."

"That's great news. Did you get... I mean... Is it too soon for an ultrasound?"

"Doc gave me one." She cleared her throat. "I got to hear the heartbeat." *I wanted you to hear it too. I wished you were there, seeing this baby. Our baby?*

Josh's hands tightened around her elbows. "And the doc said it sounded good?"

"She said everything's perfect. I worried a bit, not having realized I was pregnant, that I might have hurt the baby hauling around stuff at the feed store or riding around on Bitsy. But she said everything's okay. Just no more horseback riding until this little one comes."

"Guess we'll have to find something else to keep you occupied on the ranch."

Amy opened her mouth, closed it. Did he mean that or was he trying to let her down easy?

"I'm sorry it took me so long to call," Josh said. "Truly."

"No, it's okay… It's…" Her voice broke, and Josh reached for her, gathering her into his arms. Amy melted against him. The embrace felt right, like coming home, and her insides twisted so painfully she just barely managed to bite back a sob. She was clinging to a thread of hope, but this reunion still felt so tentative. Would Josh really hold her like this while ending things?

"I wanted to call you every day. But every time I picked up my phone, I chickened out." He wove his fingers through hers. "Who knew something so simple could be so scary?"

"I assumed all this time that you had been questioning whether you could raise another man's child. Or whether you even wanted to have kids at all. That's a big question to answer. So I wanted to give you time and space to think about it, or else I would have called too."

"I've known for a while now that I wanted a family. A wife. A couple kids running around the ranch, hearing their laughter spill across the pasture. Keeping them from getting up to mischief." He chuckled softly to himself. "Well, some of it, at least."

Amy let out a strangled breath, swiping at the single tear that slipped free. He painted a beautiful picture, but just because he wanted a wife and kids didn't mean he wanted her. "If it wasn't the baby that kept you away, then was it me?"

"God, no, Amy!" He cupped her jaw, running his thumb over her cheek. "Mostly I was thinking that it's a little hard to compete when your opponent is an internationally renowned heart-throb. I can't jet you off to private islands or shower you with luxuries. Not the way Tru could. And I guess I didn't feel good enough for you. I also sort of thought that by fighting for you, I might be depriving you of the life you and this baby could have had with Tru."

"Good enough for me?" Amy practically choked on the words. "Oh, Josh. You're *too* good for me if anything."

"Amy—"

"I'm serious." Amy couldn't believe that's what he'd been worrying about. "Tru and the jet-setting were a distraction from what I really wanted out of life. It was never real. It was never going to be anything. We were never going to work."

"So what do you really want out of life?"

"Someone solid and down-to-earth. Someone who's going to be there for me, that *wants* to be there for me." Not someone that was running around the globe, chasing fame. At one point she'd thought that Tru was something special, but now she knew he wasn't a real hero. He wasn't the kind of guy who would tend to her when she was sick, or make her laugh till she cried, or even ask her what she was thinking. "Until I met you, I didn't even realize what I was missing out on. And now, I can't imagine my life without you. I know that's a selfish thing to say, consider-ing the circumstances."

"It's not," Josh assured her. "I promise it's not."

Amy plowed on. Whatever happened now, at least she could say she'd told Josh exactly how she felt. "I've done a lot of think-ing lately, and the globe-trotting life is fine, for some. Maybe even for me, once upon a time. But that was then, and this is now. Now I want a quiet life…with you. Something simple and happy."

"Amy, that's all I wa—"

"Wait," she said. "Please. I just want to say that I also under-stand if you don't want to be a parent to this baby. I know you said you want kids, but maybe you want your own children, and that's okay. But I *am* going to have this baby, and if you're not all in, I won't hold it against you. It's a big change and a lot of responsibility in a short amount of time. It's asking for twice the commitment and we both know how new this still is between us. There is no pressure." Everything shook—her voice as she forced the words out, her hands where they clutched his sides, her chest as her heart rattled uncontrollably. She was almost dizzied by the intensity of her feelings. By how much these words hurt her to say. "We can part as friends."

"No," Josh said immediately. "We can't be friends."

Amy just looked at him, silently wishing and pleading, wanting him to choose her.

"I'm not young and naïve," he continued. "I spent a long time looking after a piece of land, wondering what my dad really meant when he said all that mattered is having good people to call home. But now I finally understand. You're my home, Amy. I know it's soon, but I also know my mind and my heart, and I love you too much to ever let us just be friends. And I will love this baby too, if you'll let me. So, in case it's not clear yet, I'm all in."

"Josh—" Her voice trembled.

"And I've already told my mom you're my person. She's really excited to meet you." He grinned. "Please don't make me go back on my word."

A laugh of disbelief tore up her throat, and Amy dove into his arms. This time she couldn't stop the tears that flooded down her cheeks. They were happy tears, though. Tears of joy. She tilted her face up and kissed him. Again and again. She kissed him in a way that hopefully told him there was no one else in the world for her.

She kissed him until he knew just how much she loved him too.

CHAPTER TWENTY-ONE

JOSH KISSED HER BACK, feeling her lips part in a gasp. It felt like it had been ages since he'd kissed her, and he sank into her touch like a starving man into a meal. He wanted to devour her. To make her tremble in his arms. To make up for all the moments he'd made her question his intentions.

Josh deepened the kiss until it was all tongue and teeth, soft and sweet. When Amy finally turned her head to gasp for air, he pulled back, giving them both some space.

"Is this okay?" he asked, stroking his thumbs along her cheekbones. There were unshed tears in her eyes. "Are you... Are you okay?"

She nodded, her smile watery. "It's better than okay."

"You're sure?"

She laughed a little. "I'm just so happy."

"Good," he said, pecking her on the lips again. "I want to keep making you happy, for as long as you'll let me."

"I mean it, Josh," she said, her hand pressing gently against his chest, her fingertips brushing over the place where his heart beat. "*You* make me so happy."

Josh wanted to laugh and scream and cry. He didn't know where to start first. Mostly he just planned to keep kissing her. Then he was going to make Amy feel all the ways in which he wanted her. He was going to make her feel good and safe. He was going to make sure she knew that she belonged with him and only him.

Her and her baby.

"Come inside?" he asked, his voice low.

She bit her bottom lip, grinning as he kissed her cheek, nuzzling against her. "Why? You have something fun in mind, cowboy?"

"I think I could come up with an activity that we might both enjoy."

"Oh, yeah?" She slid her hand beneath his shirt, her fingers sliding around to his back, smoothing across his skin. "Dinner and a movie?"

"Not quite."

"Too bad. I'm quite ravenous."

"Well, I'm ravenous for something else."

Amy giggled as he pulled her close, kissing his way down her neck.

He hummed against her, feeling more than hearing the soft sigh that left her lips.

She smiled at him. No, she beamed at him, and Josh knew right then that he wanted to spend the rest of his life waking up beside that smile. Amy followed him through the door. He closed it after her, and she surprised him by pressing him up against the back of the door. She ran her hands up his chest and over his shoulders, lifting up on her toes to whisper her lips along his jaw.

"God, I missed you," he grumbled.

"I missed you more."

"Not possible." Sure he'd missed this, but it was more than that. He'd missed having Amy in his space. He wanted traces of her in the bathroom and touches of her in the living room. He wanted to find her books left by the couch and her dishes in the sink and her hair ties around the gearshift in his truck.

And one day soon he wanted to be tripping over baby toys and looking for the last clean bottle in the middle of the night. He wanted to live that life with her. That hectic, crazy life filled with so much love that he'd gladly lie awake all night just listening to these people breathe.

He wanted little feet on the stairs and in the barn. He wanted this family so much it was a pain between his ribs.

"You okay?" Amy asked, looking up at him.

"I'm perfect," he said. He caught her hand and kissed every one of her fingers. Then he nudged her with his hips, and Amy backed them toward the couch, stripping out of her clothes.

"Thought we were aiming for the bedroom?"

"You should have known we were never going to make it that far," Amy laughed. She tugged Josh down to the couch and climbed into his lap.

Josh took his time with her, lingering in places that made her squirm and listening to the way her breath hitched as his fingers danced across her skin. He was gentle and reverential and unhurried, knowing, somehow, that they had forever to do this now. He had all the time in the world to worship her the way he wanted, to love her.

Amy threw her head back, and he lavished her neck with kisses.

"Touch me," she begged. "*Please*."

So he did. When they came together Amy let out a pretty little sigh and Josh echoed it, relieved as the blood rushed past his ears.

He moved against her and Amy moved against him, finding a rhythm that worked, that left them both wanting more, and when Amy cried out, Josh stilled long enough to watch her unravel. It was quickly becoming one of his favorite sights in the world.

Josh followed her into oblivion a moment later, then pulled her close, simply breathing in the moment as bliss washed through him.

They lay like that for a while, Amy tracing patterns into his forearm, humming contentedly whenever he pressed a kiss to her shoulder. She shivered as he ran his stubbled chin over her soft skin.

"That feels nice," she murmured.

He reached up and kissed the space behind her ear, then her throat, then shifted, so she was lying beneath him.

He studied her face.

All he saw there was contentment. How had he gotten so lucky?

Amy ran her hands through his hair, smoothing it back from his forehead. "What are you thinking?"

"That one day I'll be old and you'll be gray, and I'll still be looking at you like this."

Amy opened her mouth but no words came out. Instead she kissed him again, softly, stirring warmth in his gut. "That sounds lovely."

Josh wormed his way down her body, pressing his hand to her belly. Her breath hitched again as he kissed her stomach. There was a small, soft bump and he considered the fact that he was going to be a father to this baby. He grinned against Amy's stomach. He thought about how Amy had healed the wounded part of his heart, the same way he'd proven that she could trust him, and how wonderful it was that he'd found someone content to share this simple little life with him.

"I can still feel you thinking very hard," she said.

"I want us to be married before the baby comes." He heard her sharp intake of breath. "So the child can have my name."

Her lips twisted. "Is that a proposal, Josh Aventura?"

"It will be, if it's something you want?"

Amy hummed happily. "I think I could warm up to the idea."

"Only warm up to it?" he said, climbing back up her body. She giggled as he took her in his arms, nibbling at her neck. "You know, I didn't think I'd be able to give you a life filled with adventure, but now I think that life with you and our baby"— their baby!— "will be the best damn adventure either of us has ever gone on."

Amy looked at him, her eyes glassy. She pressed her hand to his cheek. "I would marry you tomorrow, but maybe we should wait until we can arrange for the families to be here."

"How about next month?"

Amy laughed. "Eager there, cowboy?"

"Eager to spend all the days of my life calling you my wife."

Amy kissed him again. "What am I going to do with you?"

"Hopefully many wonderful things," he said, eyeing her in a way that made them both laugh. And he smiled, knowing he would get to hear that laughter every day for the rest of his life.

TWILIGHT SPILLED ACROSS TENACITY, painting the Strom and Son Feed and Farm Supply sign in soft yellow shadows. The bell rang over the door in the feed store as Josh pushed inside, Amy right behind him. He'd hardly let her go since she showed up at the ranch, her hand still entwined with his own.

"You sure you want to do this now?"

"Yes." She squeezed his hand and he could feel her certainty and her joy radiate through him. Josh didn't think he'd stopped floating all afternoon. He was going to be a husband and a father.

"We're closing up shortly!" he heard Caleb call from somewhere in the store.

"So make it snappy," Faith added.

"It's just us," Amy called.

"Us?" Faith poked her head out of an aisle, a massive grin splitting her face as she eyeballed their joined hands. "Us as in…"

"We talked," Amy said. "Sorted ourselves out."

"Thank God." Faith came toward them. "Caleb, get out here! It's about damn time."

Josh chuckled at her antics. "Made some big decisions, too."

"Oh?" Faith said as Caleb jogged over.

"What's happening?" he asked, breathless.

"Big things supposedly," Faith said.

"In that case," Caleb waved them over to the cash desk, "step into our office. And tell us all about these big decisions."

Amy sucked in a breath, then let it out as she announced, "We're getting married."

Faith put her hand to her forehead and feigned shock.

Amy broke down laughing and hugged her sister. "You out of anyone should not be surprised. You've been meddling in this relationship the entire time."

"She is very good at meddling," Caleb said, pecking Faith on the temple with his lips.

"Because I could see this moment coming from a mile away," Faith agreed. She squeezed Amy tightly. "Congratulations. I'm so happy for you." She reached for Josh, finding his hand. "And for you too."

Amy pulled away as Caleb clapped Josh on the shoulder. "We need to tell the families, obviously. And it'll probably be a small, quick little thing." She glanced at Josh and he nodded.

That suited him just fine. If Amy wanted a fuss, he'd give her a fuss, but he was just as happy with something small. Something with their favorite people and each other. "But you'll be my maid of honor?" Amy continued.

"Of course," Faith said. "The others would have had to fight me for it."

Amy chuckled.

"Sure you're gonna be able to handle *all* the Hawkins sisters?" Caleb asked Josh. "They can be a lot."

He reached for Amy and pulled her close. "I think it'll be one hell of an adventure."

* * * * *

Don't miss the stories in this mini series!

MONTANA MAVERICKS: THE TENACITY SOCIAL CLUB

Welcome to Big Sky Country! Where spirited men and women discover love on the range.

All In With The Maverick
ELIZABETH HRIB
March 2025

A Maverick Worth Waiting For
LAUREL GREER
April 2025

Maverick's Full House
TARA TAYLOR QUINN
May 2025

MILLS & BOON

A Rancher Of His Own

Brenda Harlen

MILLS & BOON

Brenda Harlen is a former attorney who once had the privilege of appearing before the Supreme Court of Canada. The practice of law taught her a lot about the world and reinforced her determination to become a writer—because in fiction, she could promise a happy ending! Now she is an award-winning, RITA® Award– nominated, nationally bestselling author of more than sixty titles for Harlequin. You can keep up-to-date with Brenda on Facebook and X, or through her website, brendaharlen.com.

Books by Brenda Harlen

Montana Mavericks: The Trail to Tenacity

The Maverick's Resolution

Match Made in Haven

Claiming the Cowboy's Heart
Double Duty for the Cowboy
One Night with the Cowboy
A Chance for the Rancher
The Marine's Road Home
Meet Me Under the Mistletoe
The Rancher's Promise
The Chef's Surprise Baby
Captivated by the Cowgirl
Countdown to Christmas
Her Not-So-Little Secret
The Rancher's Christmas Reunion
Snowed In with a Stranger
Her Favorite Mistake
A Rancher of His Own

Visit the Author Profile page
at millsandboon.com.au for more titles.

Dear Reader,

Welcome back to Haven! A lot of years have passed since I first introduced this northern Nevada town, and writing those words now, for (probably) the last time, has put me in a nostalgic mood.

While the historic feud between the Blakes and the Gilmores was (mostly) resolved as a consequence of Brielle and Caleb's reunion in *One Night with the Cowboy*, there's been plenty of other stuff happening in town to keep the rumor mill churning. Not to mention all the weddings and babies!

Current speculation is that Sarah Stafford, recently returned to her ranching roots, is sweet on Andrew Morrow, new owner of the town's beloved bakery. Anyone who has seen them together can attest to their obvious chemistry, but each has secrets yet to be revealed...

Whether this is your first visit to Haven or your eighteenth (or some number in between), I hope you enjoy this "Match Made in Haven" and that you'll come with me to Whispering Canyon, Wyoming, in the very near future to meet some new cowboys— and the women who lasso their hearts.

Happy reading!

xo *Brenda*

For Kelly and Julie, who were integral to so many of my childhood memories. Though our paths diverged as we grew older, it has been a sincere pleasure to reconnect in recent years, not just as family but as friends, and to know that you're each the kick-ass heroine of your own story. xoxo

CHAPTER ONE

SINCE HER GRADUATION from college, Sarah Stafford's life had proceeded according to plan. Unfortunately, it took ten years for her to realize that it wasn't *her* plan but one that her parents had mapped out for her. And so today she'd doused that plan in gasoline and dropped a lighted match on it.

Metaphorically speaking, of course.

Though apparently the explosion had been heard in the farthest corners of the executive offices of Blake Mining.

As she'd walked out of the building, she'd been shaking inside. Not that anyone would know it. Sarah had a lot of practice hiding her feelings and showing the world—or at least her family—only what she wanted them to see.

The one person she'd never been able to fool was Claire Blake, formerly Lamontagne.

It was her childhood BFF who'd sensed Sarah's discontent and told her that if she wasn't happy with her life, she should do something about it. As Claire herself had done three years earlier when she left her controlling fiancé in Austin, Texas, and returned to Haven, Nevada.

Though inspired by her friend's actions and advice, Sarah had been hesitant to upset the status quo. Because even if walking into her office didn't fill her heart with joy, she hadn't exactly been *un*happy as the associate director of occupational health and safety at Blake Mining.

It was more that she'd felt...superfluous.

And indulged.

True, she'd worked hard to get her business degree from UT Austin, but almost immediately after graduation, she'd walked into an executive position that she'd done nothing to deserve. Or at least nothing aside from being born into the Blake family.

Her manicured hands wrapped around the steering wheel of her hybrid SUV as she exited through the gates of the company founded by her great-grandfather. Starting tomorrow, she was going to get those same hands dirty in her new job—and not just metaphorically speaking this time—and she was a little surprised to realize how much she was looking forward to it.

Driving into town—such as it was—she found a vacant spot in the parking lot behind Diggers' Bar & Grill and turned off the engine, then remained behind the wheel for another minute to focus on breathing in and out, waiting for the anxiety to hit.

But the familiar tightness in her chest wasn't there.

She actually felt...not quite happy, at least not yet, but definitely lighter. No longer weighed down by the expectations of her family.

Poor little rich girl.

The familiar taunt echoed in the back of her mind, but she shoved it aside in favor of her new mantra: *I am a strong, independent woman in control of my own destiny.*

And if she ended up regretting the choice she'd made—as both her parents had assured her that she would do—at least she'd know it had been *her* choice.

So resolved, she pulled out her phone and sent a text message to her BFF.

Can you meet me at Diggers'?

Almost immediately, three little dots appeared on her screen, indicating that Claire was responding.

Are we celebrating?

We are.

Her friend answered that with a trio of happy faces, followed by:

Be there in 30.
Order food before drinks!

Smiling now, Sarah climbed out of her vehicle and made her way around the back to open the hatch.

She'd done the hard part already; the next step was merely symbolic. But it was an important step to her—tangible evidence that she was shedding her old life and embracing the new.

Without hesitation—though with a silent apology to Michael Kors—she unbuttoned the crepe blazer that she wore over her sheath-style dress and tossed it into the back of her car. Then she toed off the three-inch heels she was wearing—sorry, Jimmy Choo—and discarded them, too. Now she was standing on cold (and undoubtedly filthy) asphalt in stocking feet, but she wasn't quite done yet. She reached up to pluck the bobby pins out of her hair, dismantling the knot that she habitually wore into the office so that her hair fell freely over her shoulders.

"Do you want some music?"

She jolted at the question and, with her heart pounding, pivoted to face the speaker—a tall, broad-shouldered stranger who was as distinctly masculine and undeniably sexy as his voice. Six feet, she guessed, tousled brown hair, square jaw sporting two or three days' growth and eyes the color of dark chocolate.

Her fight-or-flight response took its sweet time considering those options. On the one hand, she was a woman alone with a strange man in a parking lot. On the other hand, it was broad daylight, and this was Haven.

"Music?" she echoed, still undecided about her next move.

She caught a quick glimpse of even white teeth as he grinned.

"To accompany your striptease," he said.

Despite the heat that rushed into her cheeks, Sarah managed to respond coolly, "I'm not sure if I should be flattered or insulted, but I assure you, nothing else is coming off."

"I'm sure I'm disappointed," he said, following his remark with a playful wink that suggested he was flirting with her.

Or maybe that was wishful thinking on her part, because the man was seriously hot.

But she wasn't the least bit interested in getting burned.

Okay, maybe she was just the teeniest bit interested, but she had to trust that she was smart enough to ignore the interest that was suddenly humming in her veins. Because once bitten, twice shy—and she'd been bitten more than once.

And while her heart was still pounding a little too fast, she suspected that fear was no longer the cause—and that gave her even more reason to be wary. Because she had a history of being attracted to men who were all kinds of wrong for her and not recognizing that truth until she was left broken-hearted.

"You should know that I've got pepper spray," she told him, because she'd always subscribed to the theory that the best defense was a good offense and a woman finding herself alone with a strange man had to be ready to defend herself. (Actually, what she had was hairspray, but she'd heard that a travel-size can could be as effective as pepper spray to ward off an attacker.)

The stranger looked pointedly at her empty hands. "And where are you hiding that?"

In her purse.

Which she'd tossed, along with her jacket, into the back of the car.

Dammit.

"I've also got a black belt in karate."

That was a total lie, but she lifted her chin in the hope that her bravado would sell it.

He didn't appear the least bit intimidated.

If anything, the glint in his eye and the hint of a smile tugging at one corner of his mouth suggested that he was…amused.

"I might have been more inclined to believe you if you'd claimed to have a green—or even a brown—belt," he told her. "Do you have any idea how many hours of training are required to get a black belt?"

"As a matter of fact, I do," she responded flippantly.

Another lie.

Apparently the new Sarah Stafford wasn't exactly honest or forthcoming.

On the other hand, she didn't figure she owed a stranger in a parking lot any truths about her life.

"Please, continue with your...not stripping," he said.

She removed a pair of old cowboy boots from the back of her car and shoved her feet into the soft, worn leather. Then she grabbed the faded denim jacket—"borrowed" from Zack Kruger when they'd dated back in high school—and shoved her arms through the sleeves.

And yes, Zack was one of those guys who'd been all wrong for her—and she'd been even more wrong for him. A fact that she regretted to this day, even if he didn't seem to be holding a grudge.

"From cool business executive to sexy cowgirl in half a minute."

The stranger's quiet musing yanked Sarah back to the present; the blatant appreciation in his gaze made her blood heat in her veins.

And because she was obviously attracted to this man and didn't want to be, her response came out uncharacteristically sharp. "Why are you still here?"

"Because that—" he gestured to the vehicle parked beside hers, apparently unperturbed by her sharp tone "—is my car."

"I'm hardly blocking your path," she pointed out.

"No," he acknowledged. "But I'm wary of your black belt. And your pepper spray."

She had to press her lips together to prevent them from curving. Because the man was good-looking *and* effortlessly charming—and she really didn't want to be charmed.

She grabbed her purse and closed the hatch. "Drive safely."

"I'll be fine," he assured her, and winked again. "Yours are the most dangerous curves I've seen in this town."

THE STUNNINGLY SEXY brunette rolled deep blue eyes before walking away, and Andrew Morrow could hardly fault her dismissive response. His parting remark had been ridiculously cheesy—proof that he'd been out of the game too long and was trying too hard.

He was also late, he realized, as he pulled out of the parking lot.

And Kyle Landry knew it, too, as evidenced by his pointed look at his watch when Andrew walked into his kitchen.

"I got caught in traffic," he said by way of explanation.

His friend chuckled at that. "At least you brought your sense of humor."

"So why did you want to meet here instead of at Diggers'?"

Here was The Home Station, where Kyle was the executive chef. Before the restaurant opened, residents of the northern Nevada town had to venture beyond its borders in pursuit of upscale dining. Now people came from Battle Mountain and Elko and even farther to eat at The Home Station. As a result, reservations were typically booked weeks—and sometimes months—in advance.

"The bok choy in our produce shipment was subpar, requiring me to make some last-minute tweaks to tonight's menu," Kyle explained.

Andrew didn't need to ask what constituted subpar, because he was undoubtedly as particular as his friend when it came to the ingredients he used in his recipes. In fact, on one memorable occasion, he'd sent an assistant out for Madagascan vanilla beans and she returned with Tahitian. According to other members of the staff, Andrew had gone on a rant not unlike those seen on so many cooking shows on reality TV.

"Let's chat in my office," Kyle said, leading the way through a kitchen already bustling with activity.

He poured them each a mug of coffee from the pot behind his desk and waited for Andrew to settle in the chair across from him before he asked, "Did you and Caroline finalize terms?"

Caroline Bennett was the namesake and daughter of the original owner of Sweet Caroline's, reputed to be northern Nevada's favorite bakery.

Andrew nodded. "We did."

Kyle grinned and lifted his mug. "To new beginnings."

Andrew drank. "I'd be lying if I said I didn't have reservations, but I'm going to do it, anyway."

When he graduated from Escoffier's Austin campus of the Texas Culinary Academy—where he'd met Kyle—he'd dreamed of someday owning his own bakery. But he knew that he was going to need a lot more experience—and a significant nest egg—before pursuing that dream, and so he'd taken a job as an assistant pastry chef at Divine, a popular French restaurant in Beaumont, Texas.

Divine was a good place to work, and he was mostly given free rein when it came to the creation of his desserts. Three years later, just when he was starting to think it might be time to pursue other opportunities, Miranda Ross started to work at the restaurant. The new sommelier was knowledgeable, experienced and passionate—and not only about wine. Two years after that, they were married, and Andrew had shelved his dreams in favor of keeping the job that paid their rent.

But he and Miranda were divorced now, and when she'd moved to Napa Valley with her winemaking boyfriend, Andrew had realized there was nothing keeping him in Beaumont. And then Kyle had told him that there was a prime opportunity in Haven, if he was willing to take it.

"Of course you have reservations," his friend said to him now. "Running your own business is a lot different than making desserts for someone else's customers, but I have no doubt that you'll succeed."

Andrew appreciated the other man's confidence. Because he'd done the research, he knew that any new business was a risky venture. But he wasn't really starting a new business. Rather he was taking over a well-established one, making some minor renovations to the property, giving it a new name and updating the menu.

Still, it was those planned changes that increased the risk. People were generally creatures of habit, opting for what was familiar over trying something new. But Caroline had assured him that so long as he continued to offer her famous chocolate peanut butter banana croissants and the wildly popular raspberry bliss bars—the proprietary recipes being included as part of their deal—the local residents would overlook all else.

"Were you nervous when you took the reins here?" Andrew asked his friend.

"Sure," Kyle agreed. "At the same time, knowing that there would always be a job for me in the kitchen at Jo's was something of a safety net—albeit one I wasn't entirely convinced my mom wouldn't strangle me with."

Andrew chuckled. Though he'd only met Jolene Landry a couple times, the proprietor of the local pizzeria had made an impression. And so did her pizza, which was why her revered establishment was almost a place of worship more than a restaurant.

"Plus it wasn't my money I had to worry about losing," his friend acknowledged. "Liam Gilmore owns the inn and the restaurant, so he's the one who has to reconcile the income and expenses—I just cook."

"That makes me feel so much better," Andrew said dryly.

"You want to feel better? You should try some of the desserts left over from last night's menu."

"I'm not sure how that's going to help."

"Trust me," Kyle said, already halfway out the door.

He returned a few minutes later with a square plate upon which samples of three desserts had been arranged.

"New York–style cheesecake with macerated strawberry topping, lemon crème brûlée with fresh blackberries and a chocolate hazelnut éclair topped with chocolate ganache and toasted crushed hazelnuts."

"You can't honestly expect me to eat all of this."

"Just try a bite of each," Kyle urged.

Because it seemed important to his friend—and because each of the desserts looked delicious—Andrew did so. And then went back for a second taste.

"I have to offer kudos to your pastry chef," he said, when he finally set down his fork.

"We don't have a pastry chef," Kyle told him. "For as long as The Home Station has been in operation, Sweet Caroline's has supplied our desserts."

"What are you going to do when Sweet Caroline's closes its doors?" Andrew asked curiously.

"I was hoping to enter into the same arrangement with the bakery's new owner—which is why I'm happy to know it's going to be you."

"It's going to take me some time to pack up my life in Texas and make the move," he felt compelled to warn his friend.

"In the meantime, I think I've convinced Bonnie, who's been Caroline's right hand for more than a dozen years, to continue making the desserts for us."

"If she's that good, why don't you hire her to work here?" Andrew wondered aloud.

"She's that good," Kyle confirmed. "But we don't have the space for a pastry chef. Besides, I've heard that she's polishing up her résumé for the new owner of Sweet Caroline's."

Before Andrew could respond to that, a knock sounded on the door.

"Chef?"

"Perfect timing," Kyle said to Andrew, before issuing an invitation to his visitor to "Come in."

The door opened and a sixty-something woman with blunt-cut gray hair and sharp blue eyes entered. Over jeans and a T-shirt, she wore a long white apron with Sweet Caroline's logo embroidered in pink on the front and pink Crocs on her feet.

She offered the white bakery box that she carried to Kyle. "Per your request."

"Thank you," he said, already opening the lid to peer inside.

"Tonight's offerings," he explained to Andrew, showing him the contents. "Hummingbird cake with cream cheese frosting, bourbon chocolate mousse garnished with freshly whipped cream and dark chocolate shavings and an apple toffee tart, which will be served warm with a scoop of freshly spun cinnamon ice cream."

"I'll bring that over later this afternoon," the woman promised.

"I'm tempted to pick up my fork again and dig in," Andrew said, and it wasn't an exaggeration.

Kyle grinned. "Bonnie, this is Andrew Morrow—the soon-to-be new owner of Sweet Caroline's."

"It's a pleasure to meet you," Bonnie said politely.

"Did you make these?" Andrew asked.

"I did," she confirmed.

"Do you know how to make those banana peanut butter croissants that everyone is talking about?"

"Chocolate peanut butter banana croissants," she said. "And yes, I do. As well as the raspberry bliss bars."

Andrew wasn't usually impulsive, but he did trust his instincts—and his instincts were telling him that this was an opportunity he shouldn't let slip away. "I hear you might be looking for a job when Caroline closes the doors of her shop."

"I might be," she allowed.

"How much does Caroline pay you?"

"Not nearly enough," she told him. Then she shrugged. "Lucky for you, my husband retired half a dozen years ago with a really good pension and, as much as I love him, I need a reason to get out of the house for a few hours every morning, so I'm willing to continue working for not nearly enough."

Andrew grinned. "In that case, you're hired."

CHAPTER TWO

"I DON'T SEE any food," Claire noted, sliding into the booth that Sarah had claimed on the "bar" side of Diggers' Bar & Grill.

"I didn't know what you wanted to eat."

"I've been up since six and I worked through lunch—I want food."

Sarah had also skipped lunch, too nervous about The Big Confrontation with her parents to even consider putting anything in her knotted stomach. But those knots had since loosened enough to allow her to realize she was hungry.

Claire lifted her hand to snag the attention of their server.

"What can I get for you?" Alexa asked.

"We're going to start with the appetizer platter. And I'll have a glass of—" she looked at Sarah "—what are you drinking?"

"It's a cab-merlot blend from Washington State."

"That sounds good, too," Claire decided.

"If you're both drinking the same, do you want a carafe?" Alexa asked.

"I can walk home from here," Sarah noted.

"And Devin's picking me up later, so I don't have to worry about driving," Claire chimed in.

"I'd say that's a 'yes' on the carafe," Sarah told their server.

"I'll put your order in and be right back with that wine," Alexa promised.

While they waited for their food, Sarah told her friend about the meeting with her parents during which she'd shared her decision to leave Blake Mining to work with Claire at Twilight Valley.

"Were they supportive of your plans?" Claire asked cautiously.

Sarah snorted. "My dad accused me of going through another rebellious phase." She lifted her glass to sip her wine. "They've never considered the possibility that I might want something different than what they want for me, and I've finally stopped expecting that they ever will."

"I'm sorry."

She shrugged. "Oh, and when I gave the hard copy of my resignation to my mom, she asked for my access card."

"You're kidding."

Now Sarah shook her head. "I'm being punished for wanting to do my own thing, which is ridiculous, because I wasn't even a cog in the wheel of Blake Mining. I was more like a foreign-language sticker slapped on the outside of the machine—necessary but not particularly useful."

"But as long as you were working in the family business, they felt as if they had some degree of control over you," Claire noted.

"Maybe."

"Trust me," her friend said. "I have some experience with controlling parents—and a former fiancé who wanted to pick right up where they left off. Now you're getting the benefit of thousands of dollars of therapy for free."

"You didn't need the therapy," Sarah said. "You just needed to come back to Haven and find your own place and purpose at Twilight Valley. Although falling in love with my cousin might have also played a part in your newfound bliss."

A smile spread across Claire's face. "The icing on the cake. And that's what we need to celebrate," she decided. "Cake."

"Let's see if we can get through the appetizers first," Sarah said, when Alexa set the platter in the middle of the table.

"Speaking of cake," Claire said, reaching for a potato skin filled with bacon and cheese. "Sweet Caroline's is officially closing its doors in two weeks."

"Are you sure?" Sarah asked. "The rumors about a sale have been circulating for so long, I stopped paying attention."

"I'm sure," her friend confirmed.

"And then the era of the chocolate peanut butter banana croissant will officially come to an end," she lamented.

"I'm *not* so sure about that," Claire said. "Apparently the new owner has already hired Bonnie Reidel to work with him."

"How is it that you've been at the ranch all day and yet you still know all the latest gossip?" Sarah wondered aloud.

"Actually, me and Devin had an appointment at the bank this afternoon, after which we stopped at The Daily Grind where we heard Madison Russell dishing the details to Julie Keswick."

"How would Madison Russell know?"

"Her sister works in the kitchen at The Home Station."

"Which doesn't at all help connect the dots," Sarah told her friend.

"You're right," Claire acknowledged. "All I know is that Madison sounded as if she knew what she was talking about."

"So why did you have an appointment at the bank?" Sarah asked, circling back to pick up that thread of their conversation.

"I need a loan to build another barn at Twilight Valley."

"Your husband hasn't offered to pay for it?"

"He has," Claire admitted. "But I don't want his business propping up my business."

"You know he's got more money than he could ever spend in his lifetime—even after paying for a dozen new barns." Because Devin wasn't just family money rich; he'd made his own, equally impressive, fortune developing mobile apps.

"Well, I don't need a dozen barns," Claire said. "I only need one more. And while I might stubbornly refuse to take his money—his words—I'm also smart enough to know that having him with me when I met with the loan officer would make it next to impossible for the bank to turn down my request."

"Then you were already in town when I texted you," Sarah realized.

Claire nodded.

"So why did it take you half an hour to get here?"

Her friend lifted her wineglass to hide the smile that curved her lips.

"Forget I asked," Sarah said. "But now I know why Devin has yet to put his house on the market, more than two years after moving out to Twilight Valley. It's so that you have a convenient love nest whenever you're in town."

"We don't stop by the house every time we're in town."

"I don't need to know. And I don't want to know that you were having sex in the middle of the afternoon when I haven't had sex at any time of the day in…a very long time."

"You could end that drought anytime you want," Claire said. "Any guy in this bar would be happy to go home with you. All you have to do is communicate interest with a crook of your finger."

"Unfortunately I've known most of the guys in this bar my whole life, and I am *not* interested."

"How are we doing here?" Alexa asked, as she removed the empty platter from the table.

"Good," Sarah said.

"Still hungry," Claire countered. "We need nachos."

"Chicken or beef?"

"Chicken. With extra salsa and sour cream."

"I can't believe you're still hungry," Sarah said, reaching for the carafe to top off their wineglasses as Alexa walked away.

Claire winked. "I worked up an appetite today."

"Don't want to know," Sarah reminded her friend.

But maybe it was time to take the initiative to end the drought.

"Do you think I could borrow Eduardo this weekend?" she asked, referring to the German shepherd/collie cross that her friend had taken home from the local shelter a few years earlier.

"You want to use my dog to pick up men?" Claire guessed.

"Jenna met Harrison at the dog park," she pointed out to her friend.

And while Sarah was happy that her sister had found "the one," Jenna's new romance seemed to shine a harsh spotlight on Sarah's solitary status.

"And they've got a great meet-cute story," Claire agreed. "But it's *their* story. Instead of trying to replicate it, you need to be open to writing your own."

"I'm open," Sarah insisted.

"With guards at the gate."

She frowned as she considered her friend's claim.

"And I know that there are reasons for the guards," Claire said, not unsympathetically. "But if you really want to meet someone, you're going to have to tell the guards to stand down."

"Actually I did meet someone today. Sort of."

"How do you 'sort of' meet someone?" her friend asked, her interest piqued.

"We chatted for a few minutes but went our separate ways without introductions."

"Obviously he made an impression or you wouldn't be telling me about him now."

Sarah sipped her wine. "He thought I was a stripper."

Claire hooted with laughter. "Ohmygod—you have to tell me more."

"I threatened him with pepper spray."

"The guards were clearly on duty," her friend noted.

"Today is the day I started living the life I want," she reminded Claire. "And I don't want any more casual hookups."

"How about orgasms?" her friend asked. "Don't you want more of those?"

"I'm not sure I remember what an orgasm is."

"That's just sad."

Sarah had to smile, because while her lack of a love life *was* sad, being with her BFF made her happy. And this—hanging out with Claire and drinking wine—was exactly what she needed today.

Her smile slipped along with her foot when Claire kicked her under the table. "Serious hottie at nine o'clock."

"Is it nine o'clock already?"

Her friend laughed. "How many glasses of wine have you had?"

She stared at the garnet-colored liquid in her glass. "I think this is three."

"He's at the bar now," Claire said, her gaze focused in that direction.

"Who?"

"The tall, dark and very sexy stranger."

"You're married to my cousin," Sarah reminded her friend.

"And very happily," Claire acknowledged. "But my marital status has absolutely no bearing on his hotness."

"I'm not turning around, because Ellis Hagen's sitting at the bar, and every time he catches my eye, he thinks I'm flirting with him."

Her friend chuckled at that.

"He's chatting with Duke but scoping out the room, almost as if he's looking for someone. Not Ellis, Hottie," she clarified before Sarah could ask. "And you don't have to turn around, because he's got a mug of beer in hand now and is heading in this direction."

Sarah sipped her wine, her eyes widening as the man who'd snagged her friend's attention stepped into view. "I know him."

"Do you?" Claire sounded intrigued.

"Well, no. Not really." Before she could look away, his gaze snagged hers and he smiled in a way that made her feel tingly inside. Or maybe that was the third glass of wine. "But our paths crossed earlier today."

Claire's lips curved as he made his way toward their table. "He's the one who thought you were a stripper?"

"He's the one," Sarah confirmed.

"It was an honest mistake," Hottie said, inserting himself into their conversation. "Based on the fact that she was taking her clothes off—"

"My jacket," Sarah interrupted indignantly. "I was taking off my jacket."

"And your Jimmy Choos," he noted.

"That's where your assumption proves faulty," she retorted. "Because strippers never take off their shoes."

Claire's eyes narrowed on the stranger. "And how did you know they were Jimmy Choos?"

His brows lifted. "A man can't know shoes?"

"Not a lot of straight unmarried men do."

"How about a straight, unmarried man who grew up with a sister obsessed with designer footwear?" he suggested.

"A possibility," Claire agreed with a nod, her face lighting up when she saw another man walk into the bar. "And there's *my* hottie—I mean *husband*."

"This was supposed to be girls' night," Sarah reminded her.

"It was—and it was fun," her friend said, already sliding out of her seat. "But now I'm going to go home with my hottie husband to have a different kind of fun."

If they'd still been alone, Sarah might have reminded Claire that she'd already had fun with her husband that day. Instead, she glanced at her watch and said, "I should probably be heading home, too."

"No." Claire held up a hand. "Stay. Finish your wine." She nudged the stranger toward the seat she'd vacated. "Hottie here will keep you company."

"But—"

"No *buts*." Claire leaned down to brush a kiss to her friend's cheek, whispering in her ear as she did so. "Tell the guards to stand down and have fun."

"Hottie?" he said quizzically, when he and Sarah were alone.

"You'll have to forgive Claire. The filter between her brain and her mouth sometimes gets washed away by alcohol," Sarah told him. "Whereas I generally just say what I'm thinking even when I'm stone-cold sober."

"So now I have to ask—do *you* think I'm a hottie?"

She held his gaze for a minute before responding. "I wouldn't disagree with Claire's assessment, but I'd also deduct points for the fact that you've got no game."

"True fact," he said with a nod. "I'm seriously out of practice when it comes to flirting with pretty women."

"Acknowledging that you have a problem is the first step toward solving it."

"And the second step?"

She gestured to the bench Claire had vacated. "Practice."

He slid into the booth with his beer. "Are you inviting me to practice on you?"

"I'm inviting you to share the nachos that Claire obviously forgot she ordered," Sarah said, as Alexa delivered the platter of chips covered in shredded chicken and melted cheese to the table.

Besides, she could use the practice, too, and what was the harm in flirting with a stranger she was unlikely to ever see again?

"I won't say *no* to that," Hottie said.

"Well, dig in," she urged.

When they'd made a dent in the mountain of chips, she finally ventured to ask, "Are you new in town or just passing through?"

"Is there a right answer to that question?" he wondered aloud.

Sarah shook her head. "Either way, I'm not going home with you."

His sigh sounded sincerely regretful. "It was the dangerous curves line, wasn't it? I totally blew any chance with you with that line."

"You never had any chance with me," she said, dipping a chip into the sour cream.

"Ouch."

She grimaced. "I didn't mean it like that."

"How did you mean it?"

"This is the new me," she'd said, gesturing to the denim jacket she'd donned over her designer dress. "And the new me doesn't sleep with men she just met."

He swallowed a mouthful of beer. "Any chance we can go back in time and introduce me to the old you?"

That surprised a laugh out of her. "A tempting thought."

"Obviously not tempting enough."

She wiped her fingers on a paper napkin. "I spent the first seventeen years of my life flouting expectations and the next fifteen trying to make up for all the mistakes I made," she confided. "Finally, today, I'm starting to live the life that *I* want to live."

"And you don't want to explore this chemistry between us?" he guessed.

"I want—*I need*—to remember that every action has consequences."

"I'm sure I saw a condom dispenser when I was in the men's room earlier."

Apparently the man had more game than she'd given him credit for, because their playful banter was seriously turning her on. Or maybe it was the chemistry he'd mentioned, because the air was fairly crackling with electricity.

"Not the consequences I was thinking about, but good to know."

"So tell me what the life you want to live looks like," he suggested.

"I'm still figuring that out," she admitted. "But I can tell you that it doesn't look like a nine-to-five office job that bores me to tears.

"Although I did like the wardrobe. And the paycheck that allowed me to afford the designer labels."

"I like the denim jacket and cowboy boots," he said. "Even if the jacket's a little big, because it suggests that you've got a sentimental streak."

She scoffed. "Which only proves that you don't know me at all."

"You kept your ex-boyfriend's jacket for…how many years?"

"How can you be sure that it doesn't belong to a current boyfriend?" she asked him.

"Because if you had a current boyfriend, you wouldn't be sitting here with me. And you would have threatened me with his existence rather than nonexistent pepper spray in the parking lot."

"I do have pepper spray," she said, reaching into her purse for the travel-size can to prove it.

His brows lifted. "That looks like hairspray."

"Have you ever got hairspray in your eyes?" she challenged.

"I can't say that I have," he acknowledged. "I'm usually careful to avoid such mishaps when I'm styling my hair."

She'd always appreciated a man who could make a joke at his own expense, and a reluctant smile curved her lips now. "Well, if you had, you'd know that it would effectively repel an attacker."

"Though probably not as effectively as a black belt," he noted.

"Which you've already surmised that I don't have. Not a brown or green one, either," she confided.

"And the jacket?" he prompted.

"You're right about that, too," she finally said, her thumb rubbing over one of the metal buttons. "It belongs to an ex-boyfriend."

"Recent ex or long-ago ex?"

"Both."

He considered that for a minute. "Any chance he'll be coming back for it?"

She shook her head. "He lives in Seattle now."

"Seattle isn't so far," he pointed out.

"With his new girlfriend," she told him.

"Ah."

Somehow the single syllable managed to communicate a whole lot of understanding.

But she shrugged off his sympathy. "It was time for both of us to let go and move on. Zack just realized it before I did."

He swallowed another mouthful of beer. "Do you miss him?"

"No." She abandoned the button on her jacket to reach for her wineglass again. "But I do miss the possibility of a future with him. Or at least the possibility of a future with *someone*."

"You're only thirty-two years old," he noted. "You've still got plenty of time to build a future with someone."

Her gaze narrowed. "How do you know how old I am?"

"Math," he said simply. "Seventeen plus fifteen."

"So you were paying attention when I was talking," she mused.

"In the desperate hope that my attentiveness might somehow compensate for my lack of game."

"I think you've got more game than either of us gave you credit for." She pushed aside her still half-full glass. "Or I've had too much wine."

"How much is too much?" he asked.

"Enough to know I'm at risk of doing something stupid."

"Are you talking about me? Because I'm absolutely willing to overlook the insult if I'm the something stupid you want to do."

She laughed again, but rather than answering his question, she asked her own. "So how long are you going to be in town?"

"I'm headed to the airport in the morning," he admitted.

"Flying back to... Texas?" she deduced, hearing just a hint of the trademark Southern accent with a twist.

"Good guess," he said.

"Well, I hope you got to see some of the sights while you were here."

"There are sights?"

"Ouch," she said, feigning insult on behalf of her hometown. "We might not have the Alamo or a space center, but we've got some sights—that may or may not be of interest to anyone who doesn't live here."

"Since my time in Haven is nearing its end, I guess I'll have to take your word for it."

"Finish your beer, Tex," she said. "I've got a better idea."

CHAPTER THREE

"THAT'S NOT ACTUALLY my name, you know. My name's—"

"Don't tell me!"

Andrew was surprised by her vehement interjection. "You don't want to know my name?"

"If I don't know, I won't be tempted to try to look you up after you've gone back to Texas," she explained.

"Do you think you might be tempted?" he asked curiously.

She shrugged, as if reluctant to reveal too much. "It's a possibility."

He was surprised by the admission and pleased to know that the pull he was feeling wasn't entirely one-sided.

"Well, Texas is a big state," he pointed out. "And I might have a common name...like John Smith."

"Is your name John Smith?"

"No," he admitted.

"And that's why I'm going to stick with calling you Tex," she said. "It rolls off the tongue much easier than Not-John-Smith."

"And what should I call you? Parking Lot Peeler? Pepper Spray Wielder?"

She was obviously unimpressed with both of those monikers.

"Friend of Claire?" he suggested as an alternative.

"That one works," she decided, flagging the server to ask for the check only to learn that her friend had paid the tab before leaving the restaurant.

"Except that Friend of Claire doesn't exactly roll off the tongue," he noted. "How about F-O-C? Or FOC?"

She slid him a look. "No. For obvious reasons."

"Okay, Friend of Claire," he relented. "What's the plan?"

"We're going to start with the Main Street walking tour," she told him.

"It's a little chilly for a stroll, don't you think?" he asked, when she took a minute to fasten the buttons that ran down the front of her jacket before they exited the building.

"You have to walk to appreciate the atmosphere of Main Street." She stuffed her hands in her pockets. "Plus I've had three glasses of wine, so I don't think I should be driving."

"I've had one beer," he told her. "I could drive."

"Then you can take us to Crooked Creek Ranch after the walking tour."

Which turned out to be exactly that—a casual stroll down the primary route through the center of town. Both sides of the street were lined with buildings that housed shops or businesses, not unlike any other small town in America. What made Haven different, or at least this tour of it, was that his guide had a personal anecdote to share about each one.

"We'll start here," she said, gesturing to the doors of the restaurant through which they'd just exited. "Diggers' Bar & Grill, a landmark in Haven and favorite local eating establishment."

"I can vouch for the nachos—and the beer," he said.

"Duke, the owner and sometimes bartender, takes pride in his menu—and he doesn't tolerate fighting in his bar. The punishment for anyone who breaks the rule is banishment from the premises for a full year, which is probably why no one has dared to throw a punch inside since Doug Holland gave Jerry Tate a black eye six or seven years ago.

"More recently, however, there was a stabbing in the back parking lot. A group of out-of-towners, already drunk, stopped in for a drink. Duke refused to serve them and kicked them out of the bar, and when they started fighting among themselves, one of the guys pulled a knife."

"I understand now why you were a little apprehensive when I showed up in the parking lot."

"You caught me by surprise," she admitted. "And I'm not a fan of surprises."

"Then I'll apologize," he said. "Though I'm not sorry I got to see you taking your clothes off."

She huffed out an exasperated breath. "It was only my jacket."

He grinned. "I know, I just like seeing you blush."

"I don't blush."

"Since I'm the one looking at the pretty pink color in your cheeks, I'm going to have to disagree."

"Continuing the tour," she said, stepping away from the streetlight that illuminated her face to cross the road.

He followed.

"The hardware store." Easily identified by the sign as well as the displays in the windows.

"A staple in any community," he noted.

"This one is owned by Glenn Davis," Friend of Claire told him. "He was called out to change the locks at Frieda Zimmerman's house three times in as many months before he took the hint and asked the widow to have dinner with him. They've been almost inseparable since that first date, proving that people in their seventies can find love, too."

"Good to know I've still got more than three decades to figure things out," he noted.

"Obviously you're a glass-half-full person," she remarked, as she started walking again. "My takeaway from that story is that I've only got three and a half decades left."

"Half-full or half-empty, the important thing is that the glass is refillable," he quipped.

"A true optimist," she mused, pausing in front of The Trading Post next. "Several years ago, a young clerk was shot during an armed robbery here, setting up a conflict between local defense attorney Katelyn Gilmore and her new husband, Sheriff Reid Davidson."

"Who won?" he asked, curious about the outcome despite not knowing any of the characters.

"The client ended up pleading guilty, and Katelyn and Reid recently celebrated their seventh anniversary."

"A happy ending."

She nodded. "For Sierra Hart and Deacon Parrish, too, who battled over the last box of Frosted Flakes in the cereal aisle before falling in love."

"Apparently your grocery store is a real meet market. M-E-E-T," he was quick to clarify when she slid him a look.

"It's also where Haylee Gilmore met her future mother-in-law for the first time—when she was four months pregnant."

"Who was pregnant? Haylee or her mother-in-law?"

Friend of Claire rolled her eyes. "Haylee. With twins."

"How do you know all this stuff?" he wondered aloud.

"I get my coffee at The Daily Grind every morning."

Before he could ask her to explain that cryptic response, she gestured to Anthology Books. "Do you know who Quinn Ellison is?"

"The mystery writer?"

She nodded. "Every time Quinn launches a new book, she kicks off her tour at this bookstore."

He was a fan of the author's work and knew that her tours took her to major cities around the country. "I wonder what brings a bestselling novelist to a small town in northern Nevada."

"She lives in Cooper's Corners, about fifteen miles from here," Friend of Claire told him.

"No kidding?"

"No kidding," she confirmed. "She's also a very big fan of Sweet Caroline's chocolate peanut butter banana croissants."

"You're not the first person who's mentioned those croissants to me today," he remarked.

"I don't know what time your flight is, but if you can get to the bakery early in the morning and get your hands on one, you won't regret it," she told him.

"They're really that good?"

"Better," she said. "And possibly only available for a limited time, if it turns out that the rumors about Caroline's plans to sell the bakery are true."

It was the perfect opportunity for Andrew to confess, to tell her that he knew for a fact that Caroline *was* selling the bakery—because she was selling it *to him.*

But Friend of Claire had already moved on to Granny's Attic, a secondhand store, and the opportunity slipped away. Next up after that was Fur, Feathers and Fins for pet supplies, followed by Footloose, a shoe store.

"Across the street is our local second-run movie theater—and it looks like tonight's movie just let out," she said, as the doors opened and a stream—or at least a trickle—of people spilled out onto the sidewalk. "In the summer, the theater offers early and late screenings and sometimes weekend matinees, but during the offseason, there's only one screening—and only Wednesday through Saturday."

She was quiet for a minute, watching the moviegoers disperse. Most of them were teenagers, he guessed, hanging in groups with a few couples paired off and holding hands.

"I had my first date official date with Zack Kruger in that theater," she confided to him now. "A long, long time ago."

"The original owner of the denim jacket?" he guessed.

She nodded and smiled, a little wistfully, he thought.

"He was the first boy I ever kissed. The first boy I ever loved. But that night, our first date, we saw *Mission: Impossible III* and then went to Jo's for pizza." She gestured toward a group heading away from the theater. "Which is probably where they're going now. Jo's is famous for its pie and a popular hangout for local teens."

"Is there anything else to do for fun in Haven?" he asked, belatedly realizing that was something he should have considered before signing on the dotted line.

"There's a bowling alley on Station Street and the community center has a library, gymnasium, ice rink and swimming pool. But the most popular destination is Adventure Village, a family-friendly recreation park. It has paintball fields, a rock-climbing wall, laser tag, go-karts, mini-putt and an arcade."

"Did you have a first date with anyone there?" he asked curiously.

"No, but my cousin Jason did. And three months later, he and Alyssa were engaged for real."

"As opposed to...fake engaged?"

"Yeah. It's a long story," she said, crossing the street again and turning back toward Diggers'.

"This is The Daily Grind—formerly Cal's Coffee Shop."

"Where you get your coffee in the mornings," he recalled. "And apparently the hottest gossip, too."

She nodded. "And where Hope Bradford was enjoying a latte when she was reunited with Michael Gilmore, her high school sweetheart, ten years after leaving town and breaking his heart."

"Am I supposed to know who that is?"

She seemed surprised by his question.

"Lainey Howard from *Rockwood Ridge*," she clarified.

"That's a... TV show?" he guessed.

She shook her head. "I can't believe you've never seen *Rockwood Ridge*."

"Apparently a popular TV show," he realized.

"Very popular," she said. "And Hope was a semi-famous actor who gave up her Hollywood career to marry MG, a local rancher, and teach drama at Westmount High School."

"So you have sights *and* celebrities in Haven, apparently."

"We do," she confirmed.

As they'd wandered up and down Main Street, he'd found himself enjoying her company so much that he'd almost managed to forget the air temperature was barely forty-six degrees. But now that they were standing outside a coffee shop, the prospect of a hot drink was decidedly appealing.

"Since we're here, do you want to grab a cup of coffee?"

"I wouldn't mind a latte," Friend of Claire said. "But we can't walk in there together."

"Why not?"

"Did you not hear what I said about The Daily Grind being the source of all the hottest gossip?"

Of course he'd heard, but he'd been certain she was exaggerating, at least a little.

"Do you really think that if you walk in there with me, people will start talking?"

"You sat at my table at Diggers'—I guarantee that people are already talking," she told him.

He was surprised—but not bothered—by the idea that people might be talking about him in conjunction with Friend of Claire. Although maybe that was because he didn't actually live in this town.

Not yet, anyway.

But apparently she *was* bothered by the idea, so he said, "Do you want to wait out here while I go in to get the drinks, then?"

"If you order two coffees, Madison—the barista working tonight—is going to crane her neck peering out the window, trying to see who the second one is for," she warned.

"Paranoid much?" he asked, amused rather than concerned.

"Trust me, I'm doing you a favor. *You* wait out here, *I'll* get the drinks."

"Madison won't crane her neck peering out the window to see who's with *you*?" he challenged.

"Sure, but she doesn't know you, so her efforts won't gain any traction."

"Okay, I'll wait here," he relented. "Just regular coffee, black."

"Got it." She nudged him back a few steps, away from the coffee shop windows, and winked at him. "Might as well make Madison work for it."

A few minutes later, they continued on their way with paper cups in hand.

"The Stagecoach Inn—which is probably where you're staying because it's the only decent hotel in town," she noted, pausing on the sidewalk in front of the boutique hotel. "In fact, the only other option for short-term rental accommodations is the Dusty Boots Motel, out by the highway."

"I can neither confirm nor deny in an effort to minimize the risk of revealing information you don't want to know about me."

She chuckled softly. "Okay, so I'll pretend that you didn't hear the history of the inn when you checked in and tell you that the original building dates back to actual stagecoach days. Sadly, it was quickly forgotten when rail travel became more popular and, by the time Hershel Livingston bought it some fifteen years ago, it was falling apart."

"Now *that* name sounds familiar," he said. "Didn't he make his fortune in casinos and brothels?"

"Ironic, don't you think, that he planned to settle in Haven, one of only a few places in Nevada where gambling and prostitution are illegal?"

Apparently it was a rhetorical question, because before he had a chance to respond, she continued, "Anyway, Hershel spent millions on the rehab of the building, then abandoned the project just as it was nearing completion."

"Why would he do that?"

"No one knows for sure," she told him. "One theory is that his Las Vegas bride visited Haven during the renovation process and immediately hated it here. Another is that she caught the billionaire dallying with a local woman—or wo*men*."

"That would explain why she wasn't fond of the town," Andrew surmised.

"Whatever the reason, Hershel abruptly ordered his crew to vacate the property and put it up for sale. Eventually Liam Gilmore decided to finish the renovations and reopen it as a boutique hotel."

"There seem to be a lot of people in this town named Gilmore," he noted.

She nodded. "I probably should have started the tour with the fact that the Blakes and the Gilmores were two of the founding families of Haven more than one hundred and fifty years ago. Samuel Blake was a down-on-his-luck businessman from Omaha, Nebraska, and Everett Gilmore was a struggling farmer in nearby Plattsmouth. Both came to Haven after purchasing a parcel of land from a developer, only to discover, when they arrived in Nevada with their respective families and worldly possessions, that they'd purchased the same parcel of land.

"Both title deeds were stamped with the same date, making it impossible to know who had the legitimate claim to the property, so they agreed to share it, using the natural divide of Eighteen Mile Creek—more commonly known as Crooked Creek—as the boundary between their lands."

"At least they were able to come to a peaceful resolution," Andrew remarked.

Friend of Claire smiled wryly. "Except that it wasn't. Because the Gilmores arrived first and had already started to build their home in the valley on the west side of the creek, the Blakes had to build in the rocky hills on the east side. The Gilmores' cattle immediately benefited from grazing on more hospitable terrain, while the Blakes struggled from year to year to keep their herd viable. Then they discovered silver and gold in their hills and gave up ranching in favor of mining.

"Now we're back to where we started," she noted, pausing in front of the bar and grill to drop her empty cup in a trash can.

"And now I have to admit that you were right—Haven has some sights."

And he was staring at the most beautiful one of all, though he managed to keep *that* thought to himself this time for fear that she would roll her eyes and walk away again.

"Are you still good to drive?" she asked, when they'd made their way around to the parking lot at the back of the restaurant.

He nodded.

"Then I feel confident in saying, you ain't seen nothing yet."

CHAPTER FOUR

ANDREW WAS SURPRISED when Friend of Claire pulled out her own keys, but she only unlocked her vehicle to retrieve a blanket before climbing into the passenger seat of his rental car.

She'd said that they were going to Crooked Creek Ranch, but she hadn't given him a street name and number to punch into his navigation app.

"The address will take us to the main house, and that's not where we want to go," she'd said, when he asked.

Which left him entirely dependent on her directions. Not that he was worried she might lead him astray, just that he liked knowing where he was going. After about twenty minutes and several turns, he discovered that they'd abandoned asphalt streets in favor of gravel roads.

As his midsize sedan bumped along over the ruts, he cringed at the sound of the stones kicked up by the tires pinging against the undercarriage.

"I'm not sure the rental company is going to appreciate me taking this vehicle off-road."

"We're not off-road," she denied. "We're just on a private—and rarely used—road."

He jolted as the front driver's side wheel dropped into a pot-hole—or maybe it was a sinkhole—and again at the scraping sound when it managed to crawl out again.

"And now I know why there are so many trucks in this town," he noted, grateful that he'd paid for the extra insurance when he rented the vehicle.

"City boy," she said, sounding amused.

"Guilty," he agreed.

They drove for another five minutes or so along the rutted surface. There were no streetlights out here; no signs of any civilization.

"You can stop here," she told him.

He pressed on the brake and leaned forward to peer out the windshield. "Right here? In the middle of nowhere?"

"Sure," she agreed.

"I thought you said we were going to Crooked Creek Ranch."

"This is it," she said.

All he could see was…nothing.

And when he shifted into Park and turned off the engine, killing the lights, nothing but dark.

"I expected a ranch would have buildings. And cows."

"We're near the northern boundary of the property," she said. "Far away from the house and the barns and the cows—though sometimes the small herd is brought up here for grazing later in the season."

"Are you sure we won't get arrested for trespassing?"

"I'm sure," she said. "Jesse Blake might come around with his shotgun if he thinks strangers are nosing around on his property, but he won't call the sheriff."

"Am I supposed to feel reassured that we won't get arrested but we might get shot?"

She chuckled as she tucked the blanket under her arm and opened the door. "We're not going to get arrested *or* shot, I promise."

Though still wary, when she reached for his hand, he knew that he'd willingly follow wherever she led.

But she didn't lead him anywhere just yet.

"Give your eyes a few minutes to adjust," she told him.

"Adjust to what?"

"You'll see."

"I don't think I'm going to see anything in the pitch-dark," he countered.

But after those few minutes, he realized that it wasn't pitch-dark.

And while they were definitely in the middle of nowhere, with no streetlights or other artificial light sources to illuminate their journey, there was a narrow sliver of moon shining bright in a sky filled with more stars than he'd ever seen.

She tugged on his hand then and guided him away from the car. He stepped cautiously, aware that the terrain here was likely even rougher than the supposed road they'd driven in on and that falling and breaking his leg was not how he wanted this evening to end.

"This spot looks good," she said, stopping in the middle of the field. He could see the dark outline of trees in the distance and, beyond the trees, the peaks of the mountains spearing up to the sky.

She started to unfold the blanket and he took the opposite end to help her spread it over the grass.

Because apparently forty degrees (he was certain the temperature had dropped since they'd left town) was ideal weather to sit outside.

Or lie down, as she was now doing, stretched out on the blanket, her boot-clad feet crossed at the ankles and her hands clasped behind her head, her gaze focused on the sky.

When in Rome, he thought, and dropped to the blanket beside her, mirroring her pose.

"What do you think, Tex?" Her voice was little more than a whisper in the dark, her reverent tone not unlike that used to communicate in church.

"I think... I've never seen anything like this," he confided in a similar whisper.

He didn't consider himself a particularly religious man, but staring up at the stars, he felt certain that God did exist, and the certainty filled him with peace.

And that was before she reached her hand out to link her fingers with his again.

When tomorrow came, he'd have to focus on his future plans

and other priorities, but for tonight, he was going to enjoy the company of this fascinating and beautiful woman.

And while he was admittedly a little disappointed that she'd nixed the idea of sleeping with him, the truth was, he wasn't that man anymore, either. Casual hookups and dead-end relationships had been left far in his past, even if spending time with Friend of Claire tempted him to wish things were different.

"I hear water," he realized, after several minutes had passed in companionable silence.

"That's the creek," she told him. "It always gurgles in the spring, fed by the snowmelt from the mountains. Later in the summer, the flow will be little more than a trickle, almost inaudible."

"Have you always lived in Haven?" he asked her now.

"Always—aside from four years at college," she confirmed. "I was so excited to go away to school, to be anywhere but here. And then, when I was gone, I couldn't wait to come home.

"Because the big cities might have more in the way of amenities and opportunities, but they don't offer a view of the stars that can compare to this."

"It's truly spectacular," he agreed.

The sound of howling in the distance made them both still.

"What was that?" Andrew whispered.

"Sounded like a coyote," she said. "They tend to hunt between dusk and dawn."

"And we're stretched out on this blanket like a picnic spread," he realized.

"It's not interested in us."

"It? Or they?" he wondered aloud. "Don't they travel in packs?"

"Coyotes live in family groups but generally hunt alone or in pairs. Wolves travel—and hunt—in packs, but Nevada doesn't have an established wolf population," she told him. "We do see foxes and bobcats and even the occasional mountain lion out here, though."

"And now I'm ready to head back into town," he said.

She chuckled softly.

They were silent for several minutes, looking at the sky and listening to the quiet murmur of the creek—and the occasional howl of a coyote in the distance.

"I'm glad you brought me out here," he said. "I'm freezing my ass off, but I'm glad."

"You drove," she reminded him. "So technically, you brought me out here. And it's not *that* cold."

"You're a northern Nevada resident. I'm from southern Texas," he felt compelled to point out.

"You can go back to the car if it's too cold for you out here," she said. "Or...we could move a little closer together to conserve body heat."

"I choose option B," he immediately replied.

She laughed softly as she shifted to his side of the blanket. He put his arm around her, holding her close.

"Better?" she asked.

"So much better," he confirmed.

And it really was.

In fact, now that her body was aligned with his, he wasn't just feeling warmer but in danger of overheating.

"Can I ask you a question?"

"Sure," she agreed. "But I'm not promising to answer."

"I got the impression you wrote me off after our brief interaction in the parking lot earlier today, but when I came back to Diggers' later, you invited me to sit down with you. Why?"

It was a good question, Sarah acknowledged, and not one to which she was entirely sure of the answer. Or maybe she didn't want to admit—even to herself—that she'd found herself immediately and intensely attracted to the man now stretched out on the blanket beside her.

"As I said at the time, I knew Claire's nachos were coming and there was no way I was going to be able to eat them all myself."

"And then you took me on a walking tour of Main Street."

She shrugged. "I didn't have anything else to do."

"And then you brought me out here—or at least gave me the directions so that I could bring you out here," he clarified.

"That surprised me, too," she admitted softly.

Tex shifted so that he was propped up on an elbow, looking at Sarah as she continued to look up at the stars. "What do you mean?"

"This is one of my favorite places in the whole world—and where I come when I want to be alone. Aside from Claire, I've never brought anyone here."

"So why me? Why tonight?"

"Three glasses of wine?" she suggested lightly.

And could immediately tell by the flatness of his gaze that her response had disappointed him.

"Or maybe I realized that I've spent a lot of years keeping people at a distance and I decided it was time to let someone in."

"And so you chose someone who won't be in town long enough to expect more than you're willing to give," he guessed.

"That's a distinct possibility," she allowed. "It's also possible that I realized you're charming and funny and, for some inexplicable reason, you seemed to like me without knowing anything about me."

"I'm not opposed to knowing about you," he said. "But you won't even tell me your name."

"People often make assumptions about others on the basis of their name."

"Are you someone famous? Were you on that TV show with Hope Bradley?"

"Hope Bradford," she corrected. "And no, I'm not famous. Infamous, perhaps, but not famous."

"Sounds like there's a story there."

"More like lots of stories. You could ask anyone in town, and they'd have a story about me."

"About Friend of Claire?"

She smiled. "That would be a dead giveaway, because she was my partner in crime most of the time."

"What if I don't want to hear the stories that everyone knows? What if I want to know something that no one else does?"

"I'm not sure that's possible," she said lightly. "Because Claire knows everything."

"Okay, tell me something that only a handful of close friends know," he suggested.

"Hmm." She took a minute to consider his request before responding, "I have a tattoo."

"Do you?"

"I do," she confirmed.

"Where is it?"

"That's something even fewer people know," she told him.

"Shoulder blade?"

She scowled. "Why was that your first guess?"

"Shoulders, ankles and wrists are the most common places that women choose to get ink."

"How do you know that?"

He shrugged. "I know a lot of useless information."

"Well, if I'd known that, I might have opted to be inked somewhere else," she confided. "I hate being predictable."

"So what is it? A heart? Flower? Butterfly?"

"For your information, it's a lion."

"Not so predictable, then," he mused.

"I wanted something that symbolized strength and courage."

"I suspect you have plenty of both."

She felt her cheeks flush with pleasure at the unexpected compliment. And while she didn't often feel strong or courageous, she was aspiring to be both.

"Now it's your turn," she said.

"Sorry, no tattoos," he told her.

"Tell me something that only a handful of close friends know."

"Hmm…" he said, echoing her quiet musing.

Or maybe he really couldn't think of anything he wanted to share.

But after another minute, he finally replied, "When I was a kid, I wanted to be a rodeo star."

Which was when she realized that she had no idea what kind of job he had, though considering the taut muscles she could feel pressed against her, she wouldn't have been surprised to learn that he'd followed that dream.

"Saddle bronc? Steer wrestling? Bull riding?" she asked, naming the events that immediately came to mind.

He shook his head. "I can't tell you anything more specific than that. You'll laugh."

"I won't laugh," she promised.

"Rodeo clown."

She laughed.

He gave her a look.

"I'm sorry," she said, not sounding sorry at all.

"For your information, the job of a rodeo clown is physically demanding—and incredibly dangerous."

"I know," she agreed. "That's why, in the business, they're actually considered bullfighters rather than rodeo clowns."

"Apparently you know stuff, too," he mused.

"So what derailed your rodeo clown aspirations?"

"My parents took me to the LRCA Rodeo and I realized that bulls are huge—and terrifying."

She laughed again. "I'm tempted to ask what career path you decided to follow instead, but I'm afraid that would violate our rule about revealing potentially identifying personal information."

"It was your rule, not mine," he reminded her. "So it's your call."

She hesitated, considering, then shook her head. "Instead I'll tell you that Spencer Channing, two-time PBR and PRCA bull riding champion, now raises and trains horses right here at Crooked Creek."

"No kidding?"

"No kidding," she confirmed.

"You really do know something about everyone in this town," he mused.

"My family has lived here as long as any other."

"Be careful," he said. "You're revealing personal information that I might be able to use to track you down in the future."

"This is Haven," she reminded him. "It's next to impossible to remain anonymous here. If you ever came back and wanted to find me, it wouldn't be difficult."

"When I come back, I'll definitely find you," he promised.

As much as Sarah wanted to believe he meant it, she wasn't going to let herself hope that it might ever happen. Because in her experience, expectations only led to disappointment.

And so instead of wondering what might or might not happen in the future, she decided to enjoy this moment right now.

But he'd picked up the thread of their conversation again and was talking about other places he'd visited in Nevada and around the country.

"You're not listening to me, are you?" Tex realized.

"I'm sorry," she said. "My mind was wandering."

"What were you thinking about?"

She lifted her gaze to his. "Truthfully... I was wondering if you were ever going to stop talking and kiss me."

He stopped talking and kissed her.

CHAPTER FIVE

Six weeks later

SARAH HAD NEVER been a morning person. But her habits quickly changed when she started working at Twilight Valley Equine Rehabilitation and Retirement Facility with Claire and discovered that being at the horse rescue early meant having time to indulge in a morning ride. And so those rides became part of her new routine, serving the dual purposes of exercising the horses who lived at the ranch and giving her some one-on-one time with her friend. Because working together didn't actually afford much of that as Claire spent most of her time outside with the horses while Sarah was usually in the office, focused on fundraising initiatives for the not-for-profit facility and handling other administrative tasks that her friend had been only too happy to abdicate to her.

They weren't the only two people who worked at Twilight Valley, but they were the only ones who were there every day. Claire's husband, Devin, helped out when he could, but his work as a security systems analyst and his hobby as an app designer kept him busy. There was also a handful of local residents who volunteered on a regular basis and a greater number who showed up on a less frequent schedule. Weekends and the summer months inevitably brought more help to the ranch, including high school students in need of volunteer hours.

This morning, they'd headed to Eagle Rock, one of the highest points on the property. Claire, riding Mystic—a now nine-year-old gelding who'd come to Twilight Valley in its first year of operation—stopped at the top of the ridge to watch the sun rising over the mountains in the distance. Sarah, on the back of a twenty-two-year-old retired broodmare named Jezebel, took a few minutes to catch up with her friend. When she did, she exhaled softly, her breath stolen by the view.

"Missing your office job yet?" Claire asked her friend.

Sarah continued to gaze out on the horizon, truly awed by the beauty of the land around her, backdropped by the majesty of the Silver Ridge Mountains and an impossibly blue sky.

"The day I walked out of Blake Mining was the second-best day of my life."

"What was the best?"

Sarah shifted her attention to her friend now and grinned. "The day I met you."

"Aww," Claire said, her eyes misty. "That was one of the best days of my life, too."

"Only one of?" she said teasingly.

"The day I married Devin bumped it out of the top spot."

"But only because we're now cousins by marriage in addition to being BFFs, right?"

Claire laughed. "A definite bonus."

It filled Sarah's heart with joy to know that Claire and Devin had each found their perfect match in the other, even as she wondered if she'd ever be so lucky.

But she was focused on other priorities right now. After too many years going through the motions, she'd finally realized that she needed to be happy with her life before she'd want to share it with anyone else. Besides, the options in Haven were limited, and every time she met a great guy, it turned out he was from somewhere else. California or Washington or... Texas.

She shoved the memories of Tex to the back of her mind. She'd only spent a handful of hours with the man, but he'd obviously made an impression because, six weeks later, thoughts of him continued to pop into her mind during the day and hijack her dreams at night.

And anyway, she was happy right now working alongside her best friend in a job that gave her a feeling of purpose and a sense of satisfaction.

I am a strong, independent woman.

"Did you say something?"

"Just reminding myself that I don't need a man to make my life meaningful."

"Any particular man you don't need?" Claire wondered.

"Nope," she answered quickly.

Too quickly.

Her friend tipped up the brim of her cowboy hat to show Sarah her narrowed gaze. But Sarah kept her mouth firmly closed, and Claire didn't press her to expand on her response.

And really, there was nothing more to say.

The day after she'd met Tex—the day he'd left Haven—Claire had wanted to know what happened between her friend and the hottie from the Lone Star State, and Sarah had told her.

Almost everything.

"Any plans for the weekend?" she asked Claire, deliberately steering the conversation away from her solitary life as they began to walk the horses back to the barn, the slower gait serving the dual purposes of cooling the horses down and allowing for easier conversation.

"We're going to my parents' house for dinner tomorrow night."

"I'm sorry," Sarah said, understanding that family get-togethers were always a source of stress for her friend.

Growing up, Sarah had pulled out all the stops to get the attention of parents who were so preoccupied with the family business they had little time for their family. Claire, on the other hand, had done everything she could to fly beneath her parents' radar. Not an easy task when Paul and Elsa Lamontagne monitored every aspect of her life, from the amount of time she spent in front of the TV to the programs she watched, from the books she read and the clothes she wore to the friends she spent time with.

It was hardly a surprise that the preacher's daughter rebelled against her controlling parents. And Sarah had been right there with her, every step of the way. They'd truly been partners in crime—or at least accomplices in misbehaving.

"My mom expects me to bring dessert, because I always do, but the bakery's still closed."

"The grand reopening is the twenty-eighth," Sarah said. "I stopped at The Daily Grind to grab a latte on my way home yesterday and got the latest."

"And what is the latest?" her friend asked.

"According to Jana Beatty and Harper Langdon, the new owner is making big changes to the menu to put her own stamp on things."

"Change is good for everyone—and long overdue in this sleepy town," Claire said. "But apparently you didn't get all the latest news, because the new owner isn't a *she*—*his* name is Andrew Morrow."

"How do *you* know that?"

"I ran into Laurel Walsh at the grocery store earlier in the week," Claire confided, naming a mutual friend who worked at Jo's Pizza. "She said that the new owner has been into the restaurant a couple times already and is *very* handsome."

"Did Laurel know anything else about him?"

Now Claire shook her head. "Apparently all her efforts at conversation were politely rebuffed, but she did tell me that he always ordered a large pie, so she assumed he had someone to share it with."

"Or he wanted leftovers for the next day," Sarah suggested.

"That's what I figured, too. Oh, and according to Ayesha Dhawan, he stops by The Daily Grind for a coffee sometime between two and three p.m. every day, which is usually when she's there for her afternoon pick-me-up."

"Sounds like everyone has something to say about this guy."

"Everyone always wants to play with the shiny new toy," Claire noted.

Sarah choked on a laugh.

"It's true," her friend said. "And when I saw Beverly Clayton at the bookstore, she told me to tell you to elbow your way to the front of the line."

Now Sarah snorted. "Last time I saw Beverly Clayton, pushing her youngest grandbaby in a stroller through Prospect Park, she told me that even though I was looking at thirty in the rearview mirror, I shouldn't give up all hope that I might someday meet a nice man with whom to settle down."

"The words were obviously poorly chosen but you know her intentions were good," Claire said.

"I know. And there are days that I think I wouldn't mind settling down, but I don't want to settle."

"And you shouldn't," her friend agreed. "But maybe you should at least take a stroll by the bakery to check out this new guy before someone else calls dibs."

"I have," Sarah admitted. "Not because I wanted a glimpse of the new owner but because I wanted to see what was happening inside. Unfortunately, the windows are covered in paper."

"Then I guess you're going to have to walk over to The Daily Grind and linger over a latte one afternoon."

"No doubt, if his habits are known—as they apparently are—the coffee shop is packed between two and three. And obviously that explains why I had to wait twenty minutes for my coffee when I was there yesterday afternoon," she realized.

"But no sightings of handsome strangers?"

"No," Sarah confirmed. "But I wasn't looking, either. I just ordered my drink and, when it was finally ready, walked out the door with it."

"You need to always be looking," Claire told her. "Because the pickings in this town are slim, especially for those of us who grew up here and have known most of the local guys all of our lives."

"And yet you managed to find someone."

"With a little help from my friend."

"A *lot* of help from your friend," Sarah said immodestly. "In fact, I'm thinking if this job doesn't work out, I might offer my services as a matchmaker."

"You better hope this job works out," Claire teased, as she hoisted herself out of the saddle and dropped to the ground. "Because no one wants a matchmaker whose love life is a mess."

"My love life is *not* a mess," Sarah denied, following her friend's lead in dismounting. "It's simply nonexistent."

"Definitely put that on your business cards."

"Shut up, Claire."

Claire shut up—but she was grinning widely as she began to untack her mount.

They worked side by side in companionable silence, grooming the horses. When they were done, Claire wrapped her arms around Mystic's neck and hugged the gelding for a long minute.

"You're in a melancholic mood this morning," Sarah noted.

"I guess I just realized how much I'm going to miss him when he goes to his new home."

"Of course you'll miss him," she agreed. "But he's not leaving until the fifteenth of June."

"Which is Sunday," Claire informed her.

"Apparently time really does fly when you're having fun," Sarah remarked, startled to discover that the month was almost half over already—which meant that it was almost her friend's birthday.

And now she had an even bigger incentive to meet the bakery's new owner.

FIVE MINUTES.

After working practically from sunup till sundown for the past few weeks, all Andrew Morrow wanted was five minutes to enjoy a cup of coffee that didn't need to be reheated half a dozen times before he swallowed the last mouthful.

So when another customer paused near his table at The Daily Grind, he didn't look up. Instead, he kept his attention focused on the screen of his phone, as if he was unaware of her presence.

And even without looking up, he knew it was a woman. And while it would be polite to invite her to sit down—because it turned out that the afternoon was a busy time at the local coffee shop and vacant chairs were in limited supply—he wasn't in the mood to be polite. Because he'd learned that being polite led to meaningless chitchat, which often took a turn in the direction of more pointed inquiries.

Some of the women—and it was almost always women—

wanted to know about his plans for the bakery. Some made discreet inquiries about his sexual orientation and relationship status; others were less discreet in their offers to set him up with a daughter or a niece or a neighbor.

Maybe he was being rude, but he wasn't in the mood for any of it today. He had no interest in being set up and no time for any kind of romantic entanglements right now.

And yet, thoughts of Friend of Claire had intruded on his mind every day—and night—since he'd left Haven, and now that he was back, those thoughts came even more frequently.

She'd assured him that he wouldn't have any trouble finding her if he wanted to, and Andrew definitely wanted to. But there were only so many hours in the day and there was so much that he had to do before the bakery's grand opening at the end of the month that he'd decided to wait before doing so.

Of course, the simplest solution to avoiding unnecessary attention would be to take his coffee back to the bakery where he could lock the door—and lock out his intrusive neighbors. But he was trying to remember that those same intrusive neighbors would hopefully become paying customers when he opened for business. Not to mention that when he was at the bakery, there was always one task or another that required his attention, leading to his coffee being abandoned and growing cold.

Over the scents of freshly ground beans and yeasty doughnuts and toasted bread, he caught a whiff of perfume. Something subtly fruity with warm undertones. Sexy...and somehow familiar.

His chin jerked upward and his gaze locked with Friend of Claire's.

She was wearing a long-sleeved Henley-style top tucked into dark jeans that hugged her narrow hips and long legs today, with her long dark hair in a ponytail and her face bare of makeup. Still, she looked every bit as stunning as the day they'd first met—and just as surprised to see him as he was to see her.

Her blue eyes went wide. "Ohmygod... *Tex?*"

Andrew had known it was only a matter of time before he crossed paths with her again, and he'd been looking forward to that eventual meeting. But it hadn't occurred to him that she might find him before he was ready to be found.

"I've relocated, so maybe you should call me Nevada now," he said, in a deliberately casual tone. "Or you could use my actual name, which is Andrew. Andrew Morrow."

She blew out a breath. "You're the new owner of Sweet Caroline's?"

"I am," he confirmed.

"I came in here looking for you. For Andrew Morrow, I mean. I didn't know... I'm going to need a minute," she said. "My head is spinning."

And though he hadn't done anything wrong, he felt a ridiculous need to apologize, because it was obvious that she was as blindsided by his presence as he was by hers. Maybe more so.

"Why don't you sit?" He gestured to the vacant seat across from him.

She set her cup down, then pulled the chair away from the table and sank into it.

After she'd taken the minute, she lifted her gaze to meet his again. "I never would have guessed... You don't look like a baker."

"What does a baker look like?" he asked curiously.

She shrugged. "A chef's hat and neckerchief and a round belly that makes him giggle when it's poked."

A smile tugged at his lips as he realized she was describing the Pillsbury doughboy. "How do you know I don't giggle when you poke my belly?"

"I guess I don't," she said lightly.

"So what can I do for you, Friend of Claire?"

Her cheeks colored. "My name's Sarah. Sarah Stafford."

He shook her proffered hand and experienced the same jolt of awareness he'd felt when she took his hand at Crooked Creek Ranch. And when her eyes lifted to his again, he knew that she'd felt it, too.

"It's nice to meet you, Sarah Stafford."

She looked away first and pulled her hand back.

"You said you were looking for me," he reminded her.

"Right." She wrapped her hands around her cup. "Well, not you you—because I didn't know you were you—but the new owner of the bakery."

"Because?" he prompted.

"Because I need a cupcake."

"*A* cupcake?" he echoed, certain he hadn't heard her correctly. She nodded.

"Singular? As in one?"

She sipped her coffee, then responded with another nod. "For June fifteenth."

"The bakery doesn't open until June twenty-eighth. I'd be happy to talk cupcakes with you anytime after that, but until then, I can't help you."

"But I need a cupcake for June fifteenth."

"I'm sure there's somewhere else that you can get a cupcake," he said reasonably.

"It can't be from anywhere else," she told him. "It has to be from Sweet Caroline's."

"Then you should have bought it four weeks ago," he pointed out to her.

"If I had, it would be stale by now."

"Most cupcakes freeze pretty well," he said.

"That advice doesn't do me much good at this late date."

"Well—" he picked up his mug again "—that's all I've got for you."

She pursed her lips while he sipped his coffee.

"You do know how to make cupcakes, don't you?" she finally asked.

"I've made a few in my time," he acknowledged in a dry tone.

"Then you can no doubt handle my request for a chocolate cupcake with caramel and walnuts and chocolate chips inside, topped with chocolate frosting drizzled with caramel sauce."

"Sounds like something you should be able to figure out how to make yourself."

"You'd think so," she agreed. "But while I'm a fairly decent cook, baking is not my thing."

"And I've got too much to do before the grand opening without adding one more thing to the list."

She rearranged the sugar packets in the caddy in the center of the table, so they were all facing the same way. "What if I offered to buy a whole dozen cupcakes?"

"Same answer," he told her.

"What if I bought a dozen *and*—" she plucked a paper napkin out of the dispenser and used it to wipe a drop of coffee off the table "—made dinner for you?"

His brows lifted at that. "Like a date?"

"No!" Her cheeks immediately flushed with color. "Like a meal that isn't pizza."

"Apparently my visits to Jo's have not gone unnoticed," he remarked.

"Not just your visits to the pizzeria," she told him. "Your trips to the grocery store and your afternoon coffee breaks have been the subject of much speculation."

"Speculation about what?" he wondered.

"Where you came from. How you ended up here." Now she scrubbed at an imaginary spot with the napkin. "If you're single or married."

"I told you I wasn't married."

"Actually what you said was that an unmarried man could know something about women's shoes."

"And you suspect that was a clever way of hiding my true marital status?"

She shrugged. "A lot of guys are less than forthcoming about their relationships. And the absence of a ring isn't definitive proof of anything."

"Do you have a theory about where this wife has been hiding while I've been out and about around town?" he asked curiously.

"She could be unpacking and settling in at home. Or maybe you keep her tied up in the attic. All those old houses on Morningstar Road have fabulous attics."

His brows lifted. "How do you know I live on Morningstar Road?"

"Small town," she said again.

"Well, you have a creative mind, Sarah Stafford," he mused, not sure if he was amused or insulted by her outrageous speculation.

"I watch a lot of crime shows," she confided. "And somehow, we've gotten way off topic."

"What was the topic?"

"My cupcake request."

"Which now comes with an offer to make dinner for me?"

She nodded.

"You must think your cooking's pretty good," he mused.

"My chicken marsala is legendary," she assured him.

He'd been eating a lot of sandwiches lately—and pizza from Jo's, and the promise of a real home-cooked meal was undeniably appealing. The prospect of spending more time with Sarah was even more so.

"So—do we have a deal?" she asked.

"I guess we do," he finally agreed.

She smiled. "If I could pick up the cupcakes on Saturday, that would be great."

"Saturday being...tomorrow?"

Now she nodded.

"Custom orders usually require forty-eight hours' notice."

"I'll keep that in mind for next time," she said lightly. "When do you want your chicken marsala?"

"Why don't we say Saturday for that, too? You can pick up your cupcakes when you deliver my food."

She swiped across the screen of her phone, opening her calendar app. "What time?"

"Six o'clock?"

She added that information into her phone. "Address?"

"I thought you knew where I lived."

"The rumor mill only gave me the street name, not the actual house number."

"Twenty-seven," he told her, holding out his hand for her phone. "To give you my phone number, so you can contact me if anything changes."

She gave him her phone. He added his contact information, then sent himself an empty text message so that he had her information, too.

"Can you make enough chicken for two?"

She lifted a brow.

"Even my rumored wife deserves to be fed, don't you think?" he said.

"You said you weren't married."

"But you're still not entirely sure you believe me, are you?"

"Well, in case you're not joking, you should know that I have a brother and several cousins who are ranchers, and all of them will be made aware of my plans so that they know where to start looking if I go missing."

"Tempted to renege on our bargain now?" he asked, fighting against the smile that wanted to curve his lips.

"No," she decided, after an almost imperceptible hesitation. "I need that cupcake."

"Cupcakes," he reminded her, emphasizing the plural. "You said you'd buy the whole dozen."

"Right." She pushed her chair away from the table and stood up. "So I guess I'll see you at six o'clock tomorrow."

He nodded again, already looking forward to it.

CHAPTER SIX

SARAH LEFT THE coffee shop feeling as if she'd made a deal with the devil. And perhaps she had. Lord knows, Andrew Morrow tempted her more than any man had in a very long time.

After the night they'd gone to Crooked Creek Ranch, she'd tried to forget about him, certain she'd never see "Tex" again.

Relieved to know she'd never see him again.

Just one more mistake to be left in the past as she moved forward with her life.

Except that he was suddenly back in Haven—to stay this time!—and whatever spark had ignited between them that first night at Diggers' continued to crackle six weeks later.

Which should have been all the proof she needed that he was completely wrong for her, because she'd only ever been attracted to men destined to break (or at least dent) her heart.

But they'd struck a bargain, and so, twenty-seven hours after leaving the coffee shop, Sarah found herself headed to Andrew's house with a pan of chicken marsala.

Obviously taste was the most critical factor, but offering a dish that looked and smelled appealing heightened anticipation. So she sprinkled fresh parsley over the chicken, dusted the potatoes with paprika and glazed the baby carrots with brown butter.

When she was satisfied with the appearance of the meal, she turned her attention to herself. She brushed out her hair, dabbed some mascara on her lashes and some gloss on her lips, then dressed in a pair of dark blue jeans with a loose-knit short-sleeve sweater on top and leather sandals on her feet.

Not that she was trying to impress him or anything. But before she'd tracked him down at The Daily Grind, she'd stopped home for a quick shower after leaving Twilight Valley so she wouldn't approach him smelling like hay and horses. Aware of her time constraints—needing to be at the coffee shop between 2:00 and 3:00 p.m. in the hope of crossing paths with him—she hadn't taken the time to put on any makeup or do anything more than towel-dry her hair before pulling it into a ponytail.

And maybe she'd wanted to make it clear to him—and everyone else at the coffee shop—that she wasn't trying to impress the new owner of the bakery.

She wasn't trying to impress him tonight, either, but she did want to remind him that she was capable of looking better than a freshly scrubbed stable hand. And the appreciative look in his eyes as they skimmed over her when he opened the door confirmed her efforts had not gone unnoticed.

Then he spotted the faux fur bear paw oven mitts on her hands, and his lips twitched, as if he was fighting against a smile.

"The pan's hot," she said, by way of explanation.

"As you can see, I've held up my end of the bargain."

"All I can see is a baking pan covered in foil," he pointed out.

"Maybe you could invite me to come in so I can put the pan down?" she suggested.

He stepped away from the door so that she could enter.

"Kitchen's this way," he said.

He looked good, too, she noted, as she followed him down the hall to the back of the house. He was casually dressed in jeans and a T-shirt, the former hugging his really great butt and the latter showing off his strong arms.

In the kitchen, she saw that two places had been set on the island, complete with a bottle of wine, uncorked, and two glasses waiting to be filled.

She set the pan on top of the stove and removed the bear paw mitts. "The chicken can be kept warm in the oven at three

hundred and twenty-five degrees while you wait for your dinner guest."

"My dinner guest is here," he said.

"Oh. Okay, then. I'll just take my cupcakes and get out of
your way."

He smiled, and *damn* if her knees didn't turn to jelly.

"You're my guest, Sarah."

"Oh."

"Assuming you don't have other plans," he added.

"No. No other plans. Not tonight," she said, which she knew
suggested that she had plans on other nights but was preferable
to admitting that her social life was pretty much nonexistent
these days.

"Does that mean you'll stay and have dinner with me?" he
prompted.

"On one condition."

"What's that?"

"I get a tour of the house before we eat."

He grinned. "Absolutely. Although there's not a lot to see. I
mean, it's a big house, but it's mostly empty right now."

First, though, he programmed the temperature she'd suggested, then picked up the oven mitts she'd set on the counter to
slide the hot pan into the oven to keep it warm until they were
ready to eat.

"Let's start at the top," he suggested, leading her to the staircase.

She followed, enjoying the view.

"Isn't there a saying—something about not trusting a skinny
chef?"

He glanced over his shoulder. "Are you checking me out?"

She shrugged. "It occurred to me that a man who makes his
living baking sweet treats should be a little soft around the middle from sampling his own product."

"The key is to sample," he told her, when they reached the
top of the first flight of stairs. "To taste a little bit of filling or
nibble on a bite of pastry rather than consuming a whole beignet or croissant."

She followed as he turned and started up the second flight,

thinking that she wouldn't mind nibbling on her tour guide. She pushed the thought aside, asking instead, "And that's enough to prevent the carbs from taking up residence in your midsection?"

"That and the fact that I'm on my feet—measuring and mixing and kneading and rolling—for most of the day."

"I guess that would do it," she acknowledged, walking through the door he opened at the top. "I've only been working at the ranch six weeks, and already I can feel the difference in muscles that only ever got a workout at the gym—and not very regularly at that."

He gave her a minute to inspect the room, which was more time than she needed as the space was surprisingly—and perhaps disappointingly—empty. There was no antique furniture draped with dust cloths, no hope chests—or even cardboard boxes—filled with mementos of times past, not even a lost button or dropped hairpin.

"You're disappointed?" he guessed.

"Maybe. A little."

"The previous owners did a very thorough cleaning job before they moved out."

"I can see that." But she could also see wear marks and scratches on the old random-width plank flooring that attested to the home's age and history. She crossed that floor to look out the tall narrow windows at the opposite end of the room. "But at least the floor creaks."

"I don't think a creaky floor is a selling feature."

"That depends on your buyer," she acknowledged. "To me, it's a testament to the history of the building."

"And you said you weren't sentimental," he reminded her.

She shrugged. "I like old houses. They have stories to tell."

She thought of her parents' three-story mansion on Miners' Pass and how, when she looked at it, the only thing she saw was how much money they had. She didn't begrudge them their lavish style of living, and she couldn't deny that they put a lot of money back into the community, but apparently she still had some unresolved issues when it came to their prioritization of the business over all else.

"Let's see what the next level tells you," he suggested.

She took a cursory peek in each of the first three bedrooms. Each had obviously been freshly painted—probably before the house was put on the market, though the color choices (pale lavender, powder pink and steel blue) were a departure from the neutral tones that real estate agents usually recommended for optimal buyer appeal—and were empty of furniture. The lavender and pink bedrooms shared a bathroom with two sinks and a tub-and-shower combo, and the third—the smallest of the three—had its own (much smaller) en suite with pedestal sink and corner shower.

The fourth bedroom was obviously the master and gorgeously furnished with dark raw wood furniture, including floating nightstands that flanked a queen-size bed and two tall dressers on the opposite wall. The simple linen drapes hung on a wrought iron rail over the window coordinated with the duvet cover and pillowcases. A Kindle sat on top of one of the bedside tables, a pair of dark-rimmed reading glasses beside it.

"Why do I feel as if I've seen this furniture before?"

"Do you ever go shopping in Battle Mountain?"

"The front window display of Garrett Furniture," she realized. He nodded.

She was pretty sure the woven rug on the floor and the earthenware vase with the branches on his windowsill had been part of the showcase, too.

"I'm extremely detail-oriented in the kitchen," he confided. "Not so much in other aspects of my life. So when I found something I liked, the simplest solution seemed to be to buy all of it."

"Was the Kindle part of the display, too?"

"No. But I think there was a Quinn Ellison book on the nightstand—which happens to be what I'm reading on my Kindle right now. And the glasses are mine."

She could picture him in them and found the image incredibly appealing. "I'll bet you look cute in the glasses."

"Cute?" he echoed dubiously.

"What's wrong with cute?"

"Nothing, I guess. It just seems like a significant demotion from hot."

And suddenly she knew that they were both thinking about the night they met.

Or maybe those thoughts had been lingering in the background all along. But now they were front and center—as obvious as the big bed in the middle of his room.

"Not necessarily," she decided, forcing her attention back to their conversation. "I think it's more a matter of context."

"The context being that you'd drunk three glasses of wine that night?" he guessed.

She should have agreed, dismissing her attraction to him as something induced by alcohol. Instead, she shook her head. "I thought you were a hottie when I first saw you in the parking lot, before I'd had any wine."

"So what's different now?" he asked her.

"The difference is that you're no longer a stranger I'll never see again—now you're someone I'm likely to cross paths with on a regular basis."

"Which would make it a lot easier to meet for coffee or dinner or…whatever," he noted.

"I'm on a dating hiatus," she told him, as she moved deeper into the room to check out the en suite. "There will be no meeting for coffee or dinner or…whatever."

The bathroom boasted a simple wood counter with a square vessel sink on top and open shelves beneath, a glass-walled walk-in shower easily big enough for two and a separate freestanding bathtub.

"I would have bought this house for the bathroom alone," she told him.

"I don't see myself ever using the tub," he admitted. "But the shower is great."

And suddenly her very active imagination was painting a picture of him in that tub, and the graphic image was causing the blood to heat inside her veins.

She cleared her throat. "We should finish the tour before the chicken gets cold."

"I put it in the oven, per your instructions," he reminded her.

"Oh. Right."

But he took the hint and led her back down the stairs to the main level.

At the front of the house was the living room—which she'd caught a quick glimpse of on her way to the kitchen. A closer perusal revealed that she hadn't missed much as it was furnished with a couple of folding lawn chairs and a huge flat-screen TV mounted to the wall. Across the hall from the living room was a home office/den with built-in bookcases, currently empty, and a Murphy bed that allowed space to do double duty as a guest room.

"Because the three guest rooms upstairs aren't enough?" she couldn't resist teasing.

"They don't come with beds," he said, pulling down the wall panel to reveal the double mattress hidden inside.

"This is a really great house," Sarah said, as they moved from the den to the dining room—also empty of furniture. "The previous owner obviously put some money into renovating and upgrading but without destroying its individuality and charm."

"That was one of the things that most appealed to me," he told her.

"I looked at a house down the street before I bought mine on Fieldstone," she confided. "But as much as I loved it, it just seemed like too much house for one person."

"Yeah, I'm probably going to question my choices when I have to pay the heating bill in the winter, but the proximity to the bakery was really what sold me on this place. That and the fact that it was available for immediate occupancy."

"You might want to go back to Garrett Furniture before then," she said, "Unless you don't mind watching TV from the questionable comfort of a metal frame covered with plastic webbing."

"Most of my stuff is being shipped from Texas," he told her. "It should arrive early next week. In the meantime, the lawn chair works. And I haven't had much time to sit around watching TV, anyway."

He retrieved the plates from the island to dish up the meal she'd prepared.

"Do you want me to do that?" she offered.

"I think I can handle the serving," he told her. "Why don't you pour the wine?"

So she poured the wine. When he carried the plates back to the island, she was sampling the pinot noir he'd chosen.

"I went with the red, because I remembered that's what you were drinking at Diggers'."

"You really are a man who pays attention," she mused.

He pulled out a stool and gestured for her to sit. "Is that such a rarity?"

"As much as a unicorn galloping over a rainbow."

"How is the wine?" he asked, as he took his seat beside her.

"It's nice," she said.

He picked up his glass and sampled, then nodded to indicate his agreement.

"So tell me about your new ranch job," he said, as he cut into his chicken.

"That question came from out of the blue," she remarked.

"You mentioned it when I was giving you the tour of the house. I figured my follow-up questions were better left until we were sitting down to eat."

She stabbed a baby carrot with her fork. "It's an equine retirement and rehabilitation facility or, as most people around here refer to it, a horse rescue."

"And how did you end up there?" he asked curiously.

"I'm still not entirely sure," she admitted. "But I suspect that Claire started to recruit me—subtly but relentlessly—when the doors of the rescue opened three years ago."

"Your friend Claire works there, too?"

"It's her ranch," Sarah told him. "Formerly her aunt and uncle's spread. But they raised cattle and saving horses is Claire's passion.

"For several years, she volunteered at a horse rescue in Austin that rehabilitated and rehomed horses that had been injured, abused or neglected. When she came back to Haven, she wanted to continue that work here."

"The two of you have been friends for a long time?"

She nodded. "Since grade school. We were pretty much inseparable growing up. I used to love going to Claire's house, where her mom always had homemade cookies for us to snack on while we did homework. Claire preferred hanging out at my place, because there we were pretty much free to do whatever we wanted without anyone reminding us to do homework first."

"The grass is always greener," he mused.

"Apparently," she agreed. "Anyway, after high school, we both chose to go to UT Austin to study business, because neither of us could imagine going away without the other. But after graduation, I came back to Haven and Claire, believing herself to be in love with a guy she met in our final year, opted to stay in Texas."

"I'm getting the impression you weren't too fond of the guy," he noted.

"He wasn't right for Claire," she said. "Thankfully she realized it, too, before she walked down the aisle. And now she's married to my cousin, so we're not just best friends, we're family, which is why I was so desperate for the cupcake."

"The cupcake is for Claire?" he said, seeming surprised by this revelation.

"Didn't I tell you that?"

He shook his head.

"It's been our tradition since eighth grade, when I found out her family never had a cake for her birthday."

"You can't celebrate a birthday without cake." Andrew sounded scandalized.

"Which was my thought," she agreed with a smile. "But at fourteen, I couldn't afford a whole cake, so I bought her a cupcake. A chocolate caramel nut cupcake from Sweet Caroline's, because it was her favorite. And every birthday since, I've bought her the same."

"You were so desperate for the cupcake, I wondered if it was for a boyfriend," Andrew confided now.

She shook her head. "No man is worth that much effort."

"Ouch."

"Sorry," she said, aware that she didn't sound the least bit remorseful. "I haven't had the best of luck in the romance department and it's possible that experience has colored by opinion."

"Possible, huh?" He studied her for a long minute, obviously hoping for more details than what she'd already given him.

She just shrugged and nibbled on another bite of chicken.

"So how long have you been on this dating hiatus?"

"Eight months," she told him. "With only one little blip."

The corners of his mouth twitched. "Is that what that night was—a blip?"

"Whatever it was, it's not going to happen again," she assured him.

He didn't argue the point, instead asking, "So what did you do before you started working on your friend's ranch?"

"I worked at Blake Mining," she told him. Which was the truth, if not the whole truth.

"And what prompted your career change?"

So many things.

But none that she wanted to get into with him now.

"Maybe I got tired of being paid too much money for doing too little work," she responded lightly.

"Said nobody ever," he assured her.

"My job mostly entailed research, assessments, reports and meetings," she told him. "To sum up, it was pretty boring—and still, sadly, the most exciting part of my life."

"I'm sure that's not true."

"I assure you, it is."

Because while Sarah had been living it up in her twenties—with zero regrets—she was now in her thirties and discovering that her friends were all planning weddings or already married and looking forward to starting families or already parenting the little ones running around. And while it was true that a few were already divorced—or heading in that direction—at least they'd had the experience of falling in love and planning a life with someone special.

"So it wasn't an office romance gone bad that made you leave the company?" he pressed.

"No."

Her immediate reply made his brows lift.

"Have you never been in love?" Andrew asked.

"Sure," she said. "Probably too many times. Unfortunately, I have a tendency to be swept off my feet by handsome and charming men looking for nothing more than a good time. And while that's always fun while it lasts, it never lasts long, and then I'm alone again."

"Being with someone isn't always a buffer against loneliness," he noted. "In fact, it can highlight the distance between you."

"It sounds as if you're speaking from personal experience," she mused.

"I've had some failed relationships," he acknowledged with a shrug. "And yet, I keep trying."

"Why do you think that is?" she asked, genuinely interested in his response. "Are human beings unable to learn from their mistakes and decide they'd rather be alone than risk heartbreak again?"

"None of the mistakes were mine," he deadpanned. "The blame lies entirely with the women I've dated."

She laughed. "Even if that was true, wouldn't you bear some responsibility for choosing to get involved with them?"

"Okay, maybe I do have a weakness for blue-eyed women with great smiles."

"You're wasting your time flirting with me," she told him.

"I don't think so," he said. "But if I am, isn't it my time to waste?"

"You're getting ready to reopen the bakery—your time is at a premium," she reminded him, carrying her plate and wine-glass to the sink.

Andrew followed with his own. "Thanks for dinner," he said. "I have to admit, your chicken marsala was excellent."

"Excellent?" she echoed with a frown.

"Is that inadequate praise?"

"It's several grades below legendary. The scale starts at 'good' then goes to 'really good' followed by 'excellent,' then 'excep-tional' and 'amazing' and then 'legendary,'" she said, ticking each of the descriptors off on her fingers.

"So kind of like how 'cute' is lower on the scale than 'hot,'" he noted.

"That would depend on whose scale it is," she argued. "To a six-year-old cuddling a puppy, cute is probably at the very top."

"Well, you're not a six-year-old and I'm not a puppy, but the cuddling part sounds pretty good," he said.

"There will be no cuddling."

"That's not what you said at Crooked Creek Ranch."

"It was cold that night," she reminded him.

"I remember."

"Also, I'd had three glasses of wine."

"How many glasses have you had tonight?"

"Only two. I never have more than that when I'm driving. Although I do live close enough that I could walk," she admitted.

"Or you could stay."

"You said some things that night, too," she recalled. "Including that, if you ever came back to Haven, you'd find me."

"I said that *when* I came back to Haven, I'd find you," he clarified. "And I had every intention of doing so, but you found me first."

"Only because I needed a cupcake."

"I don't care about the reasons," he said. "I'm just glad you're here."

"I'm not going to sleep with you, Tex."

His lips curved. "Do you always lead with that?"

"Actually, the first time we met, I said I wasn't going to go home with you."

"And you didn't," he acknowledged.

"But since we're already at your house, I thought it important to clarify."

"That you're not going to sleep with me...*tonight*?"

"Or *ever*."

His gaze heated; his lips curved. "Challenge accepted."

"It wasn't a challenge but a statement of fact."

"Since I returned to Haven, I've been preoccupied with the renovations of the bakery," he admitted. "But not a day has gone by that I haven't thought about you and looked forward to seeing you again."

"You expect me to believe that you've been thinking about a woman you know nothing about?"

"You think I didn't know anything about you because you refused to tell me your name?" he challenged. "Your Main Street walking tour gave me plenty of character insights."

She frowned at that. "Like what?"

"The stories you shared showed interest and character. Instead of highlighting the potentially scandalous aspect of two seventy-year-olds having an affair, you focused on the fact that they'd found love together."

"I'm pretty sure they make the bedsprings creak, too. Because Frieda Zimmerman blushed like a schoolgirl when Donna Bradley asked how she injured her hip."

"And you're only telling me that now because you're obviously uncomfortable being depicted as a romantic."

She couldn't deny it.

"Then there's your enduring affection for the ex-boyfriend," he continued. "Which shows not only that you're loyal but also suggests that you might hold on to relationships that have already failed because it's less risky than taking a chance on a relationship that might work."

"Apparently I'm an open book," she said dryly.

"If you are, I've barely had a chance to skim the first chapter. There's still a lot that I don't know but that I'm very much looking forward to discovering."

"Sorry, you missed your chance, Tex."

"You're telling me that you don't think about that night under the stars?"

"My new philosophy is to look forward, not back."

"Which isn't actually an answer to my question," he noted.

"I'm not interested in picking up where we left off."

His fingertips brushed over the fluttering pulse point on her throat, making it race. "So why is your heart beating so fast?"

"Apparently there's some chemistry between us," she acknowledged.

"Some very potent chemistry that tells me our being together isn't a question of *if* but *when*."

Before she could argue the point, he dipped his head and brushed his lips over hers.

It was as much a question as a kiss, and she didn't answer by pulling back or pushing him away. She responded by rising on her toes to fit her mouth more firmly to his. Following her cue, he wrapped his arms around her middle and drew her closer, so that their bodies were aligned, their hearts beating in tandem.

Her lips parted beneath his, allowing him to deepen the kiss. A soft moan emanated from deep in her throat, destroying any illusion that she didn't want this. Didn't want him.

He continued to kiss her, long and slow and deep, until they were both breathless. When he finally eased away to draw air in his lungs and was able to speak again, he simply said, "Stay."

And for almost half a second, she considered his request.

Then, somewhere in the distance, she registered the sound of a door opening, followed by footsteps in the hall.

She pulled out of his arms and took a quick step back just as a gorgeous woman appeared in the doorway.

"Surprise!"

CHAPTER SEVEN

"SURPRISE!" LILAH ECHOED, rushing into her dad's arms.

Tilda followed her younger sister with markedly less enthusiasm, while Rachel remained in the doorway, grinning mischievously as her gaze bounced between Andrew and Sarah.

He hugged his daughters tight, sincerely happy to see them if not overjoyed by the timing of their arrival.

"I wasn't expecting you guys until tomorrow," he said, looking at Sarah and trying to gauge her reaction to this surprise.

"The girls got out of school on Wednesday and finished packing by Thursday. Since they were obviously eager to see you, we decided to start our journey yesterday," Rachel explained.

"Lilah was eager," Tilda said. "My vote was to stay in Texas."

"Well, I'm glad you're here," he said.

And he was.

He also wished someone had apprised him of their revised ETA. But, of course, that would have ruined the surprise.

He watched as Rachel's gaze shifted to the remnants of their dinner, including the two wineglasses and half-empty bottle of red.

"Apparently our early arrival was a bigger surprise than we anticipated," she remarked dryly.

His daughters, having clued into the same thing, were uncharacteristically silent, though he didn't expect that would last long.

"You always did like to make an entrance," he noted, silently cursing himself for not explaining his situation to Sarah when he had the chance. Now he could practically see the gears turning in her brain, no doubt leading her to all kinds of wrong conclusions.

"For a minute, I thought the wine was for me, even though you know that I prefer white," Rachel continued. "But apparently, while I was schlepping your kids across state lines, you were enjoying a romantic evening."

She shifted her attention to Sarah then. "And since Andrew isn't making the introductions, I guess I'll have to do it," she said, offering a hand. "I'm Rachel Morrow."

"Sarah Stafford," she responded politely. "And I was just leaving."

SARAH COULDN'T GET out of there fast enough.

Whatever she might have anticipated when Andrew asked her to stay and have dinner with him (and her imagination had admittedly gone down several different paths), it wasn't that the evening would end with the arrival of his wife and two kids. Because she hadn't known that he had either a wife or kids—and what kind of a fool did that make her?

She breathed a sigh of relief that she'd parked on the street rather than pulling into the driveway; otherwise, she'd be boxed in. And wouldn't that have been fun—having to ask the wife of the man she'd just been kissing to move her vehicle so that Sarah could get out of the way of their happy reunion?

I'm not married.

His words echoed in the back of her mind; the obvious lie making her blood boil.

She felt betrayed by his deceit and her own willingness to trust him. Because he'd seemed not just like a really nice guy but one who was genuinely interested in her.

How could she have been so completely wrong about him?

Maybe the problem wasn't a lack of decent single men in Haven but the fact that her own judgment was lacking when it came to interactions with the opposite sex.

The one person—the only person—she could always count

on was Claire, and when she got home, before she was even out of her car, she reached for her phone to call her BFF.

Then she remembered that Claire and Devin were having dinner with Claire's parents tonight. And even if they'd returned home by now, Sarah was trying to be respectful of the fact that they were married, to remember that she shouldn't just walk into their home and intrude on their time because she was feeling out of sorts.

Before Claire and Devin exchanged vows, the bride had promised her best friend that the change in her marital status wouldn't affect their relationship. But, of course, it did. And it would be foolish—and selfish—to wish otherwise.

And just because she couldn't lament her poor choices over a glass of wine with her best friend didn't mean she couldn't have that glass of wine.

So resolved, Sarah dropped her phone back into her purse, pushed open the driver's side door and climbed out of her vehicle. She'd leave her friend alone tonight and see her tomorrow to celebrate her birthday—

Dammit.

Without the cupcakes that she only now realized she'd left behind when she made her escape from Andrew's house.

She was lamenting that oversight when an unfamiliar vehicle—with Texas plates—pulled into the driveway behind her SUV.

Rachel popped out of the driver's seat, a smile on her face and two white boxes in her hands. "You forgot your cupcakes."

"Thank you," Sarah said, a little warily, as she accepted the offering.

"Andrew asked me to bring them to you," Rachel explained. "He seemed to think that if he came, you might throw them back in his face, and apparently it was important for you to have them for tomorrow."

"My best friend's birthday," Sarah heard herself say.

Rachel smiled again, and Sarah was struck anew not just by the other woman's beauty but her grace and poise. Or maybe she was just a really good actor who was secretly thinking of various and painful ways to make her husband pay for entertaining another woman in their new home.

"You're obviously a good friend," Rachel said now.

Sarah hoped it was true. Certainly the longevity of the friendship suggested that she'd had good instincts when she'd decided, way back in fifth grade, that Claire would be her BFF. It was only later in life—or maybe only in her relationships with men—that her instincts seemed to fail her.

"I peeked in the box," Rachel admitted now, still smiling. "Chocolate caramel nut?"

Sarah nodded.

"Any chance you'd invite me in for a cup of coffee and a cupcake?" the other woman asked hopefully.

Invite her in?

The wife of the man who'd been kissing Sarah when she'd walked in the door?

No way was that going to happen, if for no reason other than that Sarah wanted to spare her neighbors the sight of crime scene tape strung up around her property in the morning.

But, of course, she couldn't say any of that to the woman standing in front of her. Instead she asked, "Aren't you eager to get back to your family?"

"The girls need some time to catch up with their dad and, after twenty-eight hours on the road with them over the past two days, I need a break. I mean, they're my nieces and I love them to bits, but twenty-eight hours is. A. Very. Long. Time."

Sarah blinked. "Your...nieces?"

Rachel laughed. "You heard the last name and assumed I was his wife, didn't you?"

"It seemed a reasonable conclusion to draw, considering that in combination with the rings on your left hand and the fact that you showed up with two girls calling him dad."

"My husband's surname is Kuczerepa, which, after three years of marriage, I still struggle to spell, so you can guess why I decided to keep mine when we married. As for the girls, Andrew wanted them to finish out the school year in Beaumont, but obviously he needed to be here to oversee the renovations. So being the wonderful sister that I am, I offered to stay with them and finish packing up his house. Now we're here and the moving truck should be arriving on Monday."

"He did mention a sister," Sarah suddenly recalled.

When Claire had questioned his knowledge of women's shoes, he'd said that he had a sister with a fondness for designer footwear.

"That would be me," Rachel confirmed.

And, sure enough, the sneakers on her feet were unmistakably Tory Burch.

So he'd been telling the truth about that, which meant that maybe he wasn't the lying rat bastard she'd accused him of being—if only inside her own head.

But he'd definitely never mentioned having kids, and while she'd be curious to hear him attempt to explain *that* oversight, Sarah decided that what she needed right now was some female companionship.

"Would you like to come in for a cup of coffee and a cupcake?" she offered.

"Twenty. Eight. Hours," Rachel said again. "Any chance of upgrading the cup of coffee to a glass of wine?"

"It so happens that I have a really nice bottle of chardonnay in my refrigerator."

The other woman grinned. "Now you're speaking my language."

THE ONLY WAY Andrew could have blown things more spectacularly with Sarah would have been with a brick of C-4 and a blasting cap.

But how could he have known that Rachel and the girls would show up early?

Still, he blamed himself for Sarah's obvious surprise—and the flicker of hurt—he'd seen in her eyes. Because it wasn't as if he hadn't had opportunities to tell her.

When she joked about him having a wife tied up in the attic, he could have told her that it was actually his ex-wife. Not living in his attic, obviously, but in California with her new boyfriend. Instead, he'd let the moment pass.

And when she commented about his house being big for one

person, he should have told her that he wouldn't be living alone for long, that he had two kids who would be joining him as soon as they were out of school for the summer. Another opportunity missed.

He'd never outright lied to her, but he hadn't been honest, either. And he knew he couldn't blame her for walking out.

He also couldn't go after her to explain, even if she was willing to listen to him. Because how would he explain that to his kids?

Hey, it's great to see you, but I'm going to chase after Sarah— who you've never heard me mention and only met for the first time right now—in the hope that she'll let me apologize for being an idiot, and I'll catch up with you later.

Obviously that wasn't an option, because as much as he might want to make things right with Sarah, his daughters were and always would be his number one priority. The reason for everything he did—including this recent move to Nevada.

So after he sent his sister off with Sarah's cupcakes, he tried to put her out of his mind to focus on Tilda and Lilah, starting with a tour of their new home—in which they showed much less interest than Sarah had done.

"It's old and creaky," Tilda said, as the stairs seemed to groan in protest of being trod upon.

"It's older than the house in Beaumont," he agreed.

"And bigger," Lilah noted.

"Plus it has character," he told them.

"Are you referring to the ghosts in the attic?" Tilda asked, with a sly look toward her sister.

Lilah sucked in a breath. "Ghosts?"

He gave Tilda a pointed look before turning to Lilah. "There are no ghosts in this house."

"How do you know?" she asked worriedly.

"I asked the real estate agent. Their professional code of conduct requires them to disclose any evidence of paranormal activity."

Tilda snorted at his obvious fabrication.

Lilah looked at him hopefully. "Is that true?"

"I don't know," he admitted. "But I promise there are no ghosts in this house."

"But how do you know?" Lilah pressed.

"Because everyone in this town seems to know everyone else's business and if there were any rumors about it being haunted, I would have heard them."

"There's something else this house doesn't have," Tilda noted.

"What's that?"

"Beds."

"They're being shipped with the rest of our furniture."

"How come *you* got new furniture?"

Because he hadn't wanted to move the bed that he'd shared with his wife to his new home. "Because Aunt Rachel needed somewhere to sleep while she was staying with you guys, and I didn't want to sleep on the floor for two weeks."

Tilda's jaw dropped. "Are you saying we have to sleep on the floor tonight?"

"No," he said. "You can have my bed." (Conveniently made up with fresh sheets before Sarah had arrived.) "And Aunt Rachel can have the bed in the den."

"Where will you sleep?" Lilah asked worriedly.

"On the floor in the spare room," he decided.

"That doesn't sound very comfortable."

"It's only for a couple of nights."

Apparently the girls were tired out from their two days of travel, so after he made them a snack of scrambled eggs and toast—they'd always got a kick out of breakfast for dinner—they said good-night and went upstairs to crash in his bed.

Andrew had tidied up the dishes from his dinner and theirs and was settled in the living room with the baseball game on TV when his sister finally returned from delivering Sarah's cupcakes.

"Did you get lost?" Andrew asked, as she lowered herself into the second lawn chair and stretched her legs out in front of her.

"Nope," she said easily.

Of course, he'd sent a text message when he realized she'd been gone nearly an hour, simply asking "OK?" and she'd responded with a thumbs-up emoji.

"I gave you a three-minute errand and you've been gone almost two hours. Where have you been?"

"At Sarah's."

"For two hours?"

Rachel shrugged. "We had a glass of wine together. Actually, a couple of glasses."

"You had wine with Sarah?" He wasn't sure if that revelation was surprising or just unnerving.

"A really nice chardonnay from Oregon with aromas of apple and pear, subtle spice and vanilla."

"I didn't ask for your tasting notes," he said dryly. "Which I suspect you got from the label on the back of the bottle."

"What were you asking, then?" she said.

"I wasn't really asking anything. I guess I was just…surprised that Sarah invited you in."

"Truthfully, I invited myself," Rachel confided. "Because I wanted to get to know the new woman in your life."

"I'm not sure she'd agree with that title, especially after your untimely arrival."

"Well, there was a definite vibe when we came in. And she was clearly reluctant to let me over the threshold at first—probably because she suspected I was a jealous wife who would stab her in the back when she was pouring the wine."

"Why would she think you were a jealous wife? I told her I'm not married."

"Did you tell her you had kids, though? Because I got the impression that was a surprise to her."

"My parenthood status didn't exactly come up in conversation," he hedged.

"Uh-huh," she said, in a tone ripe with disapproval. "And that kind of secret is a major red flag, especially to a woman who already has trust issues."

He frowned at that. "What makes you think Sarah has trust issues?"

"I can recognize a kindred spirit," she assured him.

Of course he knew at least some of what his sister had been through. Married for five years to her high school sweetheart who worked in sales and cheated on her every time he had a business trip out of town. And there were a lot of business trips out of town. Following her divorce, she dated a few other guys, none of those relationships lasting very long, until she found herself alone at a bar one night, having been stood up by a guy she'd met online, and ran into her former divorce attorney. Six months after that, they were married.

"Do you think she'll ever forgive me?" Andrew asked his sister now.

"I'd say that depends on what you do next."

"I could use some advice here."

"Do you really need me to tell you to be honest with her?"

"No, I could figure out that part," he assured her.

"Belatedly," she muttered.

"I was hoping for something a little more concrete," he prompted.

"Start with an apology," she said. "And make it a good one."

THOUGH IT WAS tradition to give Claire a single cupcake on her birthday, Sarah decided to package up four of the treats for her friend to share with her husband. That left her with six out of the original dozen, after she'd offered one to Rachel the night before, and the other woman had enjoyed it so thoroughly, Sarah had been unable to resist the temptation of sampling one herself. But she had no intention of keeping the extra cupcakes, because she didn't need any more temptation—or any reminders of her ill-advised bargain with Haven's new baker.

It was a relief to know that he hadn't lied about his marital status—she couldn't bear the thought of being "the other woman" again—but he'd still been less than forthcoming about his relationship history and that made her wary. Not that she'd expected him to offer up details of all past romantic contacts, but a passing mention of an ex-wife and kids didn't seem too much to ask.

"I've had some failed relationships," he'd said. Neglecting to mention that one of those failed relationships—a nearly ten-year marriage, according to his sister—had made him a father twice over was an unforgiveable oversight.

And she'd really liked him, *dammit*.

Not to mention that his kisses were even more amazing than his delicious cupcakes.

But she determinedly pushed all thoughts of him out of her mind as she made her way to Crooked Creek Ranch, continuing past the main house to the old bunkhouse that her grandfather had renovated for his personal use when he vacated the primary residence for Spencer and Kenzie after their wedding. Because the Blake name might be synonymous with mining in northern Nevada, but Jesse Blake's heart would always belong at Crooked Creek Ranch. He'd turned over the reins of Blake Mining to his kids long ago and gone back to ranching, motivated by pleasure rather than the need for profit this time around.

He now had a small herd of cattle and a stable full of horses, and he'd taught each and every one of his grandkids to ride, instilling in them an appreciation and affection for the gorgeous animals that were essential to ranching operations. And now he was doing the same for the next generation.

In addition, he continued to help his grandson Spencer—another of Sarah's numerous cousins—at Channing Horse Trainers as well as enjoying a romance with Helen Powell. And no, it wasn't lost on Sarah that her eighty-year-old grandfather was in a committed relationship of half a dozen years when most of her romances expired more quickly than a jug of milk.

Collecting the box of cupcakes, she pushed open the car door. Before her feet even hit the ground, Luke was there, dancing around, begging for attention. As if Gramps's now five-year-old Labradoodle didn't have people fussing over him 24/7. But she crouched down to rub the soft curls on his head and scratch behind his ears, then she gave him one of the doggy treats she'd learned to always carry in her pocket, and he happily trotted off.

A glance toward the nearby paddock revealed that Gramps was working with a young paint horse. He gave her a nod, acknowledging Sarah's presence, but carried on with the lesson. So she waited and watched while her grandfather put the yearling through its paces.

"Who's this?" Sarah asked, when Gramps led the sorrel beauty over to the fence.

"Rembrandt." He rubbed a hand over the animal's flank with obvious affection.

"He's gorgeous," Sarah noted. "But what do you need with another horse?"

"What do I need with all the money I've got?"

She laughed. "So you bought him just because you could?"

He shrugged. "And because I knew Claire could use the cash—and a vacant stall at Twilight Valley."

Which hadn't remained vacant for long, hence Claire's plans for a second barn.

"I thought the name sounded familiar," Sarah said, recalling now that she'd seen it on paperwork at Twilight Valley. "But he wasn't at the rescue for long, so I don't think I ever got to meet him."

"I scooped him up before you started working with Claire," Gramps admitted. "I asked if she had a mount that might be suitable for a young barrel racer, and she invited me to come out to the ranch to meet Rembrandt."

"Dani wants to barrel race?" Sarah guessed.

Gramps nodded again.

"How do her parents feel about that?"

"Spencer rose to fame and fortune on the back of bulls, so he's hardly in a position to object," he pointed out. "Kenzie wants to be supportive, but I think she's worried about Dani following in her mom's footsteps."

Because Kenzie was Dani's stepmother, having married Spencer six years earlier, less than a year after his return to Haven with his four-year-old daughter in tow.

"So what brings you out to Crooked Creek today?" her grandfather asked.

Sarah held up the bakery box.

Gramps winced. "Oh, honey—you didn't try your hand at baking again, did you?"

She huffed out an indignant breath. "No, I didn't."

Evidently relieved by her assurance, he accepted the box and lifted the lid to peek inside. "So where'd you get the fancy treats? Because last I heard, the bakery wasn't reopening until the end of the month."

"Then there's obviously nothing wrong with your hearing."

"But I still haven't heard you say where these came from," he noted.

"I made a deal with the devil."

His bushy white eyebrows lifted.

Sarah shook her head. "Never mind. It's a long story."

"I've got time," Gramps assured her.

"I don't," she said. "I'm on my way to Twilight Valley where, by the way, that cold saltwater spa you funded is already getting lots of use."

Now those bushy eyebrows drew together in a scowl. "That donation was supposed to be anonymous."

"And it was," she confirmed. "I wasn't one hundred percent certain the money came from you until just now."

"You think you're clever, don't you?"

"I *know* I'm clever. I take after my grandfather. Grandpa Stafford, I mean."

"You're sassy, too," he said, an unmistakable note of pride in his voice.

She grinned and touched her lips to his weathered cheek. "Share those cupcakes with Dani and Owen."

He tucked the box behind his back. "What cupcakes?"

Sarah was laughing as she turned toward her car.

"Before you rush off," Gramps said, halting her in her tracks, "make sure you keep your calendar open the first weekend in November."

She accessed the app on her phone to check the date. "So far so good."

"And try to rustle up a date for yourself," he said.

"A date for what?" Sarah asked warily.

He puffed out his chest and grinned. "My wedding."

"Really?" She was grinning now, too. "You and Helen are finally getting married?"

He nodded as he accepted her hug.

"I've been trying to get Helen to move in with me for years, but she refused to do so without a ring on her finger—so I finally put a ring on her finger."

"I hope your proposal was a little more romantic than that," she said dryly.

"Don't you worry," he said. "Your old grandpa's still got some moves."

"I'll take your word for it," she decided.

"You don't have to take my word, you can take hers," he told her. "It was *yes*."

"And I'm happy for you both," she said. "But now I really have to run."

"Since you're making deals with the devil, maybe you could ask him to find you a date for the wedding," Gramps suggested, with a wiggle of his bushy brows. "Better yet, you could invite him."

Not going to happen, Sarah vowed.

But the idea lingered in her mind, tempting her, long after she'd driven away from Crooked Creek.

CHAPTER EIGHT

KIDS HAD A way of changing a man's perspective. And the morning after his dinner with Sarah was unceremoniously interrupted, Andrew was refocused on his priorities.

He'd woken up early—partly because he was trying to get accustomed to the early morning hours of a baker and partly because he'd slept like crap on the floor of the guest room. He still had work to do at the bakery, but he was on-track for the grand opening and felt it was important to spend some time with his daughters on their first day in their new home.

Lilah had been the first one up after him, and when she made her way downstairs, her disposition was as bright as the sun. Rachel had wandered in a short while later, drawn by the scent of coffee, as he was pouring batter into the pan on the stove. And now, finally, Tilda found her way into the kitchen.

"I'm making pancakes," Andrew said.

"I'm not hungry."

"You don't have to be hungry to want pancakes," he said easily.

"I'll have another one, Daddy," Lilah said, holding up her empty plate. "Please."

Andrew flipped the cake out of the pan and onto her plate.

"Yay, breakfast theater," Tilda said dryly.

"And here I was worried that the happy mood you took to bed last night would be absent this morning," he remarked.

"Did you really expect me to be happy that we moved half-way across the country?"

"No," he admitted. "But I expected—or at least hoped—that you'd come here with an open mind."

Tilda didn't respond to that as she tugged on the door of the refrigerator.

"Juice is already out," he told her.

She retrieved a can of diet cola from the fridge.

He glanced at the clock on the stove. "It's not even nine thirty in the morning."

"I'm thirsty."

"Pour yourself a glass of juice."

She made a face. "Juice is full of sugar."

"At least it's natural sugar. That stuff is nothing but chemicals." But he'd bought it for her, anyway, stocking both of the girls' favorite treats so the place would feel more like home when they arrived.

"Chemicals that taste good," she said, defiantly popping the top and taking a long swallow.

Rachel got up to make another cup of coffee, clearly signaling her intention to stay out of this battle. Andrew bit his tongue, deciding to save his energy for the next one. Because lately, it seemed as if there was always another battle with Tilda.

Once upon a time, she'd been as easy to please as her little sister. The onset of adolescence had changed things, but she'd been even more difficult since her mom announced she was moving to California—and downright ornery since Andrew decided to move them to Nevada.

"So how did you girls sleep last night?" he asked now.

"Great," Lilah said.

"Horrible," Tilda immediately countered. "She thrashes in her sleep."

"I'd forgotten that," Andrew admitted. "Whenever she had a bad dream when she was little, she'd crawl into bed with me and Mom—and I'd go sleep on the sofa rather than wake up black and blue."

Lilah frowned. "I don't do it on purpose."

"I know." He dropped a kiss on her forehead, to ensure she knew there were no hard feelings. "And you," he said to Tilda, "would turn yourself around so that you were sleeping sideways—so I got kicked out of the bed by you, too."

"I did?" Tilda asked, surprised.

"You did," he confirmed.

"And that's why Rob and I have already agreed that, if and when we have kids, there will be a strict no-sharing-our-bed policy," Rachel chimed in.

Andrew smirked at his sister. "A policy that will go out the window the first time your child wakes up crying in the night and can't be consoled with anything but cuddles."

He set a plate with a pancake on it in front of Tilda.

"I said I didn't want any."

"But you love pancakes."

"No," she denied. "Lilah loves pancakes."

He bit his tongue again, despite the fact that he couldn't count the number of weekend mornings that he'd made stacks of pancakes for the girls—and they'd both gobbled them up, slathered in butter and maple syrup. But Tilda clearly didn't want to remember those mornings right now.

"Do you want me to make you something else?" he offered.

"I told you I'm not hungry."

"You need to eat."

"Tilda doesn't eat breakfast anymore," Lilah remarked.

"Since when?"

"I eat if I'm hungry," Tilda said defensively. "I'm just not hungry."

"You weren't hungry at lunch yesterday, either."

Tilda glared at her sister. "My hamburger tasted like it had been sitting under a heat lamp all day."

"Mine tasted fine."

Andrew sent an apologetic look at Rachel, having a whole new appreciation for the journey his sister had endured with his bickering daughters. "I'm realizing that I can't thank you enough for everything you've done for us over the past two weeks."

"You're right," she agreed. "But you can give me a ride to the airport this afternoon."

As SARAH MADE her way down the long drive toward Claire and Devin's house, she caught a glimpse of her friend in the distance, racing over the rolling hills on the back of a horse that looked surprisingly familiar. She parked behind Devin's truck and, before she'd even opened her door, Ed was there.

The German shepherd/collie mix was always excited for visitors, though Sarah liked to think that she and Ed had formed a special bond as she'd been the first person to visit after Claire brought him home from the shelter. And even though he saw her almost every day now that she was working at Twilight Valley, he never failed to greet her with enthusiasm. Another reason she should consider abandoning any thoughts of romance in favor of a canine companion.

"Eduardo!" She crouched to give the dog the attention he craved—and one of his favorite treats.

When he trotted off with his biscuit, she straightened up and attempted to brush the dog hair off her pants.

"Good luck with that," Devin said dryly.

She glanced over to see him leaning against one of the support posts on the porch.

"Good afternoon to you, too," she replied to her cousin.

"There's coffee, if you want," he told her. "Claire just went out for a ride, but she'll be back soon."

"Coffee sounds good." She opened the passenger side door of her SUV to retrieve the remaining bakery box from the front seat, then followed him into the house. She set the box on the counter and washed her hands before accepting the mug of coffee he offered with a "thanks."

"You know where cream and sugar are, if you want them."

"I do—and I do," she said, adding some of each to her cup before joining him at the table. "I saw Claire as I drove in—on a horse that looked a lot like Mystic."

"Probably because it is Mystic," he admitted.

She frowned. "Did his buyer back out of the sale?"

"Not exactly," Devin hedged.

"So why don't you tell me—*exactly*—what happened?" she suggested.

"The buyer, Tom Broadbent, is a friend of mine from Stanford. I asked him to inquire through the website about Mystic because I knew Claire wouldn't admit that she wanted to keep him until someone else showed an interest. But then she insisted that it would be good for him to move on, that Twilight Valley was always meant to be a temporary home for the horses that came here. So Tom agreed to buy the horse, with the understanding that when Claire realized she missed him, I'd buy Mystic back."

"So it was all just a subterfuge?"

He frowned. "*Subterfuge* is a rather harsh word."

"What would you prefer? *Lie? Deceit?*" She folded her arms on the table. "And what is it about a man's DNA that renders him incapable of being honest with a woman?"

"Why do I get the feeling that you're mad...but not necessarily at me?"

"I *am* mad at you," she said, because she was. But he was right in that she was madder at Andrew. And since Andrew wasn't here, she refocused her attention on the topic at hand. "Because I wasted my time doing a thorough background check on your friend to ensure that Mystic would be going to a good home."

"Instead, he's staying in a good home," Devin pointed out.

"And that's great," she agreed. "I'm just saying, you could have told me what you were up to and saved me the trouble of checking the guy's references."

"I thought about it," he admitted. "But I didn't trust you not to open your big mouth and spoil the surprise."

"I can keep a secret," she told him, a little indignant that he would suggest otherwise.

"From Claire?" he challenged.

She considered that as she sipped her coffee. "Probably not," she finally conceded. "Especially not when she started crying over Mystic the other day."

Devin grimaced. "She cried?"

"Did you think she wouldn't?"

"I thought—*I hoped*—I'd have a chance to put the bow around Mystic's neck before she got to that point."

"Well, you thought wrong," she told him.

"Anyway, she's happy now that she knows Mystic is staying," Devin said, a defensive note in his voice.

"Of course she is," Sarah said. "And it's a fabulous gift because it shows that you know her heart."

"I'm learning, anyway," Devin said, flushing a little in response to her praise.

A happy bark sounded from outside—Ed's signal that Claire had returned from her ride.

"I'll go take care of Mystic, so you and Claire can visit," he said, rising to his feet.

"Thanks, Dev."

"You can thank me by telling Claire that one of those cupcakes has my name on it."

"Only one?"

"I not only know her heart, I also know not to get between my wife and chocolate," he said.

Sarah was laughing at that when her friend walked into the kitchen.

"Happy birthday!" she said, greeting her friend with a hug before presenting her with the bakery box.

Claire lifted the lid, her eyes growing wide. "Ohmygod! I don't believe it."

"You thought I'd forget your birthday?" Sarah teased, choosing to forget that she'd almost done exactly that.

"Never," her friend promised. "But I thought you'd have to stick a candle in a muffin from The Daily Grind this year."

"Well, the cupcakes aren't from Sweet Caroline's, obviously, but they are chocolate caramel nut."

"Did you make them?" Claire, unlike Gramps, only sounded a little wary.

Sarah laughed. "I love you too much to do something like that—especially on your birthday."

"So where did they come from?"

"I'll tell you," she promised. "But first, I want you to tell me how dinner was with your parents last night."

"Surprisingly pleasant," Claire said. "It helps that my parents really like Devin. And he earned bonus points this time by solving the dessert dilemma."

"How did he do that?" Sarah wondered.

"He sweet-talked Bonnie Reidel into making a lemon cheese-cake."

Why hadn't it occurred to Sarah to go to Bonnie for cupcakes?

If she'd done so, the whole scene with Andrew and his sister and his kids would have been avoided.

And she would have still been in the dark about him.

So maybe the whole scene had served a purpose, after all—if only to remind Sarah that she was better off alone rather than with a man who couldn't be honest.

"And Bonnie confirmed that she'll still be working at the bakery when it reopens as Sugar & Spice. Apparently the owner has two daughters who inspired the new name, because 'sugar and spice and everything nice.'" Claire licked caramel off her thumb. "Isn't that sweet?"

"It is," Sarah agreed. And then, "I slept with him."

The words spilled out of her mouth as if of their own volition.

Claire choked on a mouthful of coffee and had to grab a napkin to wipe the liquid dribbling down her chin.

"Who?" she asked, when she managed to speak.

"The new owner of Sweet Caroline's."

"Last night?"

Sarah shook her head as she refilled her coffee mug. "Six weeks ago."

"Six weeks ago?" Claire echoed indignantly. "And I'm only hearing about this *now*?"

"Because I didn't know he was the new owner of Sweet Caroline's at the time, and I thought he was leaving town the next day. For good, I might add."

"Six weeks..." Claire said again, her tone speculative now. Then she obviously put the pieces together, because her eyes went wide. "The hottie who thought you were a stripper is the new owner of the bakery?"

Now Sarah nodded.

"Well, well, well." Her friend lifted her mug to her lips again, sipping cautiously this time. "I guess he wasn't entirely wrong, was he? Assuming you did take your clothes off before you did the deed, of course."

"The only reason it happened is that I didn't think I'd ever see him again."

"You didn't find him the least bit attractive or charming?" her friend challenged.

"Okay, it's not the *only* reason I invited him to come home with me," she acknowledged. "But it was a significant factor."

"And now there's a chance you could cross paths with him on any given day."

"Exactly," she said.

"I still don't understand why you seem to think that's a problem," Claire admitted.

"Because I was in the process of making changes to my life," Sarah reminded her. "No more doing a job I didn't want to do. No more worrying about other people's expectations. And definitely no more falling into bed with hot guys who made me feel good in the moment."

"You planned to fall into bed with not-hot guys who made you feel good? Or hot guys who didn't make you feel good?"

"You know what I mean."

"What I know is that you're too hard on yourself," Claire said gently. "So what if you've had a few relationships that didn't work out? If you like this guy and he likes you—and it seems obvious there's an attraction on both sides—why not give it a chance?"

"Because I promised myself that I wasn't going to get involved with a man unless there was more than physical attraction."

"Physical attraction can be a solid foundation for a relationship."

"It was a one-night stand."

"So you're not interested in hooking up with him again?"

"He's got an ex-wife and two adolescent daughters."

"Everyone has a history," Claire pointed out.

"History suggests something in the past. His kids are very much in the present. And they're not little kids—they're fourteen and twelve."

"So you're not going to win them over with story times and snuggles," Claire acknowledged. "But maybe trips to the mall or mani-pedis at Serenity Spa?"

"I don't think there's much hope of winning them over. They did not look at all happy to discover that their dad had company when they showed up last night."

"I think you skipped that part of the story," Claire said. "So spill it now, Stafford."

Sarah obliged by summarizing the events of the previous evening for her friend.

"I can see how that would have been awkward," Claire admitted. "And he definitely should have given you a heads-up about the kids. But before you completely write him off, maybe you could give him a chance to explain?"

"Maybe," she allowed.

"And when he does, you can tell him that his are the best chocolate caramel nut cupcakes I've ever had."

"I don't think his ego needs the stroking."

"Well, you can stroke other parts, if you'd prefer," Claire said with a wink. "But I'm going to be at the grand opening of Sugar & Spice in two weeks to see what other magic he makes in the kitchen."

TILDA STOOD ON the porch, watching as her dad's car pulled out of the driveway. He was taking Aunt Rachel to the airport in Elko so that she could fly back to Texas, and Lilah had decided to go with them. Tilda had been invited, too, but after the twenty-eight-hour drive from Beaumont, the last thing she wanted was to spend more time stuck in a vehicle.

Her dad had been hesitant to leave her alone but had finally relented, giving her strict instructions to stay at the house. He didn't want her wandering off in an unfamiliar town, especially when he wasn't going to be around.

As far as Tilda could tell, there wasn't anywhere to go, anyway. There wasn't even a mall in Haven—just a handful of shops on Main Street. Apparently the nearest shopping mall was in a town called Battle Mountain. But she had no idea how to get there and when she punched the address into her Uber app, she got zero available drivers.

Zero.

"I'm in hell."

"If the rumors are to be believed, hell is a lot hotter than Haven, Nevada."

She'd been certain she was alone, so when she heard the response to her muttered remark, she sucked in a breath and spun around.

"Sneaking up on someone like that is a good way to get kicked in the balls," she told the boy standing at the bottom of the steps leading up to the porch.

"You'd need a lot longer legs than what you've got," he pointed out. "Considering that I'm at least fifteen feet away from you."

He was tall—close to her dad's height, she guessed, which she knew to be six feet—but skinny. His shoulder bones were visible through his shirt and his knees were knobby beneath the hem of his cargo shorts. On the front of his T-shirt was a graphic of a d20 with the words "this is how I roll." His hair was somewhere between dark blond and light brown, his green eyes were amplified by the wire-rimmed glasses he wore, and he carried a foil-covered tray in his hands.

A stereotypical D&D geek, she decided.

The type of guy she wouldn't have been caught dead talking to at Wharncliffe Middle School.

And though she was a long way from there now, she scowled at him. "And anyway, I wasn't talking to you."

He made a show of looking around, highlighting the fact that there was no one else nearby. "So who were you talking to?"

"Myself," she snapped.

"Do you do that a lot?" he asked curiously.

"Sometimes it's the only way I can have an intelligent conversation."

His brows lifted. "Someone has a high opinion of herself."

"What are you doing here, anyway?"

"I live there," he said, nodding toward the house next door. "My mom made a chicken broccoli casserole to welcome your family to the neighborhood."

"I stand corrected," she said. "This isn't hell, it's worse. It's a fifties sitcom neighborhood."

"Are you going to take the casserole?" he asked, a little impatiently.

She stomped down the steps to accept the dish. "Thanks."

"My name's Warren."

He reminded her of Lilah—open and approachable. Willing to make friends with everyone who crossed her path.

Yin to her sister's yang.

"I don't care."

He took a step back, startled by her blunt response. "O-kay, then."

She'd been rude—inexcusably rude—and felt the prickle of embarrassed heat crawl up her throat.

"I just want to be alone right now," she said.

Not an apology but an explanation.

"I'll leave you to it," he said, and walked away.

And she was glad.

Really.

CHAPTER NINE

WHEN SARAH RETURNED home after her visit with Claire, she found Andrew sitting in one of the turquoise Adirondack chairs on her porch, holding a branch?

As she made her way to the door, she looked at the stem covered in silvery green leaves—and then him—warily.

Or perhaps quizzically, because he said, "It's an olive branch."

And he offered it to her.

Not just a proverbial olive branch—a real one.

Though she was willing to give him credit for creativity, she refused to be charmed.

"Claire loved the cupcake," she told him, accepting the branch and extending her own. "In fact, she said it was even better than the one I gave her from Sweet Caroline's last year."

"I'm happy to hear it."

"So thank you—for making them and also for having your sister deliver them to me."

"You're welcome."

"And now that we've dispensed with those pleasantries, why don't you tell me why you're here?"

"I'm hoping you'll give me five minutes of your time to apologize and explain," he said.

"Not necessary," she said.

"My mother taught me to apologize when I did something wrong. Five minutes," he said again. "Please."

She turned her wrist to tap the face of her Apple watch, starting the timer. "The clock is ticking."

"Can we go inside? Or do you want the neighbors to see me groveling on your front porch?"

After a brief hesitation, she unlocked the door and led him inside.

"Four minutes and fifty seconds."

"I'm sorry."

"Look at that—you didn't even need half a minute."

"Any chance I could get a cup of coffee in the time I have left?"

"Apparently your mother didn't teach her kids not to invite themselves into other people's houses and offer themselves beverages," she remarked dryly.

But she selected a pod and dropped it into the single-serve coffee maker, then set a mug beneath the spout.

"Do I need to apologize for my sister as well as myself?" he asked.

"No, just yourself," she told him. "It turns out that I like your sister."

"Ouch," he said, as she handed the mug to him. "But as it turns out, she likes you, too."

"Cream or sugar?"

He shook his head. "This is fine."

"She told me that you're divorced."

"About four years now," he confirmed. "Me and Miranda both knew it was over long before we went our separate ways, but we tried to stick it out for Tilda and Lilah."

"And you have custody?"

"Officially, Miranda and I have joint custody, which worked well when we were all living in Beaumont. Eight months ago, she decided to take a new job in Calistoga, and the girls have only seen her three times since the move."

"That must be hard on them," she noted.

He sipped his coffee. "It has been," he agreed. "And I worry that I might have made things worse by moving them out of Texas and completely upending their lives."

"But that's why you moved from Texas to Nevada," she realized, setting a second mug beneath the spout of her coffee maker. "To be closer to her."

"To facilitate visitation between the girls and their mom," he clarified.

"Most people would have found a way to work some of that information into a conversation," she said.

"You're right," he acknowledged.

"We spent *hours* together. You told me that you wanted to be a rodeo clown when *you* were a kid but somehow you never got around to mentioning that you *have* kids."

"You didn't want to know anything about me," he reminded her. "You wouldn't even let me tell you my name."

"Because I didn't think I'd ever see you again after that night," she pointed out.

"You mean you didn't *want* to see me again after that night," he guessed.

Apparently the man was more intuitive than she'd given him credit for.

"Maybe you're right," she allowed, "Maybe we should both just chalk up that night as a mistake and forget it ever happened."

"I don't think I could forget that night if I wanted to—and I don't want to. But the reality is that I'm a single dad of two daughters who aren't thrilled with the move halfway across the country."

"I understand," she assured him.

"I'm not sure that you do," he said. "Because notwithstanding all of that, I don't want to pretend the connection we have doesn't mean anything, because it's been a long time since I've felt the way I feel when I'm with you."

"That feeling is chemistry," she said dismissively. "Common enough and destined to fizzle out."

"Chemistry doesn't always fizzle out," he argued. "Sometimes it makes magic—like when the heat of an oven transforms the molecular structure of batter into cake."

"That's not magic," she said dismissively. "And anyway, you

have other things that require your attention right now and I'm not looking for a relationship."

"Sometimes we don't know what we're looking for until we find it," he pointed out.

"Now you're a philosopher as well as a baker?"

"Or maybe just a man who doesn't want you to shut the door on the possibility of something between us."

"You shut the door when you lied to me," she told him.

"I never lied."

"But you didn't exactly tell the truth, either."

"You're right and I'm sorry."

"And now we're back to the beginning again and your five minutes were up a long time ago."

He set his empty mug on the counter. "Thanks for the coffee."

Sarah watched him walk to the door and told herself it was better this way.

But she didn't really believe it.

When Andrew was gone, she googled "how to care for an olive branch." Then she filled a vase with water, placed some river rocks from her front garden in the bottom and carefully sliced the bottom of the branch upward to assist with the intake of water before sliding it into the vase.

The branch had an earthy fragrance, slightly bitter with just a hint of smokiness, and she smiled as she breathed in the scent—then immediately chastised herself for mooning over the stupid branch like it was a bouquet of roses.

But the truth was, she would have been less impressed with roses. While the perennial flowering plant boasted gorgeous blooms, roses were a common sight in any florist shop. And perhaps olive branches were, too, but Sarah didn't think so, and she was touched by Andrew's thoughtfulness—even if she didn't want to be.

But she'd listened to his explanation, and she was willing to admit that she might bear some responsibility for shutting him down the first night they met. But there was no excuse for him not telling her when she was with him the night before.

And now that she thought about it, she realized it wasn't the sellers who'd painted the upstairs bedrooms pink and purple—

it was Andrew who'd done that for his daughters. Which would have been the perfect opportunity to tell her about them—saying this is Tilda's room and this is Lilah's room. Instead he'd said nothing, allowing her to be completely blindsided when they walked through the door.

He'd evidently been surprised by the timing of their arrival, too—but at least he'd been aware of their existence.

But it was water under the bridge now.

He was a divorced, single dad on the verge of opening a new business and she was a never-married thirty-two-year-old woman who was only now starting to take control of her own life. She couldn't imagine that he had time for a romantic relationship, even if he wanted one, and she wasn't willing to open up her heart to yet another man whose own was otherwise engaged.

I don't want to pretend the connection we have doesn't mean anything, because it's been a long time since I've felt the way I feel when I'm with you.

It had been a long time since she'd felt that way, too.

And though she'd dismissed the feeling as chemistry destined to fizzle out, after six weeks, it showed no signs of fizzling.

But Sarah was accustomed to wanting what she couldn't have, and so long as she remembered that the town's sexy baker fell into that category, she had nothing to worry about.

The problem was that her subconscious wasn't willing to fall in line with that plan, and when she slept, she dreamed about him. And in her dreams, she remembered how completely he'd turned her on with just a kiss, how she'd yearned to feel his hands on her and his hard body moving in tandem with her own.

"We should probably be heading back," he said, when he'd eased away after kissing her until they were both panting and breathless.

She nodded, more than a little disappointed that their limited time together was already at an end.

"You've got an early flight in the morning," she remembered.

"Not all that early."

"Then maybe, instead of dropping me off at my car, you could give me a ride home?"

It was an invitation offered—and accepted.

He ignored the speed limit on the drive back to town, following the directions she gave him to her place. The door was barely closed behind them before they were tearing at one another's clothes, leaving a trail of garments all the way to her bedroom.

They tumbled onto the mattress together, their mouths fused, their bodies straining.

His hands stroked over her skin, stoking her desire. His thumbs brushed over the already tight peaks of her nipples through the lacy fabric of her bra, sending sharp, shocking arrows of pleasure from the tips to her core. Then he replaced his hands with his mouth, suckling her through the fabric barrier, first one breast, then the other, until she was practically whimpering.

He responded by releasing the clasp at the front of her bra and peeling back the cups. Then his mouth was on her bare skin, teasing and tasting, and she did whimper.

But he wasn't finished yet. He made his way down her body, exploring every inch of her with his hands and his lips. Touching and kissing, stroking and sucking.

He brushed his lips over her belly button, then continued his downward trajectory. When he parted the soft folds of skin at the juncture of her thighs, everything inside her tightened in anticipation.

His fingertips danced over the ultrasensitive nub at her center, more of a tease than a touch. And then again and again, taunting her with the promise of something more.

She had a moment—when he was sheathing himself with the condom she'd taken out of the drawer of her nightstand—to wonder if she was making a mistake. And she acknowledged, if only to herself, that she might very well regret this in the morning. But right now, in this moment, there wasn't anything she wanted more than to be with him.

Then he was rising over her, thrusting into her. Again and again, long and deep strokes that pushed her ever closer to the edge of the abyss...and over.

He found his own release immediately after, collapsing on top of her. She welcomed his weight, her own body thoroughly sated, though her silly heart still yearned for more...

"THANKS FOR MAKING dinner tonight, Tilda," Andrew said, as they sat down to a meal of chicken tacos.

"I shredded the cheese," Lilah chimed in.

"And you did an excellent job," he responded.

"Yeah, you have a special talent for sliding a block of cheddar over a grater," Tilda told her sister.

Andrew gave his eldest daughter a disapproving look.

"You've both been great about picking up the slack around the house while I've been busy at the bakery," he continued. "And I appreciate all the help."

"Maybe you could show your appreciation by buying pizza for dinner tomorrow night?" Tilda suggested hopefully.

According to her, Jo's Pizza was the only good thing about this town.

"We had pizza on Sunday," he reminded her.

"I could eat pizza every day," Lilah chimed in.

"And if I let you, I'd no doubt get a visit from child services."

"They only take away your kids if you don't feed them, not if you feed them pizza," Tilda said.

"Well, I'm not taking any chances with my favorite girls," he said.

"We're your only girls," Lilah pointed out.

He winked at her. "Probably why you're my favorite."

Tilda snorted as she added salsa to her taco.

"Are you looking forward to camp at Adventure Village next week?" he asked Lilah.

She nodded. "I found out today that Rory's going, too."

Rory—short for Aurora—was the same age as Lilah and lived next door. They'd been introduced only a few days earlier but were already fast friends.

"I've got some plans for you, too," he said to Tilda.

"I can't wait to hear all about them," she said, sarcasm fairly dripping off her words.

"Since you insisted that you're too old to go to camp—"

"Because I am," she interjected.

"—and you're not thrilled with the idea of helping out at the bakery—"

"That's an understatement."

"—I downloaded an application so that you can volunteer at Twilight Valley this summer," he finished, choosing to ignore her interruptions.

Tilda bit into her taco. The hard shell cracked, spilling the contents onto her plate.

"Twilight Valley?" She made a face as she pushed the chicken, lettuce and cheese into a pile. "It sounds like somewhere old people go to die."

"Actually, it's where old horses go to live out their final years," he told her.

"Before they die."

He held back a weary sigh. "I've filled out most of the information. You just have to sign it."

"Thanks but no thanks," she said. "Volunteering is just another way of saying 'working without pay.'"

"It wasn't a suggestion or a request," he told her.

She scowled across the table. "You can't make me."

"You're right," he acknowledged. "But I'm not going to let you hang around the house all day doing nothing, so it's Twilight Valley or Sugar & Spice. And Twilight Valley is only two days a week—Tuesdays and Thursdays."

"How do you even know about this place?"

"When I had lunch with Kyle last week, he told me that a lot of local students do their mandatory volunteer hours at the horse rescue."

"Isn't *mandatory volunteer* an oxymoron?" she challenged.

"And there's proof that you earned that A-minus in English."

She pushed away from the table, grabbed a can of diet cola from the fridge and stomped out of the room.

"I kind of feel sorry for the horses," Lilah said. "They shouldn't have to live out their final years in the company of angsty teenage girls."

SARAH DIDN'T HEAR from Andrew again until Tuesday. And that was fine. Truthfully, she had no expectations about when—or even if—he'd reach out to her again.

She was mixing supplements into the horses' feed when her phone signaled receipt of a text message and she saw his name on her screen. Her heart skipped, and then raced as if to make up for that single missed beat.

At the same time, Claire wandered into the barn and leaned over Sarah's shoulder to see what her friend was looking at.

"Is that...a ransom note?"

"Andrew thinks he's funny," Sarah said.

"Apparently you do, too, because you were smiling when you opened the message."

"Maybe I'm just easily amused."

"'Be at 27 Morningstar Road at 6 pm tonight if you want to see your paws again,'" Claire read aloud.

Sarah swiped the screen of her phone to show her friend the photo he'd sent with the message: a picture of her faux fur oven mitts tied together with rope.

Claire laughed.

"I guess you're easily amused, too," Sarah remarked.

"You have to give him points for creativity," her friend said.

"Or deduct points for playing juvenile games," she countered.

"He's making it hard for you to stay mad at him, isn't he?"

"I'm not mad at him," Sarah denied. "I'm simply not interested."

"The problem with lying to your best friend is that she knows when you're lying," Claire said.

Sarah closed the screen on her phone and set it aside without responding to Andrew's message.

"You have to show up to get your oven mitts," Claire said. "I bought those for you."

"I know you did. And I love them, but..."

"But you're so chicken you could be marsala?"

Sarah stuck out her tongue.

"Now who's juvenile?" Claire said.

"Anyway, he's not really going to harm my oven mitts."

"Of course not," her friend agreed. "This is his way of telling you that he likes you. And obviously you like him, too, or you wouldn't think twice about brushing him off."

Sarah sighed. "I do want my oven mitts back. But the whole situation is...complicated."

"Because he's got kids? Or because you already did the horizontal naked mambo?"

"We did *not* mambo."

"Cha-cha? Rumba?" Claire suggested as alternatives.

"Someone's been watching *Dancing with the Stars* again."

"My guilty pleasure," her friend admitted.

"I'm not judging," Sarah assured her.

"I'm not judging, either," Claire said. "But I do think you should give the guy another chance. Give *yourself* a chance to be happy."

It was good advice, Sarah acknowledged. But she didn't know if she was brave enough to take it.

CHAPTER TEN

"You're punctual," Andrew noted, when he opened the door in response to Sarah's knock at 5:59 p.m.

"I didn't want to give you any excuse to harm my paws."

"I assure you, they are completely unharmed." He frowned when she handed him an envelope. "What's this?"

"The ransom."

His brows lifted when he opened the flap and saw what was inside. "I didn't ask for any money."

"I know, but I realized that I never paid you for the cupcakes," she told him now.

He handed the envelope back to her. "Your legendary chicken marsala was payment enough."

"You're not going to stay in business long if you give cupcakes away to anyone who asks," she pointed out.

"I wouldn't give them away to just anyone," he said. "But I'm always happy to help out a friend."

"Are we friends now?"

"I hope so."

"Does that mean I can have my oven mitts back?"

"Of course," he said. "But I'm hoping that, before you go, you'll stay for a meal you didn't have to cook this time."

"Pizza from Jo's?" she guessed.

"No, lasagna from the freezer section of the grocery store."

Sarah hesitated.

"With salad and garlic bread," he added, aware that the offer of a prepackaged entrée probably wasn't overly appealing.

She looked at him warily. "Why are you doing this?"

"I want you to have a chance to get to know my daughters."

"Did you ever consider just asking instead of holding my oven mitts hostage?"

"I considered it," he admitted. "And I didn't like my chances of getting a positive response."

"Next time, just ask," she advised.

"I will," he promised, pleased that she seemed willing to consider the possibility of a next time.

"Okay."

"You'll stay for dinner?" he prompted.

She nodded.

He grinned and gestured for her to make her way to the kitchen.

"You've got furniture," she noted, glancing into the living room.

"You like the leather sofa better than the folding chairs?"

"It works better for the overall aesthetic of the room," she said.

"I've got a dining room set now, too," he pointed out.

"And now this place actually looks lived in."

"You want to see lived in? You should see the girls' bedrooms," he told her.

"Or you could respect our privacy and not let strangers into our personal space," Tilda said, appearing in the doorway of the kitchen.

Andrew managed a smile, but Sarah could tell that it was forced.

"My eldest daughter, Tilda," he said, then turned to the teen. "Tilda, this is Sarah."

"It's nice to see you again," Sarah said.

"Yeah," Tilda agreed.

"I'm Lilah," his younger daughter said, her greeting bright and friendly as she exited the kitchen with a big bowl of salad in her hands.

"Hi, Lilah."

"Lilah, why don't you take Sarah into the dining room while Tilda helps me serve up dinner?"

"Okay," she agreed easily.

"Dad sits there, Tilda sits there and I sit there," Lilah said, pointing at the chairs around the table. "That leaves that one for you."

"Thank you," Sarah said, settling into her assigned seat.

Lilah took the seat adjacent to their guest and started chatting away while Andrew dished up the pasta and Tilda carried the plates to the table.

He hadn't dated much since his split from Miranda, and he'd never before brought a woman home for a meal with his family. And while this wasn't a date, because Sarah had made it clear that she wasn't interested in dating him, he could see that Tilda wasn't happy that there was a woman who wasn't her mom at the table with them.

And while he wished she'd at least make an effort to be polite, he knew that calling out her behavior would only exacerbate it.

"So what do you girls have planned for the summer?" Sarah asked, as she tore off a piece of garlic bread.

"I'm going to camp at Adventure Village next week," Lilah said. "And Rory, my new best friend who lives next door, is going to the same camp."

"That sounds like fun," Sarah said, then shifted her attention to Tilda. "Are you going to camp, too?"

"No. But in July we're going to spend two weeks in California with our mom."

"I told you it might not be two weeks this summer," Andrew cautioned. "Your mom just started a new job and she's not sure how much time she'll be able to take off."

"She doesn't need to take time off," Tilda said, pushing her pasta around on her plate. "It's not like we need a babysitter."

"Where in California does your mom live?" Sarah asked.

"Napa Valley."

"One of my favorite places in California."

"You've been there?" Lilah asked.

Sarah nodded. "A few times."

"We haven't been yet," Lilah confessed. "Mom's new house is under renovation."

"Well, I'm sure you'll love it when you get to visit."

"Our mom's a sommelier," Tilda said. "She knows a lot about wine."

"I'll bet she does," Sarah agreed.

"What do you do?" Lilah asked.

"I work at a local ranch."

Tilda made a face as she poked at a tomato wedge with her fork. "So you're like...a cowboy?"

"Actually, I mostly handle the business side of things, but I'm happy to help muck out stalls and groom horses when help is needed."

"Do you get to ride the horses sometimes?"

"Every day," Sarah said.

"Lucky," Lilah said.

"Can I be excused?" Tilda asked.

Andrew frowned at the food left on her plate but nodded.

"You may both be excused," he told his daughters. "We'll clean up later."

"Or I can help you clean up now," Sarah said.

"That's not necessary," he protested.

She shrugged. "If you don't want my help, then I'll take my oven mitts and go."

"Do you want to rinse or load?" he asked.

Sarah chuckled at his abrupt change of tune.

A short while later, she decided that she should have taken her oven mitts and made a quick escape when she had the chance, because helping Andrew tidy up after dinner turned out to be an exercise in sexual frustration. Somehow while they ate, the huge kitchen had shrunk to a fraction of its previous size, so that every time they crossed paths, there was some kind of physical contact between them. And no matter how unintentional or fleeting that contact, it had the effect of sending currents of electricity sparking through her veins.

She scraped the remnants of food off Tilda's plate—had the girl eaten any of her lasagna?—then rinsed it under the faucet.

As she was doing so, Andrew sidled by to return the container of Parmesan to the refrigerator.

His hip grazed her bottom, and the plate slipped out of her grasp. Thankfully it didn't break, but it clattered loudly enough to catch his attention.

"Sorry," she said.

"No worries." He retrieved the plate from the sink and placed it in the dishwasher.

She wondered if the heightened attraction was a result of her determination that the single dad of two was off-limits, similar to how someone on a diet might obsess over the foods they wanted to avoid.

Thankfully, Sarah had some experience in turning away from the things she wanted, and she took a step back now.

"I think that's everything," she said.

He slid the rack into place, then closed the door.

As Sarah dried her hands on a tea towel, she spotted a glass dish on the counter. "Is that my baking pan?"

"It is," he confirmed.

She stepped closer to look at the sugar-dusted squares of fried dough in the pan, tightly covered in plastic wrap. "What are those?"

"Those are what all the kerfuffle is about," he told her.

"Beignets," she realized.

And he was right that they had been the subject of much kerfuffle when Haven's residents learned that the new baker was replacing doughnuts with its French cousin.

"More specifically, those are my chai latte beignets."

"Why are your chai latte beignets in my pan?"

"Because one of the other things my mother taught me was never return a food dish empty."

"They're for me?"

He nodded.

"Thank you," she said, surprised and pleased by the gesture.

"You can have one now, if you want. I just realized that I didn't offer you anything for dessert."

"I don't usually eat dessert, anyway," she confided. Or doughnuts, though she couldn't deny that the beignets were tempting.

"Or maybe, since there are two in the pan, you were hoping that I'd offer one to you?"

"Nope, they're both yours."

"That's right—you don't eat what you bake. You only sample."

"As we discussed when I caught you checking me out."

"That was before," she told him.

"Before?"

"Before I found out that you were a single dad of two kids."

"And my parental status somehow changes the appearance of my butt?"

"No, but it changes everything else."

"You're no longer attracted to me?"

"It's not about attraction. It's about the fact that we're at different stages of our lives, with very different priorities."

"So you *are* still attracted to me."

She blew out a breath. "Did you hear the part about different stages of our lives and different priorities?"

"I heard it," he said. "I just don't happen to think that matters as much as the chemistry between us."

"And on that note, I'm going to take my baking pan and my oven mitts and go," she decided. "Please tell your daughters it was a pleasure to meet them and goodbye."

He followed her to the front door. "How about a little wager?"

She eyed him warily as she slipped her feet into her shoes. "What kind of wager?"

"You try one of those beignets, and I bet you come into the bakery on the day of the grand opening for more."

"And if I do?"

"If you do, then you agree to give us a chance to see where the attraction between us leads."

She didn't need a map to see where the attraction would lead—straight to the bedroom.

"And if I don't show up at the bakery?"

He smiled. "You will," he assured her. "But if you don't, then I will defer to your wish to ignore the attraction between us."

"You specified the grand opening," she noted. "So if I were to come in the day after for more beignets—or two days after that—I'd still win the bet?"

He nodded. "Is that a wager you're willing to make?"

She shifted the baking pan to one hand and offered him the other.

After a perfunctory shake to seal their deal, he tugged on her hand, drawing her closer.

"I look forward to seeing you soon—and definitely on the twenty-eighth."

"The twenty-eighth?" she echoed, feigning surprise. "Is that the grand opening?"

His gaze narrowed. "You know it is."

"I think I'm going to be out of town that weekend."

His gaze narrowed, then he shook his head. "I don't think you are."

"Did you take a peek at my calendar when I wasn't looking?"

"Of all the things I'd like to take a peek at, your calendar isn't one of them," he assured her.

"Then how do you know I'm not going to be out of town?" she challenged.

"Because you're not the type to cheat to win."

"There you go again, thinking you know me."

"Maybe I'm wrong," he allowed. "And maybe I'm wrong, too, in thinking that you're drawing out this conversation, hoping I'll clue in to the fact that you want me to kiss you goodbye."

"I haven't been—"

The rest of her indignant protest was muffled by his kiss.

WHEN DAD TOLD her and Lilah that he'd invited a friend for dinner, Tilda had assumed it was a guy friend because he'd never before invited a female friend to eat with them. (She specified "female" rather than "girl" in her mind because she didn't even want to think "girlfriend" for fear that might make it true.)

She knew it was silly to feel hurt that he might be involved in a romantic relationship. After all, her parents had been divorced for more than four years and Mom had dated several different guys in that time.

But Dad hadn't had much of a social life since the divorce. In fact, she didn't know for certain that he'd even been on a single date. Tilda had always suspected that was because he was still in love with her mom, and she'd always believed that they'd eventually get back together again.

But that was before Mom moved to California with Perry.

Before she claimed that he was her only chance for real happiness.

Was that why Dad was suddenly interested in dating? Had he given up on reuniting his family?

The thought made her uneasy, because if Mom and Dad weren't together, she didn't know where she was supposed to be.

But the thought of them getting back together made her uneasy, too, as she remembered the tension and the arguments and feeling as if she needed to tiptoe around the house so her mom didn't find a reason to yell at her, too.

They tried not to fight in front of the kids, but sometimes Tilda heard them, anyway. And when you heard things you weren't supposed to hear, you learned things you didn't want to know.

She was scowling at the ground when her phone pinged with a text message. She yanked it out of her pocket to peer at the screen.

Hey

The message was from London.

When she first told her BFF that she was moving, London promised that they'd text all the time. And for the first few days after school finished, she'd kept that promise. Then she'd been hanging out at the beach with Damien or shopping at the mall with Kellie or sipping Frappuccinos at Starbucks with Tanya. There was always a reason she was too busy to reach out—as she'd explained when she finally responded to Tilda's overtures. As if sending a text message to say "hey" took more than three seconds.

But this was the first time any of her friends had initiated contact in four days, and Tilda had started to feel as if she was already forgotten.

Maybe she should wait to reply, so that London didn't think she'd just been sitting around waiting to hear from her. But she was afraid that if she delayed, London might get bored and move on to something else.

So she replied:

Hey

How's haven?

I HATE it

She didn't usually bother with capitalization or punctuation in her text messages, which drove her dad nuts, but the depth of her emotion warranted the effort this time.

Not surprised

I looked on a map—it's the middle of nowhere!

U don't have to tell me

When r u coming back?

I wish!

U should come for the 4th

Party at D's

D was Damien, London's sometimes boyfriend.

I'm 1800 miles away

Actually, the specific number was 1,892 miles, according to Google Maps. Because yes, she'd looked it up, needing to know exactly how far away from civilization she was.

U could hitch

No way.

Tilda wasn't so desperate to get out of Nevada that she'd risk her life getting into a stranger's vehicle. She'd heard too many horror stories about girls being abducted and trafficked, and she wanted to live to see her fifteenth birthday—and not locked up in a garden shed in some trucker's backyard.

My dad would KILL me

He should've asked if u wanted to go to NV before he dragged u there

That was the truth.

And it wasn't only that he hadn't asked but that, when she protested his plans, he'd responded that he was sorry she wasn't looking forward to the move but she was a kid and therefore didn't get a say.

It wasn't fair.

Mom had moved to California, which sucked, but at least Tilda and Lilah and Dad had stayed where everything was familiar.

Then, just when she was getting used to the new normal, Dad decided to move to Nevada to open his own bakery, claiming it had been a longtime dream or something like that. But he didn't pick Las Vegas, the interesting part of Nevada, where she might meet lots of cool people and maybe have something resembling a social life. Instead, he dragged them to the middle-of-freakin'-nowhere.

And apparently she'd taken too long to respond to her friend, because London messaged again.

Gotta run
Mtg D at Starbcks

Have fun

Hope to see you the 4th

Yeah, like that was ever going to happen.

She tucked her phone back into her pocket.

"That was a heavy sigh."

She glared at Warren, who'd apparently decided it was okay to invade her peace—and her backyard.

"Why don't you leave me alone?" she asked, not so much because she wanted to be alone but because she couldn't understand why he'd make a second effort when she'd shot down his first.

He shrugged. "Apparently I have a soft spot for sad girls."

She folded her arms over her chest. "I'm not sad."

"You don't look happy," he noted.

She glared at him.

"That's better," he said, lowering himself to sit beside her on the wrought iron bench.

"Seriously—why are you here?"

"Because I think you need someone to talk to."

"You think I'd talk to you?" Her tone dripped with derision.

He shrugged, unfazed by her attitude. "I might not be your first choice, but it looks like your options are limited."

He was being nice to her—for no reason. And she didn't want him to be nice to her, because suddenly her throat felt tight. As if she was going to cry. And no way was she going to cry in front of him.

"Why don't you go play D&D with your geeky friends?"

"At least I have friends," he retorted.

Ouch.

"I hate you," she told him.

"Do you?" he wondered. "Or do you hate yourself?"

She felt her heart pinch. "You don't know anything about me."

"And you know even less about me," he pointed out reasonably. "So why are you so sure that you hate me?"

"I know your type."

"What is my type?" he asked curiously.

"A straight-A student who does his homework during his lunch period so he can help Mom and Dad around the house after school and who never misses curfew because his only social activities are D&D with his geeky friends and playing trumpet in the high school band."

"How do you manage to make those things sound like character flaws?" he asked, sounding more amused than insulted by her assessment.

"It's a gift."

He surprised her by laughing at that.

"FYI, I play alto sax, not trumpet." He rose to his feet. "If you change your mind about wanting to talk, you know where to find me."

Then he was gone.

But Tilda stayed outside, watching YouTube videos on her phone until Sarah got into her SUV and drove away.

CHAPTER ELEVEN

ANDREW GLANCED UP from the list on his iPad when Tilda stomped into the house, letting the screen door slam at her back.

"Sarah said to tell you goodbye," he said.

Tilda pulled a can of diet cola out of the fridge and popped the top. "How do you know her, anyway?"

"I met her on my first visit to Haven."

"Is she the reason we're here?"

"Her name is Sarah," he said again. "And no. Of course not."

Tilda didn't look convinced. "Mom followed Perry to California."

"I promise you, I didn't follow anyone here. We came to Haven because it was the best choice for our family."

"According to you."

"According to me," he confirmed. "Because I'm the dad, I get to make those tough choices."

Tilda swallowed another mouthful of soda. "Is she—*Sarah*—your girlfriend?"

He shook his head. "No."

Not yet.

His daughter didn't look convinced. "So what was with the wine at dinner?"

"Sometimes it's nice to have wine with a meal."

"Since when?"

"Actually, there's evidence to suggest that wine has been drunk since humans created the first permanent settlements."

She rolled her eyes. "I meant, since when do *you* have wine with a meal?"

"Not often," he acknowledged. "Not anymore."

"You and mom used to drink wine with dinner all the time," she remembered.

"We did," he confirmed.

"Back in the days when we all used to have dinner together. When we were a family."

"We're still a family, Tilda. We might not live under the same roof anymore, but your mom's still your mom and I'm still your dad."

Her gaze skittered away. "We don't even live in the same state anymore."

"That's just geography."

"Yeah, well, geography is wreaking havoc on my social life."

"I know this move hasn't been easy for you."

"You know nothing," she said. "You've been here three weeks and you're already dating."

"I'm not dating," he said. "Sarah is a friend who happens to be a girl but she's not my girlfriend and we haven't been on a single date."

"But do you want to date her?"

He put down the iPad and looked his daughter in the eye. "What's with all the questions, Tilda?"

She shrugged. "I just think I have a right to know if you plan on adding a stepmom to our family."

"Not anytime in the near future," he assured her.

"But you like Sarah?"

"Yes, I like Sarah," he confirmed. "And I think, if you gave her a chance, you'd like her, too."

She tipped the can to her lips again before asking, "What happened with you and Mom?"

"You want to know why we got divorced?"

She nodded.

He pushed back the stool next to him—a silent invitation for her to sit. After an almost imperceptible hesitation, she did so.

"Sometimes people grow apart, no matter how much they love one another, and realize they're better off alone than together."

"Mom's not alone. She's with Perry."

"Well, I'm not alone, either," he pointed out. "Because I've got you and your sister."

She traced the logo on her can with a fingernail. "Did you want us...or did you get stuck with us?"

He was sincerely shocked that she would ask such a question. "I wanted you. *Always*," he assured her. "And your mom wanted you, too."

Tilda rolled her eyes at that.

"It's true," he said. "But we agreed that, because of your mom's late hours at the restaurant, I could provide a more stable home for you and Lilah."

"And did you agree that she should quit her job at the restaurant and move to California?"

"Your mom wasn't happy with her job in Beaumont."

"She seemed happy enough until she met Perry."

"And now she's even happier," he pointed out, because there was no doubt it was true. By all accounts, Perry adored Miranda, and there was nothing Miranda liked more than being adored. But there were some things about their marriage his children didn't need to know, and he wasn't going to say anything that might negatively alter their perception of their mother.

"And now she doesn't have any time for us," Tilda noted.

"She's been busy with the new house and the new restaurant," he acknowledged.

At least that was the excuse she'd given every time he tried to pin down a date for their daughters to visit. But finally the renovations were complete on the house she shared with Perry so they could visit, whenever her schedule might allow.

"You're busy with the bakery," Tilda pointed out.

"Yeah, but you live with me, so you get all my free minutes," he said, hoping to earn a rare smile.

"Until you get a girlfriend," she guessed.

"Tilda," he began, not quite sure what else to say.

But she didn't stick around to listen to anything more.

THE NEW SIGN was installed at the bakery the next day, and several passersby stopped to watch the unveiling. Kyle's wife, Erin, had designed the logo for him—*sugar & spice* in lowercase script flanked by inward-facing silhouettes of two little girls created from pictures of his daughters in their younger years.

When he showed them the design, Lilah had been thrilled and Tilda mortified. Apparently being immortalized as a five-year-old was cool when you were twelve but not when you were fourteen.

But he got several compliments from the passersby—followed by even more inquiries about the menu offerings. He responded to all the latter with the suggestion that the potential customer should be there for the grand opening to find out.

But today, he was taking a break from the last-minute preparations to meet Kyle for lunch again, and he was perusing the menu when his friend settled on the barstool beside him at Diggers'.

"This time I'm late," his friend acknowledged. "I took the kids to the park so Erin could have some peace and quiet to get some work done and then had trouble dragging them away."

"Enjoy every one of those moments while they last," Andrew advised his friend. "Because before you know it, your kids will be tweens and teens and they won't want to spend any time with you and you won't be able to do anything right."

"Is it really that bad?"

"Not always." He shrugged. "Some days it's worse."

"Something to look forward to, then," Kyle said dryly.

They paused their conversation to order.

"It's been a rough year for the girls, and I get that," Andrew said, after the bartender had set their drinks in front of them.

"Having second thoughts about the move?" his friend asked.

"About everything," he confided.

"You can't expect the pieces to fall into place overnight. You all need some time to adjust. In the meantime, me and Erin are here, if we can help in any way."

"You've both already done so much," Andrew said. "You put me in touch with Caroline when you knew she wanted to sell, and Erin designed a kick-ass website for Sugar & Spice."

"My wife has real talent—and the website is kick-ass," Kyle agreed, nodding his thanks to the bartender when he set their plates in front of them. "And although you haven't shared the details of your opening-day menu, I thought I would mention that Erin loves your sticky buns."

"All the women do."

"Hey—that's my wife you're talking about," Kyle protested.

"You're the one who said she loved my buns," he felt compelled to point out. "And they are on my list for the grand opening, so I'll put some aside for her."

"That won't be necessary. She plans to be there when the doors open."

"I appreciate the support," Andrew said sincerely. "It will be nice to see a familiar face."

"I would think they're all familiar faces now, since everyone's been making the rounds of The Daily Grind when you go for your afternoon coffee run."

"It's not just my imagination, then?"

Kyle chuckled. "Definitely not."

"That doesn't mean any of them will show up next Saturday," Andrew noted.

"Are you kidding? There's going to be a line out the door."

"Because the residents of Haven have been deprived of peanut butter banana croissants for so long?"

"Chocolate peanut butter banana," his friend corrected him. "And that might be part of it, but the biggest part is that they're all curious about the new owner of Sweet Caroline's."

"Sugar & Spice," he corrected.

"You can put whatever name you want on the sign," Kyle cautioned. "It's going to take the locals a while to get used to calling it anything but Sweet Caroline's."

"I knew what I wanted when I came to Haven—a business of my own and a new start for the girls. Maybe for me, too." Andrew nibbled on a fry. "Now I find myself wanting things I have no business wanting."

"Sounds to me like you've got a woman on your mind," Kyle said, lifting his burger from his plate.

"Yeah," he admitted.

"What's the problem? Your interest isn't reciprocated?"

"I think it might be," he said cautiously. "But with everything else going on, it's probably not the right time to pursue a relationship."

"There's gotta be more to life than work."

"I've got more," Andrew reminded him. "I've got Tilda and Lilah, and they need to know that they come first with me." He sipped his beer again. "Although Lilah seems to be doing just fine. It's Tilda that I'm most worried about."

"How old is she now?" Kyle asked. "Thirteen? Fourteen?"

"Fourteen," he confirmed. "She'll be starting high school in September."

"Tough time," his friend said sympathetically.

"For the move?"

"For life in general," Kyle clarified. "In some ways, high school was the best time of my life. In others, it was a nightmare—especially freshman year. Starting a new school at any age can be hard. Walking into high school without knowing anyone is going to be even harder."

"That's why I wanted to make the move at the beginning of the summer. So she'd have time to make friends before school starts."

"It's only been a few days," his friend pointed out.

"You're right. But she's so mad that she had to leave her friends in Beaumont, she's stubbornly refusing to put any effort into making new friends here."

"Maybe she could invite one of her old friends to come here for a visit," Kyle suggested.

Andrew shook his head. "Aside from the fact that there's no direct transportation from there to here, her friends were one of the reasons that I jumped at the opportunity to move both girls out of Texas." London, in particular, had been testing her parents' boundaries and encouraging Tilda to do the same, leading to ignored text messages, missed curfews and the smell of cigarette smoke—and sometimes weed—on her clothes when she finally did come home.

"Erin suspected that you made the move to be closer to Miranda, possibly in the hope of a reconciliation."

"She's half-right," he said. "I did want to be closer to Miranda, but only to facilitate visitation between Tilda and Lilah and their mom.

"They've seen her all of three times since she left Texas—and each time, she made the trip to Beaumont because she was temporarily living in a one-bedroom apartment with the boyfriend while their house was being renovated, which meant that they didn't have a spare room for guests."

"Do Tilda and Lilah get along with the boyfriend?"

"They haven't really spent much time with him. And when Miranda came back to Beaumont for those visits, he didn't come with her."

"Have they spent much time with your new girlfriend?" Kyle asked.

"I don't have a girlfriend, and that wasn't a very subtle fishing expedition," Andrew chided his friend.

"At least tell me who she is—this woman you're thinking about who isn't your girlfriend."

"No way," he said.

"Because I know her," Kyle immediately guessed.

"Odds are good, considering that you know almost everyone in this town," Andrew pointed out.

And then she walked into the bar—and right into the arms of another man.

He frowned. "Who's that?"

"Sarah Stafford," Kyle said, having followed the direction of his friend's gaze.

"I mean the guy she's with."

"Zack Kruger."

The high school boyfriend.

He didn't realize he'd spoken aloud until Kyle responded, "Yeah, they were an item back then. But how do you know about Sarah and Zack?"

"She mentioned him in passing," he said, silently cursing himself for the giveaway.

"I didn't know you knew Sarah."

"We actually met here, at Diggers', the first time I visited Haven."

His friend didn't have any trouble connecting the dots. "I have to say, you're setting the bar pretty high if that's where your interest lies."

He dragged his gaze away from Sarah and Zack. "What do you mean?"

"You've heard of Blake Mining?"

"Of course." When Kyle first told him about Sweet Caroline's being offered for sale, he'd done some cursory research on the northern Nevada town.

"Well, Sarah's last name might be Stafford, but her mom was a Blake."

Apparently the woman who claimed to be a stickler for honesty had some secrets of her own, Andrew mused.

ZACK ROSE TO his feet when Sarah approached the table he'd snagged and greeted her with a fierce hug. "Damn, you're a sight for sore eyes."

"You, too," she said, aware of the curious glances other diners cast in their direction as she slid into the booth across from him. Some of them were no doubt wondering about the identity of the man she was with—because at thirty-two, he didn't bear much resemblance to the skinny kid he'd been at sixteen. Others would remember, and they'd talk, because people always had something to say about Sarah's unlikely friendship with Zack.

A lot of them said that Zack Kruger was all wrong for Sarah Stafford. The truth was, she'd been all wrong for him.

Though they'd grown up in very different worlds, the attraction had been real. And maybe part of the attraction was the knowledge that being together was a great big middle finger to the rest of the world. Sarah had used Zack to get a reaction from her parents; he'd used her for the veneer of respectability their relationship gave him in the community.

And they'd both gotten what they wanted, at least for a while.

They ordered lunch when their server came to the table, then picked up their conversation again.

"So how's life in Seattle?" Sarah asked.

"Good," he said. "Business is *really* good, which means I'm working longer hours, including evenings and weekends sometimes."

"How does Imani feel about that?" she asked, naming the girlfriend he'd mentioned on his last visit.

"She puts up with it. Not just the long hours but my distraction when I'm prepping for trial and my frustration when I lose—" he grinned "—which thankfully isn't very often. And through it all, she still loves me."

"Sounds like you've got a keeper there," Sarah said lightly.

"You're right about that," he said with another grin. "Which is why we're getting married in October."

"Wow."

Zack was getting married?

Sarah was...surprised.

And perhaps more surprising, genuinely pleased for him.

"Congratulations."

"Thanks. In light of our...history, I wanted to tell you in person, before you heard it from anyone else."

"I'm happy for you, Zack."

"I'm happy, too," he said. His gaze moved around the bar, no doubt as aware as she was that they were the subject of much scrutiny. "I'll bet no one around here would have guessed that I'd actually make something of myself someday."

"I would have," she said.

He laughed.

"I would have," she insisted. "I always knew you were capable of so much more than anyone gave you credit for."

"Plenty of folks gave me lots of credit for causing trouble."

But she knew he didn't cause trouble so much as he'd been unwilling to walk away from it. Yeah, he'd been suspended from school a few times for fighting, but it was usually in defense of a smaller kid being picked on by bullies.

And maybe it was true that he'd been quick to use his fists, but it was also true that he looked out for his mom and his little brothers, giving his mom more than half the pay from his part-time job toward household bills. And every week, he took Mrs. Sanchez's list to the grocery store to do the shopping for his elderly neighbor, always ensuring she got back the correct amount of change to the very last penny.

And when Sarah finally decided that they should go all the way (and it had been *her* decision—Zack might have made it clear that he wanted her, but he'd never put undue pressure on her), he didn't brag about it after the fact. Another guy might have told his friends that he'd nailed Sarah Stafford, but Zack hadn't said a word to anyone, ensuring that her first intimate experience remained intimate.

"You were one of the good ones," she said now. "Even if I didn't realize it at the time."

"I was crazy for you," he admitted.

"We were both more than a little crazy back then," she noted. "But we had some good times together."

He smiled. "We had some *really* good times—and not only back then."

She smiled, too. A little sadly because she knew those good times had already come to an end. And even if she'd realized, a long time ago, that there was no going back, the letting go was still bittersweet.

"Do you want your jacket back?" she asked him now.

"What jacket?"

"Your vintage Levi's jean jacket. The one you gave me the night we went up to Lookout Point, because—in a ridiculous effort to look sexy—I was wearing only a skimpy little top and miniskirt."

He smiled at the memory. "The top was pale blue, with a ribbon that laced up the front. The skirt was a slightly darker shade, with a little ruffle at the bottom. And you were sexy as hell," he assured her. Then he winked. "Still are."

She rolled her eyes at that. "Do you want the jacket or not?"

"It was vintage sixteen years ago," he noted. "You really still have that old thing?"

"Not only do I still have it, I still wear it," she told him.

He shook his head. "You always did have a sentimental streak."

"You're not the only one who's accused me of that in recent months."

"Sounds like there's a story there," he mused.

Now she shook her head. "Not even a first chapter."

"Don't close the book before it gets interesting."

"Too late."

"I hope that's not true," Zack said. "Because if this guy is worth it, he won't let you go that easily."

And that was the story of her life: every man she'd ever been with—even the ones who'd claimed to love her—had let her go. And maybe she bore some responsibility for pushing them away, as she'd admittedly done with Andrew, but the result was the same.

She always ended up alone.

CHAPTER TWELVE

"THIS *SUCKS*," TILDA SAID, delivering the line with all the considerable disdain a fourteen-year-old could muster.

"You've been here less than two weeks and that refrain is already sounding tired," Andrew told his daughter. "Could you at least mix it up a little? Use different words? Expand your vocabulary?"

"Child labor is illegal in this country," she protested, as she pushed the mop over the pink-and-white checkerboard flooring.

It wasn't what Andrew would have chosen, if he'd picked out the flooring, but he couldn't justify the expense of replacing perfectly good tiles. And, as it turned out, the soft sage color he'd selected for the walls worked well with the tile flooring and the off-white bistro tables and chairs for the seating area.

"A parent is allowed to employ a child in a family business," he responded to his daughter now.

She dunked the mop in the bucket, sloshing water over the sides. "An employee gets paid to work."

"You're being paid room and board."

He could practically hear her eyes roll as she responded, "That. Is. So. Lame."

"That's reality, kiddo."

"I *hate* reality." She lifted the mop again and pushed it around the floor. "I wanna go back to Beaumont."

"Well, that's not happening," he told her.

"Then let me go to California, to live with Mom."

He ignored the pain that slashed through his heart like a jagged knife, because he knew she hadn't intended her words to hurt him. It wasn't that she didn't want to live *with him*, it was that she didn't want to live *here*: a town in northern Nevada without a Starbucks or a McDonald's or—horror of horrors— a shopping mall.

So he didn't point out that his ex-wife hadn't shown any interest in having either Tilda or Lilah make the move to Napa Valley with her and her winemaker boyfriend. The girls were hurting enough without being reminded that their mom had prioritized her new romance over maintaining proximity to— and her relationship with—her children. In fact, Miranda had been scheduled to visit the previous weekend and canceled at the last minute, which he suspected was a contributing factor to his daughter's current mood.

"That's not happening, either," he said, keeping his tone deliberately casual. "Also, you missed the far corner by the front window."

"It's too dark to see what I'm doing."

"There's plenty of light."

"But no natural light," she pointed out. "Why'd you paper over the windows, anyway?"

"Because I didn't want anyone passing by to see what we're doing here until we're ready to open."

"You mean, you don't want the local authorities to see you exploiting child labor," she grumbled.

"Our grand opening is Saturday—the local authorities can see you working behind the counter then," he responded mildly.

She huffed out a breath as she pushed the mop into the corner. "It's not fair that I'm stuck working here while Lilah's at a birthday party."

"It's not," he agreed. "But your sister still has a couple of years before she turns into a sullen teenager, which is probably why she's already managed to make friends."

"She made friends with the kid next door," Tilda noted dryly. "That didn't require much effort aside from moving in."

"And yet you've put considerable effort into ignoring Rory's brother."

"Because he's totally lame."

"How can you possibly know that when you've never had a conversation with him?" he challenged.

"I've had a couple of conversations with him," she said. "And the first time I talked to him, he was wearing a D&D T-shirt."

"So?"

"So...totally lame," she said again, dropping the mop back into the bucket. "Can I be done now?"

He wasn't sure the floor was clean, but it was definitely wet. His gaze shifted to the clock on the wall showing that it was almost six o'clock.

"Sure." He pulled a couple of twenties out of his wallet and handed them to his daughter. "Why don't you go to Jo's to grab a pizza for dinner?"

She pocketed the money. "Okay."

The bell over the door jangled as she let herself out.

He felt confident that she knew her way around town, and if he worried about the fact that she'd yet to make any friends, that fact was less worrying than the friends she'd said goodbye to when they left Texas.

Miranda's decision to move to Calistoga might have been the unwelcome catalyst that precipitated his recent move and career change, but once he'd had some time to think about it, he'd decided that a fresh start could very well be the best thing for all of them. And if he'd chosen Nevada because it was close to California and he was (perhaps foolishly) optimistic that his ex-wife would soon realize how much she missed her daughters, well, that wasn't anyone's business but his own.

In the meantime, he was going to do everything in his power to let Tilda and Lilah know that they were still—and always would be—his number one priority.

"I'M SO GLAD you were able to meet," Jenna said, giving her sister a hug before sliding onto the barstool beside her.

"I'm glad you called," Sarah said. "It's been a long time since we've done this."

"We used to do it all the time, when you worked in the office beside mine."

"You mean when we'd leave at the same time and equally desperate for a drink?"

Jenna laughed as Duke came over to take their order. "Yeah. Good times."

"If you invited me to meet to try to convince me to go back to Blake Mining, I'm leaving," Sarah warned, when their wine had been poured.

"I didn't," Jenna hastened to assure her. "I wouldn't. I'm not sure I'd ever be brave enough to venture out on my own, but I'm proud of you for doing it. For following your dreams."

"Thank you," Sarah said.

When Jenna reached for her glass, Sarah finally spotted the diamond on her third finger.

"Ohmygod." She snatched Jenna's hand for a closer inspection of the ring. "You're engaged?"

Jenna smiled and nodded.

"When? How?"

"Today. At lunch. Harrison packed a picnic basket and took me to the park for our four-month anniversary."

"You had a picnic in the dog park?"

Her sister laughed. "Not in the off-leash part, obviously, but the other side of the park that's actually set up with picnic tables for people."

"That makes more sense," Sarah noted.

"We had sandwiches with lettuce and tomatoes from his greenhouses and homemade potato chips and fresh lemonade."

Harrison was an organic farmer who offered his produce for sale through The Trading Post and also supplied fresh fruits and vegetables to The Home Station. He wasn't likely to get rich doing what he did and didn't seem to have any ambitions in that direction, but he was passionate about his farm, his dog and Jenna.

Sarah was thrilled for her sister, who was obviously as head over heels in love with Harrison as he was with her. But as she listened to Jenna recount every detail of the oh-so-romantic proposal, she realized that she was a little envious, too.

And she hated that, because Jenna deserved every happiness.

But didn't she deserve happiness, too?

"You'll be my maid of honor, won't you, Sarah?" Jenna asked now.

"Absolutely," she immediately replied.

"We don't have a date yet," the bride-to-be said. "But I know that I don't want a long engagement—I want to be Mrs. Harrison Raczynski as soon as possible."

"First you have to learn to spell it," she said, recalling Andrew's sister's explanation for her continued use of her maiden name.

"R-A-C-Z-Y-N-S-K-I." Jenna rattled the letters off easily.

"Someone's been doodling her future husband's name in her notebook," Sarah couldn't resist teasing.

"It did take some practice," her sister admitted. "But taking his name ensures our future children will be one more step removed from everything implied by the Blake name in this town."

"Speaking of... Have you told Mom and Dad?"

"Not yet." Jenna glanced at her watch as she finished her wine. "But Harrison's picking me up so we can go to Miners' Pass to do just that, so I have to run."

"Don't you want to savor your engagement status for a while longer before they trample all over your joy?"

"I do," Jenna agreed. "But I won't hear the end of it if they happen to hear about our engagement from anyone else."

"That's true," Sarah acknowledged, standing when Jenna did to give her sister a hug. "Just remember, whatever happens with them, I'm here for you—whatever you need."

"I know. And thank you."

Sarah settled back on her stool as Jenna hurried out the door to meet her fiancé.

"Is everything okay?" Duke asked Sarah, as he tipped a glass under a tap to pour a draft beer for Jerry Tate, a regular seated at the other end of the bar.

Sarah managed a smile for the bartender. "Everything's great."

"Are you sure? Because you've hardly touched your wine."

"Too busy chatting with my sister, I guess," she said, picking up her glass now.

"You want anything to eat?" Duke asked, when he returned after delivering Jerry's beer.

"No, thanks. I'll get something at home." She pulled some money out of her wallet and set it on the bar to pay for her drink.

As she exited the restaurant, she realized she couldn't remember what she had in her fridge and decided she didn't feel like prepping and cooking, anyway. Instead, she pulled out her phone and ordered pizza.

Jo's Pizzeria had a front entrance with a sign over the door that said "Restaurant" and a side door designated for "Takeout." Sarah walked in the side entrance, her stomach growling as she breathed in the heady scents of tomato sauce and oregano.

Laurel Walsh, working behind the counter, found the order with Sarah's name on it and set the box on the counter.

"Large pizza," she noted, a speculative gleam in her eyes. "Are you planning to share that with someone?"

Sarah shook her head. "The large with three toppings was the special tonight, and leftover pizza freezes well."

"That's disappointing," Laurel said. "Especially following reports that you were cozied up with the hunky new baker at The Daily Grind a couple weeks back."

"I had a three-minute conversation with him while we both drank coffee," Sarah said, determined to nip any rumors in the bud.

"A three-minute conversation about…?"

She pulled out her wallet to pay for her pizza. "Cupcakes."

Laurel wiggled her eyebrows as she rang up the order. "Is that a euphemism?"

"It is not."

"Then you're not calling dibs on the hunky new baker?" Laurel asked, passing Sarah's change across the counter.

"Definitely not."

"If I wasn't still reeling from my divorce, I might be tempted," Laurel said. "Because the number of desirable, eligible men in this town seems to be dwindling with each day that passes. And apparently Harrison Raczynski was recently spotted looking at engagement rings in The Gold Mine, so if your sister says yes, he'll be off the market, too."

"She did say yes," Sarah said, smiling to ensure the other woman could see how happy she was for Jenna and Harrison. "They got engaged today."

"She's only been dating the guy—what? Four months?"

Sarah nodded. "Apparently when it's right, you know."

"Or when you want it to be right, you convince yourself it is. I don't mean your sister," Laurel hastened to clarify. "I was just thinking about my personal history. Of course, I was barely out of high school—and pregnant—when I walked down the aisle."

"Funny how you think you know everything as a teenager and only realize how much you don't know until you've grown up," Sarah mused.

"Isn't that the truth?" Laurel agreed, as Sarah's cell phone vibrated inside her purse. "Anyway, tell Jenna 'congrats' for me."

"I will," Sarah promised, reaching for her phone to check the display.

"Excuse me a sec," she said, stepping away from the counter to connect the call.

Laurel nodded as she collected another order from the pass-through window.

After a brief conversation with Twilight Valley's insurance agent regarding additional coverage for the incoming group of summer students, Sarah turned around again—just in time to see her pizza walking out the door.

"THAT WAS QUICK," Andrew said, when his daughter returned to the bakery with a large flat box a short while later.

Tilda shrugged. "They weren't too busy."

"I'm not complaining," he said, his mouth watering in anticipation as he lifted the lid. He'd worked through lunch—*again*—and had even skipped his usual afternoon coffee break at The Daily Grind because the hours that remained before the grand opening were rapidly dwindling.

"Sausage, peppers and olives?" he said, inventorying the toppings on the pie from which a single slice was missing. Apparently his daughter had been so hungry, she'd dug into their dinner on her way back to the bakery.

"What's wrong with sausage, peppers and olives?" Tilda asked.

"It's not our usual order."

She shrugged. "You didn't ask for the usual order. And besides, you're always telling me to try new things."

"Yeah, but since when do you listen to me?"

She rolled her eyes. "Take the win, Dad."

He decided to take the win.

"It would have been a bigger win if you'd waited to eat with me," he said.

"I was hungry," she said. "You made me work through lunch."

"I didn't make you work through lunch," he denied, feeling guilty nonetheless that he'd lost track of time and hadn't realized that she was working through lunch right along with him.

"Is that what you're planning to tell the Labor Board?"

She was obviously joking, and he was grateful for the rare glimpse of humor, so he responded in kind.

"That's my story and I'm sticking to it," he confirmed.

He took a big bite of the pizza while Tilda began to unpack a box of take-out containers, transferring them to the cupboard beneath a display case.

"You don't even like olives," he noted, after he'd chewed and swallowed.

"I don't like *green* olives," she clarified.

The bell over the door jingled, startling Andrew.

He didn't lock it during the day, because he figured the paper covering the windows and doors would keep people out.

"We're not open," he said automatically.

"I know."

"Sarah." He dropped the half-eaten slice of pizza into the box and stepped away from the counter.

"I'd apologize for interrupting your dinner," she said, "except that it's *my* pizza you're eating."

He frowned. "Your pizza?"

"Hot sausage, roasted red peppers and black olives."

"I'm sorry," he said, immediately apologetic. "There must have been some kind of mix-up at Jo's."

But when he glanced at Tilda for confirmation, he realized that his daughter was paying far more attention to aligning stacks of napkins than the task warranted, and the sinking feeling in the pit of his stomach warned him that maybe he was wrong.

"There wasn't a mix-up," Sarah said, and he was struck again by the fact that her voice managed to sound sexy even when she was obviously annoyed. "I ordered the pizza, I paid for the pizza, and when I turned away from the counter to take a phone call, your daughter walked out of the restaurant with my pizza."

"I'm sure you're mistaken."

Sarah shifted her attention to his daughter. "Am I mistaken, Tilda?"

His daughter finally abandoned the cupboard and straightened up.

"It was a harmless prank," she said, in the defensive tone he knew only too well.

Andrew was mortified. "You stole Sarah's pizza?"

"I didn't *steal* it," she denied.

"Did you pay for it?" he challenged.

She didn't meet his gaze. "I didn't have to. It was already paid for."

"Because *I* paid for it," Sarah said. "Because it was *my* pizza."

"I gave you money," Andrew reminded his daughter.

"And told me to grab a pizza, so I grabbed a pizza."

"I'm so sorry," he said to Sarah.

"It's just a pizza," Tilda said. "What's the big deal?"

"I think it's probably a good idea for you to go home now, Tilda," he told her. "We'll talk about the big deal later."

"What more is there to say?" she challenged.

"I'm sure I'll think of something," he promised. "Likely starting with the word *you're* and ending with *grounded*."

"Grounded from what?" she grumbled, turning toward the kitchen to exit through the back door. "There's nothing to do in this town, anyway."

"You're letting her off the hook pretty easily," Sarah noted, when Tilda was gone.

"She's not off the hook yet," Andrew assured her.

"You didn't even make her apologize."

"I apologized."

"You didn't steal my pizza," she pointed out. "And now that you've given her a free pass on this, what do you think she's going to do next?"

"I didn't give her a free pass," he said, pulling his wallet out of his pocket. "And I'm not having this conversation with you."

"It's not about the money," she said, when he thrust a handful of bills at her. "It's about the fact that your daughter is pushing against your boundaries and she's going to keep pushing until you push back."

"Here's an idea," Andrew said. "When you have kids of your own, you can tell me how to raise mine."

With a huff of frustration, Sarah turned on her heel and walked out the same door she'd entered, leaving him alone with her pizza and no appetite for it.

WARREN WAS OUTSIDE, washing his mom's car in the driveway, when Tilda walked past on her way home. He glanced up, but she pretended she didn't see him.

So what if he was the only person close to her age in the neighborhood?

She wasn't that desperate for a friend.

She stomped up the steps and flung open the screen door, letting it slam shut behind her.

If Dad was home, he'd give her hell for that for sure.

But he wasn't home and she was already in trouble, so what did it matter?

She stomped up the stairs to her room and slammed that door, too.

She hated her new room.

So what if it was bigger than the room she'd had in Beaumont?

She didn't want a new room—she wanted her old room in their old house in Texas.

But that house was gone now. Sold to a young couple with a three-year-old son and a second baby on the way. A couple looking to make happy memories, blissfully unaware that they could apparently fall out of love as easily as they'd fallen into it, go their separate ways, tear their family apart.

"This isn't working, Andrew."

"So let's figure out what we need to do to make it work."

"Maybe I don't want to make it work."

"What are you saying?"

"I want a divorce."

"We've got two daughters, Miranda. Maybe you should think about what they want instead of what you want."

"I'm not going to let my children hold me hostage in a marriage that isn't working."

"Hold you hostage? Isn't that a little melodramatic?"

"It's how I feel. I'm not happy, and I haven't been for a long time."

"Then let's try counseling."

"I don't want to go to counseling. I want a divorce."

Tilda felt tears burn behind her eyes, blinked them away.

A tentative knock sounded. "Tilda?"

"Go away."

Instead of doing as she requested, Lilah turned the knob and pushed open the door. "What's wrong?"

"Nothing."

Her sister held out a bag of sour cherry blasters. "Want some? I got them in my goody bag from Rory's birthday party."

"No." Tilda knocked the bag out of her sister's hand, spilling sugary gummies all over the floor.

"Hey!" Lilah's lower lip trembled, as if she was going to cry. "Why'd you do that?"

"Because I don't want any of your stupid cherry blasters."

Lilah dropped to her knees and began picking the candy off the floor. "You could have just said 'no, thanks.'"

"I don't want any candy and I don't want any company."

"Why are you mad?"

"I'm not mad!" Which she realized might have been more believable if she hadn't yelled the words at her sister.

Lilah opened her mouth, as if there was something else she wanted to say.

"Go away," Tilda said again.

This time, Lilah went away.

Leaving Tilda alone with all kinds of uncomfortable feelings churning inside her.

CHAPTER THIRTEEN

SHE COULD HAVE handled that better, Sarah acknowledged, as she walked home from the bakery.

Andrew said he'd talk to Tilda later, and she should have left it at that. But there was something about his daughter that set off her internal radar. Something that warned her the girl was either trouble or in trouble. Maybe both.

Because she knew it wasn't a mix-up, as Andrew tried to explain it away. The girl had blatantly stolen her pizza.

Okay, maybe theft under twenty dollars wasn't a felony, but it was definitely an annoyance and one she didn't need at the end of a long day.

Her heavy mood lifted when she turned onto Fieldstone and saw Claire's vehicle in her driveway.

"This is a nice surprise," she said, managing a smile for her friend.

"Devin had plans with Trevor tonight, so I decided to come into town with him to hang out with you."

"Come on in," she said, sliding her key into the lock. "I'll open a bottle of wine."

"Dev will probably have a couple of beers with his brother, so I'll stick with tea in case I need to drive back."

Sarah filled the kettle with water and set it on the stove before selecting a bottle of cabernet franc from her built-in wine rack. As she uncorked the bottle, she remembered that she hadn't eaten since breakfast.

"Do you want a grilled cheese?" she asked Claire.

Her friend shook her head. "No, thanks. We had dinner before we came into town."

She started to collect the ingredients for her sandwich, then pivoted to the stove when the kettle started to whistle.

"I've got it," Claire said, turning off the burner and pouring the hot water into her mug. "You make your sandwich and tell me why you haven't stopped scowling since I got here."

"I think I'm hangry," she admitted, dropping her sandwich into the pan.

"You didn't have lunch today, did you?"

"No. I wanted to finish up the grant proposal before I had to leave to meet Jenna at Diggers'."

"They have food at Diggers', you know."

"I did hear something about that," she said, flipping her sandwich.

"Is everything okay with Jenna?" her friend asked cautiously.

"Yeah, she's doing great," Sarah said. "In fact, she's getting married."

Claire sipped her tea. "When?"

"They haven't set a date yet, but soon, she hopes."

"Something else is on your mind," Claire noted.

"Yeah," she said again, turning her sandwich onto a plate.

"Want to share?" Claire asked, when Sarah sat down across from her.

Sara nibbled on her sandwich. "Do you remember when I stole that bottle of wine cooler from The Trading Post in high school?"

"I was your lookout," her friend reminded her.

"I knew it was wrong, but I did it, anyway. Even though I had the money to pay for it."

"You were underage. There was no way Mr. Hawkins would have sold it to you."

"That's not an excuse."

"Of course not," Claire agreed. "But it was fifteen years ago—I'm sure the statute of limitations has run out so that even if you went to Mr. Hawkins today and confessed to the crime, you wouldn't be thrown in jail for it."

"I was a troublemaker."

"You sometimes acted out in an effort to get your parents' attention," her friend acknowledged.

"I stole a car."

Claire rolled her eyes. "*You* didn't steal a car. *Zack* stole a car."

"I was in the car with him when he got pulled over." And fifteen years later, she still remembered the terror that had gripped her heart when she spotted the red and blue lights flashing in the mirrors—followed by a combination of dread and anticipation twisting in her belly when the arresting officer told her that her parents were on their way to get her.

"Not that I don't appreciate this trip down memory lane, but where's this coming from?" Claire asked.

Sarah summarized her interaction with Andrew and Tilda for her friend.

"I think this is about more than his daughter stealing your pizza," Claire guessed. "I think you're still upset that he never told you he had a daughter—never mind two of them."

"Maybe," she allowed.

"And you have a right to be upset," her friend assured her. "Especially because I'm sure you told him all your secrets."

Sarah popped the last bite of sandwich into her mouth and took her time chewing before she responded, "I don't have any kids that he doesn't know about."

Claire swallowed another mouthful of tea. "Have you told him about your parents?"

"I'm sure he could guess that I have parents," Sarah said dryly.

"But would he guess that your parents are filthy rich?"

"They are. I'm not."

"So he doesn't know that you're a Blake?"

"My mother's a Blake," she clarified.

"That's a fine line you're balancing on," her friend cautioned.

"I would have got around to telling him eventually, but I'm not sure it matters now. He seemed pretty mad at me for being mad at his daughter for stealing my pizza." She sighed. "I know I overreacted… I think I was feeling a little sorry for myself after

Jenna shared her news, because it seems like everyone I know is married or getting married or having babies."

Her friend fell silent.

Uncharacteristically silent.

And somehow, Sarah knew.

"You're pregnant," she realized.

Claire nodded.

"Ohmygod." She pushed away from the table to hug her friend tightly. "This is so...*wow*. You're going to have a baby. You're going to be a mom." She grinned. "And I'm going to be an auntie."

Claire laughed at that. "You're already an auntie to your brother's kids."

"And I love them to bits, but my BFF is going to make me an auntie again and—" she had to swallow around the lump that rose in her throat "—I really couldn't be happier for you and Devin."

"It's early days yet. The baby's not due until February," her friend said. "But you're the first person I wanted to tell—after Devin, obviously, and I'm sorry for the timing—"

"No," Sarah interjected. "Don't you dare apologize for sharing the best news ever."

"Yeah?" Claire said hesitantly.

"Yeah," she confirmed, and hugged her friend again. "And I'm going to be your baby's favorite auntie."

"As if there was ever any doubt."

ANDREW WAS ROLLING out the dough for sticky buns Friday night when there was a knock on the open kitchen door. He glanced over his shoulder, surprised to see Sarah standing there.

It wasn't fair that any woman should be so effortlessly beautiful. And she was even more so today, as instead of her usual jeans and T-shirt, she was wearing a sleeveless summery dress with a skirt that flirted with her knees and Louboutin sandals with a skinny ankle strap that added several inches to her height and gave him a second jolt.

He must have been staring, because she explained, "There

was a reception at The Home Station tonight—a thank-you to some of Twilight Valley's big donors."

"You have to spend money to make money," he agreed.

"Anyway, since I was in the neighborhood, I stopped by your place. Lilah told me you were here—and to come to the back door."

"She should have also told you that I was busy," he said.

"I knew you would be." She stepped over the threshold to peruse the trays on the counters. "You've got a big day tomorrow—and it smells amazing in here."

He appreciated the compliment, but he remained wary—and at a distance, because he really wanted to haul her into his arms and kiss her until they were both breathless.

"Why are you here, Sarah?" he asked instead.

"You might recognize this," she said, holding up the olive branch he'd given to her the day after his sister and daughters crashed their dinner.

"It does look vaguely familiar," he acknowledged.

"I owe you an apology. I overstepped the other day and some of the things I said obviously rubbed you the wrong way."

Finally, he turned to give her his full attention, a slow smile curving his lips. "And you want to make it up by...rubbing me the right way?"

A flush of pink color spread across her cheeks.

"I want to *explain*," she clarified.

"That doesn't sound nearly as much fun," he lamented, "but I'm listening."

"It's kind of a long story," she warned.

"I've got lots of baking to do."

"Okay." She nodded. "It starts a few years back, when a pregnant Labradoodle took shelter in the barn at Silver Star Ranch. Five weeks later, my brother, Patrick, had a dog and six puppies.

"Brooke Langley, one of our local vets—and now Patrick's wife—helped with the birth, and her son, Brendan, named all the puppies after *Star Wars* characters. And like everyone else who saw them, I fell head over heels and laid claim to the one named Han.

"But when it came time to actually take him home, I started

to have second thoughts about the amount of time that I spent away from home and whether that would be fair to the puppy, and I balked. So my sister, Jenna, snapped him up."

Andrew was a little confused as to how her story related to the pizza incident with his daughter, but he figured she'd get to the point eventually and only said, "It's nice that Han stayed in the family."

"That's what I thought, too," she agreed. "Until, four months ago, when Jenna met Harrison at the off-leash dog park, courtesy of Han getting up close and a little too personal."

He chuckled. "As dogs have a tendency to do."

"It is kind of funny," she acknowledged, with just the hint of a smile. "A real meet-cute, according to Claire. And I'm happy for my sister, of course. Because she's dated her share of duds, too, and absolutely deserves a happy ending. It's just that there's a part of me that wonders…"

"If the man of her dreams might have been the man of your dreams if you'd been the one at the dog park?" he guessed.

"It sounds silly when you say it out loud, but yeah."

"It's human nature to wonder about the path not taken," he said.

"And now, instead of shopping for a wedding dress, I'm going to be a bridesmaid. Again."

"They're getting married?"

She nodded. "Jenna told me when I met her for a drink on Wednesday. And all the time I'm asking about her wedding plans, the back of my mind is echoing the warning—three times a bridesmaid, never a bride.

"And while I've never put much stock in old sayings like that, considering this will be my sixth time standing next to a bride, I have to wonder if that means I'm twice as unlikely to ever marry."

"I'm sure that's not true," he said.

"It's not even the wedding, though," she told him. "It was the sudden and depressing realization that I might never find someone to share my life.

"Of course, I know that isn't the worst-case scenario. Being alone is certainly preferable to being in a toxic relationship like my parents' first marriage."

"I didn't know your parents were divorced."

"Divorced and remarried," she told him.

"They both remarried?"

"They remarried each other," she clarified. "But only after hooking up with various other partners and ensuring their kids had an intimate understanding of relationship dysfunction.

"Sorry—that was an unnecessary tangent and probably more information than you ever wanted to know about my family. But that's the convoluted story about why I was in a mood when I went to Jo's to pick up my pizza."

"And my daughter walking out with the pizza you'd paid for did nothing to improve your mood," he acknowledged.

"I was hangry," she admitted. "And feeling much more like my usual self after I had a grilled cheese."

"You didn't go back to Jo's for another pizza?" he asked, surprised.

"And have to explain to Laurel what happened to the first one?" She shook her head. "None of us needed to deal with the potential fallout from that."

He hadn't considered how that might have affected Tilda. It was bad enough to be the new girl without being the new girl who stole a pizza from Jo's.

"Thank you," he said, sincerely grateful for her discretion.

"Anyway, I shouldn't have presumed to give you parenting advice just because your daughter reminds me of myself at her age."

He finished arranging the cinnamon rolls on top of the base of brown sugar and butter and pecans. "It seems to me that you turned out okay."

"You wouldn't have given me favorable odds if you'd known me when I was a teenager," she told him. "The truth is, it took a long time and a lot of work to break some self-destructive habits. And some I'm still working on."

"Such as?" he wondered.

"Falling into bed with men I barely know."

"You don't have to worry about that with me," he told her,

wiping his hands on a towel. "Because you know me a lot better now than you did eight weeks ago."

"That's true," she acknowledged. "But still not very well."

He drew her into his arms. "So let's spend some time together."

"I think, between your daughters and your bakery, most of your time is already accounted for."

"I seem to have a few minutes right now."

"Be still, my heart," she said dryly.

He smiled at that and lifted a hand to cup the back of her head, his thumb brushing over the pulse point at the base of her jaw. "Your heart *is* racing."

She swallowed. "You're invading my space."

"Actually, you invaded mine."

"I brought an olive branch," she reminded him. "A symbol of peace and friendship."

His gaze dropped to her mouth, and he knew it would taste sweeter than anything on his menu. "And I'm suddenly feeling very friendly toward you."

She laughed, a little breathlessly. "I can't believe I ever accused you of not having game."

"The first time I saw you, I couldn't help but trip over my tongue," he said. "You completely took my breath away."

"You had enough air to imply that I was a stripper," she remarked dryly.

"I was definitely intrigued by the possibility that you might take more clothes off." Thinking back to that night, he couldn't help but smile. "And then you did."

"That was much later," she pointed out.

"And later still after that before I realized that I never got to see your tattoo."

"It's not exactly hidden," she said. "You'd already guessed that it was on my shoulder blade, but that's on my back and..."

He quirked a brow. "I was on your front?"

She swallowed. "Yeah."

"Next time we won't be so rushed," he promised, lowering his head to brush his lips over hers. "And I'll be sure to appreciate every inch of your body."

"There's not going to be a next time," she said, even as her body swayed into his. "I don't do one-night stands anymore."

His mouth skimmed over her jaw, down her throat. "But we've already spent one night together, so when we get naked together again, it won't be a one-night stand."

"That's a rather self-serving argument," she noted.

"But also persuasive, don't you think?"

When she opened her mouth to respond, he covered it with his own. A hum sounded low in her throat as she lifted her hands to his shoulders, holding on to him as he deepened the kiss. Their tongues danced together in an erotic and arousing rhythm that had all his blood migrating south...and an annoying buzzing sound echoing in his head.

With obvious reluctance, Sarah eased her mouth from his.

"Oven timer," she said.

"What?"

Then reality returned and he swore under his breath as he stepped away from her to pull the trays out of the oven.

He examined the mini cakes, tested a random sample and breathed out sigh of relief.

"What are they?" Sarah asked, peering over his shoulder.

"Right now, they're just white cakes. Tomorrow they'll be Chantilly cakes."

"With whipped cream and berries?"

He nodded as he removed two more trays from the oven. "And these chocolate cakes will be layered with milk and dark chocolate mousse and frosted with chocolate Italian buttercream."

"Obviously you've got a lot of work to do before you open."

"Bonnie will be here to help in the morning."

"And the beignets?" she asked, her tone deliberately casual. "When do you make those?"

He grinned. "Not until tomorrow."

She sighed with obvious regret, and he knew he'd be seeing her the next day.

"I should get out of your way so that you're not stuck here all night," she said now.

"I wouldn't mind being stuck here all night if you were with me," he told her.

She rolled her eyes, but she was smiling. "Good night, Andrew."

"Good night, Sarah." He followed her to the door. "I'll let you know when the girls make their plans to go to California so we can schedule our date."

"You seem pretty confident that I'll be here for a beignet tomorrow," she mused.

"My fingers are crossed."

"If I do show up, you should know that it's because I'm tempted by more than your fancy doughnuts."

And then, after one last, all-too-brief kiss, she walked out the door.

CHAPTER FOURTEEN

ANDREW DIDN'T STAY at the bakery very long after Sarah had gone, because he knew he'd be back there at 4:00 a.m. the following morning to ensure all the display cases were full before the doors opened at eight o'clock. But he had too much on his mind to be able to sleep right away, so he turned on the TV and decided to unwind with the baseball game before bed.

Kyle was right—running his own business was a lot different from simply making desserts for someone else's menu. Of course, he would still be making desserts for The Home Station, and he was grateful to his friend for offering an arrangement that guaranteed at least a minimal income for Sugar & Spice even if no customers walked through the door.

But worries about the opening weren't even the biggest part of what preoccupied his mind. Tonight, like almost every night since he'd met her, he was thinking about Sarah.

"Dad?"

The softly spoken query jolted him back to the present, and he turned to see his youngest daughter at the foot of the stairs.

"Why are you still awake?" he asked Lilah.

"I couldn't sleep."

He patted the empty cushion beside him, inviting her to sit. "Something on your mind?"

She shrugged as she dropped onto the sofa to snuggle against him.

"You don't know if there's something on your mind? Or you don't know if you want to tell me what's on your mind?"

"The second part," she admitted.

"Well, I'm here," he said. "If and when you decide you want to talk about it."

She was quiet for a minute—perhaps watching the ball game playing on TV or perhaps preoccupied with her own thoughts.

When the Rangers jogged off the field at the middle of the fifth inning, she finally said, "Tilda doesn't like it here."

"If you're worried that you're talking behind her back, don't be. She's made her feelings on the matter perfectly clear."

"Okay," Lilah said, seemingly relieved by this bit of information.

"What about you?" he asked now. "Do you like it here?"

She nodded.

"You don't miss your friends in Beaumont?"

"Sure, but we message and chat online, and I've already made some new friends here. Rory and Kylie and Teagan."

"I'm looking forward to meeting them."

It had always been his rule for both his daughters: if they wanted to spend time at a friend's house, he had to meet that friend—and the friend's parents—beforehand.

"You've met Rory. And her mom and dad," Lilah reminded him.

The day after Rachel arrived with Tilda and Lilah, Rory's mom had sent over a chicken-broccoli casserole so that they wouldn't have to worry about putting together a meal while they were unpacking. She'd even included a list of ingredients—in case anyone had allergies to worry about—and instructions for reheating in both the microwave and the oven. It had been hearty and delicious, feeding all three of them for dinner that night and leftovers for Andrew for lunch the next day.

"That reminds me, we've still got Mrs. Aldridge's casserole dish," Andrew said now.

"I can take it over tomorrow," she offered.

"You can't take it back empty."

"We could put some of your sticky buns in it," Lilah suggested.

"Or you and Tilda could make your famous peanut butter cookies," he suggested as an alternative.

"They're not famous," she said. "And Tilda doesn't want to do anything with me these days."

He'd noticed that his eldest daughter had been uncharacteristically snappy with her sister, but he'd hoped that Lilah might remain oblivious.

He brushed a hand over her hair. "I'm sorry, Lilah."

She shrugged as she nibbled on her thumbnail.

He gently pulled her hand away from her mouth. "I thought you stopped biting your nails a couple years ago."

"Mostly."

"I know there's been a lot of upheaval in your life these past few months."

"It would be more upheaval to go back again," she said.

"We're not going back," he told her.

"That's what you say now, but Tilda always gets what she wants."

He was stunned, not just by the words but by the resigned tone that warned she believed them. "I'm sorry if it seems that way to you, but I assure you, it's not true. And I promise that we're not going back to Texas. This is where we live now."

"Okay."

She'd always been an easygoing child, sweet-natured and quick to smile. Of course, puberty hadn't hit her with its full force yet, and he had no doubt it would all change soon enough, but for now he was happy to appreciate her sunny disposition.

She snuggled in again. "Can we get a dog?"

"Is this a test? To see if I'll give you what you want?"

"If you said yes, I'd have to admit that I sometimes get what I want, too."

"What if I said *someday*?"

"*Someday* works," she said. "If you really mean it."

"Why not?" he decided. "I'm not saying someday soon, but once the bakery is up and running and we've settled in, we could take a trip to the local shelter and see what dogs they've got available."

"They might have cats, too."

"I'm sure they do."

"Just something to think about," she told him.

He chuckled softly and hugged her close.

PEOPLE SHOWED UP.

The grand opening of Sugar & Spice was scheduled for 8:00 a.m., but there was a line of customers waiting outside the door an hour before that. On Bonnie's recommendation, he'd hired another former employee of Caroline's to work the counter. And from the time Andrew unlocked the doors at seven thirty, he and Bonnie and Mabel had been running nonstop. Tilda and Lilah had been enlisted to help, too, and they spent several hours bussing tables and doing dishes.

For the grand opening, he'd decided to offer three kinds of beignets—plain sugared, lemon filled and chai latte with cinnamon sugar—all of which proved popular. He'd also made sure there were chocolate peanut butter banana croissants (thank you, Bonnie), and nobody was more surprised than him that his sticky buns sold out before the croissants. In fact, by three o'clock that afternoon, his display cases were almost empty and Andrew was giddy with happiness and relief and exhaustion.

He knew that business wouldn't always be this brisk. That half the people who came through the door were motivated by curiosity. But he had faith that whatever they'd chosen to sample on their first visit would entice them to come back again.

Sarah had stopped by for a couple of chai latte beignets—and left with a box filled with various other treats, too. But while she was there, she offered to cook dinner for him and the girls—an offer he was quick to accept. Not just because it saved him having to come up with a dinner plan, but because it meant that he would get to see her again later that day.

Unfortunately, he forgot to tell the girls that Sarah would be bringing dinner over, and when he made his way down the stairs after stealing a quick shower, she was already at the door.

"Dad didn't tell us that we were having company tonight," Tilda—always the gracious hostess—said.

"Well, I assure you that he was aware of my plan to bring dinner so that he'd have one less thing to worry about on the day of the grand opening."

"Aware and grateful," Andrew interjected, nudging his daughter aside so that he could take the slow cooker from Sarah's hands and she could cross the threshold.

"Mrs. Aldridge sent over a casserole the day we moved in," Tilda remarked, following them to the kitchen. "But she didn't expect to sit at the table and eat it with us."

"Tilda," Andrew admonished, mortified by his daughter's rudeness.

"I'm just saying."

"Sending food is a neighborly thing to do," Sarah responded to his daughter. "Bringing food is a friendly thing to do."

"So how long have you and Dad been...friends?" Tilda asked.

"I promise, she has manners," Andrew interjected again. "But I think they might be in one of the moving boxes yet to be unpacked."

"All my stuff is unpacked," Tilda said. "Lilah's the one who still has boxes in her room."

"So maybe your manners ended up in one of her boxes," he said. "Why don't you go see if you can find them? And while you're up there, tell your sister to come down for dinner."

Tilda stomped up the stairs, clearly aware—and unhappy—that she'd been dismissed.

"I'm sorry," Andrew said.

"I already told you that you don't have to apologize for your daughter."

"Well, now that we're alone." He leaned in and touched his mouth to hers. "Hi."

She smiled. "Hi."

But when he went to kiss her again, she took a deliberate step back.

"Your daughters are upstairs," she reminded him.

"Believe me, we'll hear them when they come down the stairs."

Sure enough, almost before the last word was out of his mouth, heavy footsteps sounded.

"What did I say?"

She responded with a smile. "Why don't you get out the plates so I can dish up dinner?"

Per their dad's instructions, Lilah set out napkins and Tilda got the cutlery, and in short order, they were seated around the dining room table.

"What is this?" Tilda asked, poking at the meat on her plate.

"Apple butter and sage pork roast with sweet potatoes," Sarah said. "There's also spinach salad with a red wine vinaigrette."

Tilda began to separate the apple slices from the potatoes. "I don't like sweet potatoes."

"They're just like regular potatoes," Andrew told her. "Only... sweeter."

"And orange," Tilda noted.

"Do you suddenly have a bias against orange food?" her dad asked.

"I don't like sweet potatoes," she said again.

"I like sweet potatoes," Lilah chimed in, not wanting Sarah's feelings to be hurt by her sister's rejection of the meal she'd prepared. "Especially sweet potato fries."

"Those are my favorite, too," Sarah said.

"Have you decided what movie you're going to see tonight?" Andrew asked his daughters.

"There are only two screens and since one of them is showing a horror flick, which Lilah won't watch, we don't exactly have a choice," Tilda told him.

"We're not officially on the payroll at Sugar & Spice," Lilah explained to Sarah. "But because we worked hard today, Dad gave us each twenty dollars so we can go see a movie."

"Twenty dollars will buy you a movie ticket and a popcorn-drink-candy combo at Mann's Theater," Sarah told her.

"Do they have cherry blasters?" Lilah said.

"I don't know," Sarah admitted. "I'm more of an M&M's girl myself."

"Plain or peanut?"

"Peanut all the way."

"Those are my favorite, too," Lilah said. "If I'm going for chocolate. But my first choice is always cherry blasters."

While they chatted, Tilda scraped the sauce off her meat, ate three tiny bites of pork, complained the apple was mushy and pushed the sweet potatoes around on her plate.

"I hope you're at least going to eat some salad," Andrew said, when he saw the remnants of the meal on her plate.

She acquiesced by taking one small scoop of salad, claiming that she wanted to leave room for popcorn.

"What time is the movie?" Sarah asked.

"Seven thirty," Lilah said. Then, as the idea suddenly struck, "Do you wanna come with us?"

Tilda sent her sister a dark look across the table.

"Thanks, but I think I'll help your dad tidy up here and then head home. I imagine he's got another early day tomorrow."

"Another very early day," he confirmed. "And now I'm suddenly wondering what was so bad about starting my day at noon and making desserts for somebody else's restaurant."

"Nothing was bad about it," Tilda immediately jumped in. "That's why you should think about going back to your old job in Beaumont."

"We're not going back to Beaumont," Andrew said firmly.

"We're staying here and getting a puppy," Lilah told her sister.

"A puppy?" Tilda echoed skeptically.

"And maybe a kitten, too."

"We can't have a cat," Tilda reminded her. "Mom's allergic."

"Mom doesn't live here," Lilah pointed out.

"But she might decide she wants to come back."

Sarah quietly pushed her chair away from the table and carried her plate to the kitchen, giving Andrew and his daughters some privacy.

"Your mom isn't coming back," he said, his tone gentle but firm.

"How do you know?" Tilda challenged.

"Because she lives with Perry in California now."

"She lived with Alvin in Westbury, too, but that didn't last long."

"You're right," he acknowledged. "But even if things don't work out between your mom and Perry, she and I are not going to get back together."

"Why not?"

"Because as much as we love both of you, we don't love each other anymore."

"But if you fell in love once, why can't you fall in love again?"

"I think that's a question for another day," Andrew said. "Because if you guys don't leave for the movie soon, you're not going to make it on time."

Chairs scraped against the floor as the girls pushed away from the table.

"Money and phones?" Andrew asked, as they were getting their shoes on.

"Check," Tilda said.

"Check," Lilah echoed.

"Text me when you get there," he said.

"Yes, Dad," they intoned dutifully.

Sarah heard the door shut. Then, a few minutes later, Andrew carried the rest of the plates into the kitchen from the dining room.

"Was that as much fun for you as it was for me?" he asked her.

"Real life is messy—and there's nothing more real than life with kids," she said. "Also, it's perfectly normal for kids to fantasize about their divorced parents reconciling."

"Is it?"

"And sometimes it actually happens—which isn't necessarily a good thing."

"You're talking about your parents," he realized.

She nodded.

"Parents divorcing really does a number on their kids, doesn't it?"

"It doesn't have to," Sarah said. "And for what it's worth, I thought you handled that really well."

"And now I have a two-hour reprieve that I'd like to spend with you— if my daughters haven't made you want to run for the hills."

"They're not going to run me off that easily," she promised.

"I'm very glad to hear that," he said, drawing her into his arms.

TILDA HAD BEEN trying to work up the nerve to ask her dad about the Fourth of July for more than a week. She'd already told London that she would be there, so she needed to figure out a way to get Dad to say yes to her plans—and soon—because the holiday was coming up fast.

The grand opening had been a huge success and the Day Two crowd equally impressive—with a surge of customers through the door following each of the local church services, people wanting sweet treats with their coffee or tea or cakes or pies or assorted pastries to take home for dessert after their Sunday dinner.

She crossed her fingers, hoping that his happy mood would work in her favor. And when Dad said that he needed to go back to the bakery after dinner, to prep doughs and batters for the next day, she'd volunteered to go with him.

He'd always been willing to let his daughters help in the kitchen, and by the time Tilda started kindergarten, she knew how to beat, blend, combine, fold, stir and whisk, and her vocabulary included words like *fondant* and *ganache*. By third grade, she could make a birthday cake from scratch—without a recipe card. And by the fifth, she could frost that cake with homemade Italian meringue buttercream.

She had so many happy memories of time spent in the kitchen with Dad and Mom.

Before everything had fallen apart.

It hadn't happened all at once, like the collapse of a soufflé out of the oven, but a more gradual deterioration, like an ice cream cake melting in the sun.

Tilda pushed that unhappy thought to the back of her mind as she filled the pastry bag with pink buttercream.

Tonight Dad had put her to work frosting a batch of cupcakes, always one of her favorite tasks. She liked how she could create totally different effects depending on whether she used an open or closed tip and whether she started on the outer edge or in the center. For this batch, she was using a closed star tip to create a pretty ruffled effect, then adding a sprinkle of sanding sugar.

"Those look great," he said approvingly.

"Thanks." For the next batch, she switched to an open star tip and pale blue frosting, then blurted out the question before she lost her nerve. "Can I go to London's next weekend?"

Dad glanced up as he continued to knead the dough he was working with. "London?"

She rolled her eyes. "You know, my best friend for the last ten years?"

It was admittedly something of an exaggeration. Because while she'd known London for more than ten years, they hadn't really started hanging out much until middle school.

"I know who London is," he said. "I'm just a little surprised you think I'd say yes to taking you back to Texas when you moved to Nevada only two weeks ago. Not to mention right after we opened the new bakery."

"I didn't ask you to take me anywhere," she said. "I asked if I could go."

He returned the dough to the bowl and the bowl to the proofing drawer. "You're suggesting that I should buy you a ticket and put you on a plane?"

"A plane would be faster than a train," she agreed.

"No."

"No, it's not faster?" she said dubiously. Because she'd looked at the train schedule and found that there was no direct route from Haven to Beaumont. As a result, it would take several transfers and almost three days to make the trip by train. Bus options had been similarly limited.

"No, you're not going to Texas," he responded bluntly.

She folded her arms over her chest. "Why not?"

"Because you live here now."

"My friends live in Texas."

"You'll make new friends here," he said confidently.

"You have no idea how hard it is to be a teenager plunked into a new town where everybody's known everybody else practically since kindergarten."

"You have to make an effort," he acknowledged. "And it wouldn't hurt you to smile."

She scowled at him.

"Just like that," he said.

Her scowl deepened. "I bet Mom would let me go to Beaumont." Using the other parent as leverage was something she'd learned from her friend Kellie, whose parents had been divorced a lot longer than they were married.

Except that Dad didn't take the bait.

"Well, you don't live with your mom, so it's not her decision," he said.

"Maybe I should go live with Mom."

But they both knew it was an idle threat, considering that Mom hadn't even invited Tilda and Lilah to visit since moving to California.

"What's going on in Beaumont next weekend?" Dad asked now.

"London's having a Fourth of July party."

"Is it July next weekend already?"

"It follows June every year," she told him.

"Well, it turns out they celebrate the Fourth of July here, too," he said. "Sarah was telling me about the activities at Prospect Park, and I thought it would be fun if we all went together."

"*All* meaning you and me and Lilah…and Sarah?"

He nodded.

"Doesn't sound like fun to me."

"It's that or stay home," Dad said, in a tone that told her the subject was firmly closed. "Because you're not going to Beaumont."

WHEN TILDA DROPPED the subject of a potential trip to Beaumont, Andrew wasn't reassured. And though she stuck around to decorate a third batch of cupcakes, he knew that she wasn't happy with him. When she finished and said she was going home, he promised to follow soon after.

And though he still had filling to make for his beignets and choux pastry to bake for his cream puffs, he took a break to call Miranda first, knowing that she'd likely be at work when he finished.

"I've got ten minutes before I have to be out the door," she said, apparently having no time to waste on pleasantries.

"We need to talk about Tilda."

"You wanted custody," she pointed out. "If there's a problem, I have no doubt that you're capable of handling it."

"We have shared custody with the girls' primary residence being with me," he reminded her. "If either of us has a concern, we try to figure out solutions together and present a united front."

"So what's the concern?"

He knew Miranda loved their daughters, but she'd been an only child doted on by parents who always put her needs first, and even now she expected everyone else to do the same.

"Tilda's not happy about our move to Nevada," he confided.

"Well, of course she's not," Miranda said. "She's a fifteen-year-old girl who's been taken away from her friends and everything familiar."

He had to bite his tongue to hold back from reminding his ex-wife that their eldest daughter was still only fourteen, choosing to focus instead on the bigger issue.

"You were as worried as I was about Tilda's so-called friends," he reminded her now. "Friends with whom she'd skipped classes and stayed out past curfew and snuck out of the house to hang with when we grounded her."

"You're right," Miranda acknowledged. "But they're her friends, not ours. Maybe what we think doesn't matter."

"We're her parents."

"Exactly."

He frowned at that unexpected response.

"Did your parents like all of your friends?" she challenged.

"Yeah." He didn't have to pause to think about it. He and Calvin and Stuart had walked to school together, played on the same soccer team and camped out together in one another's backyards.

"Well, mine didn't," Miranda confided.

Which didn't really surprise him. It had taken nearly half a decade of marriage before her parents started to warm up to him—but they cooled off quickly again when Miranda decided that she didn't want to be married anymore.

He pushed those memories aside to refocus on the point of this conversation.

"Tilda wants to go to Beaumont for a party at London's on the Fourth of July."

"So let her go," Miranda said easily.

"I'm not letting her go."

His ex-wife sighed. "If you didn't want my opinion, why did you call?"

"Because I think she could benefit from some one-on-one time with her mom."

"In other words, she's giving you a hard time, and your solution is to dump her on me," Miranda guessed.

"I don't want to dump her anywhere," he immediately denied. "I'm only trying to think about what our daughter needs and how we can meet those needs."

"I'm almost five hundred miles away," she reminded him, "so I'm not sure how much *we* can do."

"Make some time for her, Miranda. Please. If she had plans to spend the Fourth of July weekend with you, I know she'd forget all about Beaumont."

She sighed. "I'll let you know when I've got time, but it's not going to be the Fourth of July. The winery hosts special festivities that weekend and I'll be working Friday, Saturday and Sunday."

Andrew said goodbye and ended the call, frustrated that she wouldn't make their kids a priority. And even more annoyed to realize that while he'd initiated the call to specifically discuss his concerns about Tilda, she hadn't once asked about Lilah.

CHAPTER FIFTEEN

MAYBE THIS WASN'T the best idea, Tilda acknowledged, as she cast another glance at the oversize clock on the wall.

The guy at the counter hadn't blinked when she said she needed a ticket to Reno. He didn't even ask for ID to prove that she wasn't a minor. Probably the makeup that she'd applied did the trick of making her look older. Just some mascara to darken her lashes and lipstick to color her mouth, both of which she'd "borrowed" from Mom's stash the last time she visited, since Dad wouldn't let her wear makeup until high school. (Though he'd reluctantly let her put some gloss on her lips for her middle school graduation.)

But high school wasn't too far away now, and the prospect of reaching that milestone—and being in a different school from her little sister—made her stomach feel funny. Somehow excited and scared at the same time.

But it was the journey in front of her that was making her stomach hurt now. And with every minute that ticked past, the pain grew sharper.

Because Haven wasn't on any of the major rail routes, her trip was going to take a lot longer than the twenty-eight hours she'd spent in Dad's car with Lilah and Aunt Rachel. From Reno she'd have to get on a different train to Sacramento—because apparently going west was the only way to travel east—then transfer to Los Angeles and again for the final leg of the journey to Beaumont. She'd made careful notes on the station names and departure times to ensure she arrived in time for the party, but it was going to take more than three days!

Once she got to Reno, her transportation options expanded. She could even fly to Texas, which would get her there in a matter of hours rather than days. But she didn't have high hopes that she'd be able to get through airport security without a parent and only her middle school ID card, so she was stuck traveling by train. Or bus, which was even less appealing.

London had promised that the weekend would be fun like she'd never experienced, but if Tilda was being honest, she was more apprehensive than excited. Maybe it was the circuitous train route that made her uneasy. Or maybe it was that she'd snuck out of the house without telling Dad where she was going. Most likely it was that London's idea of fun had started to diverge from her own.

Yeah, she wanted to see her friends again. To feel as if she fit in somewhere, because she definitely didn't belong in Haven. She wasn't even sure she belonged in her family, anymore.

And London had been so excited to hear that Tilda was going to be at the party that she had to believe whatever trouble she might get into for disobeying her dad would be worth it.

But now that she was actually at the station, about to embark on a three-day journey, she was a lot less certain.

She double-checked the app on her phone, to confirm that the train was on schedule, and breathed a sigh of relief that she only had another eight minutes to wait. Because once she was on the train, there would be no chickening out. No turning back.

She dipped her hand into her front pocket, where she'd put all her money. Every single dollar she had—and what she'd borrowed from her sister—because it was ridiculously expensive to travel by train. At least she wouldn't have to spend any money on food, because she'd tossed a few granola bars and her refillable water bottle in her duffel bag.

She glanced at the clock again—and caught a glimpse of a sheriff's vehicle. Suddenly her armpits were damp and her heart was pounding really hard against her ribs.

But the vehicle only cruised slowly through the parking lot, then pulled out onto the main road and drove away.

A whistle sounded in the distance, and other passengers on the platform began to move around in anticipation of the train's arrival. Tilda exhaled a shaky sigh of relief as she slung the strap of her duffel bag over her shoulder.

Then she turned around and found herself face-to-face with Sarah.

"WHAT ARE YOU doing here?" Tilda demanded.

Beneath the panic, Sarah thought she detected a hint of relief in the girl's voice.

Relief that she'd been found before she could board a train that her dad probably didn't know she had a ticket for?

Or maybe Sarah had imagined the relief, because the expression on Andrew's daughter's face was one hundred percent defiant.

"Funny, that's what I was going to ask you," she responded lightly.

"I asked first."

She nodded, an acknowledgement of the fact. "I'm here to pick up my grandfather's fiancée's great niece who's coming to celebrate the Fourth of July with the family."

Tilda's gaze narrowed. "That sounds totally made up."

"Truth," Sarah promised, raising her right hand as if taking an oath.

"Why didn't your grandfather—or his fiancée—come to pick her up?"

"Because Crooked Creek Ranch is a long way out of town and I don't like my grandfather driving any further than he has to, so I volunteered to play chauffeur."

"How old's your grandfather?"

"Eighty."

"That's kinda old to be driving," Tilda agreed.

"Your turn now," Sarah said to the teen.

"I'm going to visit a friend," Tilda hedged.

"In Beaumont?" she guessed.

"That's where all my friends are."

"And your dad approved of this plan?"

The teen's gaze flitted away. "Yeah."

"I'm surprised he didn't say anything to me," Sarah mused.

"He doesn't have to tell you everything," Tilda shot back at her.

"No," she agreed. "But considering that we were talking about the four of us spending the holiday together at Prospect Park, it seems like something he would have mentioned."

"It was a recent change of plans."

"That's your story and you're sticking to it, huh?"

The girl's cheeks flushed, but she folded her arms over her chest.

She was a study in contradictions: guilty and defiant. Uncertain yet determined. Scared and brave.

Sarah could see everything Tilda was feeling, and her heart ached for her. Because despite having grown up in Haven, she'd been that girl—out-of-sorts and overwhelmed and desperately wanting to feel as if she belonged…somewhere.

She'd had no shortage of friends—because she was a Blake and, even at a young age, she'd understood that the Blakes were akin to royalty in Haven. At the same time, she was aware that most of her friendships were superficial. That the same girls who invited her to hang out at Jo's or asked to be part of her study group always expected her to pay for the pizza and questioned whether her parents had bought her a spot on the honor roll.

She didn't think she would have survived those years without Claire—her one true friend. Even with Claire, she'd struggled with anxiety and insecurity. And those struggles had taken her to a dark and dangerous place.

The same dark and dangerous place she suspected was beckoning the girl in front of her.

"Question," Sarah said now.

Tilda eyed her warily.

"Do you really want to go back to Texas to see your friends or to punish your dad?"

"I want to see my friends," Tilda responded.

"Did you think at all about the fact that your dad would freak out when he realized you were gone?"

"I'm not sure he'd even notice..."

Busted.

"I mean, if he didn't know I was going, because he said I could go," Tilda hastened to add.

A quick recovery, Sarah mused, if not exactly a credible one.

"Change can be tough, especially when you're a teenager," she noted. "If you ever want someone to talk to—"

"If I want someone to talk to, it won't be you," Tilda interjected.

"I'm not your enemy, Tilda."

"You're not my friend, either."

"I could be."

"Thanks, but no thanks." The teen pulled her phone out of her pocket, clearly indicating that she was finished with their conversation.

But Sarah wasn't giving up just yet.

"I can't imagine that there's a direct train from Haven to Beaumont," she remarked, her tone deliberately casual. "So you're probably going to... Reno first?"

Tilda nodded.

"And then..." she prompted.

"Los Angeles," the girl admitted.

Jesus. Just the thought of this pretty, young—and obviously naïve—girl on her own in a big city made Sarah's blood run cold.

Before she could decide on an appropriate response (because forcibly wrestling Tilda into the backseat of her car to prevent her from getting on the train now visible in the distance was probably a little over the top), Andrew stepped through the station doors and onto the platform.

Tilda obviously spotted her dad at the same moment, because she sucked in a breath and whirled on Sarah.

"You called him," she said accusingly.

"When would I have done that?" Sarah challenged.

The teen frowned.

"Then you texted him," Tilda decided.

"I didn't. But I was planning to," she admitted, in the interest of full disclosure.

Tilda scowled. "Then how did he know where to find me?"

"You told me that he knew you were here—and where you were going," she reminded the girl.

Color flooded the teen's cheeks again.

Andrew stopped in front of them, glancing from Tilda to Sarah and back again.

"Popular place today," he remarked idly.

"Apparently," Sarah agreed.

Tilda remained silent, her gaze fixed on her sneakers.

"Let's go," her dad said.

The girl sighed wearily as she lifted her backpack from the ground and slung it over her shoulder.

"Give me your ticket, Tilda," Sarah said.

"Why?" she asked suspiciously.

"Just give her your ticket," Andrew advised. "You don't have any use for it."

Tilda thrust the ticket at Sarah and walked away with her dad.

SARAH'S ORIGINAL PLANS for the Fourth of July had included Andrew and both his daughters. She'd been looking forward to spending the day at Prospect Park and showing them that, despite being a tiny dot on the map, her hometown knew how to throw a party that brought the whole community together.

But as a result of Tilda's secret excursion to the train station and attempted defection to Texas, she was grounded until her dad said otherwise. Of course, she blamed Sarah, even though Andrew admitted that he'd tracked his daughter's location via an app on her phone—and even after Sarah gave her the money she'd made the ticket agent refund (despite it being a non-refundable ticket) because he'd failed to ask for ID before letting a minor purchase it.

Anyway, it didn't seem fair to Sarah that Lilah should be punished along with her sister, so after she finished her usual morning workouts with the horses at Twilight Valley—and showered and changed—she picked up Andrew's youngest daughter to attend the celebrations with her.

"I kind of feel bad that Tilda's missing all this," Lilah said, dipping her hand into her bag of kettle corn as they wandered around the park.

"You shouldn't," Sarah told her. "If you want to feel bad for someone, it should be your dad. He actually wanted to be here. Your sister would rather be in Texas."

"You're right," Lilah agreed, munching on her snack. "And the truth is, part of me feels sorry for her but a bigger part is glad she's not here."

"Emotions are rarely simple and straightforward," Sarah noted.

"We used to have a lot of fun together, but now she just complains about everything and makes everyone else unhappy."

"Unfortunately we can't control how other people think and feel, we can only control how we respond."

"You're saying she can't make me unhappy if I don't let her?" Lilah guessed. "Like choosing to come here today to have fun with you instead of staying home and then feeling sad that I missed out?"

"Like that," Sarah confirmed, as they finished their tour of the food booths—offering everything from foot-long hot dogs and pizza slices to candied nuts and snow cones—and turned toward the activity stations. There was a dunk tank and pie throwing booth and half a dozen carnival-type games with all the proceeds going to local charities. There was also a clown making balloon animals for the kids, a bouncy castle and an enormous inflatable slide.

Of course, there were permanent play structures in the park, too. Swings and climbers and a splash pad where dozens of little ones were dancing in the fountains and shrieking with laughter when an unexpected spray erupted.

At the face painting booth, they crossed paths with Macy and Liam Gilmore, whose kids were waiting their turn in line.

"At my school in Beaumont, there was a sister and a brother in the grade below me who were twins, but I've never met any triplets before," Lilah said to Sarah, as they continued on their way.

"Ava, Max and Sam are the only triplets I know, too," Sarah said. "But there are several sets of twins in my family."

"Several?" Lilah said skeptically.

She nodded. "In fact, one of my cousins—the woman supervising the little boys in the sandbox—has two sets."

Sarah introduced Lilah to Regan and Sawyer and Sutton.

"Where are Piper and Poppy?" Sarah asked, naming the boys' older sisters.

"At the bouncy castle with their dad," Regan said.

"He didn't have to work today?"

"Tonight—which is why we brought reinforcement baby-sitters," she said, as Deacon Parrish and Sierra Hart, recently engaged, wandered over to join them—the latter in the third trimester of her second surrogate pregnancy.

"Are you having twins, too?" Lilah asked the expectant mom.

Sierra laughed. "Nope. One at a time works for me."

"We can't all be overachievers," Regan said with a shrug.

"And I'm okay with that," her sister-in-law said.

"Have you seen either of my brothers?" Regan asked Sarah now.

"Jason and Alyssa were at the splash pad with their kids and Spencer and Kenzie were heading over to the dunk tank."

"Caleb Gilmore volunteered to sit the first shift at the dunk tank," Sierra noted, her eyes dancing with amusement. "Sky Kelly paid for five balls and dunked her brother five times."

Sarah had to laugh at that. "Well, she was the star third base-man of Diggers' softball team for a number of years."

"The best, though, was when Brielle took a ten-dollar bill out of her pocket and offered it to her sister-in-law so she could throw five more.

"Poor Caleb must have been waterlogged by the time she walked away."

"She didn't walk away. Jake had to drag her."

Sarah laughed again.

"So what do you think of Haven?" Regan asked, turning her attention to Lilah.

"I've only been here a few weeks, but I like it so far," she said.

"What grade are you going into?"

"Seventh."

"Same as Brendan," Regan noted.

"My nephew," Sarah explained. "We haven't met him yet, but we're headed toward Patrick's usual site—where he hopefully has burgers grilling—right now."

"Then we'll no doubt see you again in a while," Regan said. "But if not, it was nice meeting you, Lilah."

"And all of you," she responded politely.

But of course they crossed paths with several other people en route who wanted to say a few words to Sarah or be introduced to the girl by her side. Including Olivia and Adam Morgan, whose three sons—Easton, Hudson and Colton—were kicking a soccer ball around a field. Easton was also going into seventh grade and so was his buddy Elliott, who jumped into the game with his sister Avenlea, while their parents—Lindsay and Mitchell Gilmore—joined the adults' conversation.

"Do you know *everyone* in town?" Lilah asked, when Sarah dragged her away from the game.

She laughed. "Not everyone, but Haven's a pretty small town and my family's lived here a long time, so I know a fair number of them."

"I only ever lived in Beaumont before we came here," Lilah said. "But Dad and Aunt Rachel grew up in Louisiana before Grandma and Grandpa moved them to Texas."

"Louisiana, huh? I guess that would explain the beignets."

Lilah nodded. "He said they were his favorite treat when he was a kid."

"Do your grandparents still live in Texas?"

Now the girl shook her head. "Grandma got cancer a few years back and Grandpa died a few weeks after she did. Aunt Rachel said it was 'cuz his heart was broken and that we shouldn't be too sad, because now they're together again."

"That's a nice way of looking at it," Sarah decided.

By the time they got to where Patrick had spread his blankets on the lawn—claiming viewing spots for the fireworks later— Jenna and Harrison were there, along with Trevor and Haylee and Aidan and Ellie (Lilah's mind was boggled by yet another set of twins!), Devin and Claire and Gramps and Helen and Francesca, Helen's great-niece of the train station errand.

"I haven't seen you since the engagement was official," Sarah noted, greeting her future step-grandmother with a warm hug. "Congratulations."

"Thank you," Helen said. "When I lost my Harold, I was sure I'd never fall in love again—and then I met your grandfather."

"He's one of a kind," Sarah agreed.

"The very best kind," Helen said. "And though it seems a little silly to me, to be planning a big wedding at our ages, Jesse insisted that we celebrate."

"Well, if you need any help with anything, let me know."

"I appreciate the offer, but Jesse's decided to put all the details of our big day in the hands of a professional."

"The best of the best," Gramps chimed in.

"That would be Gilmore Galas," Haylee said.

"I thought your sister's company was based in California."

"It is, but Finley couldn't resist Gramps's charm."

"Very few ladies can," he said immodestly.

"Of course, it also gives her an excuse to visit her niece and nephew in Haven—and Lachlan's going to come with her to make a holiday of it," Haylee said, mentioning her sister's husband.

"Speaking of the wedding," Gramps said, turning his gaze on Sarah again. "You got a date yet?"

"I've still got lots of time," she pointed out.

"Are you working on it?"

"Thinking about it," she said.

"Try less thinking and more doing," he suggested.

"You should ask my dad," Lilah chimed in.

Gramps considered this for a minute. "Her dad's the baker who made the cupcakes for Claire's birthday?"

"He is," Sarah confirmed.

He nodded. "Ask him. And ask if he'll give your grandpa and his bride any kind of discount on a really big cake."

"Always working the angles, aren't you, Gramps?"

He winked at her. "You know it."

"I bet Dad would give you a discount on the cake," Lilah said, when Gramps's attention had shifted elsewhere.

"My grandfather can afford to pay full price—and then some," Sarah assured her.

"You could ask him anyway," Lilah said. "I mean, to be your date to the wedding."

"I don't know if that's a good idea," Sarah hedged.

"Why not? You like him, don't you?"

"Sure," she agreed, keeping her tone deliberately casual.

"And I know he likes you."

She bit her tongue, because no way was she going to pump Andrew's twelve-year-old daughter for information. But there was one question she needed to ask. "You wouldn't mind if I asked your dad to be my date?"

"I hope you do," Lilah said. "He needs someone in his life."

"He's got you and your sister," Sarah pointed out.

"That's what he says," the girl acknowledged. "But eventually we're going to grow up and go away to school and I don't want him to be alone."

"I'll keep that in mind."

"HOW WERE THE FIREWORKS?" Andrew asked Lilah, when Sarah finally brought his daughter home later that night.

"Awesome!" Lilah enthused.

"You had a good time?"

"The. Best. Time." Then she wrapped her arms around Sarah and hugged her tight. "Thank you for taking me."

"You're very welcome," Sarah said, hugging her back.

"And it's very late," Andrew said to his daughter. "Go on up and get ready for bed."

"Okay." But Lilah hugged her dad first, too. "G'night, Dad."

"Night, sweetie. I'll be up to check on you soon."

"No need to rush," she told him. "I'm sure you and Sarah have lots to talk about."

"Do we?" he asked, when his daughter had disappeared up the stairs.

"Lilah's trying to play matchmaker," she warned.

"Well, I can't fault her choice," he said. "But I'm curious to know how this came about."

"You can blame my grandfather. He asked if I had a date for his wedding and when I said no, Lilah suggested that I should ask you."

"And what did you say?"

"I promised to think about it."

"Are there any other candidates in the running for your potential date?"

"Not at the moment," she said.

"Let's keep it that way," he said, and lowered his head to kiss her.

"Mmm…fireworks twice tonight."

He grinned.

TILDA WAS SITTING on the wrought iron bench near the stand of trees in the backyard when Warren came over. She kept her gaze focused on the book in her hand, pretending she didn't know he was there. Pretending she wasn't desperate for someone to talk to.

Without waiting for an invitation, he sat down on the opposite end of the bench. She turned the page and kept reading.

He broke the silence first, saying, "I didn't see you at the park yesterday."

She lifted her gaze from the page to him. "Why were you looking for me?"

"I wasn't looking for you," he denied. "But I saw your sister with Sarah and noticed that you weren't there."

"You're right. I wasn't."

"Why not?"

"Why do you care?"

He shrugged. "I wouldn't say that I care so much as that I'm curious."

"Well, it's none of your business."

"Your dad ground you for trying to run away?"

She slammed her book shut with a frustrated sigh. "I *hate* this town."

"Obviously."

"I wasn't running away," she denied. "I just wanted to go to Texas to spend some time with my friends."

"How'd that work out for you?"

She glared at him.

"Maybe instead of trying to go back, you should look to the future and think about the opportunities you have right here."

"I wish I could say that I appreciate your fortune cookie advice, but I don't. And someone with a perfect family and a perfect life has no right to pass judgment on anyone else."

He seemed surprised by that. "You think I have a perfect life?"

"Are you saying you don't?" she challenged.

"Every family has secrets," he told her.

"Yeah? What's yours?"

"If I told you, they wouldn't be secrets anymore, would they?"

She rolled her eyes. "You're weird."

"You're judgy."

She scowled.

Warren's phone chirped and he glanced at the screen. "And there's another snag in my perfect life."

"What snag?"

"My mom's running late and I need her car to go to the drive-in tonight."

"Haven has a drive-in?"

He shook his head. "It's in Cooper's Corners."

She didn't know where that was and she wasn't going to ask. "Don't tell me you've got a date tonight," she sneered instead.

"Okay, I won't tell you," he said.

"With an actual girl?"

He ignored the question. "I wonder what happened to make you so mean."

"I'm not mean," she denied.

He laughed, though the sound was without humor. "The mean girls never think they're mean."

"I'm *not* a mean girl." But the heat that burned her cheeks denounced the lie. Because even if she didn't believe she was a mean girl, she had been mean to him.

"Your sister was at my place hanging out with Rory earlier today and we all ended up playing *Mario Kart* together."

"Are you trying to make a point? Or do you just like to hear yourself talk?"

"My point is that it's hard to believe the two of you are sisters," he said.

"Would it be easier to believe that we're only half sisters?" she challenged.

He nodded slowly. "Actually, yes."

"Well, there you go," she told him.

"Same dad, different moms?" he guessed.

"No, same mom, different dads."

His brows lifted. "But you live with your dad."

"Lilah's dad," she clarified.

"You call him Dad," he noted.

"Because I didn't know any different until a few months ago." And she hadn't told a single soul—so why had she opened her big mouth and blabbed to him? "Lilah still doesn't know, though—and he doesn't, either—so you better not say anything to anyone."

Warren was quiet for a long time before he asked, "So why did you tell me your big secret?"

"I don't know," she admitted. Maybe because it was a big secret—the biggest one she'd ever held on to—and the truth was eating away at her. "Maybe because, like you said, I don't have anyone else to talk to."

He took off his glasses, used the hem of his T-shirt to rub a spot of one of the lenses. "Henry's not my dad, either."

She blinked, surprised. "He's not?"

He shook his head. "My dad was a mean drunk who used to knock my mom around. She put up with it, determined to keep her family together, until I was five years old and he started hitting me, too."

"Did he—" She swallowed. "Did he hurt you?"

"Not that I can remember. Truthfully, I don't have many memories of him at all—and that's probably a good thing," he said. "We lived in Branson, Missouri then, and when my mom decided to leave him, we moved to Lakewood, Colorado, where her sister lived with her family. That's where she met Henry, a widower with a three-year-old daughter."

"So Rory's not really your sister," Tilda realized.

"Rory *is* my sister," he insisted, an unexpected edge to his tone.

"But...you don't have the same mother *or* father."

"We have the same mother *and* father," he countered. "Just because we don't share DNA doesn't mean we're not family."

"You're right," she said, feeling chastened. "I'm sorry."

After another minute, she asked, "Do you have any idea where your dad—your biological dad—is now?"

He nodded. "In prison in Missouri."

Prison? *Yikes.*

And she'd been upset when her mom moved to Napa Valley.

"Because he knocked your mom around?" she guessed.

Now he shook his head. "Because he killed a guy in a bar fight."

"My mom lives in California now—with her new boyfriend. Not that that compares to having a dad in prison," she realized.

"It's not a contest," Warren said. "And I didn't tell you so that you'd feel sorry for me or be nice to me. I told you so that you'd know that everyone has stuff going on behind the scenes, and you should think about that before you pass judgment on anyone else."

CHAPTER SIXTEEN

"YOU AND DEVIN left the park early on Saturday," Sarah commented to Claire Tuesday morning, as they were untacking their mounts after their morning ride.

"Ed's not a fan of fireworks," Claire explained.

"You didn't have him with you," she pointed out.

"I know. But the neighbors behind us sometimes set off their own, and I didn't want him to be alone if rockets started exploding in his backyard."

"Well, you missed a good show."

"Did Lilah enjoy it?" Claire asked.

"She did," Sarah confirmed, as she examined and picked Bella's hooves. "Not just the fireworks but the whole day."

"She seems like a nice kid."

"She is. And she likes me, which helps balance out the fact that her sister hates me."

"I'm sure Tilda doesn't hate you," her friend said.

"She definitely blames me for ruining her Fourth of July plans," Sarah noted. "Even though Andrew tracked her through an app on her phone."

"Another reason to be glad we didn't have smartphones when we were her age," Claire remarked. "On the other hand, I shudder to think of a fourteen-year-old girl trying to navigate her way across state lines without the ability to call 9-1-1 at her fingertips. Actually, I shudder to think of a teenager making that trip even with a phone."

"Andrew yelled at her. I think it was probably the first time in his life that he ever did."

"Sometimes yelling is warranted," Claire noted.

"Exactly what I said," Sarah told her friend. Finished with the mare's hooves, she picked up a curry comb. "Anyway, Tilda is going to be here today."

Claire nodded. "I know. I signed off on her application."

"And I know you thought I should do the orientation—"

"And you will," her friend interjected.

Sarah continued to brush the horse's coat. "Did you hear me say she hates me?"

"If she does, it's only because she doesn't know you. Working here will give you both a chance to change that."

"I really think it would be better if I stayed in the background, at least for the next couple of weeks."

"You can think whatever you want, but you're not the boss here," Claire said.

"Really?" She looked over the horse's back at her friend, who was busy grooming her own mount. "You're going to play the boss card?"

"It is fun to pull it out every now and then," Claire said, a smile in her voice.

"I thought we were friends."

"Best friends," Claire confirmed. "Which is why I know you're not intimidated by a fourteen-year-old girl."

"Maybe not a normal fourteen-year-old girl with a normal amount of teenage attitude," Sarah allowed.

"I have complete faith in you."

Which is why Sarah was in the yard with her clipboard at nine thirty, the recommended first-day arrival time for student volunteers so that they could be checked in and their necessary paperwork collected before orientation began at ten.

Warren Aldridge was one of the first to arrive, along with Dylan Spears and Heidi Garwood, whom he'd apparently picked up en route. Though this was Sarah's first summer at Twilight Valley, she knew it would be Warren's third and that Claire considered him trustworthy and dependable. The other volunteers on the list were Bryce Holland, Whitney Kirk and Tilda Morrow.

When everyone was accounted for, Sarah introduced herself, then led the students on a tour of the facility so they could meet the animals in residence—the horses and goats and Ed, who'd already greeted each of them upon their arrival.

She gave a brief summary of the tasks that they might be required to perform on a rotating basis, to ensure that those who got first crack at grooming or hand-walking also had to take a turn cleaning tack and mucking out stalls.

"Proper attire is required," Sarah reminded them, with a pointed look at Whitney's sandals. "If you don't have proper attire, you won't be able to work, and if you can't work, we can't sign off on your hours.

"There are lockers available in the lunchroom for your personal belongings and a refrigerator for your snacks and drinks. Your four-hour shift includes a half-hour break for lunch and you are expected to bring your own, except on the last Thursday of the month, when hamburgers and veggie burgers will be provided. Whatever you're eating, please don't share it with the dog. I assure you, Ed doesn't go hungry, and as much as he might like people food, his digestive system does not."

"That's the truth," Warren chimed in, proving that his time on the ranch had given him some experience in the matter.

"Tasks are pinned to the board." She gestured to the magnetic board on the wall. "Grab one and get to work."

Five teens rushed to the board, angling for their preferred assignments. Tilda lagged a few steps behind.

"Looks like you're mucking out stalls," Sarah said, when she saw Andrew's daughter staring at the last remaining pin.

The girl shrugged. "I figured that's what you'd make me do, anyway."

"It's not my job to make you do anything," Sarah told her. "And no one's forcing you to be here."

"Actually, that's not true," she said. "My dad's forcing me to be here. This was his idea, not mine."

"Should I call and ask him to come and get you?"

The teen hesitated for half a second, then shook her head. "No."

"Then put on a pair of gloves, pick up a pitchfork and get to work."

TILDA DIDN'T SAY much after her first day at Twilight Valley. When Andrew asked her how it went, she only said, "It was okay." But when it was time to go back on Thursday, she didn't grumble half as much as she'd done on the first day, and when the next Tuesday came around, she was ready and waiting when he returned from the bakery to take her to the ranch.

And so it seemed that they were finally settling into their respective routines. Sugar & Spice was doing steady business; in addition to volunteering at Twilight Valley, Tilda helped out at the bakery on weekends; and Lilah entertained them with her camp adventures over dinner every day.

If he had any cause for complaint, it was only one—that he didn't see enough of Sarah. Because exchanging a few words of greeting when he dropped off or picked up Tilda didn't count. He wanted to be able to spend some real time with her without wondering who might be watching.

And maybe Sarah wanted more, too, because when he dropped his daughter off Tuesday morning, she held up a hand—asking him to hold on a minute while she finished issuing instructions to one of the volunteers—then hurried over to his vehicle.

"Hey," she said.

"Everything okay?" he asked.

"If you're asking about Tilda, yeah, everything's fine," she said. "I was just wondering about you."

"What about me?"

"From what I hear, you've been working day and night since you opened Sugar & Spice."

"It's taking some time to optimize the prep and baking schedules, but we're getting there," he said.

"Is there any chance you might be able to steal away for a few hours tomorrow afternoon?" she wondered aloud.

"I think the chances are pretty good," he said. "What did you have in mind?"

"We could head out to Crooked Creek again, saddle up a couple of horses and go for a ride."

"What time should I pick you up?" he asked, willing to adjust his schedule as required to be with her.

"One o'clock at my place?"

"I'll see you then."

HE'D BEEN IN such a hurry to get to Sarah's on time that he didn't think about food, so he was pleased to discover that she'd packed a picnic lunch. And an hour after they'd arrived at Crooked Creek—where her grandfather had two mounts tacked and ready, they were stretched out on a blanket on the grass by the creek, munching on sandwiches and sipping soda while their horses grazed nearby.

"The first night you brought me out here, you didn't mention that this was your grandfather's ranch," he noted.

"Didn't I?" she said, with feigned innocence.

"I think you know very well that you didn't. In fact, you've never mentioned that you're a Blake."

"Obviously someone did," she noted.

"Kyle," he told her.

"And how did that come up in conversation?" she wondered.

"We were at Diggers' the day you had lunch there with your ex."

"Zack?"

His brows lifted. "Have you had lunch with any other exes recently?"

"No."

"So why didn't you tell me?" he asked her now.

"About having lunch with Zack?"

"That you're a Blake," he clarified.

She shrugged. "Truthfully, I don't think about it most of the time. But I know that other people do, and as soon as they find out that I'm a Blake, they treat me differently. Which is how I ended up dating several guys who were more interested in my family and my connections than they were in me."

"Obviously they were fools," he said.

"Maybe. But it became an instinctive defense, to keep that

part hidden, so I wouldn't have to wonder if someone wanted me or just my name."

"I guess I can understand that," he said. "And since we slept together long before I knew your name, you can rest assured that I have no interest in your family fortune—just your body."

"I think you might have to prove it one more time."

"I'll give it my best shot," he promised, and lowered his head to cover her mouth with his own.

Her lips were as sweet as he remembered, her response as passionate as he recalled, and in no time at all, they were both panting and naked and—

He rolled away from her abruptly and swore under his breath.

Then Sarah held up a little square packet between two fingers.

"I do appreciate a woman who comes prepared."

"Well, I'm still waiting for that part," she said, surprising a laugh out of him as he took care to protect them both.

Then, finally, he was inside her, filling and fulfilling her. She held on to him, her fingernails biting into his shoulders, as the world tilted and spun. The tautness of his muscles and the shallowness of his breathing told her that he was close to his release, too. But he held himself back, determined to ensure her pleasure first.

And while the creek trickled over the rocks and the horses grazed, he swallowed the cries that announced her climax. Only then did he surrender to his own.

A long minute later, he rolled off her and wrapped his arm around her, spooning her from behind. Sarah was still trying to catch her breath when she felt him press a kiss to the ink on her shoulder blade.

"You're smiling," she said.

"How can you tell?" he asked.

"I felt your lips curve against my skin."

"Okay, I'm smiling," he admitted. "Because I really like your tattoo."

She'd told him it was a lion, but it was really a lion cub. More specifically, a young Simba from the Disney movie.

He shifted so that he could kiss her lips now. "And it proves that you're not as predictable as you feared."

"And not as strong and courageous as I pretend to be," she confided. "More baby lion than king of the jungle."

"I think you're a lot stronger and braver than you realize. You're also smart and sexy and amazing and kind, and when I'm with you, I'm always right where I want to be."

And when she was with him, he made her feel as if she was all those things. And she didn't want to be anywhere else.

She'd dated a lot of men in her thirty-two years, and she'd enjoyed some pretty intense chemistry with a few of them. But only Andrew had ever turned her on so completely with just a look. Only Andrew made her insides quiver with just a smile and her knees grow weak with a casual touch.

In the beginning, the attraction had been purely physical. She hadn't known him well enough for it to be anything more. But over the past several weeks, as she'd spent more time with him, she'd discovered that she really liked him.

And if it occurred to her that her heart might be in danger, well, that was a worry for another day.

THE FOLLOWING SUNDAY, Tilda and Lilah left for California to spend some time with their mom. Not the two weeks they'd hoped for, but five days.

Sarah suspected she was as excited about the trip as they were, because it meant five days—and five nights—that she could spend with Andrew.

He suggested making reservations for dinner at The Chophouse in Battle Mountain. She countered with an offer to pick up steaks and potatoes to grill at his place. He promised to provide a bottle of wine and dessert—and extra chocolate sauce for later. When she returned from Twilight Valley, after a strenuous workout with an ornery stallion who didn't seem to appreciate his change in circumstances, she took a long shower to soothe her weary muscles then rubbed scented lotion over her body. When she dressed, it was in anticipation of being undressed, in some of her sexiest underwear and a sleeveless floral print sundress.

"My mouth has been watering for steak all day," he confided, when he met her at the door. "Now I'm only hungry for you."

"We can put the groceries in the fridge for later," she suggested.

So that's what they did, then Andrew lifted her effortlessly into his arms and carried her up the stairs to his bedroom.

"I don't need to be seduced," she said, feeling foolish because her heart had actually fluttered when he scooped her off her feet.

"Seduction isn't about necessity but pleasure," he said.

She didn't realize he'd found the zipper at the back of her dress until she felt the air against her skin. The first night they'd spent together, they'd shared a desperate passion born of the knowledge that he would be gone in the morning. Tonight was different. Tonight they had time for a more leisurely and thorough exploration.

He tugged the straps over her shoulders and down her arms, then let the dress fall to the floor to pool at her feet, before shedding his own T-shirt and jeans.

"I don't think I've ever taken enough time to appreciate your lingerie before," he said, his fingertips skimming reverently over the delicate lace.

"I like the feel of soft fabrics against my skin," she confided. "Soft fabrics and strong hands."

He eased her onto the bed. "I like the feel of you."

He straddled her mostly naked body, his knees bracketing her hips, holding her in place while his hands and mouth moved over her.

She let her hands explore him, too, tracing the hard angles and ridges of muscle. She dipped her hand into his boxer briefs and wrapped her fingers around him, stroking him slowly, making him groan with pleasure.

She'd always enjoyed physical intimacy and wasn't afraid to let a man know what she liked—and what she didn't. But Andrew didn't need any guidance. He instinctively seemed to know just where and how to touch her to maximize her pleasure, stoking the fire that burned inside her. He had a way of making her feel so much, and making her yearn for even more. From the first brush of his lips, the first pass of his hands, she was his.

His mouth moved down her throat, over her collarbone. Tasting, teasing. He suckled her breasts through the lacy fabric. His mouth hot and wet, making her the same.

He rained kisses over her belly, then nuzzled the scrap of lace between her thighs, making her gasp and yearn. He hooked his thumbs in the sides of her panties and tugged them over her hips, then nudged her knees farther apart and settled between them.

Her breath caught in her throat when he lowered his head to put his mouth on her, using his lips and his tongue to kiss and lick and drive her to the edge of reason...and over.

She flew apart, shattering like a supernova.

And when she finally came back to earth, he was there, holding her and kissing her.

"Andrew." His name was a whisper—a plea.

"Tell me what you want."

"You," she said simply.

And he gave her what she wanted. What they both wanted.

It was much later before he fired up the barbecue, and after dinner they had dessert—and then dessert again.

SHE DIDN'T KNOW what time he left for the bakery the following morning, she only knew that when she rolled over and reached for him, he was gone.

She squinted at the clock on the bedside table.

5:35.

Then rolled over again and fell back to sleep.

The next time she woke up, he was kissing her.

"Good morning, sleeping beauty."

Her eyes flickered open slowly.

"I brought you coffee and fresh beignets," he said.

"A very thoughtful gesture," she said, wriggling into a seated position so that she could take the mug and plate.

Then she set both aside and reached for what she really wanted—him.

CHAPTER SEVENTEEN

NAPA VALLEY WAS BEAUTIFUL. As they neared the end of their almost two-hour drive from the San Francisco airport to Calistoga, Tilda had to admit that Sarah had been right about that. Outside her window, everything was lush and green, with rows and rows of vines as far as the eye could see, heavy with glossy leaves and bunches of fruit just starting to ripen.

The day had started with a ridiculously early morning flight out of Elko, and though it was only midafternoon now, she was feeling the effects of the travel. Nine hours of total travel time—including the drive to the airport and the stopover in Salt Lake City—and she was beat, which made her wonder how she would have endured three days of train travel from Haven to Beaumont. And now she'd never know.

Perry had kept up a running monologue about grape growing and wine making throughout the drive. And while Tilda was sure it was a testament to his passion for his work, she really just wanted him to shut up so that she could enjoy peace and quiet for five minutes—and maybe even exchange a few words with her mom, who seemed happy enough to let her boyfriend rattle on.

"Not too far now," Perry had said, turning off the main highway.

Twenty minutes later, he turned again, this time into a long drive leading toward what looked like a freaking castle.

"Home sweet home," Mom said.

Tilda gawked. She couldn't help it.

This was where her mother lived?

But of course it wasn't.

Perry continued to drive, past the castle, past half a dozen other buildings with the same architectural style and stunning display of stone and glass until he arrived at a house that was maybe half the size of the one in Haven.

And though it was small, it was fancy—the exterior matching that of all the other buildings on the property. Glossy wood door, gleaming windows that reflected the afternoon sun.

"This is one of the original guesthouses on the estate," Mom explained, as she ushered them inside. "Originally a one-bedroom bungalow that was renovated to add two bedrooms and another bath on the second floor." She led them up the stairs and opened one of the doors with a flourish. "This will be your room while you're here."

"Mine or Lilah's?" Tilda asked.

"Both," she said. "That's why there's two beds."

"But you said there were two rooms."

"The other one's Bella's."

Isabella was Perry's seven-year-old daughter with his former girlfriend, but she went by "Bella," which Tilda knew meant *beautiful*. (It was also, she thought unkindly, the name of one of the horses at Twilight Valley.)

"Is Bella here?" Tilda asked.

"Not right now," Mom admitted. "But she's here two weeks out of every month, so her room is full of her stuff."

"I guess that's what shared custody really looks like," Tilda mused.

Mom frowned. "You know we'd love to see you more often, it's just hard with so much distance between us."

Distance she'd put between them when she decided to move to California, but Tilda knew there was no point in reminding her mother of that.

"Well, I'll let you girls unpack," Mom said. "We planned an early dinner tonight, figuring you'd be tired out from travel, so that you can get a good night's sleep before the fun starts tomorrow."

The early dinner was a salad of mixed greens with grilled fish and roasted vegetables. Tilda pushed her food around on her plate, more tired than hungry, and when she and Lilah were finally excused from the table, they went upstairs to get ready for bed.

Lilah fell asleep as soon as her head hit the pillow, but Tilda tossed and turned for what seemed like forever, unable to shut off her mind and go to sleep.

She'd been looking forward to this visit for weeks—*months*—thinking about all the things that she'd be able to do with Mom in California. But now that she was finally here, she wished she was back home in Haven.

She felt bad that Dad was alone—and then she considered that maybe he wasn't alone and felt even worse.

But she must have fallen asleep eventually, because when she woke up, it was morning. She reached for her phone, to check for messages, and found one from Dad, sent the night before to both her and Lilah.

Good night. Love you both. Sweet dreams.

The words were followed by a heart and a sleeping emoji.

One message in the past twenty-four hours, and that from her dad. It was a sad but true reflection of the state of her social life.

But she replied:

Good morning.

And added sunshine and kiss-blowing emojis.

Then she got dressed and made her way to the kitchen.

She took a seat across from Lilah at the table and Mom set a plate in front of her with a thick Belgian waffle topped with whipped cream and berries.

"I'm not hungry," Tilda said.

"Try the waffle," Mom urged. "You'll love it."

Before she could respond to that, Perry walked into the room. He smiled and wished them good-morning.

"You look like you're on your way out," Mom noted.

"I just need to check the veraison," he told her, picking up a mug of coffee he'd obviously left on the counter and swallowing a mouthful.

She pouted. "You said you were taking the day off."

"I won't be long," he promised.

"Make sure you're not," she said, tipping her head back.

While he was kissing her, he skimmed a hand down her back, then over her butt and gave it a squeeze.

Tilda dragged her gaze away—and didn't look at her mom again until she heard his footsteps move away and the front door open and close.

"We're only here for a few days," she said. "Do you think you could ask Perry to keep the PDAs to a minimum during that time?"

"Maybe I'm the one who can't keep my hands off him," Mom countered with a smile.

Tilda rolled her eyes. "I don't need to hear things like that."

Mom laughed. "You're fifteen years old—stop acting like a child."

"I'm fourteen," Tilda noted. "And I *am* a child. *Your* child."

"You'll be fifteen in February."

Which was more than half a year away.

"And definitely living up to the stereotype of a moody teenager," Mom noted. "I thought you were happy to be here."

"I was. I am." She attempted to spear a blueberry with her fork, but it rolled away. "But I thought we were coming here to spend time with *you.*"

"We've got so many things planned. Hiking and swimming. Perry wants to give you a tour of the vineyards and the winery. And shopping—we definitely need to go shopping," she said. "Honestly, Tilda, don't you have any clothes that fit?"

"I meant, *just* you." She looked at Lilah. Not that she actually expected her sister to chime in with any kind of support. Lilah didn't like conflict and tended to go along with whatever anyone else wanted to do.

"Perry took time off so that he could get to know you and your sister better, and so that you can get to know your stepfather."

Tilda's fork slipped out of her grasp and clattered against her plate. "Stepfather?"

Mom nodded. "That's right. Perry asked me to marry him—and I said yes."

Her empty stomach churned. "When's the wedding?"

For the first time since Tilda sat down at the table, Mom looked uneasy. "Three weeks ago."

"You're already married?"

"Perry wanted us to tell you together. Tonight," she admitted. "But how could I wait to share such exciting news?"

"Apparently you waited three weeks," Tilda noted. Then she counted back and scowled. "And three weeks ago was the weekend you were supposed to come to Haven to see us."

"You said something came up and you had to go to Las Vegas," Lilah chimed in, surprising her sister.

"Well, the something was that Perry proposed," Mom told them. "And we went to Las Vegas to get married."

Tilda felt hot tears burn her eyes.

Apparently Lilah wasn't too happy, either, because she pushed away from the table and stormed off to their shared room.

"I CAN PLAY hooky this afternoon if you can," Sarah said, snuggling into Andrew's embrace.

"Aren't we playing hooky right now?"

"We are," she agreed. "But I wasn't sure if you had to go back to the bakery."

"Nope." His hand skimmed lazily down her side, tracing the outside of her breast, the dip of her waist, the curve of her hip. "I told Mabel that I was playing hooky this afternoon."

"She didn't ask any questions?"

"I'm the boss," he reminded her.

"We could pack a picnic again and head back to Crooked Creek," she said.

He smiled, obviously remembering the first time they'd gone out to Crooked Creek. Or maybe the last time.

"I like that plan," he said. "But I don't know that I have the makings for a picnic."

"I'll stop at The Trading Post on my way home to get what we need."

"Why are you going home?"

"Because the dress I wore over here last night isn't really appropriate for riding."

"I'm not sure it's appropriate for grocery shopping, either," he noted.

A valid point. And while it wouldn't be the first time she'd been spotted in town wearing clothes rumpled from the night before, she knew that he was wary of any gossip making its way back to his daughters.

"So I'll go home first and then go to the grocery store."

"Or we could skip the picnic and stay here—and naked—all day."

"Hmm...another intriguing option."

"Let's see if I can influence your decision," he said, rolling on top of her.

As he kissed her, long and slow and deep, he slid a knee between her legs, parting her thighs so that he could settle between them. Her hips instinctively lifted, rubbing her pelvis against his.

He groaned, a low sound of approval that turned into a muttered curse when his phone chimed with a text message.

"Do you need to check that?" Sarah asked.

"Check what?" he asked, nibbling on her lips.

"Your phone."

"I don't have a phone. There is nothing here but you and me."

She appreciated his effort, but she could tell that he was distracted, wondering.

"Check your phone," she said. "I promise, I'll be right here when you're done."

He reached toward the nightstand to retrieve his phone.

"Just my sister," he said, setting it aside again.

"You don't want to respond to her?"

"Not right now," he promised.

Less than a minute later, his phone chimed again.

This time he sighed when he glanced at the screen.

"The bakery?" she guessed.

He shook his head. "Tilda."

Of course he couldn't ignore a message from his daughter, and she didn't expect him to.

He swiped to open the message, skimmed the content and then swore under his breath.

"Something's wrong," Sarah guessed.

Now he nodded. "Miranda just told the girls that Perry is their new stepdad."

"They didn't know that she was getting married?"

"No," he said. "And it's news to me, too."

"Are you okay?" she asked cautiously.

"To be honest, I'm not happy."

"Because your ex-wife got remarried?"

"Because of the way she handled it," he clarified. "We agreed, when we split up, that the girls would always be our number one priority. And for the first four years after, we mostly managed to present a united front, despite the divorce.

"Then she met Perry and, six months later, decided to move with him to California. There was no discussion with me or our daughters, no concern about how they might feel and no consideration of how it would impact her relationship with them.

"I was the one who had to try to explain her decision to them. And now I'm going to be the one dealing with the fallout of the surprise nuptials."

"Tilda and Lilah don't like their new stepfather?"

"They don't really know him," Andrew admitted.

"Hopefully that will change over the next few days," Sarah said, trying to put a positive spin on the situation.

His phone chimed again.

"Unlikely," he said. "Because now they want to come home." He sent her an apologetic glance. "It looks like we're going to have to take a rain check on that picnic—and our alternate plans."

She managed to bite her tongue for a whole three seconds before she said, "That's your decision? No discussion or consideration of how it affects our weekend?"

He glanced up from the screen, already open to the airline website. "I'm sorry—what did you say?"

"Nothing important." She slid out of his bed and began gathering up her clothes.

He'd already made abundantly clear that Tilda and Lilah were *his* daughters and that her opinions weren't welcome or relevant in matters concerning them. And while she knew that his primary concern was always their best interests—and, in fact, his commitment to his daughters was one of the things she liked most about him—she was a little disappointed that he wasn't willing to make any effort to salvage their plans for the weekend.

If there had been any kind of real emergency with either of his girls, she would have been right there to help him push everything else aside. But neither of them was sick or hurt—except maybe their feelings.

"If there's something you want to say, say it," Andrew told her now.

"It's just that, from everything you've told me, this is the first time they've seen their mom in weeks," she ventured cautiously. "And they've been there less than twenty-four hours. Don't you think you should give them some time to try to work things out?"

"Work things out?" he echoed incredulously. "She just dropped the bombshell of her marriage on them."

"Which blows up their hopes of a reconciliation," she acknowledged. "That aside, I don't know your ex-wife and I'm not going to pretend to understand her reasons for not sharing her plans with Tilda and Lilah in advance, but maybe you should give her some credit for telling them that she got married. And for not hiding Perry from them when they were dating."

"Is that what this is really about? You're upset that I don't want them to know we've been dating?"

"Except that we haven't been dating," she pointed out. "We've been sneaking around and hooking up. Because your daughters aren't ready to see you with a woman who isn't their mom, even though their mom was living with—and is now married to—another man."

"I'm sorry if you're disappointed that our plans for the weekend have been upended," he said coolly.

"I *am* disappointed," she said. "Not because our plans have been upended so much as the fact that you're willing to upend them simply to placate your daughters who maybe need to learn that their dad is entitled to a life of his own."

But maybe she needed to remember that she had a life of her own, too, and get back to it.

So resolved, she headed to Twilight Valley, where the horses, at least, didn't give her mixed signals.

"THAT THING'S GETTING a lot of mileage," Sarah remarked, when she returned—three hours later—from wherever she'd been and found Andrew sitting on her porch with the olive branch in his hand.

"I should probably come up with something new," he acknowledged. "But it got me in the door once before and I'm hoping it will do so again."

"I thought you'd be on your way to the airport by now."

"Not until Friday," he said.

"No flights available?"

"Could we maybe continue this conversation inside?" he asked. "I've been sitting on your porch long enough that your across-the-street neighbor has peeked through the curtains half a dozen times to ensure I know I'm being watched."

"Frank or Maria?"

"It was a man, so I'm guessing Frank," he said.

"Then I guess I'd better invite you to come in before he tells Maria, who will tell Emelia, who will tell everyone."

She unlocked the door; he followed her inside.

"After you left, I called Tilda and told her that I wasn't letting them come home early. Because you were right, they've been looking forward to this trip for weeks, and it wouldn't be fair to anyone to cut it short."

"How did she respond to that?"

"She hung up on me."

"You don't seem particularly bothered by the fact," she noted.

He shrugged. "Mad has pretty much been her mood since February, when I first told the girls that we were moving. Not that Miranda would know, because she moved to California in November, so I figure it's her turn to deal with adolescent hormones and angst."

"So where do we go from here?" she asked him.

"How about dinner?" he suggested. "I managed to finagle a reservation at The Home Station for eight o'clock."

"I appreciate what you're trying to do," she said. "But it's really not necessary. I understand why you're protective of your daughters—and why now might not be the best time for them to learn that you're dating someone."

"Except that we're not really dating until we actually go on a date," he pointed out, recycling her earlier argument.

"So then there's nothing to tell," she said.

"I feel like the luckiest man in the world when I'm with you. I *know* I'm the luckiest man in the world," he amended. "But I'm also a dad, and I need to be sensitive to my daughters' needs."

"I understand that," she promised. "I really do."

"But I also need you to know how much you mean to me," he told her. "And if I'm struggling to reconcile my identity as their father with my identity as your lover, and I know I am, it's because this is all new territory to me."

"It's possible I overreacted a little," she acknowledged. "Because this is all new territory to me, too."

"Maybe we can figure things out together?" he suggested.

She nodded. "I like the sound of that."

"So...dinner?"

"Let's see what we can rustle up in the kitchen." She glanced down at herself and wrinkled her nose. "After I shower—I smell like hay and horses."

He drew her into his arms. "I like the way you smell."

"I'm sweaty."

"You're sexy." He touched his lips to her. "My sexy cowgirl."

"Hold that thought," she said, stepping back. "Shower first, then dinner then...well, we can play it by ear after that."

And that's what they did, taking advantage of every minute of the all-too-limited time that was already ticking away.

CHAPTER EIGHTEEN

TILDA WAS BORED.

She'd been volunteering at Twilight Valley on Tuesdays and Thursdays and helping her dad at Sugar & Spice on Fridays and Saturdays—which seemed to satisfy him enough that he left her to her own devices the rest of the time. But it was Wednesday—the middle of the week—and she had nothing to do.

Nothing except check off some of the tasks on Dad's communal chore list, and she was bored enough that she was watering the flower boxes on the railing around the porch when she saw Warren come out of his house next door with a backpack slung over one shoulder.

Because she was usually home on Wednesdays, she'd started to notice a pattern in which he left the house before 11:00 a.m. and didn't come back until after 3:00 p.m.

She set down the watering can and skipped down the steps.

"Hey," she called out to him. "Where are you going?"

He paused in midstep and glanced over his shoulder. He looked surprised, and perhaps a little wary, that she'd taken the initiative to start a conversation.

She couldn't blame him. Every time he'd made a friendly overture, she'd responded with attitude and snark.

"Why do you want to know?" he said, answering her question with one of his own.

She shrugged. "I don't really."

"Then this conversation is pointless," he noted, and continued on his way.

She should have let him go, but instead, she found herself hurrying to catch up and then falling into step beside him.

He walked for thirty minutes—a whole half an hour!—without saying a word to her. She didn't say anything, either, because she'd already asked where he was going and he'd declined to answer.

But she thought she'd figured it out when the community center came into view. As if she needed any more proof that he was a geek, he spent his Wednesdays during summer break at the local library?

He paused on the steps leading into the building and opened his backpack. He took out a water bottle and drank from it.

Tilda realized then that she was thirsty, too, but she was empty-handed, not having planned to take a thirty-minute walk. Which, of course, meant she was going to have to walk another thirty minutes back home again.

Warren glanced at his watch then took another drink from his bottle, pretending he didn't know she was there.

Or maybe he really didn't.

Maybe she was as invisible to him as she felt to everyone else in her life.

She wished he'd offer her a drink.

Of course, if he did, she'd have to refuse. Because no way was she putting her mouth where his had been.

He recapped the bottle and dropped it into his backpack again before finally speaking to her. "Are you going to follow me inside, too?"

"I'm not following you," she immediately denied.

He snorted and she flushed, because obviously she had been following him.

"So why are you here?" he asked.

"I need something to read."

"Do you know how to read?"

"Now who's the mean girl?" she challenged.

He just smirked.

Then he spotted someone else walking up the steps toward the entrance—a girl with bluntly cut reddish hair and big eyes—and his attention shifted.

"Hey," the girl said, and smiled at him.

"Hey," he responded, and smiled back.

And they turned away from Tilda and walked into the library together.

She was probably a cheerleader who needed tutoring in chemistry. That was the only reason Tilda could imagine that a girl who looked like that would be hanging out with Warren.

Still, curiosity had her following them into the building.

They walked up an open staircase to the second floor. Tilda reached the top just in time to see them head into a study room together. There were narrow panels of glass flanking the door—sidelights, she thought they were called—through which she could see a long table with three chairs on each of the sides and one at each end.

Two other people were in the room already.

A guy several inches shorter than Warren with black hair that flopped over his eyes. He was set up at the far end, with a trifold cardboard screen on the table in front of him. She'd never played D&D (as if!) but she'd seen it depicted in television shows and movies and guessed the guy behind the screen was in charge. What was he called? The game ruler? Dragon tamer? Dungeon master?

Something like that, anyway.

The other guy in the room was—another girl, Tilda realized.

Blond and perky, with a ponytail and a toothpaste-commercial smile that reminded Tilda of London. Her former best friend had always been the prettiest and most popular girl in school, and Tilda had felt lucky to be part of her chosen group—one of the "in" crowd.

But she wasn't part of London's group, anymore. She wasn't part of any group now. She was on her own.

In fact, she'd exchanged only a handful of text messages with London since she'd been a no-show to Damian's big party. (Though she'd heard from Kellie that the cops had shown up and everyone had been busted for underage drinking. Some had been caught with drugs, too—and not just pot. Another reason Tilda was glad she'd never made it to Texas that weekend—Dad would have grounded her for life!)

The red-haired girl in the study room threw her head back, laughing at something Warren said, then she reached across the table and laid a hand on his arm, almost as if she was flirting with him.

But why would a girl who could probably get any guy she wanted waste her time flirting with Warren?

Maybe he wasn't bad-looking, Tilda allowed. He did have nice eyes behind the glasses. And a nice smile. And he seemed to be a decent human being—or at least a lot nicer than she was.

Two more guys wandered in to join the group, and then they settled down to business of their game.

She didn't know why she hung around.

She certainly didn't want Warren to think that she was waiting for him. Because she wasn't. And she had no intention of spending four hours at the library.

But she also had nothing else to do, and since she'd told him that she was there to get something to read, she decided to browse the stacks.

At the public library in Beaumont, you had to show photo ID and prove residency to be able to sign out materials, so she wasn't optimistic about her chances of getting a card here with only last year's student ID from Wharncliffe Middle School. But the librarian—"Mrs. Gilmore" as she was addressed by another patron and "Lindsay" according to her name tag—looked at the name under the photo and asked Tilda if her dad was the owner of Sugar & Spice. When Tilda admitted that he was, Lindsay spent the next five minutes raving about his new lavender vanilla beignets as she input the requisite information and issued Tilda a card.

"So you go to the library on Wednesdays to play D&D?" Tilda said, falling into step with Warren again after he'd said goodbye to his fellow gamers.

"It's what I do with my geeky friends," he reminded her.

"Which is at least a little less lame than going to the library to study on your summer break."

"Happy to hear it," he said. "Because your opinion means so much to me."

She shifted the stack of books in her arms. "What if I wanted to play?"

"You'd have to find another group—ours is full."

"Oh."

He eyed her curiously. "You almost sound disappointed."

She shrugged. "I guess I'm more bored than I realized."

"And you haven't made any friends so you want to horn in on mine."

"Forget I said anything," she said, annoyed that she'd let herself show even a hint of vulnerability.

They walked in silence for several minutes before he said, "Stasia goes to Cape Cod with her family for the first two weeks of August every summer, and Dylan goes to Colorado for the whole month, to spend some time with his dad. Usually we suspend whatever campaign we're in the midst of until they get back, but if you really want to learn, add the player's handbook to your reading list and sit in on the next session to see what it's all about, and maybe the others will let you participate in a starter campaign while they're gone."

"The next session being next Wednesday?" she guessed.

"Yeah."

"Okay."

"Don't you want to check your calendar first? Make sure you don't have any other plans?"

She flushed. "I think we both know that I don't."

"Then I guess I'll see you next Wednesday," he said.

"Or tomorrow, at Twilight Valley."

"Or tomorrow, on the way to Twilight Valley."

In response to her questioning look, he said, "I could give you a ride, save your dad having to make the trip."

"Okay," she agreed. "Thanks."

LIFE SETTLED INTO something of a routine over the next few weeks. Though Andrew hadn't officially announced to his daughters that he and Sarah were dating, they'd been spending a fair amount of time together and if Tilda wasn't overly thrilled by Sarah's presence, she at least seemed to have accepted it.

The closer it got to September, the more excited Lilah was about starting school. Unfortunately, Tilda was obviously dreading the same. She'd made a couple of friends through her volunteering at Twilight Valley and had even been hanging out with Warren sometimes. But he was a junior and she was only a freshman, so Tilda didn't expect him to acknowledge her presence at school. For now, though, she had someone to talk to, and Andrew was glad. And when he'd checked on his daughters before he turned in the night before, Tilda had been studying the *Dungeons & Dragons Player's Handbook* as if she expected to be tested on its contents.

"I think the girls had a good time tonight," Andrew said, settling on the sofa beside Sarah after they'd returned from a potluck barbecue at Claire and Devin's.

"It seemed like," Sarah agreed.

"Lilah's already counting the days until she can volunteer at Twilight Valley."

"Until then, I'm sure Claire would be happy to have her visit whenever she wants."

"Don't tell Lilah that—she'll be wanting to go every day."

"Mmm," Sarah agreed.

"Everything okay?" Andrew asked. "You seem a little distracted."

"Sorry."

"Don't apologize," he said. "Tell me what's on your mind."

"I'm afraid of overstepping," she admitted. "But I'm more afraid of saying nothing."

"About?" he prompted.

"Tilda."

He sighed. "What has she done now?"

"Nothing," Sarah was quick to assure him. "I was just wondering...has it ever occurred to you that she might have...an eating disorder?"

"What?" He scowled at the thought. "No. And what would make you ask such a question?"

"A lot of little things," Sarah said.

"Like what?" he demanded.

"Like the dress she was wearing tonight—she told me that you bought it for her eighth-grade graduation."

"That's right," he confirmed.

"Did it fit her better in June?" she wondered. "Because it looks two sizes too big for her now."

"She has lost some weight," he acknowledged hesitantly. "But she's been doing a lot more walking here than she ever did in Beaumont, plus whatever physical labor she's doing at Twilight Valley."

"Maybe she's been getting more exercise," Sarah allowed. "And maybe it's that she hardly ever eats."

"Isn't it normal for teenage girls to pick at their food?"

"*Normal* doesn't mean *healthy*," she pointed out. "And it's certainly not healthy for a teen who barely weighs a hundred pounds to count every calorie that she puts in her mouth."

"I don't think she's counting every calorie that she puts in her mouth."

"Just because she's not counting out loud doesn't mean she's not counting."

"Then why is she always going out for burgers and fries?"

"Is she?" Sarah asked dubiously. "When was the last time you actually saw her eat a burger? Or even a handful of French fries?"

"She had a burger tonight," he pointed out. "And macaroni salad and corn on the cob."

"No, she put a burger and macaroni salad and corn on her plate and, after she ate about three bites of the burger, she 'accidentally' dumped her plate on the ground. And she said she was going to get another one, but she never did."

He couldn't dispute what she was saying, because he didn't know that it wasn't true. Because he hadn't been paying close enough attention. And it troubled him, more than a little, to think that Sarah had noticed these things about his daughter that he'd somehow missed.

Being busy at the bakery was no excuse. Being preoccupied with Sarah was even less so. Because his daughters were supposed to be his number one priority, and if what Sarah was saying about Tilda was true, he'd somehow let her fall through the cracks.

"I'll keep a closer eye on her at mealtimes," he vowed. "But it's a pretty big leap from dumping one plate of food to assuming she has an eating disorder, don't you think?"

"Except that it's not about one plate of food," she pointed out. "Have you noticed how often she has an excuse for not wanting dinner? She had a late snack or a big lunch. And whenever you make her sit at the table, she spends most of her time pushing her food around her plate."

"She can be a picky eater," he acknowledged.

"Trust me," Sarah urged. "I know all the tricks."

I've used all the same tricks.

"What tricks?" he wanted to know.

"Cutting food into smaller and smaller pieces and then moving them around the plate so that it looks like you're eating when you're not."

Andrew frowned. "I know you took it personally that she wasn't a fan of your pork roast a few weeks ago."

"It wasn't just the pork roast," she told him. "She's done the same thing at every meal I've seen her eat."

"Which hasn't been that many."

"You're right," she acknowledged. "But you asked me what was on my mind and I couldn't continue to pretend that the things she's doing don't worry me."

"You don't have to worry about my daughter," he said, a touch of resentment in his tone. "That's my job."

"You're right." Sarah nodded as she pushed herself off the sofa, her heart aching. "For a minute I let myself forget that I wasn't actually part of your family—that I'm just the woman you screw on the side."

"That's not fair," he protested. "You know I care about you. I'm just having a little trouble balancing the different parts of my life."

"And maybe that's the problem. Maybe instead of trying to balance the different parts you should consider bringing them together."

"I don't know if my daughters are ready for that."

"I think the bigger problem is that *you're* not ready for that," she said.

"Maybe I'm not," he admitted. "In the past few months, I've moved my family halfway across the country and started a new business in a town where I knew exactly two people, so it might be that I need a little bit of time to catch my breath before I decide to jump into a new relationship without a parachute."

"That's a fair point," she said. "And probably something I should have considered before I went into freefall. Because I already love you and Tilda and Lilah."

And it hurt more than she'd anticipated to realize that he didn't feel the same way.

THE BALL WAS in his court.

That was what Sarah told herself—her justification for staying away from the bakery and the grocery store and the pizzeria and anywhere else that she might cross paths with Andrew. She spent extra hours at the ranch, but while the physical labor kept her hands busy, it didn't stop her mind from wandering or her heart from aching. Of course, she knew she couldn't avoid him forever, she just needed a little time for her bruised heart to heal before she found herself face-to-face with him again.

It turned out that the "little time" was less than forty-eight hours, which was when Claire oh-so-sweetly asked her to please stop at Sugar & Spice because the baby wanted chocolate cupcakes. When Sarah had suggested that Devin should be the one to deal with his wife's pregnancy cravings—after all, he was the one who'd knocked her up—Claire reminded her that Devin was at a conference out of town. She then offered to make the trip into town herself, but that didn't really make a lot of sense when Sarah lived so close.

She didn't bother to call out her friend's obvious manipulations, because Claire would then accuse her of being afraid to face Andrew and Sarah would end up going to the bakery anyway to prove she wasn't. Such was the joy of having a BFF who knew everything about you.

And that was how Sarah happened to be at Sugar & Spice Friday morning when Tilda, carrying a bin of dirty dishes from the seating area to the kitchen, fainted.

CHAPTER NINETEEN

OF COURSE, ANDREW freaked out. Any parent seeing their supposedly healthy fourteen-year-old daughter collapse would—and then their mind would start to go down all kinds of dark paths.

Thankfully Tilda came around quickly, and she seemed more embarrassed to realize she'd fainted than she was injured as a result of the fall. Seeing the crowd that had gathered only added to her discomfort, so Sarah ushered the patrons out of the bakery to make way for the paramedics coming in.

Despite Tilda's insistence that she was fine, Andrew wasn't willing to take her word for it. He rode in the ambulance with her to the hospital and Sarah promised to pick Lilah up from camp and meet him there.

Forty-five minutes later, they found him pacing in the ER waiting room.

"Any news?" Sarah asked.

He shook his head. "They're doing tests. Checking her blood pressure and her heart rate and running a full blood panel."

Lilah, her eyes swimming with tears, slipped her small hand into her dad's much larger one. "She's going to be okay," she said, her tone a lot less certain than her words.

He managed a smile for his youngest daughter. "I'm sure you're right," he said. "But I'll feel a lot better when I hear it from a doctor."

"The last time—" Lilah's lower lip quivered, as it did when she was trying not to cry "—the doctor told Tilda to keep a journal of what she eats each day, to help her remember not to skip meals."

Andrew immediately stilled. "The last time?"

Lilah's lip quivered again and her teary gaze dropped to the tile floor.

Her dad tipped her chin up, forcing her to look at him. "Are you telling me this has happened before?"

"Mom said she was going to tell you…" Lilah's voice was quivering now, too. "She didn't tell you?"

"No." A muscle in his jaw flexed. "She didn't. So maybe you can fill me in?"

"When did this happen?" Sarah asked gently.

Lilah's gaze shifted. "When Mom took us shopping at the outlet mall in Napa."

"So…two weeks ago," Andrew realized.

His daughter shrugged. "I guess."

"Can you tell us what led up to Tilda fainting?" Sarah prompted.

"She was trying on clothes and she did a twirl to show off a new outfit and…she just crumpled to the ground."

"Jesus." Andrew scrubbed his hands over his face.

Lilah started to cry. "I'm sorry, Daddy."

He put his arm around her and hugged her close. "It's not your fault, Lilah."

"Mom said she was going to tell you."

Sarah could imagine that Andrew was having some thoughts about his ex-wife's silence on the matter, but thankfully he kept them to himself for the moment.

"I need to know, Lilah—was that the only time something like this happened?"

"The only time that I know," she said, wiping her eyes on her sleeve.

He nodded, then hugged her again. "Okay."

A nurse came into the waiting room then.

"We've finished poking and prodding your daughter for the moment," she said to Andrew. "You can go in now to see her."

He nodded again. "Lilah, why don't you go ahead? We'll be there in just a couple of minutes."

"Okay," she said, and followed the nurse to the exam room.

"There's something you didn't want to say in front of her," Sarah realized.

He swallowed. "All those tests I mentioned… They're also doing a pregnancy test," he confided. "They asked Tilda when she had her last period and she said… April. So they're doing a pregnancy test."

"I think it's standard procedure to rule out pregnancy when treating a female of childbearing age," she told him.

"She's not of childbearing age," he protested. "She's a *child*."

"I hate to break it to you, but if she's menstruating, then she's of childbearing age."

"She's fourteen," he said again. "And she freaked out, too, when they asked if she could be pregnant—told me there's no way she could be because she's never had sex."

"So take a breath," Sarah advised. "And trust the doctors to do what they need to do to figure out what's going on."

"She hasn't had a period since April," he said again.

"She's only fourteen. It's possible that her cycle isn't regular yet."

"I do the shopping," he reminded her. "I buy the tampons when she puts them on the list. I didn't realize she hadn't put them on the list."

"This isn't your fault, Andrew."

"Then why do I feel like it is?"

"Because you're scared, and blaming yourself is easier than admitting that you have absolutely no control over the situation."

"I need to call Miranda."

"Why don't you wait until you have more information first?" she suggested.

"If you mean wait until I've gotten over the urge to yell at her, I'm not sure I'm going to live that long."

"Then at least wait until you've talked to the doctor."

"Okay." He let out a deep, shuddering breath, then reached for Sarah's hand and linked their fingers together. "Thank you for being here."

"I couldn't imagine being anywhere else right now," she told him.

And they walked into the exam room together, still hand in hand.

THE DOCTORS CONCLUDED that Tilda's recent fainting spells were caused by an electrolyte imbalance and low blood sugar resulting from extended periods of fasting. Two days later, after consultations with various professionals, she was home.

Andrew invited Sarah to his daughter's homecoming dinner, but she declined, not wanting his eldest daughter to feel as if there was one more person at the table to watch her eat. She did stop by later that evening, though, to see for herself that Tilda was doing okay and to ensure that Andrew didn't think his overture had been rejected.

After Sarah chatted for a few minutes with each of the girls, he opened a bottle of wine and the adults took it outside to sit under the stars where they could talk without worrying their conversation might be overheard.

"She looks good," Sarah commented, accepting the glass of pinot he offered to her.

"They pumped her full of electrolytes in the hospital. They also made her undergo a psychiatric evaluation."

"Standard procedure," she said.

"You seem to know a lot about standard procedure," he noted.

"I told you that I had some experience with eating disorders," she reminded him.

"So you probably won't be surprised to learn that she's going to have regular appointments with a psychologist and a nutritionist. Oh, and she's got plans to go to out Friday night."

"The last part surprises me," Sarah said. "You're letting your fourteen-year-old daughter go on a date?"

"It's not a date—it's a movie with some friends."

"Have you met these friends?"

"I know Warren."

"The boy next door," she mused.

"The others are members of his D&D group."

"Really?"

He nodded. "She's been hanging out with them at the library on Wednesdays."

"She must really be bored."

"That's what I thought, but she seems to be enjoying it," he said. "I also talked to Miranda today. She's agreed to participate in family counseling via Zoom."

"That's good news," Sarah remarked.

"The counselor said it's important for Tilda to know that we're all here to support her."

"And Lilah? How's she doing?"

"She's okay. I know what happened with Tilda freaked her out and that she felt guilty, because she saw what Tilda was doing and didn't say anything."

"It's a tough spot for a sibling—especially a younger sibling—to be in," Sarah noted. "Wanting to keep her sister's confidence and, at the same time, knowing she shouldn't."

"You're not just thinking about Lilah now but your own sister," Andrew guessed.

She nodded.

"Did she keep your confidence?" he asked.

"Jenna didn't tell my parents, but she told Zack. He then told my parents."

"Were you mad?"

"Furious," she admitted. "Also relieved and grateful. Sometimes, when everything in your life seems out of your control, you look for any little thing that you can control. Such as the food you put in your mouth—or don't put in your mouth.

"Eventually I realized that it was the number on the scale that was in control, not me. But it was a long process," she warned. "Tilda's not going to have counseling for a few weeks and suddenly be cured."

"That's exactly what her counselor told us at the first session," he confided. "That this is going to be a long—possibly lifelong—journey."

She nodded again. "At least Tilda knows that it's not a journey she has to undertake on her own—that you and her mom and Lilah are all going to be there with her, supporting her and offering a hand when she stumbles."

"Do you think it's expecting too much of Lilah—asking her to be part of that?"

"On the contrary, I think it's essential to her well-being to know that she's part of the process. Otherwise she might feel as if she's being shoved into the background while the spotlight shines on her sister."

"She said something a few weeks back that startled me," Andrew admitted.

"What's that?"

"She said that Tilda always gets what she wants."

"Does she?"

"I hope not," he said. "But the truth is, I think maybe I do indulge Tilda a little more because I don't want to give her a reason to ever think that I love her less."

"Every kid with a sibling thinks the sibling is the favorite," Sarah noted.

"And every parent with more than one child will tell you that they don't have a favorite," he assured her. "And I don't, but I worry the day will come that Tilda won't believe it. That she won't trust I could love her as much as I love Lilah…because she's not my biological child."

"I did not see *that* coming," Sarah admitted, as Andrew lifted the bottle to top off their glasses.

"Miranda wasn't the love of my life," he confided to her now. "We met because we were working at the same restaurant— she was the sommelier and I was the pastry chef. We were attracted to one another and our shifts sometimes overlapped, so we started hanging out—and hooking up—because it was easy.

"We were together for almost a year, but then our relationship started to fizzle and we decided to go our separate ways. Not long after we broke up, Miranda started dating someone else. A few weeks later, I did, too. And then, a few weeks after that, Miranda showed up at my apartment and told me she was pregnant.

"So we got married, because even if she wasn't the love of my life, the moment she told me that she was having my baby, I wanted to be there for her and our child, every step of the way. But she assured me that she could handle all the routine doctor's appointments, she just wanted me there for prenatal classes and the birth.

"I was a little concerned about the milestones throughout her pregnancy. According to the books I'd read—because yes, I was *that* expectant dad, the one who read everything he could get his hands on in preparation for the birth of his child—she should have felt movement around twenty weeks, and she claimed that she did. Four to eight weeks after that, I should have been able to feel the baby's movements, but it was nearly ten weeks before I did.

"Of course, the numbers are only guidelines, and all the books and online resources assured me that every pregnancy is different and so long as the doctor wasn't worried, I shouldn't worry, either.

"Anyway, her due date came and went, but the baby gave no indication of wanting to be born. We knew she was a girl by this point, and I teased Miranda that our daughter was already taking after her mom in being late for everything.

"Miranda reminded me that babies came when they were ready, and I tried to be patient, but I worried that she was more than a week past her due date. Then it was two weeks.

"Finally, she went into labor. Twenty-two hours later, Tilda came into the world weighing six pounds ten ounces and measuring eighteen inches. The doctor said she was a good size for a baby born at thirty-eight weeks."

Sarah blew out a slow breath.

"And that's when I knew the baby girl that I held in my arms wasn't actually my baby," he confided. "And when I looked at Miranda, I realized it wasn't a revelation to her.

"But we didn't talk about it until they came home from the hospital. I certainly didn't want the doctors and nurses who'd taken such good care of my wife and baby to know that she'd duped me into marrying her and taking responsibility for another man's child."

"I can't imagine she tried to deny it, at that point," Sarah said.

"She didn't," he confirmed. "But she insisted that, at the beginning of her pregnancy anyway, she really believed the baby was mine. It was only at her first ultrasound, when she discovered she wasn't as far along as she thought, that she realized the truth herself."

"Did you believe her?"

"I wanted to," he said. "In any event, I let her maintain the charade, because we were married and parents to a newborn— and I loved Tilda with my whole heart.

"But I felt guilty, too. Because I was experiencing the joy of being a dad to another man's child. I certainly didn't want to lose Tilda, but I felt strongly that Miranda should let the biological father know he had a child. I thought he at least deserved the chance to be part of her life, even if it would make things a lot more complicated for us.

"Miranda then confessed that she'd gone to Nigel when she realized she was having his baby, and he assured her that he had no interest in being a father."

Sarah swallowed another mouthful of wine.

"But after all of her deceptions, I couldn't be sure Miranda was telling the truth about that, so I tracked him down. Anyway, long story short, he already had two kids with two different women and didn't spend much time with either of them, so he was glad that this one had a better father than he would ever be.

"I felt sorry for him, that he couldn't appreciate the opportunity he'd been given to be a dad, but mostly I was relieved that he had no interest in Tilda, that my family would remain intact—at least for a while longer.

"But juggling the responsibilities of our jobs and our family wasn't always easy, and we inevitably went through some rough patches. During one of those patches, Miranda decided that having another baby would solve all our problems. Again, though, we didn't talk about it—she just decided to go off birth control and hope for the best. Nine months later, Lilah came along, so while I wasn't too happy with her machinations, I was overjoyed with the result.

"But, of course, there were more rough patches to come. And when we finally decided that living separate and apart was the best solution for everyone, she was surprised that I asked for joint custody of both our daughters—as if I'd feel less of a connection to Tilda because we didn't share DNA.

"Surprised and relieved, I think. Because as much as she loved her daughters, her work schedule wasn't particularly conducive to handling the day-to-day demands of parenthood, and she was happy to let me take on those responsibilities."

"Tilda doesn't know any of this?"

He shook his head. "I'm kind of dreading when she does that genetics unit in high school science where students chart Mom and Dad's eye color and figure out what options there are for baby—because blue is not an option with a brown-eyed father."

"So long as there's a grandparent with blue eyes, there's a twenty-five percent chance of a blue-eyed child," she pointed out, proving that she'd paid attention during science class.

"You're saying that she might not need to know the truth?" he asked dubiously.

"I'm saying she shouldn't find out in high school science class," Sarah clarified. "That you should tell her yourself before she starts asking the tough questions."

"I'm not sure that's a good idea. Especially not when she's dealing with so much other stuff already."

"The timing might not be ideal," she acknowledged. "But secrets have a way of coming out—and usually at the worst possible moment. The only way to ensure that doesn't happen is to tell her the truth on your terms."

ANDREW FOUND HIMSELF thinking about Sarah's advice long after she'd gone. He'd refused to heed her concerns about Tilda's eating habits—to his daughter's detriment—forcing him to acknowledge that being a parent didn't give him an inside track on making the right decisions.

Friday afternoon, determined not to make the same mistake again, he knocked on Tilda's partially open door.

"Come in," she invited.

He stepped over the threshold. "Are you busy?"

"Just checking my course schedule for September."

"How's it look?"

"First term I've got English, science, US history and phys ed. Second term is math, music, Spanish and computer science."

"Music? I thought you wanted to take art."

She shrugged. "Warren told me that the band gets to go on some cool trips, so I thought I'd give music a try."

"Cool trips?" he said dubiously.

"A couple years ago, they went to Disneyland."

"Sign me up for band," he said.

That earned him a small smile.

"The teachers aren't listed for second-term courses yet, but I've got Mrs. Channing for science first term, and Heidi says that she's the best, so I'm happy about that."

And Andrew was happy that Tilda finally seemed to be looking forward to the start of a new school year.

"There's a downloadable checklist of required school supplies on the website," she continued. "Do you think we could go shopping this weekend?"

"Sure," he agreed. "But can we talk about something else for a sec?"

"Okay," she said cautiously, spinning in her chair to face him as he perched on the edge of her mattress.

"I'm sorry I didn't see what you were doing. A parent always wants what's best for their child, and it's scary to admit that you had a problem I wasn't equipped to help you deal with."

"This is what you want to talk about?" She made a face. "Can't we save this for therapy?"

"We can talk about it again there," he told her. "But I want you to know that you can talk to me about anything at any time."

"Okay."

"Because secrets can eat away at us..." He inwardly cringed over his use of the word *eat* but maybe he was being overly sensitive, because it didn't seem to faze her.

"You think I'm keeping something else from you?" she guessed.

"No," he immediately replied, aware that he was bungling it. "I'm saying that you can talk to me about anything. And that sometimes parents keep secrets from their kids, too. Either because they feel the child is too young to understand or to deal with the truth."

"Like when you said that you and Mom grew apart instead of telling us that she had a boyfriend?"

"That's a good example," he admitted. "How did you know she had a boyfriend?"

"She moved out of our house and moved into his."

He nodded. "And sometimes parents keep secrets from one another—like when your mom didn't tell me that you fainted when you visited her in California."

"I asked her not to tell you," Tilda admitted. "I was afraid you'd freak out."

"And you were right—I would have freaked out," he confirmed. "I *did* freak out when the same thing happened here. Because there is absolutely nothing more terrifying for a parent than being unable to help their sick or injured child.

"But your mom and I promised one another that there would be no more secrets between us—at least not when it comes to you and Lilah. But there is something that we've both been keeping from you," he confided. "And, to be honest, I don't want to tell you now, but I've realized that if I expect you to be honest with me, then I need to be honest with you."

"Okay," she said again.

"You already know that your mom was pregnant when we got married."

"Yeah, because I can count."

"What you might not know is that your mom and I dated for a while and then spent some time apart before we got back together and decided to get married."

She looked wary. "Maybe there are some things that a kid doesn't need to know."

No doubt that was true.

But what Sarah said was also true—secrets had a way of coming out. Usually at the most inopportune times.

If he told Tilda, he could maintain control of the narrative. If she found out in some other way, she might jump to all kinds of wrong conclusions.

"The most important thing you need to know is that I love you and your sister more than anything else in the world."

"You're starting to freak me out a little here," Tilda said.

"There's no reason for you to freak out," he hastened to assure her. "It's just not easy for me to find the words…"

"Rip off the Band-Aid, Dad," she suggested.

"Okay." He nodded. "Your mom and I weren't together when she got pregnant."

For a long minute, Tilda was silent.

"You're saying that you're not my dad," she realized.

"No," he immediately denied. "I'm not saying that at all. Because I *am* your dad in every way that counts…just not biologically."

She fell silent again, for even longer this time.

"And now you're not saying anything," he noted.

"I'm…processing."

He nodded. "That's fair."

"I think it's going to take some time."

"Okay." He rose to his feet. "I'm going back to the bakery. But whenever you're ready to talk, I'm here. Whatever questions you might have, I'll answer them as best I can."

"One question," she said. "Can we have pizza for dinner?"

"You bet." He dipped his head to kiss her forehead. "I love you, Tilly."

She only nodded.

And when he came home with pizza a few hours later, she was gone.

CHAPTER TWENTY

SINCE WALKING OUT of her job at Blake Mining, Sarah's life had proceeded according to *her* plan. And even if it wasn't a flawless plan, at least she went to work every day with joy in her heart, happy to be doing something that mattered and happier still to be doing it alongside her best friend.

Maybe choosing to be a rancher wasn't going to change the world, but it had changed *her* world—giving her a sense of purpose and personal happiness. Meeting and falling in love with Andrew Morrow was the icing on the cake. (An appropriate analogy, she thought.) And after their tête-à-tête on Wednesday, she honestly believed that their relationship wasn't just back on track but on a better track.

And so, when her phone rang Friday afternoon and she saw his name on the display, she didn't even try to hold back the smile that curved her lips.

The smile immediately slipped when he responded to her greeting by saying, "Tilda's missing."

"What do you mean *missing*?"

"I mean that I came home with dinner and she wasn't here."

"Did you try texting or calling?"

"I tried texting *and* calling. And before you ask about the tracking app, that's not going to help because wherever she went, she didn't take her phone with her."

Now Sarah understood the panic in his tone. Because teenagers were rarely more than two feet away from their smartphones, and if Tilda had purposely left hers behind, it was because she didn't want to be contacted.

"I'm calling you because I wondered if you'd seen or heard from her."

"No, I haven't," she admitted. "But if she left her phone, I'm sure she didn't go far."

"Are you sure?" he challenged. "Like you were sure it would be a good idea to tell her about her parentage? Because I did that earlier today."

She reeled at the anger in his tone.

"So this is my fault?" she guessed. "Because I recommended that you be honest with your daughter rather than continue to perpetuate a lie?"

"Because I took your advice and now she's gone," he said.

Sarah sucked in a breath, unable to deny the apparent cause and effect. And she felt not only guilty but sick with worry. "I was trying to help."

"And now my fourteen-year-old daughter is only-God-knows where."

"We'll find her," she said confidently, needing it to be true.

"No," he said. "There's no *we* here."

And suddenly she saw that the new track their relationship was on had come to a dead end—the broken rails hanging over a bottomless chasm.

"*I* need to focus on my family right now."

And, as he'd made clear not even a week earlier, Sarah wasn't part of his family.

Even after everything they'd been through in that week, she remained on the outside looking in.

Though the realization made her heart ache, that was something to be dealt with later. Right now, the only thing that mattered was finding Tilda.

"I'm here," she said. "Whatever you need. I can call the sheriff. I can call everyone I know. I'm at Twilight Valley, but I can come back to town, drive around the neighborhood, knock on doors."

"Thanks," he said. "But I think you've done enough."

And then the line went dead.

SARAH TUCKED HER phone back in her pocket and resumed her chores, because so long as the world continued to turn, there were animals that needed to be tended to.

Ordinarily the evening feeding was something that Claire handled, but Devin had taken his wife to an appointment with their ob-gyn and Sarah offered to hang around until they returned.

As she went through the motions, she tried to make sense of recent events. Had Tilda been so upset to learn Andrew wasn't her biological father that she'd run away? And if so, where would she go?

She was tempted to reach out to Warren, to ask if the neighbor might have seen her, but no doubt Andrew had already done so.

Her next thought was to call the sheriff, but it wasn't her place to report Tilda missing and the girl's dad had likely covered that base, too.

Instead, Sarah finished with the horses, but when she started to close up the barn, Ed sat down smack in the middle of the open doorway, deliberately impeding her efforts and refusing to move.

"What's the matter, buddy? Are you feeling neglected because Claire and Devin went into Battle Mountain for an appointment with the baby doctor?" she asked.

He whined, a low and plaintive sound from deep in his throat.

"That sounds like more than feeling neglected," she noted, crouching in front of him. "Did you get caught in something? Are you hurt?"

As soon as she reached for him, to examine him for bumps or cuts, he backed away.

So she straightened up again and he barked.

"I'm sorry, but I don't understand what you're trying to tell me."

He tilted his head, as if to communicate that he was having the same problem.

"You know I love you, Eduardo, but I don't have time to play games," she said. "So why don't we head up to the house now to get your dinner?"

He barked at her again.

"I still don't speak dog," she told him.

He turned and trotted away, and she followed, because it seemed as if that was what he wanted her to do.

He made his way to the far end of the barn, where there was a ladder to the hayloft.

"If there are rats up here, I'm going to scream," she warned, as she started to climb.

It took a minute for her eyes to adjust to the dim lighting and another several seconds to scan the mostly open space and spot a pair of sneakers peeking out from behind a stack of hay bales.

She recognized the bright pink Converses immediately, and nearly collapsed with relief. "Tilda."

The teen wiped at the streaks of tears on her cheeks. "That dog is a worse tattletale than Lilah."

"And thank God for that," Sarah said, lowering herself to the floor beside Andrew's daughter. "How did you get all the way out here?"

"Warren gave me a lift," she admitted.

"I didn't see anyone drive up."

"He was going to see his friend Matt, who lives a little farther down the road, so I told him to drop me off at the end of the lane."

"But you didn't tell your dad where you were going—and you left your phone at home."

Tilda sniffed. "He's not my dad."

"Is that what this is about?"

The girl's eyes narrowed. "You're not surprised."

"No." If Andrew had decided to be honest with his daughter, she was going to do the same. "He told me a few days ago."

"That must be when Mom told him," Tilda realized. "And why he finally decided to tell me."

"You think your dad just found out that you're not his biological child?"

"Well, yeah. Obviously. And now that he knows, he doesn't

have to be responsible for me and he's probably going to send me to California to live with Mom, but she doesn't want me, either."

"I can't speak for your mom, but I can assure you that's not true about your dad," Sarah told her. "He would do absolutely anything for you—including tell you a truth he would prefer to deny."

"Then why did he tell me? Why now?"

"Maybe because he was trying to be honest with you, so that you would know that you can be honest with him."

"How long do you think he's known?"

"Since you were born," Sarah said gently.

Tilda seemed puzzled by that. "If that's true—why did he stay with my mom? Did he love her that much?"

"He loved *you* that much."

The teen sniffled. "Do you really think so?"

"I know so," Sarah promised.

"Even after everything I've put him through these past few months?"

"I'm not saying he's loved everything you've said and done, but I promise that he loves you. And right now, he's worried sick about you, so you need to call him and let him know that you're safe."

"He's going to be mad," Tilda noted.

"First he's going to thrilled to hear your voice," Sarah said. "Then relieved to know you're okay. The mad will probably come after that."

"He's going to ground me *forever*."

"Quite possibly," she agreed. "Because that's what parents do to make sure their kids understand that actions have consequences."

"Maybe you could call him for me," Tilda suggested.

"I could," Sarah allowed. "And I definitely will if you don't. But if you want your dad to stop treating you like a child, you have to stop acting like a child and take responsibility for your actions."

Tilda wiped her eyes again, then she took a deep breath and nodded. "I'll call him."

ANDREW SNATCHED UP the phone on the first ring, before he even saw Sarah's name on the display. "Have you heard anything?"

"Dad, it's...me."

"Tilda." Relief turned his knees to jelly. He slid to the floor, clutching the phone like a lifeline. "Where are you? Are you okay?"

"I'm fine," she said. "I'm at Twilight Valley."

Of all the places he'd imagined she might go, that wasn't one of them.

He knew his eldest daughter wasn't a big fan of Sarah, though when he'd shared his concerns about her attitude with Rachel, his sister assured him that Tilda wasn't likely to be a fan of any woman he dated in the beginning. She'd also assured him that Tilda would come around—but even if she didn't, he couldn't give his teenage daughter a veto over his love life.

But right now, it didn't matter why she'd gone to Twilight Valley—all that mattered was that she was safe.

"You're sure you're okay?"

"I'm fine. And... I'm sorry," she said. "For leaving without telling you where I was going—though I didn't know myself when I walked out the door—and for making you worry."

"Are you ready to come home now?"

"Yeah."

"Don't go anywhere. I'll be there in twenty minutes."

WHILE TILDA WAS on the phone with her dad, Sarah went to the house to get her a snack and a drink. When she came back, it seemed as if the weight of the world had been lifted off the girl's shoulders and she was throwing a ball for Ed, laughing when he returned to drop it, wet with doggy drool, at her feet.

Though Tilda had only been gone a few hours, Sarah knew those hours must have felt like an eternity to Andrew, because they'd felt the same to her as she'd desperately tried not to think about all the horrible things that could happen to a teenage girl on her own.

Ed halted abruptly in pursuit of the ball Tilda had thrown for him, his ears twitching back and forth for a moment before he barked, obviously hearing a vehicle on the laneway before it came into view.

As soon as Andrew climbed out of his SUV, Tilda ran into his arms and they clung to one another for a long time.

Sarah held back—letting Andrew have his reunion with his daughter. When he finally released Tilda from his embrace, she raced over to Sarah to give her a quick hug before returning to the passenger side of her dad's vehicle.

Andrew made his way to Sarah more slowly.

"Thank you for finding Tilda," he said, his tone a little stiff and a lot distant.

"It was actually Ed who found her," Sarah told him. "I've promised him extra treats every day for the rest of his life."

"I'm sure he appreciated that."

"Or he would, if he had any idea what I was saying."

He nodded slowly, and with every second of terse silence that passed between them, so did Sarah's hope of a happy resolution for their relationship.

Her ominous feeling was confirmed when he said, "Anyway, it's been a chaotic couple of weeks and the next few won't be any better with the girls both starting school soon."

She took a moment, not because any effort was required to read between the lines, because she needed the time to absorb the impact of the words she knew were intended as the knock-out punch to their fledgling relationship. Then she lifted her chin and met his gaze evenly. "Could you at least be as honest with me as you were with your daughter and admit that you're dumping me?"

"I'm sorry," he said, and to his credit, he did sound regret-ful. "But I have to focus on what's important. My family needs to be my priority."

Because he was a dad, and implicit in the parental role was a willingness to always put your child's needs ahead of your own. Perhaps she hadn't realized that before, because she hadn't grown up witnessing that kind of selfless love, but that was the kind of parent Andrew was.

Her actions had been motivated by love for his daughters, too.

But obviously he couldn't see that, or maybe it didn't matter. Because she was, as always, on the outside looking in.

And when their relationship hit a bump in the road, his response was to bail. Just like every other man she'd ever loved, starting at the very beginning with Zack. Maybe it hadn't been his choice to move to Seattle when he was released from juvie, but he'd gone, anyway, and she'd been alone.

Just like she was alone now.

But she didn't say any of that to Andrew.

She didn't say anything at all, because she couldn't speak around the lump in her throat.

"So... I'll see you in town, I guess," he said, his tone somewhat wooden.

She simply nodded and stood there with her heart breaking into a thousand pieces while he walked away.

WHEN TILDA GOT home from Twilight Valley, she found Lilah standing in the doorway of her bedroom, her eyes red-rimmed and swollen from crying. Tilda immediately knew that she was responsible for her sister's tears, and the realization that she'd caused Lilah so much distress made her stomach cramp—like it sometimes did when she wouldn't eat.

"Tilly!" Lilah called out her sister's childhood nickname as she ran to her, wrapping her arms around her middle and sobbing as she held her tight.

And Tilda found herself crying again as she hugged Lilah back.

After several minutes passed, Lilah finally let go and took a step back. "Why'd you run away?"

Tilda stuffed her hands into the front pockets of her shorts. "I didn't really run away. I just needed some time to think about some stuff."

"What kind of stuff?"

Tilda hesitated. But Dad was right about secrets eating way at a person—and she'd been sick about this one since February. And maybe it didn't affect Lilah directly, but she deserved to know.

"Like the fact that Dad's not really my dad," she said. "I mean, he's not my biological father."

"I don't understand," Lilah said.

"Mom got pregnant by someone else before she married Dad." Lilah's cheeks turned pink. "Oh."

Obviously the idea of their mom having sex with a man who wasn't their father was a little disconcerting—to both of them. (Although Tilda didn't really want to think about Mom having sex with Dad, either.)

"But you're still my sister," Lilah said.

"Yeah, I'm still your sister." She hugged her again. "I'll always be your sister."

"I'm glad you're home," Lilah said.

"I thought maybe you'd be glad that I was gone," Tilda admitted.

"Why would you think that?"

"Because I've been a horrible sister."

Lilah sniffed. "I'd be happier if you weren't a horrible sister, but I never wanted you to go away."

She could barely speak around the lump in her throat. "I'm sorry, Lilah."

"For leaving?"

"For everything."

"I'll forgive you if you promise to try to be nicer from now on."

"I promise to try," she said. "Maybe we can start by walking to The Trading Post to get some cherry blasters?"

"I don't know that Dad's going to let you leave the house for the next month," Lilah warned.

"Let's find out."

AFTER CONFIRMING THAT they each had their phones, Andrew did let them leave the house. And though the events of the day had scraped his emotions raw, he realized he was happy to see them go off together. How long their newfound understanding of one another would last was yet to be seen, but he was taking it as a win for now.

While the girls were out, he called his sister to let her know that Tilda was home and safe—because of course she'd been one of the first calls he'd made when he'd realized his daughter was missing.

When they were back home and tucked into bed, he collapsed on the sofa, physically and emotionally exhausted. His eyes had just started to drift shut when he heard footsteps on the stairs.

He patted the sofa beside him, a silent invitation, and Tilda sat down.

"We said no more secrets, right?" Tilda said.

"That's right," he confirmed.

"Then you should know I didn't leave because I was upset to learn that you weren't my dad," she admitted. "I've known that since February."

"Since *February*?" Andrew was stunned. "How did you find out?"

"I heard Mom talking to Daphne," she said, naming a long-time friend of Miranda's in Beaumont.

Secrets have a way of coming out.

And he could only imagine how distressing it must have been for Tilda to learn about this one, and his heart ached for her.

"Does your mom know that you overheard her conversation?" he asked her now.

She shook her head. "No."

"Why didn't you say anything?"

"Because I was afraid that if you knew, you wouldn't want me."

"Oh, honey. I would *never* not want you."

"But… You're not even my dad."

"Just because we don't share DNA doesn't mean I'm not your dad."

"That's what Sarah said," Tilda confided. "She also said that I should know that I can always talk to you, because you'll always be on my side."

"Did she have anything else to say?" he asked, feeling more than a slight twinge of guilt to realize that while Sarah was working to mend the fractures in his relationship with his daughter, he was resolving to end his with her.

"She said that if you grounded me for life it was only because you were so worried about me—because you love me."

"She's right about that, too," he noted.

"Am I grounded?"

"It's my job as a parent to ensure you know there are consequences to your actions."

She sighed. "That sounds like a yes."

"On the other hand, while I'm certainly not happy you snuck out, I'm glad you went somewhere you felt safe."

"So… Maybe I'm not grounded?" she said hopefully.

He managed a smile. "I think I need to sleep on this one."

"Okay." After another minute she said, "I'm sorry I gave you a hard time about Sarah. I was afraid that if you fell in love, like Mom and Perry, you wouldn't want me and Lilah around, either."

"I promise, even if I fell in love a hundred times, no one would ever take the place of you and Lilah in my heart."

"Nobody falls in love a hundred times," she scoffed.

"Probably not," he acknowledged with another smile. "And even though things didn't work out between me and your mom, I'll always be grateful I fell in love with her because she gave me you and Lilah."

"But you love Sarah now, don't you?"

"Yeah," he admitted, only now acknowledging the truth to himself. "But I messed things up there."

"Because of me?" Tilda asked worriedly.

"No. Because of me. Because it's been the three of us—me and you and your sister—for so long that I forgot how to let anyone else in. Or maybe I didn't want to let anyone else in."

And he'd been so terrified for Tilda that the fear had pushed everything else—including Sarah—aside.

"But you can fix it, right?" she asked him now.

"A relationship isn't like a broken appliance," he said. "You can't just order a replacement part and expect it to work like new."

She considered that for a minute. "So maybe it's like an egg," she decided. "Once you crack the shell, you have to make it into something else—something better. Like an omelet."

"That's a pretty good analogy," he mused.

"A lot of life's lessons are learned in the kitchen. My dad taught me that."

"He must be a pretty smart guy."

Tilda tipped her head against his shoulder. "He's the best."

CHAPTER TWENTY-ONE

ANDREW HAD SPOKEN to his sister several times over the past few weeks in an effort to keep her up-to-date on all that had been happening. And even when they didn't talk, she checked in almost daily via text message.

Two days after Tilda went missing (his daughter still maintained that she'd only needed some time and distance to think and had *not* been running away), Rachel called while he was finishing up a batch of cream puffs for a bridal shower. He put her on speaker so he could continue to pipe filling while they talked.

After the usual exchange of pleasantries, she asked, "Have you got a bed for the spare room yet?"

"A bed and a dresser plus a wingback chair and reading lamp," he told her. "When are you coming for a visit?"

"Rob and I want to make the trip for Thanksgiving."

"You usually go north to spend the holiday with his family," he recalled.

"That was when we saw you and the girls all the time. Now that you don't live ten minutes away, we miss you."

"We miss you, too."

"So… Thanksgiving?" she prompted.

"That would be great," he said.

"I suspect you're going to be busy at the bakery, so I'd be

happy to handle the shopping and cooking for the big meal—assuming I wouldn't be stepping on any toes."

"My toes will be at the bakery," he confirmed.

"I was referring to Sarah's toes."

"Thanksgiving is more than three months away. I have no idea where her toes are going to be by then."

"If that's true, then you're not half as smart as I've always given you credit for being," she said.

"Sarah understands that my focus needs to be on Tilda and Lilah right now."

His sister sighed with obvious exasperation. "You're my brother and I love you, but you really are an idiot sometimes."

"I love you, too," he said, deliberately ignoring the latter part of her remark.

"Sarah cared enough to see what was going on with Tilda, to draw your attention to her behavior, to forgive you for challenging her observations and to be there for all of you when the situation hit a crisis point. She was also the one that Tilda ran to when her world was turned upside down, and you responded by pushing her out of your life?"

"Tilda didn't run to Sarah," he denied. "She went to Twilight Valley."

"Because she knew Sarah would be there."

"And maybe Tilda wouldn't have felt the need for time and space if I hadn't followed Sarah's advice and told her the truth about her parentage."

"It was the right thing to do. Tilda had a right to know."

"When you have kids of your own, I'll come to you for parenting advice," he said.

"I'll bet that's what you said to Sarah, too," she retorted. "And if you did, then I hope *she* dumped *your* ass."

"I've got cream puffs to box up," he told her.

"I'll let you get to it," she said, and disconnected the call.

A few minutes later, after the cream puffs were on their way to the bridal shower, his phone chimed with a text message.

We're still coming for Thanksgiving. Hopefully you'll have your act—and your family—together by then.

WHEN ANDREW PULLED up outside Claire and Devin's house—
only a week after he'd raced to Twilight Valley to find his daughter—he took a minute to appreciate the ecstatic greeting he got
from Ed, because he suspected the dog's owner wouldn't be
nearly as happy to see him.

"Did you take a wrong turn somewhere?" Claire asked, both
the question and the distinct chill in her tone confirming his
suspicion. "Because that's the only reason I can think of that
you'd be at my door."

He straightened up slowly to face her. "I did take a wrong
turn. And I made a lot of other mistakes, too. Which is why I
need to find Sarah to make things right, because there's a big
empty hole in my life without her."

He could tell his admission surprised her, but Claire's tone
remained guarded when she replied, "Well, she's not here."

"But you know where she is," he guessed.

"I do," she confirmed.

"Will you tell me?" He offered her the box of chocolate caramel nut cupcakes in his hand. "Please?"

"Are you really trying to bribe me?" Her tone was colder now
than the inside of his flash freezer.

"They're not a bribe," he denied. "They're a *thank-you*."

"A *thank-you* for the information you want me to give you?"
she guessed.

"No, a *thank-you* for being the one person Sarah can always
count on."

She accepted the offering then and responded in a tone only
slightly less chilly. "Sarah went to Las Vegas for Jenna and Harrison's wedding."

"I didn't know they'd set a date."

"Now you do."

"And now I know why her phone's turned off," he realized.

"It might be turned off," she allowed. "Or she might have
blocked your number."

"Another possibility," he acknowledged.

"Was there anything else?" she asked, when he continued
to linger.

"I know I screwed up," he told her.

"That's something we agree on."

"I was worried about Tilda—panicked—and I took it out on Sarah."

"She was worried, too. And you responded to her efforts to help by telling her that you were done."

He winced. "She really doesn't have any secrets from you, does she?"

"We're best friends," Claire reminded him.

"It wasn't one of my finest moments," he acknowledged.

"And yet, it was no less than what Sarah expected."

"What do you mean?"

She gave an exasperated sigh, the breath escaping her lungs like air bubbles from a soufflé. "Throughout her life, whenever the going has gotten tough, instead of standing by her—as people who care about you are supposed to do—the men in her life have walked away. And so did you."

"It wasn't like that," he denied.

Except it was exactly like that, and the blatantly skeptical expression on Claire's face told him she wasn't fooled for a minute.

"Okay, I can see why it might look that way," he allowed. "And I know I'm going to need to prove myself to get her back."

"Do you have any reason to believe that she'd want you back?"

"She told me that she loves me."

"And she'll be the first to admit that she falls in love too easily, and always with the wrong men." Claire glanced at her watch. "She's been in Vegas for almost thirty-six hours—by now, she's probably fallen in love with someone else there."

"You don't pull any punches, do you?"

"Not when it comes to my best friend," she agreed.

And he knew that Sarah was lucky to have Claire in her corner. That when the going got tough, this woman at least had always stood by her.

"When is she coming back?" he asked now.

"I don't know."

"I thought she told you everything."

"And you expect me to prove that she does by sharing that information with you?" she challenged.

He shrugged. "It was worth a shot."

After a brief hesitation, she said, "She said she'd be at work on Monday. I told her there was no reason to rush back and suggested that she should take a few extra days to have some fun."

"But she'll keep you in the loop about her plans," he realized.

"Of course."

"Will you let me know when she's on her way?"

"No. But I'll tell you that she went on a private charter out of Battle Mountain."

"Thank you."

"I won't say you're welcome, but I'll wish you luck. You're going to need it."

WHOEVER SAID IT was better to have loved and lost was obviously a masochist, Sarah thought, as she gave the hand-tied bouquet of creamy white roses to her sister in preparation for her walk down the aisle.

It was better—far better—to love and be loved in return, as Jenna and Harrison obviously loved one another.

"I can't tell you how much it means to me that you could be here," Jenna said to her after the formalities were concluded.

"There was no way I was going to miss my little sister marrying the man of her dreams."

"I never dreamed of anyone like Harrison," Jenna confided. "And I've never loved anyone more."

"Be happy," Sarah said. "Always."

"I will be."

When the bride released Sarah from her embrace, the groom moved in to hug his new sister-in-law. "Thank you for celebrating with us this weekend, but especially for letting Jenna have Han. She told me the story, and if you'd taken the puppy, she and I might never have met, and my life would have been forever incomplete."

Those words echoed in Sarah's mind throughout her flight back to Battle Mountain the next day. Maybe it had been destiny that Jenna and Harrison met at the dog park—and maybe she was destined to be alone.

Not that she was ready to give up on love just yet, but she was finally considering the possibility that her life was meant to follow a different path. That she'd find her happiness in the job she loved and the friends and family who enriched her life in countless ways.

But still her heart ached, because there was a great big Andrew-Tilda-Lilah-shaped hole in it.

Because he was on her mind, as he always seemed to be these days, when Sarah saw him standing beside her SUV in the airport parking lot, she felt certain he must be an illusion. She blinked a few times, but every time she opened her eyes, he was still there. Looking every bit like the man she suspected she would always love, even if he wasn't capable of loving her back.

And then she saw that he had something in his hands.

Oversized cue cards, she realized, and her heart did a slow somersault inside her chest.

SOMETIMES I STRUGGLE TO FIND THE RIGHT WORDS

SO I'M GOING TO TRY IT THIS WAY INSTEAD

"I'd rather you didn't," she said.
His only response was to turn to the next card.

TO TELL YOU THAT I'M SORRY I EVER BLAMED YOU

AND THAT I WAS WRONG

She really didn't want to do this, but she couldn't seem to make her feet move to walk away.

MY DAUGHTERS ARE THE CENTER OF MY WORLD

BUT WITHOUT YOU—IT SEEMS AS IF THERE'S NOTHING ELSE

She felt a lump rise in her throat, because she knew exactly what he meant. It had only been nine days, but she'd missed him unbearably.

SO PLEASE SAY YOU'LL GIVE ME ANOTHER CHANCE

TO PROVE HOW MUCH I LOVE YOU

AND WANT YOU TO BE PART OF OUR LIVES

He lowered the last card and waited, obviously for some kind of response.

But how could she agree to give him another chance—even if that was what she desperately wanted to do—when her heart was still battered and bruised from the last one?

"Who told you that *Love Actually* is my favorite movie?" she asked instead. "Because I know it wasn't Claire."

There was no way her friend, understanding how much he'd hurt Sarah, would give him an inside track.

"It wasn't Claire," he confirmed. "She said that her loyalty would always be to you and if I couldn't figure out how to make things right on my own, I didn't deserve you."

"So who told you?"

"Zack," he confessed, a little sheepishly.

"Zack?" She frowned. "You mean Zack Kruger?"

"Yeah."

"How do you know him?"

"I don't know him, but I called him."

"You called Zack?" She was struggling to wrap her head around what he was telling her.

He nodded. "And let me tell you, I'm glad your first boyfriend wasn't named John Smith, because I'd probably still be making phone calls in an effort to track him down. Thankfully my search for Zack Kruger only turned up thirty-nine people by that name in the whole country. Two of them residing in Washington State and only one of those a lawyer."

"Okay, so you get an A in your efforts to track him down," she said. "But the real question is, *why?*"

"Because I knew I needed an edge if I was going to have any hope of winning you back and Claire had already made it clear that she wasn't going to be any help. To be honest, Zack wasn't too keen on the idea at first, either, and it took a lot of fast talking to convince him that I'd finally realized you were the best thing that ever happened to me and now needed to convince you that I knew it. In the end, he agreed to talk to me so long as I agreed that he could kick my ass if I ever hurt you again."

"And you agreed to that?" she said dubiously.

"If I ever hurt you again, I will absolutely deserve to have my ass kicked."

"If I let you back into my life, you will hurt me again," she said, both saddened by and resigned to the fact. "Because I want—I *need*—to be an equal partner in a relationship and you don't know how to let anyone in."

"I know I've been overly protective of my daughters—and myself," he admitted. "Perhaps because it's just been the three of us for so long and because Miranda's decision to abandon our family left some pretty deep scars."

"I can empathize with what you've been through," she told him. "But we've all been hurt. And while that's a risk you take when you open your heart, it's a risk I can't take with you again, because I know it will only end with more hurt."

"You said you loved me," he reminded her.

"And I do," she confirmed. "But love isn't always enough."

"Don't say that," he pleaded.

"How many times have you seen *Love Actually*?" she asked him now.

"Once," he admitted.

"So maybe you didn't realize that while Mark's grand gesture with the cue cards is widely viewed as one of the most romantic scenes in the movie, he doesn't get the girl in the end."

Andrew frowned. "That doesn't seem right."

"But it's realistic," she told him. "Not everyone gets a happily-ever-after in life."

"Maybe because they give up too soon."

"Or maybe because life doesn't follow a movie script."

"I'm not giving up on us, Sarah." He rifled through the cards until he found the one that said "to prove how much I love you" and held it up again.

It took every ounce of willpower she had to turn and walk away.

"FIVE DAYS," CLAIRE said to Sarah, as they moved the horses into their stalls the following Friday afternoon.

Sarah looked at her blankly.

"It's been five days since the hottie baker channeled the most romantic scene in the most romantic Christmas movie ever for my best friend, and I had to hear about it not secondhand but—" she counted silently on her fingers "—fifth hand."

"How did you hear about it?" Sarah wondered, giving Jezebel's cheek a rub as she latched the mare's door.

"Nat told Kevin who told Jason who told Devin who told me."

Nat was Natalya Dawson, who'd flown the charter from Las Vegas, Kevin was her husband, Jason was his best friend and colleague as well as being a cousin of Devin—and also of Sarah.

"I didn't realize Nat saw anything," she said now.

"She was parked not too far from you at the airport, which isn't the point and not how this friendship thing works," Claire admonished. "You're supposed to tell me these things. And when they happen, not five days later."

"Are you saying I should have pulled out my phone and sent you a text while he was going through his cards?"

"Maybe not right then," her friend allowed. "Although if you'd pulled out your phone, you could have snapped a picture. I would have paid good money to see that."

"I'm sorry I didn't tell you. I'm even sorrier that you had to hear it from Devin who heard it from Jason, et cetera."

"I'm your best friend. I would have been there for you."

"Aren't you tired of being there for me?" Sarah asked wearily.

"Never."

"Well, maybe I'm tired of needing someone to be there for me and trying to stand on my own two feet for a change," she said, offering a slice of apple to Dumbledore when the usually shy gelding put his nose over his gate to greet her.

"Which is admirable," Claire said. "But even standing on your own two feet, how did you resist throwing yourself in his arms?"

"By reminding myself that his gesture was nothing more than blatant emotional manipulation and that I didn't have time for that."

"Was it emotional manipulation?" her friend asked gently. "Or was it finally opening up his heart to tell you how he feels?"

"Maybe it was how he felt in that moment," Sarah allowed. "Because it's easy for Andrew to be sweet and charming when all is right in his world. But the minute there's any kind of crisis, he shuts me out."

"He's been a single dad for a number of years—he's probably grown accustomed to having to deal with everything on his own."

"And now he can continue doing so," Sarah said.

"That's it? You're over him? Poof, like magic?"

"It's a process," she acknowledged, as they exited the barn. "But I feel good about the fact that I've taken the first step."

She tipped the brim of her hat to better shield her eyes from the bright afternoon sunlight—and gasped softly when she saw Andrew was there.

Not just Andrew, she realized, but Tilda and Lilah, too. And the girls had cue cards in their hands.

Aware that she'd been set up, she sent her friend a look.

"I missed the first grand gesture," Claire said with a shrug. "No way was I missing this one."

"What are you doing here?" Sarah asked Andrew.

"I thought about what you said," he told her. "Then I watched the movie again. And I realized that the reason Mark doesn't get the girl is because he lets her go, because she's happy with Peter, and he wants her to be happy. Because when you love someone, you want them to be happy.

"And if you tell me you're in love with someone else—and that you're happy without me—then I'll let you go, too. But if you're even still a tiny bit in love with me, then there's no way I'm giving up on you—on us."

Behind him, Tilda and Lilah cleared their throats. Loudly.

Andrew stepped aside then so that Sarah could focus on his daughters and their cue cards.

Tilda: APOLOGIES FOR OUR DAD

Lilah: WHO DESPITE HAVING TWO DAUGHTERS

Tilda: CAN BE A LITTLE CLUELESS SOMETIMES

Lilah: IN HIS RELATIONSHIPS WITH WOMEN

Tilda: NOT THAT THERE HAVE BEEN A LOT OF OTHER WOMEN

Lilah: TRUTHFULLY, HE'S HARDLY DATED AT ALL

Andrew: YOU CAN PROBABLY GUESS THAT THEY SCRIPTED THEIR OWN CARDS

Tilda: WHICH IS WHY IT TOOK US SO LONG

Lilah: (AND TOOK HIM EVEN LONGER)

Tilda: TO REALIZE HE WAS IN LOVE WITH YOU

Andrew: AND MAYBE LOVE ISN'T ALWAYS ENOUGH TO GUARANTEE A HAPPY ENDING BUT ISN'T LOVE EVERYTHING YOU NEED TO TAKE THE FIRST STEP TOWARD A HAPPY BEGINNING?

"Now would be a good time to throw yourself in his arms," Claire said to her friend in a stage whisper.

When he'd shown up at the airport with his cue cards, Sarah had been wary of a gesture obviously designed to weaken her resolve—and very nearly succeeding. And while, at first glance, what he'd done today wasn't all that dissimilar, his willingness to enlist his daughters' help—and their willingness to give it—proved to her that he was finally ready to let her into not only his heart but also his family.

And that was an offer she couldn't refuse.

Andrew handed his cards to Tilda and stepped forward.

"What do you say?" he asked Sarah. "Is love enough to at least get us started?"

"Maybe love and…fresh beignets every Sunday morning?" she suggested, with a smile in her eyes and love in her heart.

"Whatever you want," he promised, drawing her into his embrace.

Lilah: (KISS)

But Andrew's lips were already on Sarah's.

Then Claire and Devin, who'd come out of the house to stand beside his wife, started clapping even before Tilda had a chance to show her last card.

(APPLAUSE)

And Ed barked happily as he danced around the kissing couple.

EPILOGUE

Ten months later

ANDREW DECIDED TO mark the one-year anniversary of Sugar
& Spice with free cupcakes for the first one hundred customers
through the door. Sarah didn't understand why he felt the need
to give samples away when the success of his business proved
people were willing to pay for his delectable treats, but she did
understand his desire to share the milestone with his loyal customers.

And she was happy to join the party and reflect on how much
they had to celebrate—most notably how well his daughters
were thriving in Haven. Tilda continued to have regular sessions
with her counselor and was maintaining a healthy lifestyle that
included daily walks with the dog Lilah had finally convinced
Andrew to adopt—along with two cats—from the local shelter.
In addition, the girls were enjoying regular visits with Miranda
and Perry, who (according to Tilda) still talked too much about
wine but absolutely doted on his stepdaughters.

Warren was researching colleges in advance of his senior year,
had a part-time job stocking shelves at The Trading Post, continued to volunteer at Twilight Valley and somehow still found
time to play D&D with his geeky friends—a group of which
Tilda now declared herself a proud member.

The previous fall, Sarah had been surprised to get an invitation to Zack and Imani's wedding—addressed to "Sarah and Andrew"—and even more so when he voted to go to the wedding so that he could thank Zack in person (and maybe prove that he didn't deserve to get his ass kicked).

A few weeks after that, they were in attendance when Gramps exchanged vows with Helen. And after the ceremony, the octogenarian groom expressed sincere pleasure that Sarah had finally managed to find a man worthy of her—even if that man hadn't given him a discount on the cake.

At the end of February, Claire had given birth to a baby girl, and Sarah was currently making the rounds of the bakery with four-month-old Everleigh on her hip while the new mom chatted with Jenna, who'd recently announced that she and Harrison were expecting their first child before Christmas.

But they were the only ones expanding their families. Rachel and Rob had shared similar happy news when they visited at Easter and now, at six months, the mom-to-be was absolutely glowing. Sarah had been a little surprised when Rachel and Rob said they were making the trip to Haven again for Sugar & Spice's anniversary party, but she was always happy to see them, as were Tilda and Lilah.

Feeling a slight tug on her skirt now, Sarah glanced down at Elijah, Nat and Kevin's three-year-old foster child. The little boy had been in their care since the previous Thanksgiving and, if all went according to plan, they would officially be his parents by Thanksgiving this year.

"Cupcake?" Elijah said hopefully.

She squatted beside the boy, the baby still on her hip, so that she was at his eye level. "What kind do you like?"

He pointed to a vanilla cupcake with a swirl of multicolored icing in the display case—Tilda's handiwork, no doubt—and Sarah ducked behind the counter to snag his treat, not worried that the last of the freebie cupcakes had been distributed hours earlier.

"That's his second one today," Nat said, shaking her head when she saw the little boy with the cupcake in hand and smears of red and blue and yellow icing on his face.

"Whoops," Sarah said.

"Not your fault," the other woman assured her. "I can never say no to him, either."

"I swear there are more people here today than there were on opening day," Erin Landry remarked, sidling up beside Sarah when Nat moved away.

"The really odd part is that people keep coming in but no one seems to be leaving."

"Has it happened yet? Did I miss it?" Kyle asked, joining his wife.

Erin sighed. "You didn't miss it, but you might have blown it."

He spotted Sarah then and winced.

Before she could respond, Devin swooped in.

"Mine," he said, and stole back his baby.

Over the quiet murmur of voices, someone cleared their throat. Loudly.

Then Andrew made his way to the center of the room.

"I want to take a minute to thank you all for being here today to celebrate the anniversary of Sugar & Spice, but also and especially for your support over the past twelve months without which we wouldn't be celebrating this milestone.

"I will admit to having some reservations when I moved from Texas to Nevada to start my own business here. It's hard to start over, especially in a place where you know only two people. But soon I knew three people and then four and five and—"

"Most of us here can count," Rob interrupted his brother-in-law.

"My point is that, very quickly, the residents of Haven showed me and my family what it means to be part of a community. And one particular member of that community has become an integral part of our family—offering her love and support through sickness and in health, good times and bad, for better and for worse."

Rachel stepped forward to elbow her brother. "I think you're getting a little ahead of yourself and treading on the actual vows there."

He met Sarah's gaze then and shrugged.

Tilda came to her dad's rescue, handing him some cue cards.

I SOMETIMES STRUGGLE TO FIND THE RIGHT WORDS TO KNOW
WHAT TO SAY

SO I'M GOING TO TRY IT THIS WAY INSTEAD

"Really? You're going to do this again?" she asked. But she
was smiling, her love for him and his whole family shining in
her eyes.

"Just one more card this time," he promised, and turned it
around so she could see the words he'd written.

WILL YOU MARRY ME?

Sarah lifted a hand to her chest, where her heart was suddenly so full it felt as if it might burst out of her chest. The crowd
around her was silent, waiting, as she blinked away the happy
tears that blurred her vision to accept the Sharpie Lilah offered.

Still smiling, and holding Andrew's gaze the whole way,
Sarah breached the distance between them, uncapped the marker
and wrote her response.

Of course, it was YES.

And the crowd of family and friends gathered around erupted
in applause without any prompting.

* * * * *

WESTERN

Small towns. Rugged ranchers. Big hearts.

Available Next Month

A Maverick Worth Waiting For Laurel Greer
Stone Creek Sheriff Stella Bagwell

....

Conveniently A Fortune Michele Dunaway
And Cowboy Makes Three Susan Breeden

....

 LOVE INSPIRED
The Sheriff Next Door Julia Ruth
Earning The Veteran's Trust Lisa Jordan

6 brand new stories each month
WESTERN
Small towns. Rugged ranchers. Big hearts.
MILLS & BOON

Keep reading for an excerpt of a new title
from the Medical series,
CELEBRITY VET'S SECOND CHANCE by Ann McIntosh

CHAPTER ONE

DR. JONAH BEAUMONT blinked against the grittiness in his eyes, his body aching as though he'd already worked for eight hours, although it was only nine thirty in the morning.

Besides the clinic being short-staffed and extra busy, getting out of bed to tend to a sick patient only to have the animal die on you was always a draining experience.

At least, it was for him.

Pushing the memory aside, he finished bandaging the irate duck's foot and, over the angry squawks of Jennifer Mulligan's pet mallard Hofstetter, said, "You're gonna have to isolate this baby, keep him confined and out of the water till the wound heals. Bumblefoot can become serious if it doesn't completely heal."

"He won't like that," Jennifer replied, struggling to hold the wriggling Hofstetter still. "He's used to being in charge of the flock. There'll be a mighty fuss going on all day, with him trying to boss them around from in the pen."

Jonah chuckled. "I feel for you, especially when it comes time to rebandage this foot. He doesn't much like this part of the proceedings, any more than he liked me cutting out the abscess."

Jennifer snorted. "I'll get Fen to hold him while I do it. She's the only one he'll allow to do whatever she likes with him."

Jonah straightened and peeled off his gloves. "That little girl of yours is a natural with the animals. I've never seen anything like it."

"She's already decided she wants to be a vet when she grows up," Jennifer said, shaking her head as she maneuvered the still squawking Hofstetter into a pet carrier. "Bruce and I are trying to figure out how to afford it."

"Tell her she needs to keep her nose to the grindstone at school, and when she's a little older, as long as I'm still around, she can come here as an intern after school and on the weekends. That'll go a long way toward helping her get scholarships and grants."

Jennifer's smile lit up her face and made the exhaustion weighing on Jonah lift a little.

"I'll tell her," Jennifer said. Then her smile faded. "I heard about Marnie Rutherford's mare dying this morning. What a blow that must have been to her." She hesitated a beat, then added, "And to you."

And, just like that, the weight of the world seemed to drop back onto his shoulders and, with it, that pervasive sense that no matter how hard he tried, he could never do or be enough.

"Yeah," he replied, turning away to toss the gloves into the garbage. He used the excuse of grabbing a wet wipe to keep his back to Jennifer. "She was devastated. Unfortunately, there was nothing I could do."

Behind him, he heard Jennifer pick up the carrier, and he turned to face her once more, knowing his expression wouldn't betray his real feelings. He'd had years to perfect hiding them, since his clients needed to have complete confidence in his abilities, even when he didn't.

"Torsion is like that a lot, isn't it? Quick to come on, and quick to kill."

Jennifer spoke matter-of-factly—a farmer to the core, who understood all too well the vagaries of animal husbandry. Jonah was opening the door for her and pondering how to respond to her statement when the waiting room suddenly erupted in a cacophony of barks, shouts, squeals and bleats.

With a muttered, "Excuse me," Jonah slipped past Jennifer in the corridor and ran toward the door leading to the waiting area. Throwing it open, he was in time to see a tall, dark-haired stranger put Geoffry the billy goat into a professional-looking horn hold, while his owner, old Mrs. Kimball, fluttered around ineffectually. Geoffry, not being used to such masterful treatment, seemed too shocked to do anything but stay still.

Something about the back view of the man holding the goat sparked a rush of awareness in Jonah, but he wasn't sure whether it was familiarity or something completely different. Instinct had him turn his attention, instead, to the rest of the people in the waiting room, most of whom were hanging on to their upset and anxious pets for dear life. Yet, there was also excitement on more than one face, and there'd been a smattering of applause too.

"Oh, Geoffry." Samantha, one of the vet techs, brushed past Jonah in the doorway and crossed the room to take the goat's harness. "Mrs. Kimball, we always ask you to leave Geoffry outside until it's time for Dr. Beaumont to see him. He's such a spicy guy. And he doesn't like dogs."

"That's not true," Mrs. Kimball replied. "He gets on fine with Mic and Mac at home. I'm sure that doggy must have growled at him."

Considering the dog in question had somehow wedged itself under its owner's chair despite being at least a hundred pounds, Jonah somehow doubted that statement.

The German shepherd mix looked frankly terrified.

Samantha couldn't get through the door with him standing there, so Jonah stepped back to let them pass as the goat wrangler walked away from him toward the reception desk. There was a brief shuffling of people— Sam, Geoffry and Mrs. Kimball going into the corridor, the patient Jennifer with her carrier leaving—and then the door swung shut, leaving Jonah still standing there, a little breathless and somehow confused.

Must be the lack of sleep.

But rather than go back to the examination room to see his next patient, he found himself circling over to behind the reception desk, wanting to see the strange man's face.

Hear his voice.

"Hi," the receptionist, Laura, said, while Jonah hung back out of sight behind the dividing wall, waiting to hear their interaction. She was fairly new, so if Jonah was caught spying on her, he could legitimately say he was evaluating her skills with the clients. "Thanks so much for jumping in like that. We really appreciate it."

"No problem," the man replied, amusement clear in his tone. The hair on Jonah's arms and back of his neck lifted, leaving a tingling sensation behind that made him shiver. "That poor dog didn't know what to do with itself, and the goat clearly runs the show, wherever he is."

Laura giggled, and someone else nearby called out, "You got it, man. Geoffry's a beast."

"So, what can we do for you today?" Laura asked.

"Well, I'm here in town on business, and saw your sign. I'm a vet too, and wondered if by chance your Dr. J. Beaumont is the same person I went to college with. Dr. Jonah Beaumont?"

Unable to restrain his curiosity a moment more, Jonah took the two steps necessary to get to the front desk and stood behind Laura, drawing the attention of the man standing in front of her.

Their eyes met, and Jonah's heart did a weird little stutter step before starting to pound way harder than was appropriate for the moment.

Neither of them spoke for the space of a couple of seconds, although it somehow seemed to stretch on for an eternity, during which time Jonah took in the man in front of him.

His first thought was, *expensive*.

It wasn't often you saw someone dressed that way in small-town Butler's Run. Although not much of a clotheshorse himself, Jonah knew enough to ascertain that the casual outfit—which fit to perfection—hadn't been bought in a chain store. The leather jacket alone probably cost more than all the clothes in his closet at home. And while it was paired with jeans and a flannel shirt, he'd bet both garments had designer labels in them as well.

All this he took in with a sweeping glance, down then

up, just as aviator sunglasses were being lifted to reveal the other man's face.

It was sharp, almost vulpine. Ruddy, with high cheekbones, a narrow nose that flared slightly at the end, and a cheeky, full-lipped smile. His thick dark hair fell to his shoulders and could have seemed effeminate except that the man himself exuded masculinity and sex appeal.

The consummate Latin lover come to life, with a dash of what looked like Hollywood flair added in.

But it was the eyes that brought back the sharpest memories. Light brown, almost coppery, and gleaming with good humor. Jonah remembered wanting to see them turn his way, again and again, although even when they did it was never in the way he wanted them to.

Jonah forcibly squashed that thought, and the rush of arousal that came with it.

Instead, he forced himself to remember how nice and kind the man across the desk had been to him. And also, that he'd always been so far out of Jonah's league it sometimes felt impossible they existed in the same universe, much less the same world.

"I can't believe it." Jonah finally found his voice and was amazed when it sounded fairly normal, although there was a definite edge of surprise—or shock—to it. "Rob Sandoval? What the heck are you doing here in Butler's Run?"

Rob couldn't help grinning across the reception desk at Jonah Beaumont, who looked almost the same as he had ten years before, which was the last time they'd seen each other.

About three inches shorter than Rob's six feet one inch, Jonah was broad-shouldered and barrel-chested, stocky but obviously still muscular. His scrub top hung down over a taut belly and clung to bulging biceps. There was definitely a touch of silver in his short black hair, and a few more creases in his chocolate-dark skin, especially at the corners of his mouth and eyes. But that full-lipped mouth still smiled in the same restrained way, and the deep-set eyes, with their heavy lids, gave his face a sleepy, sexy look, in contrast to what Rob remembered as a sharp intellect.

Behind him he could hear the murmuring of the people in the waiting room, and the receptionist was looking from him to the card he'd handed her, back and forth, as though trying to figure something out.

It made him grin a little wider.

Small towns, no matter where in the world they were, were all the same. Almost everybody knew everybody else's business, and what they didn't know, they'd nose out or make up.

He'd had enough experience since starting the video shorts and documentaries to realize someone would recognize him when he'd walked into the clinic. Even in the most remote corners of the States, at least one person had known about his alter ego, Vet Vic, who traveled around revealing the secret lives of animals.

Clearly there were a few Vet Vic fans in the waiting area, and they were probably waiting for him to admit to who he was.

But, instead of answering Jonah's question about why

he was there, Rob couldn't resist leaving them all hanging, just a little.

"Why would you say it like that, as though Butler's
Run was in the middle of the Kalahari or something?"

Jonah's lips twisted slightly, the surprise fading to be
replaced by rueful amusement.

Or was it annoyance?

"It might as well be. Butler's Run, South Carolina,
isn't on the beaten path like, say, New York City, is it?"

"Thank the good Lord for that," drawled one of the clients, bringing a wave of laughter and murmurs of agreement.

"True," Rob replied, then glanced over his shoulder at
the crowded waiting area. "Listen, I can see you're busy.
I'll be here for a few weeks. Want to get some lunch and
catch up?"

Jonah rubbed the back of his neck as he nodded. "Sure.
I'd love to catch up. And normally lunch would be good,
but we're short-staffed today, and I might end up working through it."

"Why not ask Vet Vic to help you out?" called someone from behind him, making Rob mentally shake his
head. "If he's not filming today."

Whoever it was obviously just couldn't take the sus-
pense anymore.

"Vet Vic?" Jonah's forehead creased with obvious confusion. "Filming?"

"I knew it!" The receptionist bounced in her seat. "I've
watched all your videos. They're great."

"Where you been, Doc? Didn't you hear they were
coming to do a piece on the Marsh Tacky?"

"Haven't you seen any of this guy's documentaries?"

"Vet Vic is the bomb."

Rob held up his hand, cutting through the overlapping chatter and hubbub. While there was a dawning of understanding in Jonah's expression, the tumult couldn't be allowed to continue. Turning so he could see the waiting room, he scanned it, making eye contact with most of the clients there.

"Come on, guys. Give Doc Beaumont a break, will you? He can't just have some strange vet come in and start working on his patients. There are liability issues."

"Oh, forget about all that legal claptrap," a woman with pink hair said. "Anyone here gonna sue if something happens?"

The resulting negative response was seemingly universal, but Rob shook his head.

"I'm not putting Jonah in that position."

"He's got interns and stuff working for him all the time. How would it be any different?"

Clearly the pink-haired lady was determined not to give up without a fight, and Rob hoped there were no emergencies in the back, waiting for Jonah's attention. The entire situation was getting completely out of hand. The best thing he could do was leave, before it went any further.

And when he turned back to the desk to apologize and tell Jonah goodbye, there was that expression again—the one he couldn't decide was amusement or irritation. But, to his surprise, before he could speak, Jonah's face smoothed of all emotion, and he said, "If you're free, I really could use an extra pair of hands today. I have two vet techs and my intern out sick."

Rob searched the other man's face, trying to figure out if he was just pandering to the clients' demands, but there was no reading him.

He hesitated for a moment, not wanting to cause a disruption to the running of the clinic. And yet, the opportunity was too good to pass up.

"You're sure?" he asked, and got a nod in return. "Well, then, can you lend me some scrubs?"

A ridiculous cheer went up from the waiting clients, and Rob glimpsed Jonah's mouth twist again as he turned away from the desk.